HARD WAY TO LOVE

ETHELBERT OFOR

HARD WAY TO LOVE

Copyright © *Ethelbert Ofor*, 2025

All Rights Reserved

Disclaimer

This is a work of fiction. All of the characters, places, organisations, events portrayed in this novel are just mere coincidence, or just product of the author's imagination.

Editorial Review:
Hard Way To Love
by Ethelbert Ofor

I. A Poignant Tale of Desire, Dilemma, and Emotional Reckoning

Hard Way To Love by Ethelbert Ofor is a thoughtfully written and emotionally grounded novel that explores the delicate and often misunderstood nature of romantic relationships, particularly within the framework of modern Nigerian society. The narrative blends desire, emotional uncertainty, ambition, and spiritual clarity, all while maintaining a reflective tone that keeps the reader both engaged and challenged.

The strength of this novel lies in its emotional intelligence and cultural authenticity. Mr Ofor does not merely tell a love story. He opens a window into the moral struggles and emotional turbulence that accompany deeply human experiences such as infatuation, regret, reconciliation, and redemption.

II. Key Chapter Highlights

From the opening pages, the reader is introduced to Jeff, a relatable and introspective protagonist whose experiences echo the emotional complexities of many readers. Several chapters stand out for their structure and message:

- Chapter One – The Capping Ceremony: A warm and culturally significant opening that sets the emotional tone and introduces Jeff's intrigue and desire.

- Chapters Two and Three – The Office Environment and Romantic Pursuit: These chapters provide insight into workplace boundaries, emotional projection, and the blurred line between admiration and obsession.

- Chapter Four – The Conflict: This is a turning point where emotional tension reaches its peak, leading to confrontation, internal collapse, and ethical conflict.

- Chapter Five – Reflection and Responsibility: A chapter that explores the aftermath of broken trust, encouraging themes of personal growth and ownership of mistakes.

- Chapter Six – Professional Maturity and Spiritual Renewal: The conclusion is uplifting and redemptive, focusing on Jeff's personal development and his renewed focus on purpose over emotion.

Each chapter carries a clear message that aligns with the overall moral of the story: love, when distorted by self-interest or unaddressed emotions, can become painful, but through reflection and renewal, it can also evolve into something enduring and meaningful.

CONTENTS

CHAPTER 1

The reception hall of the Federal Neuropsychiatric Hospital was teeming with people. It was 13:15 hours. It was the middle of June, and at that time of the day and year, especially in the eastern part of Nigeria, the sun was usually at its full strength and shining bright, and that day was no exception.

Students, teachers, and guests were all eager to reach the buffet area to get some food and snacks after hours of sitting, waiting, watching, and listening to speeches made by staff and parents of the student nurses who were being capped in this epoch-making event.

Unlike some of the speeches that were inordinately long, there was nothing boring about the music that filled the room delightfully. The DJ, Mr Ikemba, made sure of that, sweating profusely as he did.

The heat of the mid-afternoon sun blazed through the long, tired-looking reception hall like a sauna, forcing everyone in the building to use their programme booklets as fans to augment the laboured efforts of the ceiling fans. The fans looked so obsolete that it would only take a token effort to convince anyone that they were older than the students in the reception hall.

However, there was no shortage of fun despite the poor curb appeal of the building and its furnishings. As wines were being poured liberally, screams of cheers, laughter, and clinking of glasses erupted from all corners of the building as the students were being congratulated for passing the all-important permanent training section exam (PTS). There were constant clicks of the camera shutters from professional and amateur photographers who had been either contracted or just invited to cover the ceremony.

But amid the multitude of people and the heart-warming activities going on in the reception hall, was this lady next to Jeff that looked like a specimen from the outer space. She stood head and shoulder above the rest and had arrested him with her disarming beauty.

Jeff, who was one of the guests on this occasion had travelled all the way from Lagos to Enugu to stand in for his uncle and wife in this capping ceremony. Their daughter, Doris, had successfully completed the first six months of her admission into the school of nursing and had passed with flying colours the permanent training section examination that followed those agonising six months that were marked by intensive, brain-fatigued lectures from those lecturers that would not compromise their strict moral and religious principles in carrying out their duties.

Today, Saturday, the 15th of June, the successful students dressed in their impeccable white uniforms were being crowned for their efforts and success, and Doris was one of them.

Doris' parents had travelled to Dubai on an impromptu business trip and had asked Jeff to represent them in the capping ceremony. It was a request Jeff was not only happy to carry through, but he also saw it as an honour and an opportunity to reciprocate everything they had done for him. They had been pivotal to his success in life including training him up to university level with his father passing on quite early.

For these students, today was not only unique in their lives but also historic because it marked the beginning of their journey of becoming qualified nurses three years down the line, and who knows, with God on their side, they could become the leaders of tomorrow who would pave the way for the future and survival of nursing profession in the country, and perhaps, could find themselves in positions of authority and corridors of power to influence the country's polity with a view to bringing the much-desired change in governance that the masses had always craved for.

Jeff wasn't going to occupy his mind with what the student nurses would become in the future. That was the least of his problems, at least for now. What mattered most to him was this lady standing next to him who had trapped and mesmerised him with her disarming beauty. She appeared to be in her twenties. She was sandwiched by two of her friends. They were oozing with confidence and elegance and needing no fashion umpire to confirm their class. They looked trendy and elegant in all fashion sense especially when compared with other guests. But it was her delicate beauty and slender physique that set her apart from her friends and, of course, from everyone in the building.

She wore a red jacket with a pair of navy blue stretch jeans and kitten-heel black shoes. She was the kind that could bring life to a dead end and make a corpse wink, and any attempt to view her from the rear would surely get your stick out of gear. There was nothing artificial about her beauty. It was in her blood and bones.

Jeff, from that moment, fought in vain to take his eyes off her. Her beauty had knocked his socks off.

She furtively glanced back at Jeff. But there was nothing definitive Jeff could make of this look because it was neither welcoming nor repelling. It was like a look of someone caught in two minds. Though he did not know what to make of it, he was sure he wasn't the only guy staring and doing nothing. But he wasn't sure whether she looked in any other guy's direction. At least that's what it looked like to him, and he would be glad if she didn't.

For him, her presence had mitigated the stress of standing in this long, slow-moving queue in a temperature that was slowly climbing to mid-thirty degrees. He was so distracted that it took a nudge on his back and stern words to remind him he should keep moving when there was a slight movement in the queue.

"If you are not hungry, I am. So, keep moving unless you want us to swap positions," the lady standing behind him told him after nudging him, noticing that he was just standing and staring at the lady next to them.

Jeff felt embarrassed and apologised to her even though he knew that her harsh words and spiky look could have stemmed from petty jealousy.

While eating his food, he was still unable to take his eyes off this lady who now sat right opposite him.

She had stolen a few glances at him as they ate. She laughed in her sleeve when Jeff, staring at her, lost concentration and poured his Pepsi down his shirt. But seeing how embarrassed and uncomfortable Jeff had become following the accident, she looked away to spare his blushes.

But as Jeff was dabbing his shirt to soak up the wet patches of the Pepsi on it, he could hear a loud laughter from the guests opposite him. When he stopped and looked, it was the lady and her friends laughing their heads off as they watched him secretly. He believed she had said something to her friends about him staring at her and, in the process, poured down the Pepsi on his shirt. He was embarrassed by that, but neither the embarrassment nor anything for that matter was going to put him off. *I am certainly not going to be like every man in this building who is staring and doing nothing. I am going to wave at her next time I see her look at me and see whether she will wave back,* Jeff said in his heart. But there was no next time as they finished their meals as he was still ruminating on his plan.

Gathering their stuff hastily, they started for the door. They were bouncing off one other, still laughing and chatting as they left the hall in what appeared to Jeff as a subtle way to announce their departure. She was trailing behind. Just before walking through the door, she stealthily turned and gave him a cheeky look and then smiled a little.

If they were leaving, then it must be abrupt, Jeff had thought. He did not even know why they came in the first place because he didn't see them with any of the students. They might have settled with them before making their way to the reception hall, or the students they had come to see were as shy as his cousin, Doris, who was uncomfortable staying with him.

He wasn't going to let her go without taking a chance. He wouldn't forgive himself if he didn't. He knew his chance was pretty slim. To some, it might look like a wool-gathering expedition, but it was still worth a try. He believed the old saying: fortune only favours the bold, and to dare is to do. But suddenly came the realisation there was no chance in hell she was going to be single unless this was the first time she had ventured outside. He believed that he was either going to discover that she was married to somebody who came from money or at least in a relationship with the most eligible bachelor in the society. He was dispirited by the thought, but he still wanted to try, nevertheless. He wanted her to tell him of her unavailability.

He abandoned his food and drinks, grabbed his suit, and headed for the door. He had to pursue this to a logical conclusion.

As if she knew he was coming after them, she looked back again and saw him hot on their heels. Intuitively, she knew he was after her, so she stopped and faced him. That sudden halt took him by surprise, and he lost his self-composure. Before today, in addition to his self-composure, an attribute that had followed him like a shadow was his first-rate masculine features, defined cheekbones, hawkish brown eyes, and six-pack flat tummy. These ripping qualities had undoubtedly made him irresistibly endearing to ladies. So, it was no surprise he had always had his ways with girls, especially those that tickled his fancy like she did.

Jeff stood before her, speechless. But that didn't prevent him from seeing how close they were to each other as he could perceive the pleasant whiff of her perfume. The closeness also gave him the opportunity to take a closer look at her. Not that he hadn't seen enough of her to convince him she was a special specimen. None of that, but it offered him, amongst others, the opportunity to confirm even further how fundamentally beautiful she was. She wore no make-up and would never need to slap on any to look good. She was intrinsically beautiful.

Now, standing next to her, he noticed how perfect their heights were. She was almost his height, probably 6ft, about an inch shorter — perfect heights for perfect kisses —no need to stoop down or stand on your tiptoes. He also used the closeness to do other assessments, where he noticed that her newly braided hairstyle was parted into two symmetrical chunks with what looked like a Tigris statement necklace sitting magnificently between them in her faintly exposed chest. The hair cream applied to her hair made it shimmer against the reflection of the sun, revealing the details and finesse of the braiding. The flower golden stud attached to her left nostril was distinct as it highlighted the shape of her nose which looked like a crossbreed of Nubian and hawk noses—a lot more pointed than wide. Her caramel complexion skin was so smooth and translucent you would think you could see your reflection in it. Her hazel eyes sparkled like certified loose diamonds, and her glossy, white teeth shone so bright that one would think they would dazzle the sun.

Jeff couldn't believe one person could have all these attributes. For him, she was a phantasmagoria of beauty and elegance. And he was prepared to do a cartwheel and much more to make her his.

As an attempt to encourage him to speak, she delightfully pouted her lips and then swung her head from left to right and right to left before saying, "Hi." She sounded pleasingly assertive, and there was equally evidence of self-assertiveness in her posture, but she wasn't brash.

She must be a model for these big, flourishing companies, Jeff imagined in his heart as he still struggled to say a thing. His composure had practically eluded him.

Her beauteous eyes popped up distinguishably, and like her inviting pouted lips, they weren't incriminating. They were rather persuasive. And that was a further encouragement to help him rediscover his composure to say something.

The other girls moved away to give them some privacy.

Despite the distance, Jeff still Knew they were being watched and that depleted his confidence further, quite unlike him.

She ran her eye over him as if she were doing a quick assessment of his personality and code of dressing. Her gaze finally fell on his stained shirt, which he tried in vain to hide with his suit.

"Sorry about the stain on your shirt," she said amiably and fondly in her genuine attempt to ease his nerves. But all to no avail, as Jeff still remained speechless.

Opening her bag, she said, "Oh well, since you don't want to say a thing, here you go, this is my complimentary card."

He reached out for it but missed and it dropped on the ground. He put it down to nerves. They were jangling. Being so close to her and smelling her sensuous perfume got his heart racing, and the heat of the closeness zapped through him like one in a steam room.

Picking the card up from the ground, he said, "Erm, Erm…I am sorry about that."

"Not to worry. Give me a call when you are ready to talk. I don't want to keep my friends waiting for eternity. Moreover, it is getting late, and we still have other events to attend," she told him in a soft, penetrative voice that went through him like a patella hammer to the knees.

Her erotic voice made him nervously weak but, at the same time, intensified his desire to know her and make her his.

"Take care," Jeff struggled to say as he sucked in her angelic voice, which was as outstanding as her beauty.

"You too. Watch what you are doing," she said, zipping up her handbag and throttling to meet her friends.

Jeff stood there and watched them enter a Land Rover (Discovery) model and drive off.

Though feeling humiliated about his timorous behaviour, he still saw some elements of civility in her. Her modest behaviour was a sharp contrast to her beauty. Usually, a girl with all her attributes would have her tail up and would show a degree of sassiness, and that made him radiate some sense of optimism even when he knew the outcome looked bleak and hopeless.

Returning to the reception, he handed his niece the gifts from himself and her parents. "Be good, and see you when I see you," he advised her and left.

Jeff made no attempt to call her when he arrived back in Lagos that night for two reasons. First, he wasn't still composed enough. He didn't want to repeat the same mistake he made in Enugu. The timid attitude he displayed in Enugu earlier on could be put down to nerves; a repeat performance would be inexcusable. He had been given a chance to take a second bite at the cherry, and he wasn't going to make a mess of it. Secondly, he believed that she might still be somewhere enjoying her evening. So, he left it for the following morning.

He woke up with vigour and enthusiasm the following morning in his little but cosy, two-bedroom apartment in the suburbs of Lekki peninsula, Lagos — an island magnificently blessed and beautified by wonders of nature — almost hedged in by Lagos Lagoon to the north, and Lekki Lagoon to the east.

After observing his morning ablutions, he went to the kitchen and made a nice cup of tea the way he enjoyed it— strong with one sugar. He strolled back to the lounge, drew the curtains, and slightly opened the windows to let in some fresh air and some sunlight.

As he drank the tea, his mind was running riot with ideas on how to make this all-important phone call. He had finally gathered his wits and felt physically and mentally coordinated to give it a go. He set out his strategies. He didn't only plan what to say but also envisaged what would be her likely answers and possible questions. He knew it wouldn't be an easy task to win her over by mere words of the mouth, especially over the phone. Nevertheless, he relied immensely on the adage that says: Words are mightier than swords, especially when chosen wisely.

Shunning anything that would upset his nerves again, he entered her phone number. Then took a deep breath before hitting the call button. It took a few seconds before an automated voice said, "The number you are trying to call is currently not available." He took a closer look at the card just to confirm it was the card she gave him and that he wasn't putting in the wrong number. With the pace of an African chameleon, he started putting her number again, this time more carefully. He hit the call button once more. And once again the automated voice was activated, encouraging him to leave a message. He left several text messages.

Jeff watched his phone like a hawk for hours, hoping to receive a callback or a reply to his text messages, but to no avail. But on second thought, he believed that she might still be sleeping after the long journey and the events of the previous day. This thought came as a relief to his disappointment. But as the day wore on, his hope began to fade away, re-enacting his fear that he was not going to get a callback.

It all seems too perfect and easy, doesn't it? A super model stopping to talk to you, giving you her complimentary card without you asking for it, and even asking you to give her a call and all that. They all look like winning a lottery jackpot without buying the ticket. So, could this be a fluke and a mere fantasy? Jeff had thought. Then, the effect of the shattered dream hit him like a missile.

The mere thought and prospect that he had lost her made his brain foggy, his heart weak, and his thoughts uncoordinated. He had only himself to blame because the lady was courteous enough and did all she could to encourage him to talk. Her beauty had turned him into a timid boy against his natural bold self.

The burden was too much for him to bear alone. He would need to speak to somebody as quickly as possible, somebody who would offer an alternative route. He believed in the saying: "A problem shared is a problem halved." He thought of Fabian. He had been his childhood friend. They called him Fab for short. They grew up together in the outskirts of Coal City at Coal camp. He was blessed with wisdom and was popular among their mates for his ingenuity and astuteness in resolving issues at the snap of the fingers. To Jeff, he was a man sprinkled with stardust. He got a job in an oil company in Port Harcourt, Rivers State, after obtaining his master's degree with first-class honours in company law at the University of Nigeria, Enugu campus. Scrolling through his contacts, he found out that he didn't have his number anymore. He wasn't surprised because they hadn't spoken for years.

Peeping through the window, he noticed it was getting darker, as confirmed by the noises of the dark chanting goshawk birds, and that was when it dawned on him that night was around the corner and would soon be upon them, and that was when he also realised that he hadn't made any preparations towards getting back to work the next day. Up to that time, he hadn't washed his clothes, let alone getting them ironed. Things were bad enough, and going to work looking scruffy could only add insult to injury.

CHAPTER 2

At work, Jeff made a genuine effort to conceal his apathy, which had practically replaced his usual self-confidence and easy-going nature. He was known as a charismatic, bubbly, easy-going fella by most of his colleagues. Today, he was a mere shadow of himself and reflected none of those qualities he was known for. So, it didn't take his co-workers time to figure out that he wasn't his normal self as he looked unconsciously detached and lost.

"You look off colour today, Jeff. What gives? I hope nothing is the matter?" Mark asked, cutting through the silence as they stood under the mango tree on their break.

"Don't mind me. I am fine. Just a bit under the weather. Secondly, I didn't manage to get enough sleep last night."

"C'mon, Jeff, it is four days now. You should let go. No one is above mistake." Jeff had unknowingly left the gas valve on all night on Thursday after the induction of fresh staff members. A huge waste of money and a major fire risk, according to the manager.

"You could have rendered all of us jobless if the building had got on fire," the manager told him in front of the whole staff the next day.

Jeff hated himself for that. "That wasn't the best way to make a first impression on the new staff," he told Mark, as he tried to agree with him that the incident was the reason for his low mood.

Maureen and other staff who later joined them had all rallied round him to support and encourage him.

"Your lunch is on me," Maureen said cheerfully, handing him two gala meat rolls and a can of Pepsi. And he thanked and beamed her a wry smile in response.

He was still wearing the same sad face when he returned to his office. On getting to his seat, he realised there were a few conference folder files laid on his table in a most disorderly manner. You could tell they were dropped in anger. He had only one person in mind — the administrator. He linked that to the upcoming conference on the protection of human rights to be hosted by their sister company, Free Movement Alliance, which was also an affiliate of the National Human Rights Commission.

Next to the files was a cup of coffee, which he could only tell was coffee from the smell and not by any other feature. It looked so milky for his liking. He wasn't a coffee person, but when he did fancy one, he had always made sure it looked, tasted, and smelt like one. The cup of coffee on his table had none of these qualities except for the aroma.

By the way, what is a cup of coffee doing on my table? Quite unusual. Is it really for me or did somebody forget it on my table? He reluctantly inquired within himself.

"Where have you been all afternoon, Jeff? The administrator was looking for you. She kept those files and had asked me to tell you that they need urgent attention," Tessy informed him in her usual calm, and monotonous voice. "Sorry if the coffee has gone cold. I made it ages ago thinking you would be back soon from your break. I know I should have asked you how you wanted it. I can make you a fresh one if you want," she offered willingly.

"That's ok, Tessy. I will have it." Jeff's late dad had always used the saying, "You don't look a gift horse in the mouth."

"Do you like the coffee?" she asked as he took the first sip of it which now was more on the cold side.

He wondered if it would be wise to tell her what he really thought of her coffee. *Should I tell her how awful her coffee tasted and risk deepening our unfriendliness which is at rock-bottom as it were, or just pretend it is a nice cup of coffee and see if that could blossom and inject some life into our cold relationship?* Jeff thought. They had been just colleagues, nothing more, nothing less. He saw this kind gesture as an opportunity to add some fluidity to their relationship, which seemed lukewarm especially for staff that were sharing the same office for some years.

"Not bad, Tessy, considering you have never made one for me before. Thanks."

"Glad you like it. My little way of cheering you up. You have been so miserable today. How is it? Hope you are not still thinking about Thursday's incident?"

Jeff shrugged his shoulders dejectedly. "Sincerely speaking, I appreciate all the kind gestures and support from the staff, but I don't think I like all this pampering," he said, head stooped dejectedly.

"What do you mean by that?" she asked.

"That is all I got on my break from every member of staff. That's how I got this Pepsi, which Maureen bought me to cheer me up," he said glumly.

"That's what colleagues are for, Jeff," she said, countering his misunderstanding of the staff's support.

What happened on Thursday was indeed a blessing in disguise as far as he was concerned. He was glad he had no other excuses to give anybody for his low mood. How could he have explained the main reason for his deflated mood to colleagues? His sanity would have come under scrutiny if he had told his colleagues that he was hurting and getting depressed for losing someone he never had.

Thank God for Thursday's event. If a disappointment could turn to a blessing, then this surely falls into the bracket, he thought.

"Thanks, Tessy, for your immense generosity and care. Very thoughtful of you," he said with gratitude. He was touched by Tessy's concern and could not thank her enough.

You never know who a real friend is until you are in difficulty. Who could have convinced me that Tessy had such a heart of gold if the incident of Thursday hadn't occurred? He ruminated in his mind.

Jeff hurried to tackle the files in front of him. Julie, the administrator, was known for her open-mindedness— easy to talk to— eager to help if you ask for her help — and could be humorous with her banters if the situation warranted it. However, when duty called, she was a different person. She had never been scared to show her ugly side if her patience was tried or her leadership challenged. She was a fire-breathing administrator who, most of the time, had kept everyone on the edge. She was ready to drag you through the mud and make you look extraordinarily little if she noticed that you weren't putting in enough effort.

Jeff didn't want to fall into that trap. He didn't want to add anything that would escalate or reinforce Thursday's event, let alone the real cause of his low mood. He had fought perseveringly to be in Julie's good book all these years. Like he was told, he treated the files with dispatch to stay out of her trouble.

"Today is exceptionally warm. I can hardly breathe," Tessy said, noticing he had attended to the files.

"Could be one of the reasons we spent much time under the mango tree during our break without even realising that our break time was up," he replied.

"Wonder how long it will take the management to supply our offices with decent air conditioners. We work so hard, and the company is reeling in good money. In fact, everything here needs to be replaced. They have seen better days," she lamented.

"The management, as you can see, is conspicuously miserly. They don't give a toss about our welfare," he said despondently.

"That's one way to put it, Jeff. That's why we are stuck with these old ceiling fans that do nothing but circulate warm air. Such a disgrace!"

"I don't even want to deliberate on the staff salary," she added.

"Neither do I. How many times have they promised to address the meagre take-home pay of the workers, which is not commensurate with the hard work the staff are putting in? The meagre salary does not reflect the market trends and inflation in whatever form either," he replied.

"I need to whisper this because the walls have ears. They are using our money for their frivolous travels and holidays claiming they were for seminars and symposiums. Big liars. And if they think they can pull the wool over our eyes, then they had better think again because we are nobody's fools. They are only interested in feathering their nest and having your eyes out if you falter. Anyway, enough of our complaints because they can't hear us, and even if they can, they can't be bothered, can they?" she asked annoyingly.

"Exactly."

"Fancy an ice cream? I bought them in town when I went to buy some ink cartridges for Julie as if I knew it would turn this warm," she said.

"When you see an eagle, you must appreciate it because it is a rare bird and not seen quite often," Jeff responded, giving her a friendly look.

"Does that mean yes or no? You know I was brought up in the city. You better speak in clear terms or be prepared to explain the meaning. Frankly speaking, I think those born and brought up in the rural areas are in a better position to use and understand them."

"I beg your pardon. I take offence to that. Are you insinuating I am a villager then?" he asked with a hint of disappointment in his voice.

"I didn't mean it that way. It came out the wrong way. My dad has always warned me to think twice before I speak. It is still a lesson in progress. I will learn to think over stuff before I shoot my mouth off." Walking up to his seat and lifting his stooped head, she said, "C'mon, don't feel that bad. I am sorry."

Her hand felt cold but at the same time soothing.

"Your hand is cold, Tessy."

Offering no apology, she said, "It has always been…but my heart, on the contrary, is always warm, and that's what matters."

"Yes, I remember; cold hand, warm heart," Jeff replied cheerfully.

At that point, more than any other thing, it was clear they were warming up to each other. Another blessing in disguise. "I am not crossed with you. I really am not," Jeff reassured her.

"Good to know, but I still want to know the meaning of the proverb," she insisted.

"You are just like an Elephant."

"An Elephant!" she squealed.

"Better hold your peace. I used Elephant in this context to depict memory. Don't tell me you haven't heard the saying that Elephant doesn't forget. You need to work harder on your proverbial stuff. It is under par."

He could see the relief in her face as he threw more light into the contextual meaning of the adage.

"My poor understanding of proverbs is getting awkward and embarrassing. This is not the first time I have portrayed myself in a bad light for being unable to understand the contextual meaning of adages and proverbs. I will start to pay more attention to them," she said warmly.

"Do you know what? It has turned out to be an exceptionally heart-warming and exciting day. I am happy I have been able to cheer you up," she said, taking a quick glance at her watch.

"I can't thank you enough, Tessy. I don't know whether to call you a shrink, an angel, or a lifesaver. You have been amazing and supportive," Jeff said thankfully.

"Not at all. That is what friends are for," she replied warmly.

Everything that happened in the office flew out of the window when Jeff got home from work. He had used Tessy temporarily to mask his anguish of not being able to contact Jane. The sadness and distress he left at home before going to work that morning were right there waiting for his return. And there they were, staring him in the face just as a raccoon would stare at the homeowner from its hiding place in the cupboard after breaching the owner's privacy.

CHAPTER 3

Tessy had seized the prevailing situation to strengthen their relationship. She was buying snacks and drinks for the two of them while coming to work or during break time. She had also called Jeff at odd times on a few occasions just to ask how he was, calls that stirred up some suspicion in him if she was wanting something more than just a colleague relationship. She even abbreviated his name, Jeff Chibuike, to JC and called him that even in the presence of other staff, and when she did, she sounded possessive and looked controlling.

As the relationship continued to grow, he discovered that both shared the same interests in music and sports. They discovered they supported the same English Premier League team, Liverpool, and enjoyed funk and soul music. The bond continued to grow and flourish, so much so that they went to the pub together on two occasions to watch Liverpool play in the English premier league.

A few weeks later, Tessy came to work with a beautiful Liverpool football club portrait and did what surprised and intrigued Jeff. "I bought it for us, I mean for our office," she said adoringly. She came behind his corner and hung it on the wall.

"Here you go. Isn't that beautiful?" she asked excitedly after putting it up.

"Absolutely," he replied with a beautiful smile.

She pulled out her phone from her pair of jeans, sat on his lap, and posed for a selfie. He was so captivated by the portrait that he barely noticed what was going on. "You need to move a bit to the right so that we can get the portrait in the selfie," she told him with a flirtatious smile. With her cheek glued to his and arm around his shoulder, she said the Liverpool football club motto, "You will never walk alone," and then she snapped the picture.

Everything was exciting and welcoming as far as Jeff was concerned, especially now he was unable to get in touch with Jane. It was like a stopgap relief that made it harder for him to notice that Tessy was slowly but steadily becoming uncomfortably intimate with him. Her indecent jokes had increased exponentially and were as common as the way she brushed past him. There was a lot of body contact as she walked past him lately, even though there was enough space to push a hospital theatre bed in the office.

But she scaled it up a bit that hot, humid afternoon. While they were having ice cream in the office, she walked up to him and wiped off the remnant of the ice cream in the corner of his mouth with her thumb. He was transfixed and dumbstruck.

"You can at least say thank you, can't you?" she said humorously, trivialising what she had done.

He made a face and was still unable to say a thing. He was embarrassed and angry at the same time. He wondered why she didn't tell him there was some ice cream in the corner of his mouth.

There were a few similar events like that in the following weeks, but he refused to attribute them to anything sinister until that Wednesday afternoon. He had told her that he was going on his break. And she had asked him to get her some ice lollies from the nearby shop. She was walking up to him to give him some money when she appeared to have tripped over the edge of the rug on the floor, and he intuitively stepped forward and caught her by the waist while her hands rested on his shoulders. Somebody walking in at that moment would think they were doing salsa or tango dance. When she stabilised, he let go of her waist, but her hands continued to rest on his shoulders. Instead of disengaging, she looked at him as if she were smitten with him —her eyes were saturated, not with tears, but with burning desire from her raging hormones — they were piercing, desperate, inviting, and seductively provocative. He remained motionless and confused. Then she started moving her face slowly towards him, expecting him to do the same so they could meet midway for a kiss, the kind of unplanned kiss you would see in romance movies. But when he didn't reciprocate, she finally broke free and apologised. Her apology confirmed to him that his assumption was right. She actually wanted a kiss of him and in the office. That created doubts in his mind, and he wondered if the trip was accidental or on purpose.

The recent events he had thought were a blessing in disguise were now looking like or maybe turning into a premeditated curse judging by her sudden, uncomfortable moves. For a moment, he had thought if it was necessary to think outside the box, whether there were hidden agendas in her behaviours and actions, especially how she would quickly change the topic each time he wanted to share the story with her about what transpired between him and Jane in Enugu. As far as he was concerned, she seemed to be using the gas valve leak as a smokescreen to justify the kind of intimacy she was pursuing. But whatever it was, he remained resolute and didn't show her any sign of interest in that direction, though he started keeping an eye on her more than he had recently done.

Weeks later, Mark, a work colleague, had approached Jeff that morning before work started. "I came early today, so we can talk about this."

"About what?" he inquisitively queried.

"There is this rumour going around that Tessy has a huge crush on you. She told Maureen, and Maureen confided in me. But I wouldn't have bothered to be here this hour if I didn't hear what I heard yesterday where Julie, the administrator was giving Tessy quite a tongue-lashing for mistakes and gaps she had started noticing in her works. She put them down to her lack of concentration at work because she was preoccupied by the thoughts of you."

"Thoughts of who?" Jeff asked, looking bewildered.

"Thoughts of you, Jeff. I think Maureen had told a few more staff. To be honest, I think everyone knows now, maybe, except you. I don't want it to look as if I am tittle-tattling." Mark looked around him, lowered his voice, and said, "Maureen said that Tessy had the selfie portrait of you and her in her lounge, room, kitchen, and even in her bathroom. According to Maureen, Tessy's mobile phone screen saver is the same picture of you and her. Haven't you noticed?" Mark stopped to ask.

Confused and unable to grasp the meaning of what Mark was saying, Jeff could only force a smile before shrugging his shoulders and then pouting his lips.

"I don't know whether it is true or not," Mark continued, "But Maureen also told me that the ring tone on her mobile was 'get down on it' by Kool and the gang. I feel awful saying all these, but Maureen said that Tessy told her that she usually got turned on looking at the selfie, especially when having a bath, and had touched herself at times. According to Maureen, Tessy said she always wanted to get down on you each time the ringtone went off."

Jeff nearly blacked out at what Mark was telling him. The picture was now getting clearer.

"Isn't that irony of life that somebody is dying for your love this much when our Frank has done everything humanly possible to gain her attention? The other day, Frank helped her to offload the stationeries from her car. Guess what? She didn't even say thank you to him. Frank was so gutted that he told Maureen about Tessy's ingratitude. When Maureen confronted her about it, she said she never asked him to help her. She was even mad at Maureen, stressing that people should stop bothering her with anything concerning Frank. She went further to say that one should not be forced to love someone. How vile was that? I feel so sorry for Frank. Now, think how jealous and angry this development would make him feel," Mark said.

Jeff heaved his shoulders in resignation. "If what you are saying is right, then I am surprised she hasn't told me that she is this madly in love with me."

"What? You want a Nigerian babe to tell you that she is madly in love with you? Seriously? Of course, you know the title that will fetch her if she dares, don't you?"

"I have absolutely no idea. You tell me."

"C'mon, Jeff. Don't play this pretend game here. Society frowns at girls who have such boldness. We call them slappers."

"Slappers? What on earth is that? You have just accused me of playing pretend game when you know I don't. So, I am not going to pretend that I know what I do not know."

"Okay. Slappers are prostitutes if you want me to break it down."

"Now you are talking. So, girls who are bold to express their feelings towards men are called prostitutes. So, what do we call men who express their feelings towards women? There must be a terminology for them — gigolo — philanderers, or what? If men can toast ladies, I expect ladies to be free to do the same to men without prejudice and societal condemnation. Equal right. That's what I call fairness if we sincerely believe in equal rights. This is the 21st century, not the medieval age. About time we did away with this retrogressive thinking that is holding our women back. That's my argument anyway," Jeff said.

Ignoring his argument, Mark laughed and said, "Wait a minute, so, you really want Tessy to come and tell you that she loves you?"

"Of course, I don't see why not," he said, re-affirming his opinion.

"Okay, let's assume she has the courage. What will be your response?"

Jeff laughed proudly and said, "I will tell her to put it in writing to assure me she means it. You know girls nowadays can easily get you in trouble. I don't want to be accused of sexual harassment and all that. I need evidence to protect myself in the court of law in case it comes to that."

Mark laughed so hard and loud that he would have fallen if he hadn't stabilised himself with the oak tree in front of him. When he stopped laughing, he said, "You are the most sarcastic man I have ever met. What a contradictory statement! Is that your version of women's emancipation? Anyway, what will be your reply to the letter?"

"I will tell her to give me a couple of weeks to think about it."

Mark was really having fun now because he couldn't stop himself from laughing and coughing intermittently. "You are a horrible man, Jeff. You really are."

Jeff knew full well that what he was telling Mark wasn't true. He was aware, like any other person, that society thumbs its nose at women who dare say stuff like that to a man. But he continued to pretend nevertheless and said, "No, I am not, Mark. I am only trying to make her taste her own pill and see how it feels. That's what she is doing to our Frank, isn't it?" Jeff wasn't against Tessy rejecting Frank's advances, but he wasn't impressed with the way she was going about it — treating him like a piece of rubbish.

"Let's just presume that tomorrow is Valentine's Day. And let's also assume Tessy gives you a flower and a card on the day, which I genuinely think she will. What is going to be your reaction?" Mark enquired.

Jeff gave him a lengthy look.

"You aren't going to refuse, are you?" Mark asked.

"Of course not. I will take them."

Holding his heart gingerly, Mark heaved a sigh of relief because he thought Jeff was going to reject the gifts.

Jeff then continued and said, "But I will put them in the bin right before her."

Mark opened his mouth wide in shock at his response.

"No, I am only joking," he said, laughing.

"You are a proper nasty man," Mark exclaimed.

"I won't be that mean to Tessy. But I will surely tell her to give the flower to Frank, who will appreciate it."

Mark shook his head in disbelief and told him that he had heard enough and that he was returning to his office after glancing at his watch to realise he should be doing some work in his office at that hour.

When Mark left, Jeff returned to his seat. He sat for a while and ruminated over all Mark said. He remembered recent events of indecency by Tessy and narrowed them down to what Mark had just told him. *Is that why they say that familiarity breeds contempt?* he asked himself.

CHAPTER 4

Finally, the administrator had to move Jeff to a new office closer to hers as Tessy's mistakes at work continued to deepen and mount. It appeared Julie was trying to nip things in the bud. Tessy and Jeff were big assets to the company, and Julie wouldn't like the company to lose them. She knew it was only a matter of time before they were caught red-handed doing stuff they should not be doing at work, and she was aware of what the company policy said about that — instant dismissal, and she didn't want things to escalate to that, at least, not when she was the administrator of the company.

Tessy was disappointed, devastated, and livid by the move. She was consumed by the feeling of loss. Comparatively, there seemed to be no difference between her and a toddler whose favourite toy or candy had been taken away from.

Jeff was no better. He was both disillusioned and angry and saw no reason why he should be moved. It wasn't his work that was under scrutiny. It was Tessy's. So, if there was anybody to be moved, it had to be Tessy, though he wouldn't have liked that to happen, not now she was filling up nicely the vacuum created by Jane.

He felt lost on the first day in his new office despite the luxurious features of the office. Though he didn't like the obvious intimacy Tessy was showing, at the same time, he missed her. She made him laugh with her funny jokes. In her presence, he tended to forget the thoughts of Jane that usually weighed him down. Nevertheless, he knew it was the right decision by the management. After all, everyone knows that an ounce of prevention is better than a pound of cure. It seemed Julie was trying to nip in the bud, a major disaster looming.

He was impressed by everything about his new office. It had all the prerequisites and features of a modern office. The cobalt blue Panasonic air conditioner was in immaculate condition, contrary to those in other offices, including the one in the office he shared with Tessy. The upholstery and its arrangement were contemporary. There were vertical cream-coloured blinds to the windows which were overlaid by red wine-coloured curtains that perfectly matched the colours of the chaise lounge sofa and the tufted carpet. At the right-hand corner on entering the office opposite the air conditioner was a cream-coloured brand-new five-foot whirlpool fridge/freezer stuffed with assorted fruits, dairies, biscuits, and drinks. He wasn't sure all the contents of the fridge were for him when he opened it.

Julie noticed his apprehension when she walked in. "You will get used to the new environment, I promise you," she said, standing in the doorway, smiling broadly. "Do you like your new office?"

"Glorious. Really appealing," he replied with a sham smile.

"I made sure that it was exquisitely decorated to your taste. I will be on hand to ensure you adapt as quickly as possible to the new environment."

To my taste? What does she know about what I like and dislike? He asked in his mind. Trying not to look ungrateful, he nodded and thanked her.

Julie kept to her words because she was in his office probably more than she was in hers. As weeks passed, he noticed that she was upping her game and closeness. He didn't see anything wrong with that. At the end of the day, she moved him to prevent distractions, so he knew it would be contradictory and preposterous if she resorted to the same gimmicks that compelled her to move him from his previous office. But when she started asking him to come with her to shop for office stationery, drinks, and confectioneries, he started feeling uneasy.

Tessy had texted him a few times expressing her concern about the frequency at which he was going out with Julie where they had at times ended up in restaurants and coffee shops. But he reassured her she should not lose any sleep over it.

But that reassurance was dealt a blow three weeks later when Tessy walked into Julie's office that Wednesday afternoon to find her and Jeff having a meal together in her office.

"Hello Tessy, can we help you?" Julie greeted her offhandedly but with a hint of guilt in her contoured face.

"Not really. I am here to deliver a message. I don't need any help from any of you. Is he supposed to be here in your office having lunch with you? I thought the main reason for moving him to a new office was to remove any form of distraction. This surely negates the motive, doesn't it? This is more like robbing Peter to pay Paul. You have always kept your eyes on him and have always wanted him closer to yourself. But like a drowning man who would clutch to a straw, you were looking for a flimsy excuse to perpetrate your evil thoughts. That really makes you clever, doesn't it?"

"Watch your tongue, young lady," Julie interrupted her defiantly.

"Watch your manoeuvre, smart lady," Tessy replied fearlessly. "Anyway, I am here to inform you that the bank manager of Oceanic Bank would like you to call him back on his mobile. He said he couldn't get you on the line. How could he? I now know why." She dropped a piece of paper angrily on her table. "That is his number if you will ever find time to call him," she snarled. She gazed at Jeff angrily on her way out.

Julie's ego had been bruised and battered, and she wasn't going to let things stay that way. She needed to enshroud herself with some respect because she felt her dignity had been eroded. "Excuse me, Tessy," she said before Tessy exited the door. "Have you come to deliver a message or to pick a fight? Why are you sounding so bitter, like a sore loser? You feel I have taken your man, and you are going off the deep end," she concluded contemptuously.

That was when the wheels came off. Like a cobra cornered by a mongoose, Tessy spun around and placed herself in a vantage position to fend off the attack and said, "Now I know how shameless you are. You have thrown your reputation to the pigs. So, you are really on a man hunt, and you think this docile gentleman here will be an easy, perfect prey to quench your voracious masculine appetite. You want to use your administrative position to take advantage of his good nature, don't you? I can see he is already a puppet in your manipulative hands. Look at him sitting there like a lackey," she said, turning her attention to Jeff. "Are you not man enough to know what you want? Can't you spot danger when you see one? Are you that silly? I can't believe you have condescended this low to allow this cougar to be cooking for you. Only God knows what amount of love potion that food is stuffed with. It won't be long before you forget how to spell your name. She is fifteen years older than you, for God's sake. And if you haven't heard, she had just split up with her husband, whom she has left desolate, heartbroken and in a wheelchair after the poor man suffered a stroke. Now, she is on the prowl, seeking fresh blood. The same fate awaits you, lover boy, unless you make hay while the sun is still shining. Run for dear life while you can," she said, shaking visibly with rage.

Julie had heard enough of her rants, and with clenched teeth and fists and eyebrows fully retracted like that of a Madagascar lemur, she charged towards Tessy.

"Can the pair of you behave yourselves?" Jeff said as he stood in between them to prevent further escalation of the brawl.

"Get out of the way, Jeff, so that I can shut her filthy mouth up forever," Julie threatened.

"This is not right. This is the height of irresponsibility. I hope the pair of you will have the courage to tell the MD or any of the staff members the reason for this quarrel if they happen to walk in. Anyway, I am out of here. I can't stand here and watch two mature women behave like spoilt teenagers. I refuse to be a witness to that. This is an office, not a clubhouse," he reminded them, now feeling ashamed on their behalf.

"What on earth is that noise?" Mark asked Jeff when he came out from Julie's office.

"You can go in and ask the two deranged, shameless women. Anyway, I don't think I can handle this. The kitchen is too hot, and I can't deal with the heat anymore. I am too young to play this game of love and savagery. I am scared I might get burnt. No man in his right frame of mind stands before a moving train. It is time to move on. I don't mind serving in the tills in a grocery shop insofar as it will pay my bills and put food on the table."

Ignoring completely all Jeff had said, Mark asked, "Don't tell me that what I am thinking is the cause of this uproar. They are not fighting over you, are they?"

"The door is open. You can go in and ask them."

"Aren't you making a rash decision?" Mark asked, looking mystified at the unfolding events.

"It is my call, and I am sticking to it."

The management decided to suspend three of them without pay while they investigated the cause of the misunderstanding. The MD of the company described the incident as unfortunate because the three staff involved were real assets to the company, and he had hoped that the problem would be resolved amicably so that they could be reinstated.

The job hunt was the only thing in Jeff's mind from here on in. He was constantly searching the internet or going through newspapers and magazines, concentrating more on job vacancy columns. He had made up his mind not to go back to the office, irrespective of the decision of the management. As far as he was concerned, the office was a ticking bomb waiting to detonate.

It was towards the end of the first week of his suspension that he found in Vanguard newspapers an advert about a seminar on human rights to be held in Cosmo hotels in Port Harcourt. It caught his attention, not only because it related to his present job somehow, but it also had the potential for improving his CV significantly, thereby doubling his chance of landing a new, better job. It looked like something he had always wanted. But most of all, it would offer him the opportunity to visit Port Harcourt, the garden city, for the first time. Enthusiastically, he grabbed his phone and, rang the number and was told he was very lucky to have taken one of the two remaining slots.

"Many thanks," Jeff replied delightfully.

Having successfully secured a place for the seminar, he started making physical and financial provisions for the journey. He would have liked to do the journey by air, but the prevailing circumstances discouraged him from doing so. The future looked bleak, and using his depleted, meagre finance for a flight would be a bit irrational, so he decided to use public transport as it was the cheapest means of making the journey as his car wasn't in a good state for such a long journey.

CHAPTER 5

A long journey, it eventually turned out to be. It took them just under 11 hours to get to Port Harcourt. It was getting late, and Jeff wanted to get himself to his hotel before night fell. Grabbing his luggage hastily, he headed straight to the Dozie taxi depot, which was about fifty meters away from the bus stop and got a taxi to his hotel.

"Hello, welcome to Cosmo Hotel," an elegant young lady in her prime of youth greeted him. She looked to be in her mid-twenties and was evidently full of bounce and spirit.

Jeff was thrilled by her eloquence and confidence. Her English was not only polished but also gripping. But what caught his attention more than any other thing was her British accent. Most probably, she had just relocated from the UK. She looked sleek and charming in her black skirt and light blue long-sleeve shirt with a navy blue bow tie. She shot him a look of approval that made his spinal cord tighten a bit against the walls of his vertebrae.

"You must be Jeff Chibuike."

"I am. How do you know my name?" he asked, looking a bit surprised.

"Because you are the last guest we are expecting today. Others have since checked in," she told him.

Asking one of her colleagues to mind the reception area, she offered to show him his room.

He was a bit hesitant about the help. He felt a churn of discomfort and anxiety in her company.

"Let me help you with your bags," she willingly offered.

Good Lord! This is not the best way to start my stay, his thoughts sounding louder than his words. *That will be jumping from frying pan to fire if this, by any stretch of the imagination, kickstarts any kind of intimacy. I am here to seek remedy to my problem, not to compound it,* he thought.

"Here you are! This is your room," she purred sonorously as she ushered him into a vast, exquisite room. Her steamy looks and innuendos made clear she was hitting on him.

The room looked ravishingly beautiful. There was a swan lounge chair and an egg arm swivel chair both overlooking the liquor cabinet. At the far end of the wall on the right-hand side was the sleep motion bed adorned with breath-taking bed accessories. He never knew the amount he paid for the hotel could stretch that far to get him anything near the comfort of what he was seeing.

The interior décor undoubtedly complimented the tired-looking appearance of the exterior.

Their attention was simultaneously drawn to the imposing bed. Picking up the TV remote control from the coffee table, she sat on the bed and pointed the remote at the 32-inch colour television mounted on the wall opposite. Rubbing and caressing the bed with the other hand, she looked seductively into his eyes and said, "You have multiple TV channels to kill off boredom in case you become bored."

A lustful feeling ran through him, but he stifled it before it could progress any further.

"I will leave you now to settle in." Stretching out her hand for a handshake, she said, "My name is Meghan. Don't hesitate to call me if you need anything tonight. See you later, Jeff."

"See you later, Meghan," he replied with mixed feelings. She blew him a kiss and dazzled him with her provocative sidelong smile before slowly closing the door behind her. Her hand was baby-soft and warm as toast.

Jeff made sure he didn't have any reason to ask for her help through the night. He clearly saw the danger of doing so. There was no doubt in his mind that she had feelings for him. "I can't be running away from women only to run into another."

"Aren't you attending the seminar you came for?" female voice informed him when he picked up the phone that jolted him from his sleep.

"What time is it?" Jeff asked in a state of confusion.

"Others have gone in already for the seminar. It is 8.40 am. You have a clock in your room, haven't you?" she asked, giggling. "You didn't sleep in, did you?" she asked jokingly.

"I must have. I have got to go now. Thanks for waking me up, though."

"You are welcome."

He had already replaced the receiver before realising he didn't ask who it was. It didn't matter anyway. He needed to move at lightning speed if he was going to catch up with the seminar. Good job; he managed to lay out the clothes he would be wearing the previous night. He hurried into them after a quick shower.

"Where are you going? Here, you need to sign the attendance register before you can enter the auditorium," Meghan informed him with a mischievous smile.

"What are you still doing? You told me last night you finish at eight this morning. It is past 9 o'clock," he reminded her.

"I know. The person who is supposed to take over from me is running late. Possibly slept in like you."

"You must be the person that I spoke to on the phone this morning, correct?"

"Yes, I was." And there was some sense of flirt and cajolery in her voice that mimicked the one that woke him up earlier on.

Helping him to readjust his tie, she gently pushed him into the auditorium, saying, "Go in. You are late. We will talk later. Oh, sorry, here is my card. I don't know whether I will see you before you go. Good luck with your seminar."

Trying to be courteous, he thanked her even though he felt uncomfortable with her intimacy. Closing the door after her, he binned the card to nip things in the bud.

The seminar went smoothly, as he had expected. The presenters were good in their presentations— detailed, with a great deal of professional clarity. It would take a lamebrain not to take in what they taught. The morning session passed in no time, and at 1:30 pm exactly, Mr Dotubo, one of the presenters, brought the session to a close.

One day gone, one more to go, Jeff merrily told himself. He was intrigued by how much he learned about Human Resources and conflict resolution, and he knew why the company was ranked so high in Human Resources and development.

He quickly transferred and saved all he jotted on his notepad to his laptop before leaving the Auditorium. He was hungry now. He had no time for breakfast, having woken up late. Gathering all his stuff, he made his way to the restaurant.

"Oh, my goodness! Oh, my goodness! Is that you, Fab, or am I seeing double?" Jeff screamed at the top of his lungs, causing everyone in the restaurant to look in their direction. He didn't care.

"Boy, oh boy," Fab responded intensely as they clasped each other in a bear hug.

"What on earth brought you to Garden City?" Fab asked excitedly.

"I am here for a seminar."

"On Human Resources and Conflict?"

Jeff nodded. "And you?"

"Same," he said, nodding. "We came so early, so other staff members decided to go for a walk and sightseeing while we waited for the afternoon session."

"You are not looking bad, Fab," he said, taking a second look at him. "I can smell the wealth. Oil money is good. You look impeccable. Really happy for you. This is where you really belong … a place you can utilise and showcase your God's given talent and intellectual gift," Jeff complimented him.

His eyes lit up at the remark. He laughed proudly while flicking his nose with his fingers and involuntarily adjusting and readjusting his designer eyeglasses. Though he was aware of his outstanding intelligence, he would feel great each time someone reminded him of that.

"What of you? You are easy on the eye. Life must be treating you well in Lagos, Jeff."

"Wrong. On the contrary, life has been hard on me. I am learning the hard way."

"You do not look it then."

"Maybe in your eyes, but the truth is that I have been through rough patches and still not out of the wood. Part of it is what brought me here."

Fab waved the waiter over. "Would you like to make your order while I find out what your problem is? It seems to me you have a lot up your sleeve, and they appear unsettling."

Flipping casually through the menu, Jeff asked the waiter to fix him some meat pie and build a refreshing cocktail of lemonade and whiskey. He couldn't care less. After all, his session for the day was over, so he didn't mind getting a little alcohol down his system.

"So much water has passed under the bridge since the last time we saw, Fab."

"I know. Longest time indeed."

"This meat pie is super good— so tender, so delicious," Jeff complimented the baker as he took his first bite. "I wanted to contact you some time ago to seek your opinion over something but realised I had lost your contact."

"That's a bizarre coincidence because a few weeks ago, I tried to contact you but found out that I didn't have your number in my contacts anymore. We must have inadvertently cleared our numbers from our contacts."

"That's a bit telepathic," Jeff said. He was in the middle of his speech when four people walked in through the door, three men and a lady.

"Are you still here, Fab?" one of the men asked casually.

"I am. I have an August visitor, as you can see," he replied joyfully.

"The leopard will never change its spots. Why are you staring like that? I thought you said you have an issue to talk about, or is she bigger than the problem?" Fab said, pointing in her direction. He just knew why Jeff was staring.

"I believe she is," Jeff said with no genuine attempt to deny his claim.

Fab smiled affectedly and said, "I can understand. Who wouldn't? We have all stared, tried and failed woefully. She is not a casual lay, I must tell you."

"She is the issue that I wanted to phone you about. I am going to talk to her right now."

Fab burst out laughing. Tilting his head in a manner to engage his full attention, he said, "Hey, hey, don't be ridiculous. Don't tell me the little whiskey you just had is already messing up your brain. Don't go there to disgrace yourself, please. That lady is a sacred cow, to put it mildly. That gentleman in a grey suit with a striped yellow and white tie is our CEO. Even in his strictest, harshest behaviour, he protects and guards her jealously like the hen protects her newly hatched chicks. To some of us, he seems overprotective of her. Our CEO is ruthless when he is angry and has fired staff for negligible offences. He doesn't give a toss if you are the breadwinner of your family or not. Everyone avoids his trouble because it spells doom. On a few occasions, he had publicly slapped his secretary for letting in visitors without informing him first. You are unlucky if you enter his office without knocking and waiting to be asked in. We wonder at times if there is something surreptitious in his office he is protecting. The other day, he threw a cup of tea at the delivery man for the late delivery of the office furniture and attempted to stab him with his penknife when the man demanded an apology for his hostility. But having said all this, he has a soft spot for Jane and has treated her a bit differently from most of the staff. He claimed that he was protecting her from incessant disturbance from men like you," Fab said, jerking his fingers at Jeff. And Jeff laughed a little the way Fab said it.

"Huh," Jeff scoffed. "I know his kind. He is jealous of young men approaching her because he believes they have a better chance than him to win her love. I can see that in his face. I think he likes her," he insinuated.

"Don't be ridiculous. He is far too old for her. I won't be surprised if he is the same age as her dad or even older," Fab interrupted him.

"Yes, he might be too old for Jane to notice him in that sense, but I am sure that Jane isn't too young for him to make a pass at," Jeff replied, laughing.

"But frankly speaking, and in all fairness to her, I don't think she needs his protection because she is as steadfast as the sun. She has a mind of her own. Nothing impresses her, especially men. If not, Helen, our colleague, confirmed to us that she was straight. Most of us had thought she was a lesbian. Let me tell you, Jeff when this girl was employed, we couldn't believe she was single until our administrator confirmed it."

"All the male staff, including married men, went after her like one seeking a river in the Sahara Desert. We were like male bowerbirds that make the best nest to attract a female for mating. Every guy with his unique tactics. One of our staff started wearing a suit every day to look corporate and different even when the temperature was as high as 32 degrees Celsius. Jane made a mockery of him by telling one of the girls that she wondered if the guy's hypothalamus was still regulating body temperature correctly. I tried to impress her with my intelligence and as the company lawyer but failed dreadfully. She made a caricature of me that I couldn't communicate. I was mad as a hatter when she said that. But she did not even apologise. She defined what effective communication was to me and unequivocally condemned my reckless usage of Latin when I spoke to show I was a lawyer. Another guy tried a different approach altogether by ignoring her, thinking it would arouse Jane's curiosity as to why he did not show any interest in her, being the only one who seemed indifferent. His reaction formation approach backfired big time. I think Jane knew what his antic was and decided to treat him as if he wasn't even a staff. The foreign engineers made no impression as far as she was concerned. I don't know whether I would be right to say she is allergic to men. Jonathan, one of our staff at a point said he believed she was misandrous. To our surprise, it is the old gardener, Mr Tamuno, the girls, and the CEO, who is like a father to her with whom she relates well. Don't get me wrong. She isn't rude to the boys — she doesn't just want any intimacy from the male staff. We all thought she must have had a terrible experience from a previous relationship until Helen confirmed to us that she had never been in a relationship. Our female colleagues would have been envious of her beauty because no man ever looked in their direction whenever she was around, but her innate kindness and humility had protected her from such petty jealousy. Jeff, she is something else. Completely inaccessible. So, don't bother to waste your breath and energy, my good friend," he dissuaded him.

Jeff, after listening to him, spread out his hands flamboyantly and exclaimed, "Great stuff. So, she is waiting for me then. That's why she rejected all of you."

Fab laughed hysterically and nearly fell off his chair. Then he said to Jeff, "If you suffer from mania à potu, why do you drink alcohol? I can see you are heavily influenced by that little whisky you drank." He genuinely believed that the whisky had dulled his senses, and he was talking wet.

"Mania à potu, what is that?"

"You have to Google it, Jeff."

"Whatever the meaning, it is not going to stop me. I am going to speak to her, and now."

"Good luck, but stay away from me after the embarrassment because I don't want to be associated with the awkwardness that will follow."

"Stay here, Fab. I will be right back," he said, ignoring all his advice.

"Good day, lady and gentlemen," Jeff greeted them politely.

"Good day. Who are you, and how can we help you?" the gentleman in a grey suit, whom he believed was the CEO, asked him with a hawk-like look, probably having an intuition as to why he had approached them.

"I am Jeff. Jeff Chibuike."

"So, how can we help you, Mr Chibuike?"

"I only need her help, Sir." Without much ado, he looked straight at Jane and asked, "How are you doing?"

With a face painted with rage and resentment, the CEO decided to intercede on her behalf and said, "Look here, young man, we are here for business, and if you don't mind, could you please take your leave honourably?"

Jane felt a lump in her throat and was unable to speak, recognising him. She quickly got up and ran towards the restroom.

"As you can see, your presence hasn't done her any good. I am sick of men like you putting her through stuff like this."

"Like what?" Jeff boldly asked him.

"Don't stand there asking me questions, young man. I am warning you for the second and last time to find your way. I will not stand by and watch you put her through this misery."

"Okay, okay, do not blow your top. I will leave, but I am not giving up on her. No reasonable person gives up on a peerless gem. She is more than a diamond to me. My life is incomplete and meaningless without her."

"Get lost, you witless simpleton," he shouted at Jeff, trying to get physical.

"Excuse me, Mr Douglas, hope you wouldn't mind if I speak to him, please?" she politely asked after returning from the restroom, looking stunned and almost spaced out.

"What happened? Why did you do that? Why did you leave me heartbroken for so long? I thought I was your kind of girl. You left me high and dry — in the dark."

"Can you please stop putting me through the sword? I have been through a lot because of my inability to contact you," Jeff pleaded. "Can I start by introducing myself? I lacked the courage to do that in Enugu because I couldn't find the right words to describe how you made me feel."

She gave a gleeful chortle that made Fab leave his seat to join them to confirm his eyes and ears were not playing tricks on him.

"My name is Jeff."

"I am Jane," she said, stretching out her hand for a handshake. They held their hands, looking and searching through their eyes as if they were seeking to unravel a mystified puzzle. It was Fab that brought them back to Mother Earth by screaming, "You are still holding hands, guys."

She turned and gave Fab a look of, *mind your business and stop meddling with other people's affairs.*

"What is the meaning of this? What is going on here? Who is he?" the CEO asked in astonishment.

"It is a long story, Sir," she said softly.

Jeff told her that they still had thirty minutes before the afternoon session. He asked her if she could spare ten minutes of her time.

"I have waited for this moment for so long," she said with a wide smile that exposed her glittery, white teeth.

"In that case, you need to excuse me for a moment."

"Where are you going now? I am coming with you. I am not letting you out of my sight again," she insisted excitedly.

Throwing his hands up in the air and allowing them to drop floppily on his lap, Mr Douglas screamed, "He has cast a spell on her"

"I need some explanation, and quick. Somebody needs to tell me who this man is .... a man who has made Jane laugh from the bottom of her heart for the very first time. A man, Jane doesn't want to leave her sight ..."

"I know who he is, boss," Fab replied. "He is my childhood friend. We grew up in Enugu. We did things together. He had always had his ways with girls. But this is beyond my comprehension. I know eventually that a guy someday will win Jane over, but the thought that a man could tickle her fancy this much and make her feel this weak and soft would never have crossed my mind in a million years."

Throwing a lazy sideways glance at Fab, she modestly said, "Will you just shut up, Fab. Haven't I got the right to choose who I want to fall in love with?"

"Will I be right then to say that he is the reason you rejected all the men that made a pass at you?"

"What if the answer to your question is a big yes?" she dauntlessly replied.

"I won't be long, Jane," Jeff told her, interrupting the banter going on between her and Fab. He left and was back in a flash, to her relief.

"Right, I know this might not be the right place. I don't even know if I have the right. But I have always known that every rule has an exception, and I am ready to break protocols and cut corners."

"What on earth are you doing with a guitar, Mic and Speaker?" Fab asked curiously and comically, suppressing a laugh in the process.

"What do you think? I am going to serenade the object of my desire."

"I never knew you could play guitar. Never seen you with one before. So, why do you want to show yourself up before everyone here? Spare yourself the embarrassment, lover boy."

"That is the second time you are asking me to spare myself some embarrassment. You saw how the first one ended. Fab, if you want an omelette, you won't be scared to break eggs. Whoever seeks gold should be prepared to get his hands dirty. Nothing is too embarrassing when you value what you are looking for. As the saying goes, *the end justifies the means.* Like I have said before, she is worth any embarrassment and trouble. She is the purest of gems. I have always believed that someday, somehow, I will have this singular moment to open my heart to this wonderful lady. It is now a dream come true."

Jane wasn't comfortable. Her nervous look said it all. She didn't want anything to spoil the moment. Her dazzling hazel eyes were now replaced with glazed ones. She tugged and pinched her ears intermittently while shuffling backwards and forward awkwardly. Her long fingers raked through her silky hair endlessly. Finally, she approached Jeff meekly and whispered in his ears, "Don't do this, please. You don't need to serenade me. I am all yours already.

Even if you want to, there are so many comfortable, serene places to do it. Not just here, please."

"Darling," he said to her, "I made this promise to you and myself since we parted in Enugu. I promise that I will sing for you the day I meet you again. That's why I carry these musical gadgets wherever I go. I didn't care about any bottleneck. Jane, darling, you are worth any trouble. Any man worthy of you will be keen and glad to work his fingers to the bone to make you his. Remember, your boss, Mr Douglas, wanted my head on a platter some moments ago. Fab was disillusioned and distraught when I told him I was going to speak to you some minutes ago. As you can see, they have swallowed their arrogance and disillusionment and are now mere spectators. Your presence made me lose my power of speech the first time I met you. Today, on the contrary, your presence has given me so much power and confidence. With the kind of wings you have given me, I believe I can soar for eternity. Now, I feel strong as an ox and bold as a lion. Let me take you to a height you have never been before, sweetheart. Allow me if you would like to be your groove control and take you on a fantastic voyage just for this moment. Let me call your heart my home, my cutie-pie."

Laughing, smiling, and looking more relaxed, she said, "I can see you have a way with words. They just roll off the tongue and are so pacifying and catchy to the ears that I feel serenaded already."

With her permission, he quickly secured the corner of the lounge dining area where he would be in nobody's way with his instruments. With his mic firmly attached to his Innox microphone stand and his guitar connected to the pioneer speaker, he then grabbed the only vacant Stagg seat left in the area. He ran a quick test on the gadgets just to affirm that he was good to go. Everything fell into place.

He handled his guitar so professionally that it sounded not too far off from what you would expect from Jimi Hendrix. Beginning with a voice that sounded like the legend Louis Armstrong, he finished strongly with a contemporary voice that strongly mimicked Michael Bubble and Luther Vandross.

A day to remember. The day I felt the power of love, like a dry leaf, I was blown away like the desert sand blown away by the sirocco wind into uncharted territory charted by your magnetic fingers, and like a cyclone of love, I had been whirled into your presence.

Just like a dream, my soul mate came into my life, but like an eel fresh from the sea, you slipped through my fingers, but I knew a goldfish, like a fish in a bowl has no hiding place, and like an elephant that doesn't forget I caught your image and kept it glued to my brain. I had my ups and downs and my temptations, but destiny kept me unscathed and undefiled.

I hold you in my dreams and will forever do. If my heart stops, there will be no need for a defibrillator, for your gentle touch will inject enough voltage of shock to restart my ailing heart. Why do I need to breathe when you are the breath of my life? When I inhale you, I breathe in life. When I exhale you, I breathe out love.

When I am feeling low, I remember your melodious voice that makes the ocean calm its waves to listen.

When I imagine your face in my mind, it brings a smile to my face and fills my heart with joy.

Even if the ocean dries up, my love for you will continue to drip and trickle. Even if the sun stops shining, your beautiful face will continue to illuminate my world.

Now that I am in your presence let me be putty in your hands so that you can mould me into whatever you cherish. Like a wax, let me melt into your heart and solidify into your being, and let the thread at the heart of the wax that binds us together be lit up so we can glow together in glory now and forever. Now that I know you, I don't think I can live without you. As Christmas is inseparable from pine trees, so shall we be inseparable from each other.

Let the lub beat of my heart synchronise with the dub beat of yours, baby. If You hold my heart, I will nurture your soul.

Jane, you are my joy, my peace, my strength, my hope, my stronghold. You are the breath that I take, the blood that runs through my vessels, the spring in my step, the marrow of my bone, the eyes through which I see the world. Without you, I fall apart, but with you, I stand firm as a rock; like the wing of an eagle, you make me soar so high. In your presence, my happiness is complete. I will never look any further, for you are enough… enough… and enough.

Now we feel the power of love and know what true love is all about, I enjoin you to slip into my world, because I believe we have got so much to love and cherish together. Let me forever be the shoulder you lean on…

We can now gladly and proudly say, "game, set, and match."

Taking a bow, he pulled the guitar over his head before bowing again to the enthusiastic crowd.

The tumultuous ovation that followed the rendition nearly brought down the roof. As he opened his eyes which remained partially closed throughout the rendition, he realised over fifty people watched him perform. Most of them were full of emotions and admiration and still clapping. He was humbled by what he saw.

"Wao, wao, wao!" Fab and the CEO exclaimed as they scooped him up into the air in a synchronised, concerted effort. "What a performance! Where did that come from?" they asked.

"Was that good?" Jeff asked meekly.

"That was a mind-blowing rendition that could move a statue to tears. That vocal is sure weapon to woo any woman," Fab complimented him.

With rivers of tears streaming down her cheeks, Jane rushed to him with outstretched arms and wrapped them around him, and he snuggled up into the embrace, and they held each other for quite some time, whispering into each other's ears. And Jeff had some tears in his own eyes. They wiped each other's faces, smiling and crying intermittently as they did. The scene attracted another round of applause from the excited guests, who now knew what the performance was all about, and they were all pleased to see a couple so much in love.

Jeff, unable to contain his excitement, decided to roam the streets while Jane and her colleagues went in for the afternoon session.

They were coming out as Jeff was returning to the hotel. Lost in his little world of excitement, Jeff lost his way back to the hotel and had to ask passers-by for directions when he noticed he was drifting further and further away, trying to figure out the way himself. He was sweating, having walked for almost three hours, and Jane noticed.

"Why are you sweating like someone who has run a marathon?" she asked.

"It would have been better if I had run a marathon. At least in a marathon, you have all your directions mapped out for you, not this type where I wandered into unfamiliar territories." And he laughed.

"Please don't tell me you are just coming from the little walk you told us as we were going in for the afternoon session," Fab said jokingly, laughing stealthily, knowing what might have happened to him.

"You lost your way, didn't you?" Mr Douglas finally asked him, smiling mischievously.

"I did," he said, laughing with a hint of embarrassment in his face.

Jane's face lit up in amazement before collapsing into a cheeky smile that graduated into full-blown laughter seconds later.

Douglas looked at Jane and said, "You better keep an eye on him, or you will lose him before he puts the wedding ring on your finger."

"I totally agree with you, Mr Douglas," Fab said with a smirk.

"Well, lady and gentlemen, we can't stand here all day. Today is a special day that needs to be celebrated in a big way. Thank God we are in the right place at the right time. So, let's go in there to have something to eat and drink. All expenses on me," Douglas announced.

Using the lift, they went to the second floor, where a buffet had been set out for the evening guests and customers. They were ravishingly spoilt for choice … from local delicacies to European and Chinese dishes. Jeff helped himself to lamb spareribs in soy and syrup sauce while Jane, with her chopsticks, relished a slew of Chinese egg noodles served with rainbow heirloom tomato bruschetta.

At the end of the meals, Mr Douglas poured out the Frontera wine for everyone. Lifting his glass up delightfully, he said, "To what shall we toast?"

"Very simple to Jeff's and Jane's engagement," Fab declared amiably.

"Without a ring," Douglas exclaimed jovially.

"I am yet to see a ring that is more telling and effective than what I saw today. To hell with the ring. This is a relationship made in Heaven. We are only privileged to witness it," Fab comically said. They all laughed heartily before clinking their glasses.

Jeff joyously made Jane drink from his glass, and Jane returned the favour amidst clapping and cheers from others.

Douglas had to mediate when Jeff made a move to follow Jane home after the meals. Presenting himself as a father and marriage/relationship advocate, he insisted that it was improper for them to sleep together under one roof when they had just met. "It is early days, guys. We make mistakes we later regret when we do things hastily. There would be many opportunities for visits and all that. For now, I think the way forward to sustain this heartwarming relationship and make it stand the test of time would be to keep your distance from each other and let things unfold gradually and naturally. We all know that absence makes the heart grow fonder. I have heard Jeff's predicament, and I am willing to pay his hotel bills until he is able to get a new job and able to rent a house."

Jane and Jeff thanked him for his kindness and magnanimity.

"That's what friends are for," Douglas said generously. "Jane is a good lass, and I am happy to see her find love — her missing rib after rejecting ten thousand suitors," Douglas said hyperbolically. And everyone laughed heartily when he said it.

CHAPTER 6

It was a humid and warm evening and Jeff had decided to go downstairs to get some fresh air. He was relaxing on a two-seater sofa in one of the lounges downstairs, reading the Guardian newspapers, when Meghan approached him and asked if she could join him. "I am on my break and wonder if I could spend part of it with you if you don't mind." And she smiled lightly.

"Why not?" Jeff answered warmly.

She left and came back with two cans of Diet Coke and handed one to Jeff, giving him no chance to say yes or no to the offer. "It is Diet Coke. It has no sugar and has less than one calorie. So, it won't do anything to your weight," she said, as if she were a dietitian or as if she knew Jeff was watching his weight.

Jeff accepted it half-heartedly and thanked her.

"My colleagues are all gossiping about you serenading a lady they say is the most beautiful girl they have ever seen with your beautiful voice they say could win a Grammy award. Tell me about it."

"What else do you want to hear? They have told you everything unless you doubt them."

"I doubt them. I need you to sing for me to believe. I missed the action. I want to see and hear you sing."

"As in serenading you?" he asked nonchalantly.

"Yes," she said before adding, "Not really." And she winked naughtily.

They were still talking when a white BMW car pulled up, and a lady emerged from it looking radiant as the sun.

"Wow!" Meghan exclaimed, pointing at the lady. "They say your girl is beautiful, but look at that," she said, pointing in the lady's direction. "She surely will make your girl jealous. I am sorry to say that, but you must acknowledge something special when you see one."

Jeff dropped the can of Coke to see who it was.

Jane had come to pay him a surprise visit. She was tired of texting and calling. She wanted to see Jeff face-to-face. It had been three days since the last time they saw each other, and those three days were hell for her. *No one has the right to tell me how to live my life, not even Mr Douglas. I am a full-fledged lady, and I know what I like and want. I am having no sex with Jeff as yet, but I want his company, and no one is going to stop me,* she told herself before paying him this visit.

Jeff was so surprised that he didn't know how to react. He felt timid with what he was wearing — a pair of carton colour chino shorts with a grey colour short sleeve shirt and a flip flop. And that was a complete contrast to Jane's golden colour mock neck dress with yellow kitten heel sandals.

In the eyes of those watching, she unequivocally met the high standard requirements of the modelling industry and movie world as she stepped out of her car. Some eyes roved insatiably as she walked in. Some wanted to constitute themselves into mini paparazzi and were tempted to take some pictures of her without her consent. Most of them recognised her and knew who she had come to see, while some stood in awe seeing her for the first time, including Meghan.

"Hello darling," Jeff said, standing up and holding her hand before giving her a peck on the cheek.

Meghan was dumbstruck to realise it was Jane, Jeff's girlfriend.

"How are you today?" Jane asked him.

"I was bored till now," he answered. And he smiled elaborately. "Really glad to see you, Jane.

This is a pleasant surprise. Jane, this is Meghan, one of the receptionists. Meghan, this is Jane, my girlfriend."

"Oh my God. You are breathtakingly beautiful. If you want a stardust, come out of a girl's beauty and womanhood, then look no further," Meghan said in a most flattering sense.

Jane bowed humbly before thanking her for her heartwarming plaudits.

"I was just asking Jeff about you. Your story is still the talk of the town. No wonder he sang his heart out for you. You are worth anything. And for your boyfriend, I have to say he is one of a kind. I threw myself at him on the day he arrived, but he rebuffed me emphatically, and that was even before he met you, I think. Can you imagine that, Jane? Am I not beautiful?" she asked Jane warmly and comically before twirling in circles to highlight her physique.

Jane laughed unrestrainedly at her remarks and free-mindedness before fondly saying, "Who said you are not beautiful? You are damn pretty, Meghan."

"I am no longer surprised why he has no eye for any other woman now that I have seen you. Who will?"

"Thank you for your praise, but you must leave us alone, and now. Enough of your drama," Jeff told her warmly.

"With all pleasure. Just give me a buzz if you want anything. It will be an honour to dance attendance on the pair of you."

Jane knew that she was genuine and had a touch of humour and wasn't holding touch for Jeff judging by her bubbly, free-mindedness. So, she was unperturbed seeing Jeff with her.

"Can we go upstairs, Jane?" he asked subtly.

"What for? I think we are okay here, aren't we?" she answered, smiling lightly.

"No. We are not. You weren't expecting to meet me down here when you were coming, were you?" he asked her dotingly, face glittering with a longing smile.

"Not really, but I had no intention of meeting you in your room either. I would have asked the receptionist to inform you to meet me downstairs."

"I am not having this argument, Jane. We can't stay down here. We need some privacy, don't we?"

"I am not sure of that. We don't need privacy to chat, do we?" she asked, laughing.

"I want to be free to say what I want to say without bothering who is listening," he responded with a grin.

"Say what you want to say or do what you want to do?" she asked, winking mischievously and laughing naughtily.

"Will you stop putting words in my mouth and instilling thoughts in my head," he cajoled her serenely.

"Look, Jeff, if we are going to go upstairs, you must make sure you are going to be a good boy all the time," she cautioned him animatedly, suppressing a peal of laughter in the process.

"I will not force issues. I promise."

"Do I take your word for it?" she asked with pretend seriousness.

"Promise," he said again with his hand on his chest. "Before I forget, I have to say you look amazing and whimsical, Jane."

"So are you, but you must stop dressing provocatively like that," she said.

"Like what?" he asked, surprised.

"Like showing off your bare macho chest to the girls in your summery attire," she said as she moved closer to button his shirt up to reveal less of his exposed chest

When they got upstairs, Jeff ordered some battered, crispy fish and some ice cream, which they enjoyed feeding each other amidst laughter and jokes.

"How much I love you, Jane," he said after staring intimately at her for some time. And she stared steadily into his eyes without saying a thing.

"Haven't you got anything to say to that?" he asked concernedly. He was stunned by her silence.

"There are words inadequate to express how I feel about you, and love is one of them. You are larger than life, Jeff. Now that I know you, I doubt I can exist without you, and that's no exaggeration. Of course, you know I love you with all my heart, with everything I have got. I believe action speaks louder than words," Jane said with eyes filled with intimacy, tenderness, and commitment.

She paused for a moment and then asked, "You haven't told me why you didn't call me after we met in Enugu. Any reason?"

"I did. I called the number you gave me so many times the next day, but they didn't go through. I sent text messages, but the outcome was the same. Frankly, I thought you were fake. I believed that you were just the type that uses her natural endowment to lead guys on. I am deeply sorry to say this, but that's what I thought even though I blamed myself for being so shy to talk to you in Enugu."

"Are you sure you dialled the number I gave you?"

"Of course, I did. I felt the world crashing on my shoulder when I couldn't reach you."

"Same here. I was mad as a hatter, not with you but with myself, for not taking the mantle of leadership in Enugu. I knew you were shy or maybe intimidated by my presence. I just knew because I had seen it many times where men would either remain speechless or would be babbling like a child as they struggled to find their words. But you are not one of those men. My heart yearned for you the very moment I set my eyes on you. That is why my life almost came to a standstill when I didn't get any call or text from you. '*Has he lost interest in me when we haven't even started*?' I asked myself one of those days. I thought I said something irritating or behaved irrationally without knowing it in Enugu. There wasn't a day I did not think of you, and there wasn't a day I did not blame myself for not telling you how I felt about you in Enugu. Frankly speaking, I didn't know why I didn't ask for your phone number. If I had your number, I would have swallowed my pride to call you first, even though it is unnatural for a girl to make the first call or send the first text message to a guy. Most people believe that when a girl texts or calls a guy first, it means she is throwing herself ... I meant likes the guy," she reframed her words quickly, feeling shy and cheap for using throwing to express herself.

"Are you throwing yourself at me?" Jeff asked her, laughing cockily. You had better be sincere with your answer.

"Shut up, Jeff and behave yourself. I didn't say throw."

"I thought you did ..."

"Okay, what are you going do about it?" she asked demurely.

"I would catch you expertly if you ever did. Do you wanna try?" he asked her with an unassuming smile. And they giggled heartily.

He was so pleased to hear all that from someone like Jane, now his soulmate.

He got up and walked to the CD rack, flipped through it before selecting one.

"What are you doing?" she asked enthusiastically.

"You wait and see."

"Are you going to serenade me privately this time?"

"Not really. I am going to *seredance* you instead.*"*

"Never heard that before, *seredance?* You made that up, *didn't you?"* she asked with a giggle.

"At least you know what I meant, don't you? That's what counts. Words are coined by men, not by spirits," he said cheekily.

He put (*just the two of us by Bill Withers*). Then he stepped onto the floor, and like Adolfo Indacochea, the great Salsa dancer, he made his moves majestically before stopping to ask her to join him on the floor.

She marvelled at his moves and said, "If you can dance salsa so majestically with *Bill Whithers's just two of us, I wonder what you would be doing with Los Lobos's La Bamba. I* have no idea how I am going to match your moves. You are good at everything, aren't you? Guitar, vocals … Now, you are dancing Salsa as if you were an indigene of Santiago Cali."

He laughed and said, "How much do you know things I am good at?" He smiled mischievously at his remark and then said, "Anyway, less talk, more dance." She made a face. She knew what he was insinuating and was certain she wasn't going to fall prey to his charm.

"I will teach you how to dance Salsa, but you must join me here first, on the dance floor. Remember, you cannot get your moves wrong—I am not looking for perfection," he encouraged her.

Gingerly and shyly, she got up and joined him on the floor.

"This is Salsa dance, Jane. You can't stand away from me. You hold hands and sway your hip to the music when you do Salsa dance."

He took her hands, which she offered cautiously, and in a brace of shakes, he twirled her round before catching her expertly before she lost her balance.

"You see what I meant when I said I would catch you."

"But I haven't thrown myself at you, have I?" she asked, looking straight into his sensuous, ravenous eyes. And they smiled warmly.

Now, their bodies were next to each other, and both felt the heat. Bringing her up from her slanting position, he slowly moved his face closer to hers, and she moved hers towards him. Then she paused as her body stiffened as if she had been slingshotted into an entirely new terrain before melting like wax into his warm, masculine chest. Intuitively, their lips locked against each other, the kind of unplanned kiss one usually sees on a romance movie channel. He felt he had been in that position before. It reminded him of Tessy's move on him in the office that hot afternoon. The difference was this was real, mutual, and cherished.

"Bad teacher. You didn't even have time to teach me the dance steps. You just twirled me and put me in a position I couldn't resist kissing you. Anyway, we should take it easy. Nice and slow, Jeff," she said warmly after breaking away from the slow, passionate kiss that lasted nearly a minute. "We mustn't be in a rush," she reiterated. "We must wait for the right moment. Believe it or not, but my virginity is still intact, and I am ready to wait until the time is right … after our wedding," she said, noticing that Jeff's hands had started to wander while they were kissing, meaning that he wanted something more than the kiss.

His face unconsciously narrowed in disbelief that she had never been in a relationship as Fab had told him days before. Then he smiled and promised her that he would wait until she was ready. "You're worth the wait, Jane," he reassured her.

Her action was more of dangling a banana before a monkey than waving a red flag to a bull and she had wanted to use that singular opportunity to assess Jeff's self-control.

"This is the first time I have genuinely and passionately kissed a man in my life. And I am happy and pleased you are the one whom I gave it to. The first and only boy who ever kissed me before today stole it when I was distracted, and he got a slap in the face before I reported him to his parents, who inflicted more punishment on him for his rude and unacceptable behaviour. We were in our early teens then, though— as green as gooseberry."

Jeff laughed affectionately before adding, "That served the pervert right."

CHAPTER 7

A week later, at about quarter past five in the evening, Jeff had a call on the hotel phone in his room. He scooped it up from the wall. "Who is it?"

"There are three gentlemen down here to see you," one of the receptionists informed him.

He had just had a shower and was getting ready to go downstairs for his dinner when the call came through.

"Wao! Mr Douglas! Is everything okay?" he asked, shaking his hand at the same time. He was glad to see him, especially now he was more of his benefactor.

"We are absolutely fine, as you can see." The two men with him smiled admiringly before bowing down gently. "I thought it would be nice and an honour to take you round the city and show you important places in Garden City which, if I am correct, Jane hasn't been able to show you, or has she?" He laughed lightly when he mentioned Jane. "It is simply weird for you to visit us here without seeing the major landmarks the city has to offer. After the tour, we will finish the night at one of the good hotels in the city. You deserve everything, Jeff. As far as I am concerned, you are a superstar. Friends and colleagues are still talking about your performance here. And it makes me proud that I personally know who you are. So, c'mon, let's get moving," he urged him, smiling broadly and cheerfully.

Jeff felt valued and loved listening to Mr Douglas. "Well, in that case, I need to go up to get properly dressed."

Waving his hand dismissively in the air, Douglas said, "You are fine the way you are. Insofar as you have your phone, you are good to go. This is Garden City and not Lagos, where there are strict rules for everything, including dressing codes." They all laughed at Douglas' remarks.

"If you say so."

One of the men led the way to the car park.

The beauty of Douglas's car was mind-blowing. It was Porsche's latest model. Black in colour with two golden horizontal stripes that made it stand out.

"This car is beautiful, Mr Douglas," Jeff said on entering the car after one of the men opened the door for him. It was so comfortable, almost noiseless, when the engine was started. The shock absorber was so active you would think you could keep a glass of water on the seat without it spilling, even if the car was in motion. The air conditioner was instantly activated as soon as the engine was turned on, adding to the luxury and comfort.

In two and half hours, they had almost driven round the Garden City. In those hours, they visited important landmarks and facilities in the city, such as Seawall jetties, piers, Wharves, Docks, Marinas, and boat landings, amongst others, with one of the men acting as a tour guide, giving Jeff a brief history of each landmark.

They finally ended in a massive three-storey building which Jeff was unable to identify as a hotel. At best, it passed as a block of office flats. Mr Douglas did say that they would end the evening in a hotel, but there was nothing to show they were in a hotel. It was noticeably quiet and dimly illuminated. It smelled musty, with some cobwebs dangling from the light bulbs and fluorescent lights. The windowpanes and the ceilings were thickly coated with dust at the edges. *This is Port Harcourt. Perhaps their definition of posh could be at variance with what we call posh in Lagos and elsewhere,* he thought, just to conceal the fear that had gradually started brewing in his mind.

The lift came down after one of the men called it, and four of them entered. Douglas then pressed the first-floor button. When they came out from the lift, Jeff saw a lady walking leisurely in the corridor who greeted them nonchalantly. Her presence helped to douse his fear which now was slowly building up. *At least, the building is inhabited by someone known to Douglas and his friends,* Jeff believed.

Opening one of the rooms alongside the corridor, he ushered Jeff in.

Up to this point, there was nothing convincing to Jeff that they were in a hotel. There was neither a reception area nor receptionists when they first entered the building. To him, nothing was adding up, and nothing supported it was lived in except for the lady they met when exiting the lift. His mind, at this point, had started giving him negative feedback.

"Sit down, Jeff and make yourself comfortable," Douglas urged him.

Jeff sat down uncomfortably while Mr Douglas sat on the remaining chair in the room, flanked by the two men. It was when Jeff sat down that he realised that the men were more bodyguards to Douglas than his friends, as he previously thought. Their stance, their black double-breasted jackets and dark sunglasses spoke volumes. Jeff wondered how they saw through such sunglasses at night. The many (yes sirs) at everything Douglas said showed they were not only taking instructions from him but were actually dancing attendance on him. For the first time, he noticed how terrifying their looks were.

"Do you care for a drink, Jeff?" Douglas asked as he poured himself a glass of scotch whisky.

"No, thanks. I am fine." Jeff was panic-stricken now. He could feel and smell danger. The joyful and enthusiastic face of a guy on a merry-go-round had now given way for one being led to the gallows. He was seriously wondering why Mr Douglas had invited him to that solitary, ghostly-looking building amongst all the beautiful hotels in Port Harcourt as he promised.

"Well, Jeff, I wouldn't like to take much of your time. Let's get down to business."

Jeff's suspicion grew out of proportion, and it reflected in his face. His stomach churned, and his intestines knotted as adrenaline rushed through his vessels. His mind went back and forth as it tried to figure out what kind of business Douglas wanted to discuss, and what his stake would be in it.

Douglas cleared his throat, removed his eyeglasses, rubbed his eyes, then his nose, before finally pinching his two lips as if he knew he shouldn't be opening them to say what he was about to say that would be abhorrent to the ears of a sane person. It was like he had something lodged in his throat as he cleared it one more time before saying, "I am interested in Jane just as you are."

That didn't make any sense to Jeff, so he said nothing. All he could do was lift his eyebrows and pout his lips.

"Haven't you got anything to say to that, or…?"

"To what?" Jeff asked, refusing to give credence to his bizarre statement. As far as he was concerned, he hadn't heard anything, and he was right if he didn't. Douglas's interest wasn't only preposterous but also insensitive and insane.

"I want Jane," Douglas said, reframing his former statement. Now, he was direct.

Jeff smiled, still not believing what he had heard, but he was bold to ask, "How and why?"

"Before you completely misconstrue my intentions, let me clarify one thing. I just want her for six months, then you can have her back."

Jeff managed half smile and half laughter and said, "So, Jane is now a piece of equipment in a construction company which you can hire and return when you are done — a pawn in a pawnshop? Is that how low you have downgraded her — pick up and drop off material? Even if you were a pawnbroker, you should have known that

I would never involve myself in something as devilish and sordid as this."

"Language, Jeff," he cautioned him.

"That's for you. You should be the one watching what you say," Jeff said harshly.

One of the men removed his sunglasses and eyeballed him.

"I can see and feel your anger. I expected it. But before you become mad as a wet hen, there is something I want you to know. This negotiation has a handsome reward attached to it."

"Go to hell with your reward." Jeff was now bloated with anger and about to explode.

"Well, what can I say? All I know and can say is no one likes to wallow in abject poverty because it is a disease — like cancer, it eats you slowly into extinction, taking with it all that is left of your dignity and personhood. I am aware you are out of the job and running low on cash. But I will gladly turn the table in your favour if you switch on your good brain and be more reasonable."

"Reasonable by loaning Jane to you? Is that what reasonability means to you?"

"Well, all I know is, the higher the risk, the greater the reward. And don't forget that in this part of the world, what determines a man's handsomeness is how much he has got in his pocket," said Douglas defiantly.

"This is not a risk. It is the epitome of callousness and savagery. If money is the determinant of a man's handsomeness, why have you not used it to get what you wanted? After all, you have always been with Jane. You shouldn't be involving me to get her, should you? Your wealth should have done the job for you, shouldn't it?" Jeff asked him derisively.

"I was setting out my plans to woo her so I can have her with her full consent. That's what I was doing until you reared your ugly head from nowhere to reap where you didn't sow."

Jeff laughed cynically. "Me, Jeff, trying to reap where I didn't sow? Your action shows who the intruder is. But if you insist you are the one that sowed on the good soil, then go ahead and reap your produce. Just leave me out of it," he said, knowing full well that Jane would never fall in love with him.

"I wish I could, but unfortunately, I can't because you have thwarted my plans, and that's why I want you to rectify it. You have to right the wrong. You must clean up the mess you made, Jeff," he answered callously.

Jeff was boiling and about to detonate as a landmine. He thought how brazen and vulgar

Douglas was by saying he should right the wrong and clean up the mess when he was the one who needed his brain examined by a psychiatrist on the strength of obscene words that were pouring out from his defiled mouth and weird ideas going on in his depraved mind.

Convinced that Jeff was unlikely to bulge and comply with his demand, he decided to do what sent shudders down his spine. At the press of a button, Jeff was taken downstairs at a frightening pace. He couldn't tell whether it was the ground floor or the basement. Standing with scalpels in their hands were three ugly, evil-looking men. It was impossible to draw a distinction between them and zombies. They were cutting open a tied-up lady without any anaesthetic agent amidst screaming and struggling. Close by were two girls tied to a pole, possibly waiting for their turns to be cut open. It was a human abattoir.

Then he was taken upstairs, where they were at the same speed.

Jeff never knew he was sitting on an escalator. When Jeff came up, he was white as a ghost and was throwing up based on what he had seen.

"You see, what we do here is no child's play. We harvest the human organs of recalcitrant people like you and feed the remnants to the crocodiles in the pond. We send the skeletons to medical schools to help train our medical students, especially those who want to major in orthopaedic surgery. The harvested organs are sold to the highest bidder. It might sound cruel, but if you look at it from our point of view, the harvested organs are used to save lives. We don't eat them. So, you see, we are not as vicious and insensitive as you might have thought. At least, we are saving lives and contributing effectively to the training of our medical students … our little way of promoting and contributing to our health care system."

Jeff was pale faced by what he had seen and still hearing. "You take innocent lives to save lives, and you don't see anything wrong with that? Don't the medical schools bother to know how you got the skeletons? I don't want to bother about the highest bidders for the harvested organs. I am quite sure they are operating in the same satanic platform as you and your associates," Jeff said, his teeth still chattering.

Douglas gave no answer to that. All he did was to shrug his shoulders unrepentantly.

The blood-curdling events could only rekindle Jeff's resolve not to betray Jane.

"I don't want to believe you have made up your mind to give up your life because of a woman. You should stop being unreasonable, Jeff. Like I said,

I am willing to pay you 2 billion naira. I will transfer one billion now, and the remaining you will get after the six months contract. It is a promise.”

“You can go to hell with your contract and money, Douglas.”

“I am everything but a rapist. That’s why I am still here arguing with you. I have never raped anyone, and I am not going to start with Jane. But if you continue to drag this out, I will have no choice but to do away with you,” Douglas threatened. Douglas was playing down his real intention, which was to have Jane as his wife. He knew full well that it would be impossible for Jeff to agree to his plan, no matter the threat, if he was aware of his real intention.

“Yes, Kill me. But I am not yielding to your demand,” Jeff responded, eyes brimming with anger.

Douglas laughed. “You are wrong, Jeff. You will surely dance to my tune. What if I told you that we could have the head of Jane on a platter before us in the next hour if you did not comply.” He didn’t wait for Jeff’s response. He saw the answer in his face.

Jeff knew at that point that he wasn’t bragging. He knew he was devilish enough to carry out his threat. Jeff didn’t know what to think at this point. He wondered why Mr Douglas was involved in such dehumanising, devilish activity like this when he was CEO of an oil company, an enviable position. "Why are you doing this when you are holding a public office, a dignifying one for that matter? I erroneously took you as a kind, loving, and protective man, especially toward Jane. So, all along, your actions have been pretentious and evil?" Jeff asked him defiantly.

"You are dead right in your choice of word, *dignifying*. That is what it is all about. I hope you don't expect me to announce to the world that I butcher people and get all the condemnation and recriminations that go with it? Neither do you want me to tell you timidly that I was interested in Jane, having seen how madly in love she is with you? The only option left for me to actualise my long-time dream is by taking this route. It might be harsh and morally wrong, but who cares. I can't give up on her, unfortunately."

"But that's what you are doing anyway. If you don't want society to condemn you for what you are doing, why are you doing it then? And why are you not man enough to make your intentions known to Jane courageously and courteously? Is it not because conscienceless people like you are usually cowardly?"

"No, it is because we do not have willing organ donors here in our country. So, this is the only way we can get them for the bigwigs in our society who really need them. As rich as they are, most of them are riddled with all kinds of diseases. Most of their major organs, as a result, are compromised and need urgent organ transplants from healthy guys like you and me. One more thing I need to tell you is that it was through these upper echelons of society that I got this laudable job so that I could go on doing what I am doing unnoticed, with nobody questioning my source of wealth. In other words, my CEO's job status in this company cleans my money and ill-gotten wealth. But on top of all that, I personally make sure that the proceeds from the sales are equitably distributed, hence, the amount I am offering you. I won't go back to say anything about my intentions toward Jane," Douglas answered savagely.

Jeff pulled out his mobile phone to call Jane to run for dear life. He had heard enough. At this moment, Jeff couldn't draw a distinction between Mr Douglas and lucifer. With a shadow of despair written all over him, Jeff said, "I don't need any proceeds from your evil intentions. This is blood money, Mr Douglas, and you should cover your face in shame."

"What are you doing? You want to call Jane or the police, aren't you? It's a waste of time. We are untouchable and comprehensively protected even from the police."

Jeff didn't listen or look at him. He wanted to get Jane out of harm's way at all costs. "Yes, you can kill me, but not Jane," Jeff said as Jane's phone started ringing.

Mr Douglas pulled out the phone in his trousers, which was vibrating. It was Jane's phone. "I tricked Jane into giving me her phone by telling her that I was having technical issues with my network provider and that I needed hers to make an important international call this evening. You know your Jane. She is kindhearted, and I knew she would agree. I did that because I wouldn't like any interruptions from anyone, including her, while we are having this sensitive discussion."

It was a nightmare to Jeff which he would soon wake up from.

Douglas then ordered him to hand over his phone. He would only allow him access to the phone when he wanted him to text nasty things to Jane. Otherwise, the phone was switched off, making it impossible for Jane to get through to Jeff — an act that would further convince Jane that Jeff had lost interest in her.

Jeff was running out of options now. "You can't do this, Mr Douglas; do you realise that Jane is still a virgin?" he hinted as a way to dissuade him from pursuing his bizarre demand.

"How do you expect me to know? You have just informed me. I never knew. It is a piece of vital information, though, because it has added much value to my pursuit. Huge bonus, isn't it? Having Jane on its own is more than a dream come true, but as a virgin is better than winning a family lottery to the space," Douglas said shamelessly and pretentiously.

Jeff's determination to save Jane from Douglas quadrupled at that moment. He couldn't contemplate Douglas laying his filthy hands on her, much less taking her virginity. There was no other choice at that point than to take them head-on, knowing that a cat in gloves catches no mice. He was brave enough to attack them hammer and tongs even though he knew it could prove fatal. But he wanted to give it a go. If he died in the process, he would have died defending what was most precious to him.

Jeff relied on his natural strength, which was augmented by his finesse in karate and taekwondo. Unexpectedly, he sprang up from his chair and side-kicked the two men heavily in the chest at the same time, sending them crashing onto the floor with a grunt of a scream. Before Douglas could react to what was going on, Jeff swung his left fist at him but missed. Douglas ducked as Jeff's right fist followed through. He was too clever by half, not only in intelligence but also in his reflexes, especially considering he was in his mid-fifties. But Jeff's right kick to his chest took him by surprise and sent him tumbling helplessly on top of one of the men, with stars flickering in his eyes. Jeff then smashed one of the windows with Douglas's chair and jumped down like a Spider-Man. Unfortunately, it was the pond area. He landed between two ten-footer crocodiles basking in the fluorescent lights with their mouths agape. He was exceedingly frightened that he froze. But before he could decide on his next move, Mr Douglas and his men were at the other end of the pond watching him, with one of them pointing his gun at him. He wanted to pull the trigger, but Douglas put his hand up to him.

"Jeff," Douglas said, "I have exhausted my patience. If I get any more negative behaviour from you, you will only have yourself to blame because I will not hesitate to carry out my threat. If the dead could tell tales, I am sure that Jane would not be pleased that you wasted her life for a simple matter like this."

Jeff froze at his boldness and was shocked he called what he was planning a simple matter.

"Do we have a deal or not?" Douglas asked, voice loud and authoritative.

"I don't even get you, Mr Douglas. What deal? How do I even come into this? Tell Jane that you want to sleep with her for six months and that you will pay me 2 billion naira as a result? Is that what you want me to do?"

"Come on, Jeff. What do you mean? What do you take me for? … I might be a curmudgeon but certainly not a buffoon."

"That's all you have been saying unless I am deaf."

"No, Jeff, you have a significant role to play to actualise my dream. Jane, in a million years, will never accept my proposal to sleep with me."

"Haven't you contradicted yourself there? You just told me that you were mapping out a plan to woo her to sleep with you. So, you knew all along you had no chance of getting her. So, why are you blaming me for thwarting your plans? The truth is that you are being unreasonably clever to use me to realise your evil intentions."

"Whatever you make of it, Jeff. The bottom line is that I want you to be the one that connects the dots to help me actualise my dream."

"I get it. You want me to be the kingmaker that will put the dirty crown on your depraved head," Jeff said, laughing ominously.

"I won't argue any more. If I were you, I would not spare the horses. The earlier we reach an agreement, the earlier we start counting the months," said Douglas, not minding how hurting and damaging his words were to Jeff.

Jeff shook his head pitifully and helplessly before saying, "You are not only doing a number on me but also on poor, innocent Jane. What have we done to deserve all this? We are not the first couple to fall in love, are we?"

Ignoring Jeff's lamentation, Douglas said, "All I want you to do is break Jane's heart by pretending to be sleeping around with Garden City girls. Leave everything to me. I will arrange the girls and will put Jane in a position to get the rumours before finally catching you red-handed. When that happens, I am sure I will be the shoulder she will cry on. The rest will be history. When that happened, you would be on the gravy train as you join the billionaire club."

"Deal, but on one condition," Jeff finally responded. By now, he knew that it was a lost cause, and there would be no need to argue with him. He didn't want to compromise Jane's life. There was no shadow of doubt in his mind that Douglas would kill her if he didn't comply with his directives.

"What condition?" Douglas asked.

"That you pay nothing to me. Jane is not a commodity, and I don't want to reduce her to one."

"Impossible. That will make everything worthless. Haven't you heard the saying: the harder the battle, the sweeter the victory. Besides, I have a conscience and will not do a thing as significant as this without giving out something in return. It works against my conscience and belief."

Mr Douglas was nevertheless careful not to do anything that would cost Jeff's life because he knew that if anything happened to Jeff, he would lose his chance. He knew full well that not even the execution of Jeff would give him access to Jane because he was aware of how much Jane loved Jeff.

To Jeff, every word Douglas spoke carried the weight of finality. Jeff now knew more than ever before that he was in the midst of demons fresh from the bottomless pit of hell.

When Douglas was convinced that Jeff's confidence had been reduced to dust, he ordered one of the men to go back upstairs and put a ladder down the smashed window so that Jeff could safely climb up without annoying the Crocs.

"From now onwards, you are going to be electronically tagged and monitored by my men throughout the duration of the contract. Let me reiterate that you pose a dire danger to yourself and Jane if you make any false move. Hope I have made myself clear?"

CHAPTER 8

Feeling helpless, with no eureka moment in sight, Jeff had no choice but to abide by the terms of the contract, which included, amongst others, proving to Jane that he was sleeping around with the girls secretly organised by Mr Douglas. Jane was told about Jeff's infidelity by one of the cleaners in Cosmo's hotel after she had been bribed with a huge sum of money and gifts by Douglas. Jeff was forced to text her thereafter that he wasn't interested in their relationship anymore and told her that she shouldn't bother to contact him. "Don't take it personally. As you can see, I am too young to be roped into a committed relationship. I want to enjoy life a little bit more before settling down. Sorry, you gave your heart to me, and sorry if I broke it," he texted Jane indifferently, as scripted by Douglas.

Jane was dazed after reading the text. She had to tap herself a few times to make sure she was awake and not dreaming, and she wasn't. It was a harsh reality. The world had just crashed on her shoulder, crushing her confidence and pride in the process.

All attempts made by Jane to contact Jeff were futile. She would have loved at least to see him face to face to hear it directly from his mouth.

Unable to weather the storm alone, she had to inform Mr Douglas of what was going on believing he would be of help to change Jeff's mind. *If Jeff doesn't want to see me or speak with me, at least, he can't refuse to see and speak with Mr Douglas knowing that he is the one footing his hotel bill and who has also promised to find decent accommodation for him,* she thought, head hurting and turning. Little did she know that Mr Douglas was indeed the architect of her problem.

"Are you serious, or are you just messing with me?" Douglas exclaimed, looking really shocked after listening to her.

"Do you really think I would joke about something this serious, Mr Douglas?" she said, voice cold and depressed.

Seeing her reaction convinced him he had cleared the first hurdle, but the second hurdle stared him in the face. Jeff was out of the picture, and all attention now was on Jane. Douglas needed no one to tell him that he had to tread with utmost caution. He knew that any wrong move or word would give him away. Jane certainly wasn't going to sweep Jeff's memory under the carpet — not before, not now, not in the future. Her love for Jeff was authentic and immeasurable.

Days later, Douglas met up with Jane after work and lied to her that all his efforts to see and speak with Jeff to address her concern had proved abortive. He told her that Jeff would neither pick up his calls nor try to call back. He told her that he had visited the hotel where Jeff was staying and discovered he had left the hotel, and he thought he had left so that he could not be traced or disturbed. Douglas actually went to the hotel not to look for Jeff but to collect his belongings and pay off his outstanding hotel bill.

"That's the same here, Mr Douglas. It is either the phone is switched off, or he will refuse to pick up his call when I phone him," she said sadly, giving credence to what Douglas had just said. "I already knew he had left the hotel. The receptionist told me that he checked out a few days ago when I visited the hotel the other day."

"This is nightmarish. Not in a million years would I have believed that Jeff is this vicious. He looked a complete gentleman in appearance and speech you would think he could not hurt a fly. Never knew he was a wolf in sheep's clothing. Even if he was a womaniser, he has no right to treat you with such disrespect. That's very cruel of him," Douglas said deceptively.

Jane cried frantically after listening to Mr Douglas. "I love him so much. I really do, and that's why it hurts so badly," she said, voice sorrowful.

"You don't need to tell me. I know." He walked up to her and cuddled her before saying in a low tone, "Isn't it better you discover this now than later when you must have been fully committed? You have to thank your stars that he could not hide his true colour from you." He later took her to a nearby restaurant thereafter and bought her some fish pepper soup which she barely ate. Douglas continued to console her all evening, promising that he would weather the storm with her. "Don't feel this desolate. I am here to support you through this tough time," he promised her deceitfully.

Douglas was subtle and cautious with his moves, just like a smooth operator.

Jane refused to mention what had happened to her to her colleagues and friends, not even Tessy, her best friend. And that favoured Douglas's ill intention. Jane didn't want any sympathy from any of her colleagues and friends. Secondly, she didn't want her male colleagues to be aware that Jeff had deserted her, as that could unlock the door for them to take a second bite at the cherry— she didn't want to be put under such pressure again. The only person she considered fit to know was indeed the wrong man, Douglas, whom she had always seen as a trustworthy father figure.

Douglas never said anything or behaved in any way that would portray his real intention to Jane. Rather, he started taking her occasionally to the pictures and inviting her to staged engagement and wedding parties of his friends, where usually there were significant age gaps between the couples involved. He would cleverly convince her that taking her to such events and cinemas was his little way to help her deal with her present heartbreak, and she would thank him immensely for his concern and care.

"I am Brenda," the bride in one of the staged wedding parties introduced herself during the after-wedding party.

"I am Jane," she replied, shaking her hand.

"Are you here on your own … or?" she asked Jane pretentiously.

"Oh no. I came with Mr Douglas," Jane said gingerly, proving she wasn't a gate crasher.

"Mr Douglas?" she exclaimed. "As his wife … or?"

Jane hiccuped a burst of laughter the way she asked her. "Wife! No. Douglas is a colleague and a friend. In fact, he is my boss."

"I was only joking. I know Douglas. He is so scared of women," she told Jane slyly.

"Is that why he is still single?" Jane chipped in casually.

"I think so. He told my husband that he didn't believe that any woman would love him the way he would. He is so scared of heartbreak. I wouldn't blame him, especially after the messy divorce of his friend, Mr Dokubo, whose wife left for a handsome, young, rich man after a seven-year blissful and peaceful marriage. According to her, Mr Dokubo was way older than her. Guess what? The new marriage lasted only two years before breaking down irretrievably. She later discovered that the so-called young, handsome man was not only a womaniser but also a drug dealer. And anytime she confronted him about his waywardness and ostentatious lifestyle, he ended up beating her black and blue. In my humble opinion, relationship and marriage are not about age. It is all about understanding and mutual respect. At the end of the day, age is nothing but a number. I had been engaged to Mr Michael for over eight years before our wedding today and all he had done these years was treat me like royalty. It might surprise you to know that he is twenty years older than me." She paused for a moment before asking Jane, "Does your husband know you are here with another man?"

"Husband!" Jane exclaimed, looking bewildered at the question. "No. I am not married," Jane said tamely.

"If you are not married, what of your partner?" she asked pretentiously again.

"Not in a relationship either," Jane said modestly.

"I am shocked because I believe that men should be hovering around you like flies over a carcass. You are too pretty to be single. Or are you just being too choosy trying to find Mr Right?" And she smiled broadly.

Jane was close to tears when she asked her.

"I am really sorry for asking," she apologised, noticing how upset Jane had become by her enquiries.

"No. There is nothing to apologise for, Brenda. It is just that life could be cruel at times."

"We need to sit down for a moment. The party is nearly over, anyway," she said. She took Jane to a quiet corner, and they sat opposite each other. "Your countenance changed since I mentioned husband and partner. Please pardon me if I have offended you by that," she said, sounding genuinely concerned.

"You haven't. I am just paddling my own canoe."

"Paddling your own canoe? What do you mean by that?"

"I don't want to dump my emotional baggage on anyone, you the least. This is your special day, and I am not going to ruin it," Jane said, voice heavy with sadness.

"You can confide in me if you really want to. I am not putting you under any pressure. But what is love and empathy if we can't help our fellow human beings who need our help?" she asked concernedly.

"My boyfriend just dumped me just weeks into our relationship," Jane finally said, convinced she was with the right person. "I caught him sleeping around with Garden City babes. He couldn't even render any sincere apology, which would have been difficult for me to accept anyway. But it would have been much better than telling me that I should stay clear of his way. He said that he was still too young to involve himself in a committed relationship. I am distraught, Brenda. I love him so much, and I thought he loved me as much, but I was wrong." She cried when she said it.

Brenda walked up to her and gave her a hug before saying, "You see what I mean. Men are the same, especially when they are young. They don't care who they hurt in their pursuit of pleasure. They are brutal and insensitive." Then she lowered her voice and said, "Isn't it better you found out earlier than later when you must have crossed the Rubicon? I know it hurts at any time, but it is certainly more devastating when you are completely roped in after your wedding. I am not an advocate in matters like this, but personally, I would count my losses and move on if I were in your shoes."

"This is bizarre, Brenda. I have managed to turn your beautiful day into a mourning one. We should be eating, drinking, and dancing," Jane said apologetically.

"I am not complaining, Jane. Anyway, let's go and get something to eat and drink."

Brenda had managed to sow seeds of doubt in Jane's mind just like Douglas did days ago, and she was falling for their antics as she ruminated on them the whole evening, thinking that she might have been saved from a major disaster. Nevertheless, she couldn't finish a day without thinking about Jeff, how deeply she loved him, how deeply she erroneously thought he loved her too, and, of course, the manner he had abandoned her. She was haunted by fear of rejection. Jeff had dropped her like red-hot iron. Mr Douglas wasn't interested in welcoming her into his home even when she had obviously shown platonic interest. She wasn't any more sure of herself. Every now and then, she would stand in front of her standing mirror, looking at herself. Her beauty and self-worth had taken a hit and were now under her thoughtful scrutiny. To compound her condition, her colleagues, oblivious to her sticky situation could only tell her plainly how dreadful she looked lately. She wasn't sure whether the *dreadful* look they meant was because of her mood or physical appearance. She believed that her sex appeal to the opposite sex was gone, especially when she remembered the way Jeff dumped her. She knew philanderers usually would go to any length to lay a girl before casting her aside. "I must look dreadful these days that Jeff didn't even want to waste his energy to get me laid before deserting me."

CHAPTER 9

With the coast clear, Mr Douglas then placed Jeff under strict surveillance from here on out. He was moved to an unknown destination and into an old, fortified-storey building. It was more of a jail but with no wardens. All the windows and doors were iron-boarded. The only door and window that were not boarded were the front door and window that came face to face with where the guards stayed. He was assigned two men at one time who monitored his movements 24/7. They were responsible for bringing food and other necessities for him in addition to monitoring him.

Jeff's patience was overstretched after two months in captivity. The thought of what Douglas might be doing to Jane fuelled his anger and determination to act. He threw caution to the wind and decided to take the bull by the horns. He knew it wasn't going to be easy, but he was now ready to risk his life and Jane's.

Although it appeared that Mr Douglas and his men held all the cards, Jeff believed it was only a matter of time before they played one badly.

He started keeping an eye on the guards. It wasn't too long before he discovered the weaknesses of a particular set of guards — they were deeply into alcohol, drugs, and women. He had seen them bring in girls into the compound and were having fun with them after getting dopey and drunk. He knew it won't be long before he would catch them napping and would pounce to pick their pockets.

It was on a Saturday night. They had taken over from the earlier shift in an absolutely drunken, delirious state. He was excited that they hadn't come with the girls and prayed they didn't turn up later.

At about 3am, in the still of the night, Jeff sauntered his movement onto the balcony and could hear the two guards grunting like pigs in their sleep. He tiptoed back into his room and picked up an old wooden Baton left under the bed. He was sure nobody knew it was there. He saw it as an instrument Divinely provided for him to work with. He re-examined it and was convinced that it was weighty and proportionate in size for the job he was about to carry out. When he came out again on the balcony, he was glad that they were even deeper in their sleep, with their heads resting against each other. He felt it was a perfect time to strike. He wasn't sure if his planned assault would be successful, but he was certain of the consequences if it didn't. But nothing was going to deter him from carrying out this attack. His resolve to rescue Jane was top of his priorities.

He opened the door that led to the staircase gently, and the door opened noiselessly to his delight. He moved down the stairs at a pace slower than that of a sloth. He reached the downstairs landing safely. He opened the door that led to the outside as gently as he could, but unlike the one upstairs, it made a creaking sound that was enough to arouse the guards. Luckily for him, the corridor downstairs was dimly illuminated. Jeff quickly hid behind one of the big pillars of the building with his heart now in his mouth as he panicked and feared the worst. He believed it was over for him as the men tried to get up to find out the cause of the noise. They were still staggering to get up in their sleepy state when a wild, black cat ran across the compound.

"Bloody pussycat," both swore languidly and fell back to their sleep at once.

Jeff remained rooted to the same spot for the next five minutes to ensure they had fallen deeply asleep again. He prayed that the cat didn't reappear.

With both snoring loudly again, he gently stepped outside. He tried to still his breath. He knew that any mistake would spell doom. He could hear his heart pounding away as their snoring intensified. He wasn't going to be put off by anything. He was fighting for dear life but much more for Jane's.

Just two more steps to reach them, Jeff unknowingly kicked an empty can of coke on the floor, and they woke up to the noise, but before they could react in their drunken, sleepy state, Jeff was already on top of them. He had flattened one already, but the second man was now fully awake and aware of what was going on. Jeff was smarter than he was as he knocked down the gun from his hand before he could put it to any use. Jeff didn't want to rush the gun even though it was closer to him. He had never handled one before. He knew the table might turn against him if he decided to fight with it, so he continued his assault with the Baton. A rush of adrenaline had now gone through the guard like a flash flood, filling him up with hysterical strength, and he fought back doggedly, knowing his life was hanging by a thread, now seeing that his colleague was lying lifeless on the floor. Jeff panicked. He knew time was of the essence. He wanted everything over and done with as quickly as possible. He knew it was only a matter of time before a backup showed up, knowing full well what Douglas was capable of. Jeff clung tenaciously to his baton and managed to kick the gun further away from the guard each time he tried to reach it. He eventually managed to dive to reach it, but Jeff was quick enough and landed on top of him as he did, hitting him into unconsciousness with his baton. Now unconscious, Jeff finished him off like his colleague.

Jeff stood still, confused and panting vigorously as he watched the dead men on the floor. He had killed them, but he wasn't sure what next to do. He realised he was in no man's land with the building standing alone with no other building in sight. Jeff wasn't even sure whether he was still in Port Harcourt or entirely in a new area. Amid his confusion, he knew, and convincingly too, that he had to leave the place and fast.

He had started running away when he suddenly realised he still had the tag locked on his left ankle. He knew he had to get it off as quickly as possible to disconnect himself from the monitor. But he needed a key to unlock it. He thought one of the men might have it. And there it was in the pocket of one of the men. He grabbed it and unshackled himself. But that was not all because he suddenly realised that his clothes had nudges of blood from one of his victims. He had no other clothes. He had no option but to strip the other man whose shirt was unstained. He would discard his blood-stained clothes in a safe place where they would not be found.

He noticed he had no money on him when he wanted to escape from the vicinity, which he now saw as a crime scene. He knew he would need some money to embark on this dangerous, long adventure. Cardinal's goal was to get to Douglas, kill him and get Jane to safety. He searched the pockets of his victims and, lo and behold, he found rolls of five hundred naira notes in their pockets as he had expected. He took them and pocketed them.

Now, he was ready to move on to the second stage of his mission, which was to find Douglas, take him down, and then whisk Jane away to safety as quickly as possible. But that plan ended abruptly when a car with a blue light came to a stop about fifty meters from where he was with a voice screaming, "Don't move and hands up."

Jeff had been caught red-handed. Two dead bodies on the floor. The blood-stained baton was still on the floor. And he was equally sure the blood of the victim would be found on him on examination.

Asking Jeff to put his hands behind his back, the police officers handcuffed him and advised him to remain calm and say nothing, as anything he said could harm his defence in court.

Jeff didn't realise that the guards were carrying a response alarm, which the second guard activated when he attacked them. The alarms were linked to Douglas, who then alerted the police officers.

Up to now, Mr Douglas was playing his game to perfection, concealing anything that would awaken Jane's suspicion. He had portrayed himself as a perfect, caring gentleman, and that had endeared him to Jane even more. On a few occasions they had been to events, he would willingly open and close the car door for her. He had even booked tailor-made holidays exclusively for her. He refused her coming over to his house when he hosted his friends. He cleverly told her that he would be requiring some help on the day for cooking and serving the guests.

"Should I pop in to help?" Jane offered willingly.

"Oh no, you are okay. Don't worry, Jane. I have got friends that are willing to help on the day."

On a few similar occasions, he had refused her to visit his house, making her wonder if she was any good to him or any man for that matter.

"Why don't you want me to visit you?" she finally asked him, noticing that Douglas was glaringly averse to her visit. But she felt so embarrassed for asking.

"Nothing, really. I am just a prude when it comes to stuff like this. I like the way I am. I like to stay away from trouble," he said with a tinge of humility.

Jane took another look at herself. Her self-worth was now under strict scrutiny as she thought about Douglas's statement. She couldn't believe that Douglas now saw her as trouble.

Douglas's act by her assessment was in tune with what Brenda told her, and she had genuinely begun to see him not only as a father figure and boss but also as a rare gem.

Things even got better for him when Jane read about Jeff murdering two men. The police were quoted as saying that Jeff committed the murder, fighting with his victims over drugs. Jane thanked God once again for saving her from getting into a lifetime relationship with him, even though she still felt like a child deprived of her precious toy without Jeff. Her life without Jeff was a mess, and she knew it deep down in her bones.

So, when Douglas made his moves months later, it was difficult for her to resist him despite the age difference. She accepted him, though with caution. After all, all young Jeff had succeeded in doing was to break her heart immeasurably.

Jeff was locked up in Opirikom police area command, Port Harcourt, pending his trial in the criminal court months later.

The trial was straightforward, with no burden of proof required when his case finally came up for hearing. He was caught right in the act. Moreover, Douglas had strongly admonished him to keep a sealed mouth throughout the trial if he were to save his life and that of Jane. The only time he recommended that he open his mouth was to plead guilty to his crime. He advised him to be litigant in person throughout the trial. Douglas had constantly reminded him that his crime was murder, a case that carried the death penalty and had strongly advised him to plead guilty to his crime. However, he assured him that he would use his connections to ensure that it would be mitigated to manslaughter, which would only attract a specific jail term. He went further to assure him that he would ensure that he did not spend more than the time they agreed.

Jeff didn't even bother to be warned. He knew it would be a fruitless effort to put up any convincing defence in court as he believed that Douglas might have bought over the judge and the jurors.

Jeff was finally found guilty of murder by the Jury and was sentenced to death by the presiding judge.

He was heartbroken and felt betrayed when the judge delivered the verdict. All the time, Douglas had never wanted any mitigation of the case for him. He had always wanted to get rid of him so that he could keep Jane for good.

CHAPTER 10

Jeff was excommunicated from the rest of the world. No visits, no contacts. He left Lagos on a sour note, and here in Port Harcourt, a place he had come to find succour and peace, he had only succeeded in compounding his already messed up situation. In Lagos, he was a freeman. Here in Port Harcourt, he was languishing in jail with no help in sight. But he wasn't too surprised why everyone had abandoned him. He understood. *Why would anyone want to visit or communicate with a murderer? My story was in national newspapers and magazines. If only they had told the world the exact reason I killed the men. But they didn't. The word, murderer on its own is an anathema and a human repellent. But at the same time, I wonder why Jane would not want to have a word with me, at least to hear my own version of the story, or is she that distraught that she couldn't be bothered to dig out the facts, or has she been bamboozled by Douglas rhetorics, manoeuvres and lies? Is everything going to end as broken dreams?* Jeff had thought.

He had spent just over 12 months in prison following his condemnation by the criminal court. He was still alive because the governor of the state, who was supposed to sign his death warrant a couple of weeks ago, took ill and was flown to India for medical attention. It was a move that spared his life for the time being. He was living a borrowed life as far as he was concerned, one day at a time.

It, therefore, came as a relief a week later, around 3:05pm on a Tuesday afternoon, when a prison officer opened his cell to inform him that a lady had come to see him.

He was overjoyed with the news because up till that day, there was still no message from anyone. *Thank God. Finally, Jane has reconsidered* what he had thought. He knew he had little or no chance of convincing her, but it would still do him a lot of good if he could declare his innocence and tell her what happened between him and Douglas. He knew his life was only hanging by the thread. All he was happy about was that he had been given a chance to tell Jane what transpired between him and Douglas before his execution would be signed. *I will die a happy man if I am able to convince her that I didn't betray her.*

He had worn his boxer shorts and a pair of shorts a cellmate gave him for months, apart from Sundays when inmates who had no visitors were given a pair of trousers and a shirt to attend church service, where he had always prayed to God to come to his help and rescue him from his troubles. He could count on his fingers how many times he had had a shower. He could not remember the last time he had a proper shave. He brushed his teeth when he was able to borrow some toothpaste from other inmates, and that didn't happen quite often. His hair was bushy and twisted, more like unplanned dreadlocks. He stank to high heaven. But that was okay. The joy that he was going to see Jane's face again overshadowed all his negative feelings.

From the old clothes' collection from charity organisations in the prison yard, the officer took a partially torn navy blue top and a pair of jeans and flung them in his direction. "Cover yourself up with that. You do not need to scare a lady with your bare body," he said sarcastically. "Wonder if your visitor knows the details of the crime you committed, or is she your business partner?" No prison officer wanted to give him an audience each time he tried to tell them what actually happened. They would rather curse him and tell him how cowardly he was trying not to own up to his crime. Jeff pretended he didn't hear him. He rather followed him to the waiting room.

He was appalled looking at her as she stood like a statue.

He couldn't believe it was her standing in front of him, and neither did she believe it was Jeff standing before her.

"What are you doing here?" Jeff asked, unable to gather his thoughts and looking like a lost ball in the weeds. He pulled away as she tried to hold his hand and screamed, "Don't touch me."

"What have they done to you, and what have I done? Look at the state of you. I really am sorry, Jeff."

He ignored her. He sat down on the bench opposite hers with a table In between them.

"You have come to mock me," he said when they were both seated. "All your wishes have come to pass, haven't they?"

She shrank and looked like a Labrador puppy approached menacingly by a Rottweiler as she watched his countenance.

"I can't deny the fact that I should be in bad with you considering the mess I have plunged you into, but the truth is that I never intended this kind of misfortune for you. I swear."

"Really! And you want me to believe that?"

"I really am sorry for all the trouble I have caused you. It is my irrational thinking and consequential action that landed you in this mess."

"That's no news to me. I know full well you are. If you hadn't gone loopy at the office, I shouldn't have been in Port Harcourt in the first place. I don't deserve to be in this mess, do I?"

"No, you don't. But there is more to it than what happened in the office," she said softly.

"What can that be?" he asked, now getting beside himself with grief as he boiled and sputtered like water over hot oil in a pan.

"I have a confession to make, Jeff. I can't keep it any longer. It is killing me, especially considering your present situation."

He became edgy and unsettled like a cat on a hot tin roof when she said that.

"Hey, you have twenty minutes left," the rugged-looking prison officer informed her.

"I am listening, Tessy. As you have been informed, time is not in our favour." His impatience was snowballing out of control with every passing second.

Sobbing and cupping her mouth with her two shaky hands, she dropped the bomb…. "Jane is my friend — my best friend."

"Which Jane, if you don't mind me asking?"

"Jane Inemo."

"I didn't get that. Can you say that again, please?"

"Yes, we have been friends since when we were about eight years old when her adoptive parents moved to Lagos from Delta state. Even when she got this job in the oil company in Port Harcourt a few years ago, it didn't interfere much with our friendship."

"But what has Jane got to do with all of this?"

"A lot. That's why I said I am the cause of your woes and miseries."

"You have lost me. I can't think straight. You just said that Jane had a lot to do with my situation, and at the same time, you are saying you are the cause of my problems. To be fair, you are right because two of you seem to have something to do with my situation, but What I am not sure of is in what capacity and to what extent."

"Do you still remember that Saturday you were in Enugu attending a nursing capping ceremony?"

"Of course, I do. What about it?"

"I was in Enugu the same day."

"Doing what?" Jeff asked suspiciously because he could not recollect seeing her.

"Attending another event. We came to Enugu together; me, Jane, Vivian, and Doris. It was when I came to pick them up from the nursing school that I saw you and Jane through my rear mirror in a position I didn't like."

"You saw me in a position you didn't like? How? Is the position you saw me the reason you didn't want to meet me?"

"Of course, I would have loved to meet you if I didn't see you in that position. And that was where it all started and cascaded down the wrong channel. I was the driver. We drove in my uncle's Land Rover. I didn't trust my car for such a long journey, so I decided to borrow my uncle's Land Rover. I had come to pick Jane, Doris, and Vivian up from the capping ceremony after attending a wedding ceremony when I saw you through my rear-view mirror standing with Jane. And that got me on tenterhooks. It is rare to see Jane stop to talk to a guy. She is a prude. In fact, you can call her a misandry when it comes to men. But there was more to it. Jane had always made us irrelevant in the eyes of men. No man ever sought our attention or looked in our direction once Jane was with us. I was worried sick when she stopped to talk to you. But my jealousy reached a fever pitch when I saw her open her handbag and give you what I presumed was a complimentary card. The whole thing took a turn for the worse when she joined us in the car."

"I think I like him," she said when Doris asked her what she thought of you. Referring to you, she said, "He has got the rare features I like in a man."

"She never stopped talking about you throughout the journey… how you watched her all day, how you spilt your drink on your shirt, and how you were shy to talk to her and all that. The more she talked, the more jealous I became. I was green with envy, and that affected my driving. It was that jealousy that finally made me do what I did."

"Please, what did you do?" he asked impatiently. His ears now were tingling and fluttering with the information they were gathering and his whole body shaking like a pigeon perched on a swinging tiny rope.

"She had always taken the attention of all men, but the thought of her taking you away under my nose was something I couldn't handle, and that was what caused my evil acts."

Jeff felt his senses were under attack as he tried to understand the hard information filtering through his brain. "And what were the evil acts and intentions you are on about, Tessy?" he asked persuasively.

She sobbed further. Her face was illuminated in shame and despair. "I am ashamed of myself, Jeff."

"You can do it," he encouraged her. He needed to hear it all.

"I got her tipsy in the after-wedding party we attended thereafter," she continued, "And that gave me the opportunity to take her phone. I switched it off so that no one could reach her, especially you." She paused again and apologised. Now, a slimy snot was drawing a line between her nostrils and her upper lip.

"And?" Jeff prodded her.

She paused and sniffed to get the bulk of the snot back into her nostrils and wiped the remnant with the back of her hand. "And… I tried to make her buy a new phone with a new number, but she refused to use a new number when she finally did the next day. She still believed you would give her a call someday. But I didn't want that to happen."

"And?"

"So, pretending to help her set up the new phone, I added your number to her new phone and then blocked it before finally deleting it."

A fleeting moment of silence cut across the room as they locked a contrasting gaze on each other. It was so quiet you could hear a ladybird crawl up the wall. Then he snapped out of it. But before he could unleash his temper, which was at boiling point, she cut him short and said, "I haven't finished." Then she continued and said, "But before the time she bought the new phone I had the premonition that you might store her number in another device or diary or something. That was the reason I acted quickly. Remember our suddenly blossoming relationship that fateful Monday, two days after the capping ceremony? It wasn't because of the gas leak that happened on Thursday. I created that atmosphere with a view to retrieving the complimentary card Jane gave you. I knew I had to strike while the iron was still hot by encouraging and creating an endearing relationship between us so that I could visit your house as soon as possible. I knew time was of the essence. The earlier I got the card, the more unlikely anything positive would develop between you and Jane. But you cut a long journey short and made things easier for me."

"How?" he interjected.

"You wore the same suit to work the same Monday. I prayed and hoped the card would still be in your suit, and it was, as I later discovered. When I got you fully invested in our discussion, I seized the opportunity and took the card from your suit as we enjoyed the ice cream. Remember?"

"Yes, I remember, but I was so moronic not to put two and two together to know I was dealing with a dangerous man-eater and a pickpocket.

Now I know why you always switched off and changed the topic every time I wanted to say something about what happened between me and a lady in Enugu. I thought it was normal jealousy that was expected when a guy tried to discuss or show any form of interest in another girl in the presence of a girl who was showing interest, as it was in your situation. Never knew you had always known who Jane was. You are evil, Tessy. You really are," he said, face brimming with fury and disgust.

Ignoring his name-calling, she continued and said, "I then took your phone, which you forgot to take with you when you went to submit some documents at the MD's office. I had watched you all day and was lucky and clever enough to capture your passcode. I cleared all the call history and texts you made to Jane. Having successfully achieved these, I knew it would be impossible for anything positive to come out of your acquaintance with her. I did that because something told me you might use another phone number to reach her since you could not get through with yours.

Poor Jane. She became emotionally troubled when she didn't get any calls or texts from you weeks after the capping ceremony. She couldn't get you out of her mind. Once, while we were talking, she suddenly said that the only man she would have loved to spend the rest of her life had deserted her. Rather than sympathising with her, I rebuked her by telling her how absurd it was for her to be hurting for a relationship that never started."

"I thought I was going crazy when, days later, I decided to try her number again, only to discover that everything about her had disappeared from my phone. I thought I mistakenly pressed a button on my phone that cleared every history and information about her. The complimentary card was nowhere to be found either when I looked for it. I blamed myself for being so carefree. Little did I know I was dining with a remorseless soul."

"Even though I know what I did was despicable, it would still be civil if you control your anger and choose the names you call me," she said with a hangdog look.

Jeff took another lengthy look at her. He didn't know whether to cry, laugh, applaud, or jeer her satanic ingenuity or, better still, put his hands on her neck and strangle her. Then he snapped out of the thoughts. "You did all these?" he asked with a cold chill running down his spine. "You did all these, and I was eating your food and drinking your coffee and tea. Why didn't you think of slitting my throat?"

"Don't sound so horrible, Jeff. Why would I do that?" she asked, still crying inaudibly.

"You are asking me? I wouldn't put anything past you. Not when I am getting the true picture of what you really stand for. Not in a month of Sundays would I have thought you were capable of all these vile acts. I thank God for sparing my life and that of Jane's from such a malicious person like you."

"Would you stop calling me names?" she implored him rather angrily while dabbing away tears from her eyes. "After all, I did all I did because I have always had feelings for you," she said, reiterating her innocence.

That made Jeff laugh in her face. "You want me to be suckered into believing such Humpty Dumptyism of yours? I am not a sucker, has never been and will never be, Tessy. I am only trying to contain my anger, but I think I have the right to call you a clever psychopath. You never loved me. You were only jealous because you thought Jane was in love with me. You never showed me any sign of love all the years we worked together."

"That is true, Jeff. I was only trying to be a good girl, as our grandma had taught us. I thought I told you this before. My grandma made us believe that men must make a move to kickstart a relationship with a girl. But you never did. I didn't know your reasons, but whatever they were, I wasn't going to let Jane snatch you away from me. Consequently, I tossed my grandma's advice to the wind even though I had profound respect for her and had never toyed with her advice."

The more confessions she made, the angrier Jeff became and the more he wanted to do away with her.

"I don't know how many more confessions you still have to make. I think I have heard enough. But the mother of all your crimes was the fact that you were in touch with Jane all the time I was with you in that damn, God-forsaken office, and that made me look like a complete idiot … didn't it?"

"Yes, I was. Just to let you know, I didn't do it to spite you; I did it for the love I have for you," she pleaded her innocence.

Jeff looked in the direction of the prison officer as if to say to him: take her away from my presence before I murder her. He was that close.

She noticed he was boiling like a broth on a camping gas cooker. Frustrated and dejected, she put her face flat on the table and wept like a family that suddenly lost the breadwinner before pleading one more time for his forgiveness.

Jeff's heart wasn't made of stone. He had to reset his mind and view things from a neutral standpoint. The unrestrained expression of her feelings was enough to convince him that she was madly in love with him, and that might have prompted her jealous, dangerous acts. He believed that what happened was a feeling that unknowingly careered beyond the limit. He thought she acted out of desperation and, in so doing, crossed the red line.

"All I want is to clear my mind and name and hope you will find it in your heart to forgive me, and I will be out of your life for good," she promised.

It was undeniable that Jeff had a genuine liking for her despite the unparalleled love he had for Jane. The few glorious, wonderful times they shared in the past were reawakened and unconsciously reflected in his countenance. So, he had to grin and bear all that happened.

Tessy was naturally supernormal and instantaneously felt the relief in his look. A little smile showed on her tear-ridden face, and he noticed her dimples, which he had almost forgotten how they looked.

"Thanks, Jeff, for your understanding."

"Tessy, you went too far with your psychopathic love," he mocked her.

"Wash your mouth and stop calling me names," she humorously rebuked him.

"I am sorry for calling you names, but look at me. Look at the mess you plunged me into," he said as tears welled up in his eyes.

"I know. Please don't get me emotional again, Jeff." She stood up and walked up to him. Bending behind him, she gently wrapped her hands round his neck and with her head resting against his, she whispered, "I am sorry."

"What are you doing? You can't hold me, Tessy. I stink."

"I couldn't care less," she replied as tears rolled down from her cheeks onto his.

"From what I have just gathered from your confession, it means you are yet to confess your crime to your best friend. Do you intend to do that?" he asked her with a deadpan expression.

She momentarily ignored his question and ambled back to her bench. Her eyelids twitched a few times as she struggled to find the right words to express herself. Shaking her head repeatedly, she said, "I dread it, Jeff. How can I? I mean, I am dreading the fact that I am about to lose the two most important people in my life. As short as our (relationship) lasted, if I can call it that, but I have never had such feelings for any man like the one

I had being with you. About Jane, I have no choice. I will tell her when the time is right."

She paused and, took a long, hard look at him and asked in a very low tone, "Did you actually do it? I mean, did you kill the two men as alleged in the papers and television?"

He looked round the room and lowered his voice even further, and said, "I did."

"You killed them?" she exclaimed quietly, her face reflecting how startled she was. She was hoping he would tell her that it was all a set-up.

"Now listen, Tessy, you have come at the right time, or should I say God brought you here today for a reason. We are in a big mess. This visit of yours will either make or mar us."

She looked lost and petrified and said, "Who is in danger?"

"All of us, Tessy. Our lives are in real danger if a particular person finds out that you know Jane and that you visited me today."

Her panic was now palpable. "Why are our lives in danger, if I may ask?"

"It is a long story, Tessy. The prison officer had warned already you had no time left. He will be here soon to take me back to my cell. He is not our problem. Our problem is what happens when he takes me back," he said worryingly.

"You are scaring me, Jeff. I really am scared."

"That's not my intention, even though it appears so. My intention, Tessy, is to let you know the dire situation we are in and why."

"Stop talking like this, please," she pleaded with him.

"Have you got any money on you?"

"Money? Why?" she asked, fear eating her up as an aggressive tumour.

"I can't go back to the cell without telling you the details of why I murdered the two men and why I think we might be dead before the sun rises tomorrow."

She looked over her shoulders in panic before asking, "Killed? By whom?"

"Tessy, this is not time for questions. It is time to think about our safety. Have you got any money on you or not?"

"What has money got to do with this?" she asked, choking on her words.

"Because I need to tell you the full story before you go. And the only way to achieve that is to grease the palm of the prison officer to give us more time.”

“How much are we talking here?”

“About five thousand naira.”

“Oh dear, I haven’t got that much. I have only two thousand naira and my bank card. The two thousand naira is for my taxi anyway. But don’t worry, Jeff, I would rather grease his mind instead.”

“How?”

“You know what I mean. He is a man. I will give him a thought-provoking smile that is full of sexual innuendos. Believe me, that will be worth well over the amount you are asking for.” And she smiled at her jiggery-pokery.

He stared at her briefly, laughed and shook his head.

Smiling seductively at the prison officer, she told him that she needed more time to talk to Jeff since she had missed him so much because they hadn’t seen each other for a long time.

The prison officer, feeling like a jackpot winner, walked away and left them to it.

“Tessy,” Jeff began, “I killed the two men to save Jane.”

"To save Jane? From whom or for what?"

"From Douglas."

"Who is Douglas?" Jane asked, the thin air now saturated with apprehension, and the smell of death hung around them.

"I thought you knew."

"I know only one Douglas, the one Jane had mentioned to me as her boss and who has also served as a father figure to her."

"That's the one I am talking about."

She sniggered and scoffed. "So why are you defending Jane and killing people because of him?" she queried, looking more confused.

"I thought he was what you described him as until lately."

"So, what is he?"

"You don't want to know, Tessy."

"I do, Jeff," she insisted.

He again looked round him and lowered his voice even further, and said, "Mr Douglas is an occultist, killer, kidnapper, human trafficker, human organ harvester, you name it. The list is endless."

She was startled to learn who Mr Douglas really was. Still feeling squeamish, she said, "Before you continue, Jeff, I want to believe Jane is okay. Please tell me she is still alive. I haven't spoken to her for some time now, and she hasn't bothered to call me either."

"I presume she is," he said hopefully.

"Where is she then, and how did you even get to locate her?" she asked, still not sure whether he was telling her the truth.

"Forget about how I located Jane. My concern is that Jane is most likely living with him."

"Who is him?"

"Mr Douglas, of course."

"It is time I shut my mouth and listen because I am mystified and dumbstruck. The whole story is zigzagging and crisscrossing in my brain."

"Mr Douglas believed that I came all the way from Lagos to Port Harcourt to take Jane away from him. According to him, he employed Jane because of her beauty more than any other thing and had been nurturing her to become his at the right time, but I came from Lagos to Port Harcourt to thwart his plans. He, therefore, tricked me to a building that was supposed to be a hotel and told me I should hand Jane over to him. He said that if I didn't, he would kill Jane and me and feed my flesh to the crocodiles in his pond. To cut a long story short, he, with the help of his cohorts, ordered me to pretend to be sleeping around with street girls of Garden City, and he had made Jane catch me red-handed. He forced me to send derogatory text messages to Jane as to how I wasn't bothered by my actions of sleeping around after Jane allegedly caught me in the staged act. He knew that Jane would be so heartbroken if she discovered my infidelity. He said he was sure that he would be the shoulder Jane would cry on when she found out. Unfortunately, that's exactly what happened. He stole Jane from me, and to add insult to injury, I believe he must have stolen her virginity in the process. He did promise that he would keep Jane for six months and that he would make sure that he influenced the court ruling to that effect, but he lied, judging by the court ruling where I was handed a death sentence. The apple of my eye has been taken away from me in a most treacherous and deceitful manner." Jeff said, tears welling up again in his eyes.

Tessy's anger was obvious, but she wouldn't let it get the better of her. She wanted all the details first. "And the dead men? How did it happen?"

"Douglas tagged me and placed me under strict surveillance 24/7, two guards at a time. I took the chance when I noticed that a particular pair were either drunk, dopey, or frolicking with street girls while they were on duty. They tended to sleep a lot as well. Seeing them drunk and asleep that fateful night, I took my chance and murdered them. Little did I know that all the guards wore response alarms. The second man was able to activate it before I killed him. These response alarms were all linked to Douglas, who then informed the police that they arrived in no time and caught me while I was still on it. That is just the summary."

"Mr Douglas harvests People's organs for money?" she asked.

"Maybe for rituals as well. You never know with this kind of person. You can't put anything beyond him," he said dolefully.

"You now know why I said I must tell you the story today before you leave. I won't be surprised that Douglas might have an idea you are with me now as we talk. He is that cryptic, especially about anything concerning me and Jane."

Tessy pulled out her phone from her bag. She was about to dial a number when the prison officer came again and told her that she wasn't allowed to make a call inside the prison as it would be tantamount to security risk. She was smart and knew how to play the game of tease. She grabbed the officer's hand, massaged it gently and finally squeezed in a one thousand naira note into it and then gave him another round of seductive, teasing smile. The officer smiled back and walked away.

Tessy phoned his cousin, who was a brigadier at the military cantonment in Shomolu Lagos. "I need a military back up forthwith," she told him, citing the danger that stared her in the face.

"What do you mean by that?" Jeff asked, wondering who she was to be needing a back up.

"Yes, I got a job at the cantonment with his help during our suspension as their administrator." She quickly gave her cousin the low down of everything Jeff had told her.

With her brother duly informed, she turned to Jeff and said, "I need to phone Jane right away. No time to play around. The mere thought of Jane living with Douglas is driving me round the bend. It makes me cringe, visualising that old, greasy pervert shamelessly molesting her. Jane, of all girls. It's all my fault. If I hadn't done what I did in Lagos, you wouldn't have come to Port Harcourt to kickstart this ugly drama," she said regrettably.

"Are you sure Jane will answer your call? That monster might have brainwashed her."

Jane's phone finally rang on the third attempt, but she didn't answer it. The next two calls were equally ignored. They were wracking their brains on the reasons why she hadn't picked up her calls. "Could it be that Mr Douglas is with her and has asked her not to answer the calls?" Tessy said. "Or could it be that Jane had decided not to do anything anymore with anyone else? Narcissists like Douglas could gradually mould her to voluntarily shun and cut ties with everyone in her life," Tessy suggested.

Trying to cut Jane some slack, Jeff said, "Maybe, she hasn't got the phone on her at the moment, or maybe she put it on silence to catch a nap."

Tessy phoned her again on the strength of Jeff's supposition. This time it was clear that the call was rejected because the call was stopped just after two burrs of ringing.

Tessy's phone beeped two minutes later. It was Jane's text message. "How are you, Tessy? It has been ages."

"That's Jane, Jeff. Why didn't you pick up my calls, Jane?" Tessy texted back.

"Sorry, Tessy, but I can't talk now."

"I need to talk to you right now, Jane."

"You sound desperate, Tessy."

"That's one heck of an understatement, Jane. Are you safe where you are?"

"Sure thing. I am safe."

"And happy?" Tessy curiously added.

"You sound worried. Why all these questions? Is everything okay, Tessy?"

"We need to talk, Jane — and now."

"Okay, I will call you in half an hour". They panicked over Mr Douglas being aware of the contact they were trying to make with Jane. "If what I am thinking is right, then we are as good as dead," Jeff said, trembling.

"Well, lady, you have had it. Time to leave. Don't put my job on the line. If my boss realised that I had left you here for close to two hours and made phone calls, I would be sacked," the prison officer warned her.

Tessy rolled her eyes seductively at him. She got up and walked up to him. Leaning against him, she whispered something in his ear. The officer disappeared with a radiating smile on his face. He had no reason to question her offer. The officer intuitively saw Tessy as a wild street girl, the reason she was hobnobbing and visiting a killer in prison.

"What did you tell him?" Jeff asked.

"I lied to him that I would shag him tomorrow in my hotel."

"Bad girl," Jeff called her humorously.

"I had to, Jeff. We can't leave things the way they are. They are precarious."

"May God save us," Jeff prayed.

Thirty-five minutes later, Tessy's phone rang. It was Jane.

"Where are you, Jane?" Tessy asked hurriedly.

"Why are you asking?"

"You are sitting on a time bomb, in case you don't know."

"Where else am I supposed to be except Port Harcourt? And why is staying in Port Harcourt akin to sitting on a time bomb?"

"Of course, I know you are in Port Harcourt. I want to know exactly where you are now?"

"I am in my house," Jane lied confidently, unaware that Tessy was making the call from Port Harcourt.

"Good. I am in Port Harcourt, and I am getting a taxi to visit you now," she told her, pretending Jane was telling her the truth.

"No, you can't visit me now," Jane responded grudgingly.

"Why? This is Tessy, your bestie. Why can't I meet you?"

"Erm…Erm," Jane stuttered.

"What is going on, Jane? I don't think you are safe, and that's why we need to see."

"What is going on, Tessy? What's all this urgency?"

"Jane, you sound as if you are doing me a favour. I am trying to save you … save us, I should have said."

"Save us from whom?" Jane asked angrily.

"Well, there is no need for rigmaroles. I need to hit the nail on the head. "I know where you are, and that's why you are acting strange."

"Where am I?" Jane confidently asked. She knew that nobody knew she was living with Douglas, not even her colleagues at work. How could Tessy know all the way in Lagos?

"You are with Douglas, aren't you, Jane?"

Jane lost her voice momentarily and was unable to say a thing. She was shocked by Tessy's home truth. She couldn't believe that Tessy had seen through her. As if she were made of a block of butter, she was now melting under Tessy's scrutiny.

"I am making this call from the prison in Port Harcourt," Tessy informed her.

"In the prison?" Jane asked in total shock. "How did you end up in Port Harcourt prison? What happened?" she asked with deep concern for her best friend.

"I am not serving prison term if that is what is on your mind. If I was imprisoned, I shouldn't have told you that I was getting a taxi to visit you, should I?"

"What are you doing in the prison then?"

"I came to visit Jeff."

"Which Jeff?"

"The Jeff you know too well, your Jeff."

Jane laughed cynically and told Tessy to be reasonable. "You are talking wet. You better tell me why you are calling, or I will end this call. How did you even know who he is, or are you just pulling my legs?" she asked, unsure about Tessy's claim.

"No, I am not pulling your legs. I am only trying to pull the scales out of your eyes that have virtually blinded you."

"I should be saying the same thing to you, Tessy. You need your head examined because you are not supposed to know Jeff, let alone visit him in prison."

Jeff asked Tessy to pass the phone. "You need to leave Douglas' house right now in your best interest or risk being arrested alongside him when the special military squad arrives at his house," Jeff warned her firmly. There was a hint of sadness and disappointment in his voice as he spoke to Jane. But he still loved her unreservedly despite feeling betrayed by her actions. To Jeff, there was no limit to love forbearance as far as Jane was concerned because true love makes suffering and heartbreak bearable.

Jane shook visibly, hearing Jeff's voice. She never thought that Tessy was telling her the truth.

"Mr Douglas is evil, Jane. He engineered everything. He made me look like a womaniser. He orchestrated everything from start to finish. All the nasty text messages sent to you from my phone were masterminded and scripted by Douglas. He said that when you caught me red-handed sleeping around, he would be the shoulder you would cry on. He put an electronic tag on me and kept me in captivity, with two guards watching me at one time. I killed the two staff when they came on duty drunk and dopey. I killed them so that I could come and save you. Little did I know they wore response alarms that were linked to Douglas, which one of the men activated before I killed him. Mr Douglas then informed the police, who arrived at once and found me right in the act. When he asked you to give him your phone that evening, it was his sheer attempt and desire to prevent you from contacting me and vice versa."

Jane clearly remembered Douglas asking for her phone that day. She had no doubts now that Jeff was telling the truth, the truth she would have figured out herself if she had looked deeper. She broke down in tears and wailed so loudly that Jeff could hear her.

"Jane, this is not time for crying. If Douglas is not with you, then you must escape right now. Run for dear life. If he discovered that you spoke to us, then there would be no escape for the three of us. He is cryptically dangerous. He is going to murder us in cold blood," he said, fear echoing in his voice.

"I am going nowhere. He has ruined my life — he stole my innocence. He stole my virginity. He put asunder what God had put together. He doesn't deserve to live. I will wait for him to come back from wherever he went. I will kill him in his sleep, I swear. I will," Jane promised while remonstrating furiously.

"Jane, you know talk is cheap. So, please don't take up a task you can't carry out. Douglas is mysterious and oracular by nature. He is not who you think he is. Your look may give you away. If he suspects any foul play, you are dead. Run while you can," he reiterated his appeal.

When Jane gathered her thoughts, she went back to her earlier question, "How do you know each other?"

· "We were colleagues at work in Lagos," Jeff said.

"For how long?"

"For about three years."

"How come nobody told me about it, especially Tessy?"

"Jane, that's another story for another day. What is paramount now is how to save your life and ours."

Tessy's brother, for the love of his dear sister, summarily conducted a special military operation on the location where Douglas and his men were carrying out their heinous crimes and found that the story was true. They went with the press to cover the story. They were arrested and charged accordingly.

Everyone was in the know what Douglas had done to innocent citizens and had demanded justice. The youths were heavily mobilised on the day judgement was to be delivered in the court. The youths had made it clear that they would cause unprecedented mayhem if justice were thwarted. The judge and jurors knew they couldn't but deliver justice. Douglas and his men were subsequently found guilty and sentenced to death, while Jeff was released and reunited with Jane.

Jeff was over the moon that Douglas and his men had been sentenced to death, even though he knew that their execution might take forever, considering his enormous connections. His connections might even fetch him a presidential pardon during the independence celebration. But Jeff was not going to concern himself with that, at least for the time being. Douglas was in prison. That's what mattered most, and he was once again a free man.

As it were, Tessy had caused their problems, and Tessy had fixed them, and, most importantly, she had saved Jeff from execution following his death sentence.

Jane, nonetheless, was lost for words and deeply shocked that their problems were caused by her best friend, Tessy, out of jealousy, and she knew that their friendship would never be the same again. If Tessy hadn't done what she did, Jane wouldn't have lost her virginity to Douglas; Jeff, on the other hand, wouldn't have found himself in all sorts of trouble, including killing people.

Jane was completely heartbroken not to have suspected foul play from the get-go. She blamed herself and refused to forgive herself even though Jeff had wholeheartedly forgiven her. She thought she would have known better.

"I am distraught with my actions. I should have insisted on seeing you no matter how long it took before making any decisions," Jane told Jeff after reuniting with him. "I acted like someone who lacked the mental capacity to make informed decisions. I allowed my emotions to cloud my sense of reasoning. Right now, I feel dirty, sad, and worthless. I am not worthy of you. Neither am I worthy of this life anymore. I deserve to be lying at the seabed with the Goonches and piranhas feeding on my flesh," she lamented.

Moments ago, Jeff was bitter and envious about what Jane did. Now, he was panic-stricken. She was going to take her life. He could see all the signs of a person with suicidal thoughts and intent, and he made a frantic effort to prevent that from happening.

"Look, Jane, you must pull yourself together. I am not complaining. Things do happen in life, sometimes good, sometimes bad. I have got your back. You are still the one I love and will always love. Nothing can change it, not even Douglas and his evil manoeuvres. As far as I am concerned, you are still undefiled," he promised her with all his heart.

"I wish I could see myself and everything that happened that way," she said glumly.

"You can't because, at times, it is difficult for us to assess ourselves accurately without sentiments and bias. You have got to get rid of your pent-up emotions and pick yourself up from this depth of despair. I am your mirror, Jane, and you need to trust me and my judgment."

"No, Jeff. It isn't that easy. Can't you see that I have lost the most important thing in my life — my virginity— to an evil genius called Douglas? It was the depth of despair of losing you that made me take leave of my senses to allow somebody like Douglas to touch me, never mind taking my virginity. I cried right through as he did. They were not the tears of joy I would have prided myself on if it were with you, nor were they tears of pain of what he was doing to me, but they were tears of sheer agony, sadness, and betrayal. I betrayed you, whom I had always promised to give my virginity to, even though I felt desolately betrayed for what I thought was correct at the time. But I still knew I shouldn't be losing my virginity to that *scumbag* under no circumstance. I just knew it was wrong as I lay there in bed, allowing that vulture access to my body because, in my little, messed-up brain, I thought I was avenging your infidelity. What an irrational way to get even! I was completely lost in thought that I didn't even know when he finished, until I realised, I was in the room all by myself. It was a horror show, to put it mildly. Hindsight, I thought I didn't do enough to stop this from happening. I should have done a lot more, shouldn't I, Jeff?"

Still holding her delicately to his chest, he said, "Not at all. You did enough, Jane. What you did was out of profound heartbreak. There are very few people, if any, that could have acted differently in that circumstance, especially in the presence of somebody so manipulative as Douglas, whom you wholeheartedly trusted and treated as a father. As for me, you have not lost me and will never as long as this life exists. Nobody is perfect, not even me. After all, you knew I wasn't a virgin when I met you," he told her with a cheeky smile to make her feel that she hadn't done something nobody had ever done.

"You really want me to feel good about what happened, don't you? Yes, you told me you weren't a virgin. But don't forget you also told me how you lost your virginity. You lost it to somebody you loved and who loved you in equal measure. That's the difference. I lost mine to a man whom I had never loved and will never love, but whom before now I had profound respect for and looked up to as my guardian and spiritual director, and that's why it hurts so badly," she said, crying and squeezing a burst of hurtful laughter in between. I feel defiled and violated. I never knew a positive action could lead to something so negative. Hindsight, I would have given it to you the day I visited you at the Cosmo Hotel. I knew you wanted it, but I morally refused you, trying to be a good girl," she said as she broke down in tears again.

"Don't see your action as stupid. It was an honourable action and a sound decision. A decent girl with a respectful pedigree would do the same," he reassured her.

"The only thing that can make me feel a bit better is to be Douglas' executioner now he is sentenced to death. It would be an honour for me to sit in that doctor's examination chair, pumping the lethal injection slowly into his vein as he is tied firmly to a bed, talking to him all the time as I inject him, reminding him of all his evil deeds, and telling him how glad I am to see him die, and even happier to be his executioner."

"No way, Jane. You don't want his blood in your hands. The law had taken its course. Allow the people appointed for the job to carry out the execution. Don't let what he did to you make you soil your hands. You should stop worrying and blaming yourself for what happened. That is why we are human beings and not superhumans. Mistakes are part of life. We cannot avoid them, but we can at least learn from them. Again, at the heart of our Christian practice is that word, *forgiveness.* It is so powerful. That's why it is a major part of Our Lord's prayer. I have forgiven you, Jane, and If you do not know me enough to know that I love you enough to forgive and bear your shortcomings, then you don't love me enough. If you think that loving you is wrong for what you did, then I don't want to be right," he told her promisingly.

It was such a reassurance that made Jane blow off steam. His words had finally sunk in, and her mood brightened thereafter, and they went to a nearby café for a meal, holding and swinging their hands warmly as they walked.

CHAPTER 11

Jeff and Jane knew it was unsafe to continue to stay in Port Harcourt even though Douglas was now behind bars. So, they moved back to Lagos and started a new, modest life on the outskirts of Victoria Island, the less hustle and bustle area of Lagos. They quickly held a quiet court wedding to cement their relationship to help keep people like Douglas away from meddling with their affairs.

Life would have been fun and merry if Jeff had kept the huge sum in his account paid in by Mr Douglas in his sickening contract. Jeff saw that as blood money and was in haste to reverse the amount back to Douglas's account. Consequently, they were scrambling to make ends meet. He could only rely on his vocal talent and was making enough money to put food on the table by singing in pubs, nightclubs, hotels, and special occasions and events.

Jane later managed to get a job as one of the make-up artists in the Valmount movie industry. There, she grew rapidly as one of the best not only in the company but nationwide. She was awarded a scholarship to study cosmetology at the London School of Beauty and make-up after coming tops in the interview conducted by the company.

These events re-enacted Jeff's fear when Jane announced that she had been selected to travel to London to study cosmetology by her company, Valmount. Jeff didn't want her out of his sight for any reason.

"We have always wanted this," she politely protested, trying to make Jeff change his mind. "You promised to give all your support to my movie industry career. Why are you dragging your feet and feeling so cold about it now?" she asked submissively.

"Because I love you so much and can't imagine living for two whole years without you. Yes, I promised my unwavering support, but not to leave me behind for as long as two years," he said persuasively.

"The world is a global village … the computers, the phones are all out there for us to keep in touch," she said reassuringly.

"Jane, nothing can replace your presence. Nothing compares to your company. Everything about me revolves around you, and you know that …"

"Shh," she stopped him before adding, "I know that. Same here. You mean the entire world to me. It is not going to be easy for me either. As I said, we have computers and phones. We can use them for a variety of things … I mean everything. Let us not allow this opportunity to pass us by. It is a rare chance, Jeff. I want to progress in this profession please. It is going to be a huge step for me, for us, for our future if I can complete this course."

"Okay, Jane," he reluctantly agreed, seeing how impassioned she was about it.

She jumped out of the chair hysterically. Spinning around in circles with flailing hands, she finally landed on his lap, punched the air, and screamed, "Yes." Then she followed it up with a kiss and then added, "That is why my love for you is boundless."

The eve of Jane's departure was special, magical, and full of emotions. They treated and pampered themselves in the best way possible. There was no reservation of love and kisses. If they could store some in a container, they would. Two years was like an eternity for a couple so much in love. Jeff made sure he treated Jane to the best of his cooking prowess. He wanted to cook and serve her something that would linger and remind her of him for the couple of years she would be spending in England. Consequently, he asked Jane to escort him to the supermarket to buy the necessary ingredients for the meal he had in mind.

"We have got all the ingredients for fried rice. It is your favourite, isn't it?" she queried dotingly.

"Not for a day like this. We are not after my favourite. It is your departure day's eve. So, I am after something unique, something we have never prepared before."

Her eyes lit up. If there was something she was good at, it was tasting and trying new meals — local, national, continental, and intercontinental.

"How comfortable are you preparing this, Jeff? The ingredients are intricate and tricky. I know I like trying new food, but this is a special night. This is meant to be our last supper before I travel. Don't you think we need to prepare a meal we are conversant with, my darling?"

"I will get it right only if you stop putting me on the edge. Go away, Jane. I will get you when it is ready."

She laughed, gave him a peck, and left.

He prepared a rack of mutton marinated and roasted in olive oil with fresh rosemary, garlic, Knorr sauce, dried oregano, and a hint of sea salt. He served it with a warm salad made of baked beans and slow-roast tomatoes. To complete a well-balanced meal, he decided to add some homemade potato wedges as a meal side dish.

Taking a bite of the roasted mutton, she exhaled and exclaimed, "Wao! Incredible. I have never tasted anything as good as this. Your cooking ingenuity is simply surreal, Jeff. Ever considered opening a restaurant?"

"Ha-ha! Am I that good? I am glad you will believe me next time I tell you about what I can achieve in the kitchen."

"Don't blow your trumpet because you can cook," she said admiringly.

Looking at her intimately for a while, he said, "Jane, this meal is neither about creating an impression nor is it for perfection and pride. Neither does it have anything to do with taste and aroma. It is simply in honour of your departure. At the end of the day, I am positive that no food prepared by any chef can taste and smell better than you."

Jane moved closer and held him intimately before giving him a kiss for his kind words.

They decided to go local and had their traditional palm wine after the special dinner. And it did what it said in the tin… it sent their hormones raging. Like marsupial brown antechinus mouse, he engaged her in a marathon of hot, steamy romp. They tried to get as much as possible of each other. They knew it would be years before they would have another opportunity. Holding each other fondly thereafter, they finally fell asleep.

The alarm went off at exactly 6.00am. And they woke up with a start.

"We need to hurry up, Jeff, if we are going to beat the morning traffic at Bailey Street and northbound Ikorodu Road (A1)." She was quite upbeat and excited about the journey. Jeff wasn't going to spoil it. He was getting emotional, but he managed to control it and went with the flow.

"*Oyibo* girl (English girl)," he eulogised her. "Make sure you return with a British accent," he cajoled her.

"You and this English accent. What is wrong with our accent and dialect?" she protested playfully.

"So many things, Jane. For a start, we can't pronounce words correctly. We pronounce words as spelt. Again, we tend to use the wrong words for actual words and end up giving them a whole different meaning to what we really mean. You were with me the other day at Domino Plaza when a customer went to the till with one shoe he picked from the shelf and told the white lady at the till to help him find the other leg. The white lady was shocked at first before realising the poor boy meant the matching shoe. Or the other day, when a young boy stuck halfway on a tree asked his father to put him down, when he only wanted his dad to help him come down from the tree. The list is endless. You are going there to correct all these wrong usage and pronunciation of words."

She chuckled with delight and replied, "I will try."

They made it in time and got to the airport at exactly 6.40 am, giving them over two hours to spare before boarding. 15 minutes later, an announcement was made through the public address system that Blueprint plane A630 flight to London had developed a minor fault. So, the flight would be delayed by two hours.

There was a picture of disappointment on Jane's face at the announcement, contrary to Jeff's, who looked overly elated.

"Shouldn't that be a blessing in disguise? It has given us an extra few hours to be together, hasn't it?" he asked eagerly.

"That is true," she concurred on second thought. They kept discussing and encouraging each other for the next hour until Jane got tired. Improvising her folded jacket for a pillow, she put it on Jeff's lap and put her head down on it. "Wake me up when the plane is ready for boarding in case I fall asleep," she told him.

Caressing her face gently and watching travellers scurrying up and down the airport, she fell asleep on his lap.

As she slept, he kept watching her beautiful face. Such would be a thing of the past in the next few hours or so. The thought hit him hard. Then he braced up to it. He must hold his emotions even though it was glaring that he was struggling to do so. She woke up an hour later. About an hour and a half later came the announcement that the plane was now ready for boarding. They held each other warmly and then had a passionate kiss. She held back the tears, and he managed to hold back his. "Be good, and don't do what I will not do," he humbly advised her.

"I will be sensible, Jeff. Don't worry about me. Just be a good boy yourself," she responded as she joined the queue. And they waved at each other continuously as they moved in opposite directions.

Everything was bleary as he fought back the tears as he drove home. The disturbing thought of living for two whole years without Jane was equal to the envy and fear that she might fall in love in the foreign land, and he prayed that God would give him the strength and fortitude to withstand her absence while believing that she would be resilient enough to resist all temptations that would come her way because he knew that she would be pretty tested and pressured by men.

The house, like his heart, felt empty. The silver colour swivel chair was the first thing that got his attention upon entering the house. Jane personally bought it for personal reasons — for comfort and relaxation. Jeff looked at the piles of Vogue and OK magazines on the bookshelf…her favourite magazines. Then, the standing mirror she recently bought to replace the old one she said was outdated. There was something reminiscent of her wherever he looked. The loneliness was overpowering. He needed to do something to help digress his mind. He believed a cup of tea might be helpful. So, he went to the kitchen to make one. And there was even a bigger reminder of Jane…the customised mug she presented him on his last birthday stared him in the face. But more overwhelming was the inscription on it. She carefully chose every word on it: *"To someone who found me. To someone who showed me what true love truly is. Happy birthday, my heartthrob."* He picked up the mug, held it to his chest and gave it a cuddle. He appreciated it even more than the day it was presented to him. He put the kettle on and went to the room to get changed. There, he was greeted by the smell of her perfume, which still lingered. Jane was gone, but everything he touched or looked at was an instant reminder of her.

Six hours after Jane's departure, there was a breaking news on the television as Jeff sat in the lounge having his dinner. "Blueprint Airways flight number A360, en route to London, caught fire mid-air and crashed into the sea. This is a breaking news. We will be bringing you the details of the crash as we get them."

His body froze as his heart pounded and raced uncontrollably. Still unable to process the information correctly, he quickly changed the television channel. He wanted to hear it from another news source. He was hoping to learn that the news was fake or at least unverified. But such luck was hard to come by. The next channel he changed to didn't only confirm the news but was showing footage of the crash. By now, he was sweating profusely. His tummy churned violently, and he felt a sudden urge to throw up and empty his bowel. The news got worse two hours later as they began to give details of the number of people on board — 350 passengers. "346 so far confirmed dead. One passenger was rescued from the wreckage but severely burnt. The three remaining passengers are still unaccounted for. This is breaking news, and we will continue to bring you updates and details of the crash as we get them."

There was no-mentioning of the sex of the passenger rescued. He wondered if the rescued passenger was Jane. And what if it was, how badly was she burnt. The horrific pictures of victims with fourth-degree burns flashed before his eyes. He was reluctant to envisage that Jane would be in that position. It wasn't only the frightening picture she would be presenting if she were to be the rescued passenger, but the unbearable pain and discomfort she would be enduring. "Poor Jane," Jeff cried out! He cried the whole night, wandering up and down. There were mixed feelings and emotions constantly swapping positions in his mind … from anxiety to depression and, of course, hope. In between, he had listened to the news to get more details of the crash, but there was no update all night. He killed off the thought of driving that night. He was in a bad state, both physically and mentally. He knew he wouldn't make it in one piece to the airport if he chose to drive.

Not even a cup of tea could offer him any comfort. It could only warm his body, but it wasn't heart-warming.

The seven o'clock news the following morning had the much-needed update. The three remaining passengers had been found dead, washed ashore by the tide.

"Jane, my love," he said in immeasurable agony. "Is that how your journey to England finally came to a horrifying end?" He threw himself on the floor. He tore his vest off his body and wept uncontrollably. Subsequent news that followed confirmed that the rescued passenger was a male, one of the crew members. That was the last straw that broke the camel's back. That piece of news officially confirmed his nightmare and kickstarted his mourning period.

He was too devastated to do anything, driving the least. The only thing he never stopped doing was crying, lamenting as he did. It was confirmed that the victims would be given a mass burial because their remains were burnt beyond recognition except the last three that were washed ashore. If Jane were to be among the three, he would at least have the chance to see her face one more time before giving her a befitting burial, which she thoroughly deserved. He informed friends and relatives of what had just happened. Vera and Tessy cried passionately when he told them.

Everything changed at 9 o'clock, two hours later. He didn't know whether for better or for worse. The list of all the passengers on board the ill-fated plane was released in some of the national newspapers. Jane's name was missing. He took a longer time to go through it but was unable to find her name. He wasn't sure if it was a typographical error that her name was omitted or whether it was a different airline that he was looking at.

He quickly went through the details of the airline she travelled with one more time. There was no luck. It was actually the plane she travelled with. He knew at that point that the conundrum wasn't something he could resolve in his lounge. He knew he had to get himself to the airport. He grabbed his car key, dashed out, and jumped into his car and drove to the airport. He wanted a clearer picture of what was going on. He wanted to know why her name was not included in the list of the passengers that boarded the plane.

At the airport, everyone was exceptionally busy when he arrived. Staff were trying to clear the backlog of delayed and cancelled flights following the air crash. Relatives and friends of the victims of the crash were everywhere, some crying, some yelling on top of their voices. Intermittently overshadowing the cries of relatives were the announcements of flight delays and cancellations over the public address system. Consequently, it took him some time to get the attention of one of the staff members to lodge his concern.

"Just to find out why my wife's name, who was one of the passengers of the crashed airline, was missing from the list of passengers just released," he told staff when she had a moment to listen to him.

The lady suspended everything she was doing and paid full attention to him. "Just a second," she said, leaving him and dashing across the lounge to the other wing of the waiting room. She resurfaced three minutes later with a middle-aged lady.

"Can we know who you are?" One of them asked him.

"I am Jeff Chibuike."

The lady went through the list of passengers on her laptop. She scrolled down and suddenly stopped when she got to the name Jane Chibuike. "So, you are the husband and next of kin of Jane Chibuike?"

"Yes, I am."

"We do not know what it was, but Jane, your wife, didn't make the trip," she said. "The plane had to leave without her after repeated calls to inform her that she was the last passenger yet to board the plane. We decided to remove her baggage before the plane took off. Since you are not here with her, we will be requiring proof of identity to hand over her baggage to you. What a lucky lady. Both of you should be going to the church to do a thanksgiving for her good luck," she said, smiling lightly.

Jeff took a hasty breath and, looked at the two ladies in dismay and said, "What thanksgiving and with whom? I have come to ask what has become of my wife, and you are there talking about luck and thanksgiving."

"Excuse me. What are you on about, young man? You have got us completely confused," one of the ladies said.

"What confusion? There is no confusion here. I am only asking what happened to my wife. She was left in your care, and now no one can tell me where she is. Where is my wife?" Jeff screamed out in anger and frustration.

"We would appreciate it if you could lower your voice and be more civil," the other lady advised him politely. "How is it our business that your wife decided not to travel?" one of the ladies asked.

"My wife is not with me if that is what you want me to say to get the picture straight. For God's sake, I have not seen or heard from her since I left her here in the airport yesterday morning," he said out again.

"Well, I think you must make up your mind, either to join the screamers on the left or the coolheaded on the right. We know this is a tough time for everyone, but yelling is never going to help anybody. Would you have preferred your wife as one of the deceased passengers or the only surviving passenger with fourth-degree burns? I don't want to sound horrible, but I am convinced beyond all doubt that he would have preferred to be among the dead than live the rest of his life like that. Have you seen his picture? No team of plastic surgeons in the world can do anything to reconstruct him."

"Why are you mentioning reconstruction here? I am of the opinion that he is never going to make it," the other lady cut in.

"But at least the relatives of the victims now know what has happened to their loved ones. I don't know what has happened to my wife," Jeff responded defiantly.

"Strange!" One of the ladies said.

"Strange indeed. So, you prefer your wife to be among the dead? I am certain you are speaking out of frustration. The truth here is that she is not one of the passengers and could be alive somehow, somewhere," the other staff gently chipped in.

It was difficult to clearly understand what they were on about, but it made some sense. He wondered if Jane could be alive as they were suggesting. *But how can she be alive without contacting me since yesterday?* he wondered.

"Now that we know your position and that of your wife, we are going to take an official statement from you, and then we will contact our security department and the police to take over the investigation of what might have happened to your wife. They will be contacting you for more details as they carry out their investigations," the other staff added.

Jeff couldn't settle. There were different thoughts going on in his mind. *If Jane wasn't one of the passengers of the crashed aircraft, where is she then? What has happened to her? If she were safe, why hasn't she bothered to contact me?* Jeff thought in his mind. So many questions with no answers.

The police officers, true to type, were in his house two hours later. They interrogated him for over an hour and recorded some of his statements on their electronic device and some on their notepad. He could understand that they left every option open, including pencilling him down as one of their suspects.

"This is the beginning of our investigations. We are heading back to the airport to gather more information. We will keep you updated with any new developments and findings. We may call again if we consider it necessary to gather more information during our investigation. This is our hotline number in case you hear or come across anything that might help our investigation," one of the officers told him, handing him a card with their phone number and address.

CHAPTER 12

Days passed, weeks passed, but there was nothing optimistic from either the police or the airport.

"We are on it." That was the only response he got each time he went to the police station to get an update on their investigation about his wife.

He has been living as a recluse since Jane went missing. It appeared as if the world was on his shoulder. He wanted to leave the house to visit the pub, cinema, or club rather than visit the police station and the airport and get no encouraging update. He needed to see and hear something different because he was slowly drifting into an empty world with shadows of depression hovering over it.

He, therefore, visited the Cubans club that Friday evening just to have a drink and dance his sorrow away for a moment. Cubans club was packed to the ceiling with revellers. The icing on the cake was it was Motown night with some interludes of funk and disco music. It had all the elements of Soul Train as presented in the 70's and early 80's by Don Cornelius. At about 2 o'clock in the morning, just as people were starting to show signs of tiredness, the DJ announced the *line dancing*. A loud cheer welcomed the announcement. It seemed as if everyone was waiting for it. Jeff had watched line dancing on Soul Train on television so many times, including a few times it was mimicked at Hotel Emporium in Enugu, but he had never had the opportunity to take part in it. That was the very first time any club or pub he had been to had it on their list. Just as in real Soul Train, it was the line of girls facing a line of guys. It was an opportunity for everyone to display one's dancing skills. It was hilarious and heart-warming at the same time. By the time it got to Jeff and the girl opposite, the music had changed from "*The Beat Goes On by the Whispers*" to "*Celebration by the Kool and the Gang.*" Though there was nothing to celebrate as far as he was concerned, it didn't change the fact that it was one of the most danceable tunes you could ever wish for if you were a Motown or funk music lover. Forgetting his misery momentarily, he hit the floor with the girl opposite. She danced like Donna Summer while he mimicked the footsteps of Jeffrey Daniel of the group Shalamar.

Line dancing over, the music changed to a slow, romantic tune — *let's Get It On*, and the revellers reflected the mood created by the tune in their moves and dance styles — there were a lot of body contacts and holding of hands by the dancers. To him, it was more of smooching than anything else. That was okay. But it wasn't okay in his eyes, watching this particular girl completely sandwiched by two repulsive men. They wrapped themselves around her in a manner that she could scarcely breathe. He saw she was clearly uncomfortable as she made some efforts to break free.

Still sandwiching her, they craftily moved her, though dragged should have been a more accurate description, to a darker corner of the ballroom where they would be less noticeable. Their intention now was obvious, at least from Jeff's perspective, because no other person in the room seemed to be bothered. Their hands were all over her as if they were trying to fix a jigsaw or find a needle in a haystack. What was going on was visible to the blind, and the noises the men were making were audible to the deaf, yet nobody bothered to bat an eyelid.

He couldn't stand the abhorrent sight and decided to do something because he was convinced that they were literally taking advantage of the girl as she continued to offer some resistance.

"Hey, guys," Jeff shouted at them. "What's going on here? Can't you see she is not enjoying whatever game you think you are playing?" Face hard as nails.

Audaciously, they said, "What's going on is we want to get it on. At least that's what the music is saying unless you are unable to understand the lyrics."

"Do you really find what you are doing comical?" he asked, his temper simmering now.

"It sounds like you can play a better game than us, young man," they contemptuously retorted, laughing heinously as they said it.

He left them and went to the bouncers at the entrance and notified them of his observation.

They laughed sacrilegiously at his complaint. Tapping him on the shoulder, one of them said to him, "Guy, boys and girls are here to have fun."

"Fun? Like that? By force …?" he asked, feeling insulted by their response.

"Yea, like that. Let me tell you what you don't know because it seems to us you are new to nightlife and things that go with it, like what you are seeing now. Some girls prefer rough handling like that — we call people like her sadomasochists." And they laughed contemptuously when they said it.

When Jeff looked back to where the molesters were, he couldn't see them, but he could hear a voice saying, "Let go of me." Even the sound of the music couldn't drown her resentment and resistance. They had now dragged her behind the DJ's corner and were about to force themselves on her. He had seen and heard enough. He wasn't going to see this innocent, vulnerable girl being molested and raped in his presence. Abandoning the bouncers, he jumped over the DJ's table and into the scene. "Guys, you have to pack it in right now, knock it off or…," he warned them.

"Or what? You are breaching our privacy, silly man. Get out of here before you feel so sorry for yourself," they warned him callously.

"I will leave if you let her go," he told them emphatically.

"So, she can go with you, huh? Is that what you want? If you want her, go out there and wait for us. We won't be long. We will be happy to hand her over to you when we are done," they shamelessly ordered him.

The girl was half-naked at this point. From her compromised position, she looked at Jeff as if to say he should leave with his life. She didn't want him to risk his life because of her. She knew he was putting himself in harm's way, trying to stop these sociopaths whose hormones were already through the roof and who had got the full approval of the security men who should be preventing stuff like this from happening in the first place.

He was having none of that. He couldn't imagine himself present where an innocent girl was being molested.

He pulled out his belt from his jeans and whipped one of the men so hard across the face that it left a bump on his face. That was enough to show them he was not showboating. But that was equally the beginning of what the girl was trying to prevent.

The other guy quickly pulled up his trousers and rushed towards Jeff with a clenched fist. Jeff dodged his punch, and the momentum of his swing carried him past him and, in the process, exposed the back of his neck to him, slapped him hard in the occipital region of his head, and he fell face down on the floor, unconscious. The other fella jumped over the DJ's table and started for the exit.

Jeff grabbed the girl and headed for the door. "You are not supposed to be visiting a place like this, young girl," he advised her, now realising he had made a wrong choice to be there himself.

The two bouncers were scared to make any move on him, seeing what he had done. They instinctively knew his type. They could only watch him leave with the girl.

One of the bouncers screamed before Jeff left, "What of this hippie you left in a heap here?"

"Look after him. At least I have got you something to keep you busy instead of standing there and doing nothing. You are paid to do a job, not to stand and watch vulnerable people molested," he cursed them.

"Don't think you are clever. We know your type. Guys like you usually intimidate others to get what they want. Just be gentle with her wherever you are taking her to," the other bouncer told him, sounding mischievous.

Jeff stuck up a finger at them in derision and walked away with the girl.

"Where are we going?" she asked as they moved to the car park.

"To your house, of course. You need to get yourself home safely especially now you are a bit tipsy."

"Can you take me to your house instead?" she pleaded with him.

"Hey, be careful. If you want to be silly, I will quietly take you back in there and be on my way."

"Please don't," she pleaded once again.

"Make up your mind, girl. Your address or back to the club?"

"I haven't got a home," she said uneasily.

He stopped and gave her a stern look.

She looked at him and then on the floor. Her look was defining and revealing. He knew her situation. He wasn't ready to discuss it in the street. He needed to get her to safety first.

"I need to go back in there to get my little luggage," she said, realising that he was ready to take her to his house.

"Your luggage?"

"Yes, I carry it everywhere I go. I have no safe place to keep it."

He felt so sorry for her situation as the picture of what her profession was became much clearer.

While driving home with her, he asked her what she would have done if he wasn't there to rescue her.

"They would have taken me home if they felt they didn't get enough in the club, or another guy would have done. I have no choice. That's the way it goes when events of life push you into this undignified trade," she replied despondently.

He felt very touched about her situation, and he seemed ready to do whatever it was to keep her off the streets.

On getting home, he showed her the bathroom, where she had a shower and then changed into her nightie.

He made her some toast and a chocolate beverage drink. And she thanked him.

"I know I am not supposed to say this."

"Say what?" he asked.

"Don't take it the wrong way. I won't blame you if you see me as an ungrateful jerk, but can I urge you not to touch me, please. It is for your own safety. I believe that I might be riddled with…"

He looked at her and left.

"Are you angry at me for what I said? I am sorry …"

"Go to sleep when you have had your toast and drink. I will see you in the morning. Good night," he interrupted her and went to his room.

He was up with the crows the following morning. He prepared some plantain with custard. He woke her up and gave her a brand-new toothbrush and toothpaste.

"You can join me in the dining when you are ready."

"Thanks," she replied with gratitude and a little smile. She saw him as unique. She couldn't remember the last time she was served breakfast by a guy, never mind one as young and handsome as her host.

He looked at her pitifully before asking her how she found herself in her kind of trade.

"It is a long story," she replied.

"As long as it may seem, but I am ready to listen to it," he said persuasively.

"Please, if I may crave your indulgence, I wish you would not put me in a position to tell my story. I am not trying to be rude, but I would very much appreciate it if you could shelve this topic. I know I am very hungry, but I would prefer to forgo this beautiful breakfast rather than tell my story," she said, now fighting back the tears that had started gathering in her eyes.

"Just two questions, and I will leave you alone. Where do you come from, and where are your parents?" he asked her, wondering if she was motherless to be in this dire strait and doing this debasing job.

"I don't know," she answered, feeling compelled.

"You don't know where you come from, and you don't know who your parents are?" he asked her, feeling that she wasn't telling him the truth.

"Please, sir, can you forget about all this if you don't mind?" she pleaded humbly.

"Eat your food. We will revisit this topic at a better time. For now, I am heading to the police station."

"Police station? This early? And on a Saturday?" she asked concernedly.

She looked petrified when he mentioned the police station because she wondered if his going to the police had anything to do with her, especially with regard to what happened at the Cubans early that morning. "Why are you going to the police station this early?" she finally asked.

"My wife has been missing for about three weeks now. She was supposed to travel with the plane that crashed three weeks ago en route to England."

"I am sorry to hear that. I know about the crash, but I didn't know your wife was the girl that was kidnapped on the day."

"Kidnapped? Who told you that? How do you know she was kidnapped?"

"Because I know."

"How can you know when the airport has no idea of what has become of her? The police are still investigating and trying to find out what had happened to her."

"I am not pretty sure, but I heard she was kidnapped and had been trafficked to Europe by some sex traffickers."

"Kidnapped? Trafficked? Who told you all this? How did you find out about all these, if I may ask?" he asked, eyes twitching in astonishment and fear at the news she was breaking to him.

"If there is any advantage about this goddam profession, it is fishing out information which the police and security officers cannot get their hands on. Some of our girls are just like the American FBI, especially this lady whose name I am going to withhold for personal reasons. At times, I marvel at how deep she goes to find information."

Jeff didn't know when he sat down. He then asked, "What do you know about Jane, my wife?"

"Not much, sir. I just overheard some girls in the dormitory a couple of weeks ago discussing the crash where one of the girls who was supposed to travel with the flight was kidnapped. That's why I knew it must be the same girl when you said she was supposed to travel with the plane that crashed."

"Do you know who kidnapped her, why she was kidnapped, and to which country in Europe?"

"No, sir. None of that. To be honest, I did not pay much attention. If I knew I would meet her husband, I would have listened to every detail and possibly asked relevant questions about the kidnap. But the destination, I presume, isn't hard to know, sir. Over eighty percent of girls kidnapped for sex trafficking are usually shipped to Italy. I am not saying that she is in Italy. I am only suggesting that she is likely to be there."

"It is not your fault. But can you stop saying this, *sir?* It makes me look older than my age, and that is unsettling."

A smile escaped from her lovely face the way he cautioned her. "I am sorry," she said, stopping herself just in time before putting *sir* again.

"Just call me Jeff." Just then, he realised he didn't even know the girl's name.

"I am Becky," she told him before he asked her.

He didn't want to let her out of his sight in case she went back to street life again, but now he was going to. He believed that she stood a better chance of finding who kidnapped Jane, and the reason she was kidnapped. "Are you willing to do me a big favour?"

"What favour, sir? Sorry, Jeff?"

"You are going to be my FBI. You are going to gather more information from this person who knew that Jane was kidnapped. Something tells me that she might know who masterminded this evil act and the rationale behind it, but most importantly, where the kidnappers had taken her to."

"I will try, Jeff."

He nodded gratifyingly, knowing there was a glimmer of hope that she could be the medium through which he could unravel the mystery surrounding Jane's disappearance. "I am ready to play ball. I will do anything. I will pay any amount to get to the bottom of this case and get my wife back, even if it means borrowing from an archenemy."

"You don't need to, Jeff. Good begets good. You are unique — different from other men I have met. I never knew that decent men like you still exist."

"No need for all these accolades. They make me uncomfortable. Nobody is good. Only God. As humans, we can only strive towards perfection. So, do I count on you to help get more information with regard to my wife's disappearance?"

"Let's not get ahead of ourselves. I am not promising a moon on a stick. Like I said, it will all depend on this lady and how much she will be willing to reveal. But I know her weak point. She loves cognac brandy with fish pepper soup. And that's where you need to come in. I will need some money to provide that for her. Little alcohol usually gets her tongue rolling. If you make her happy, she will reveal information that will shake you to your bone marrow. She is that good. From her comments, she knows who killed Senator Akintola and his boys, but she won't mention the name to anybody because she knows that she would be endangering her life if she did. Up to now, the police are still investigating his death with no success. You see, it is just over three weeks since your wife went missing, and they are yet to make any breakthrough. No identification, no arrest. They don't even know what happened to her, let alone know what to do about it. Such is their inefficiency that I wonder at times why they get paid for doing nought." And she laughed to deride the police.

"That's no problem, Becky. I have enough money to buy her enough brandy and fish pepper soup."

"Then we are on it. You will have to give me a couple of days to smoothen things up before introducing the topic. The worst mistake I will make is to present the case in a manner that she will understand that I am getting the information for someone. If she understood that I am a news informant, then I would be in trouble, and her trouble is a nightmare."

"Take your time, Becky. No rush. Just get it right, and let's take it from there."

In all of this, he had only one person in mind – Mr Douglas. He knew being in prison would not be enough to keep a monster of his calibre from his evil ways. He believed that Douglas must still have some secret agents carrying out his orders, and he knew full well he would be top on his list because it was because of him that he was behind bars, awaiting execution. And his suspicion was eventually confirmed by Becky. He had vowed to make Jeff's and Jane's lives miserable. To him, there was no better way of perpetrating this evil than to ship Jane to Italy, where she would be used as a prostitute. "If I can't keep Jane, no one can, and that includes Jeff," he vowed.

Douglas colluded with the security agents of the airport and the technicians in charge of the CCTV to carry out his heinous plan. He concluded that sending Jane abroad for prostitution would be his best shot yet at tarnishing her integrity and making her worthless to everyone, especially Jeff. "Let me hear the song you will be singing to her when she is able to regain her freedom on completion of the two-year pimping contract in Italy, Mr lover-boy," he cajoled Jeff in his mind. "It is fair we all bear the brunt and share the pain: Now, I am a prisoner, Jane, a prostitute, Jeff with the heartache. From the statistics available to me, you shall have slept with about two thousand, one hundred and ninety men by the time you complete the two-year contract, based on three customers per day, each against your will. Isn't that much worse than just sticking with me, the man you lost your virginity to, huh?" And he sniggered shamelessly at his bizarre thought.

Douglas' agents managed to take Jane's passport when she was asleep on Jeff's lap after one of them distracted Jeff.

When Jane couldn't find her passport on demand, one of the Douglas's agents dressed as an airport staff member offered to help her sort things out so that she would not miss her flight. She asked Jane to follow her to her car, where she was supposed to speak to a certain person who would help with her situation. In desperation, Jane followed her anxiously and sheepishly to the car park, where two armed men were already waiting, and they whisked her away in their red Mercedes car.

CHAPTER 13

A week later, Becky came in dressed in a beige hoodie top and ripped black jeans that almost gave her a badass status. But more worrying was her downcast look.

"Hey, Becky, are you okay?" Jeff asked.

She slumped onto the sofa without uttering a word, and then she got up as quickly as she sat down. She took off her leather boots before excusing herself to go to the kitchen to make a cup of coffee. She looked odd and behaved weirdly. Her hangdog looks infected Jeff's countenance at once.

She put down her cup of coffee on the coffee table and then gave Jeff a look that startled him. "Sit down, Jeff," she said persuasively. "I am afraid I haven't got good news," she continued.

His heart raced and pummelled against his rib cage. He knew it was bad news the way she said it, looking gloomy.

"You are a brave man from the little I know about you. So, I want to believe that you are going to handle well what I am about to tell you."

Conversely, her last statement knocked out any little courage left in him.

"I think Jane is no more," she announced dolefully and almost apologetically.

Momentarily losing his power of speech, he fixed his gaze on her as if he were encouraging her to say she didn't mean what she had just said, but she meant it, as revealed by the sadness that continued to linger on her face.

"No more, as in dead or …?" he asked.

"Jane is gone, I am afraid," she told him, reframing her sentence.

"Gone to where?" he asked, now sounding ridiculous just to buy time to process the information, which wasn't sinking in, or perhaps he wasn't courageous enough to understand.

"In that case, I must be direct. Jane is dead," she said remorsefully. "She died en route to Italy on a boat."

"Jane cannot be dead. How could she? My Jane is too young to die. She is too good to die. She is too beautiful to die. Of course, she is dammed too innocent and too caring to die," Jeff lamented.

"You really need to hold yourself, Jeff. I feel your pain," she sympathised with him.

"Impossible. You can't feel my pain. You know nothing about her. All you know about her is that she is missing. So, how can you sit there and tell me you feel my pain? What I feel is more than pain. It is an irreparable loss, Becky. Part of me has just gone and gone forever. I can't bear it. I can't ..."

"You can, Jeff. Worst things have happened to people in the past, and they forged on without committing suicide. For example, are you aware that a family of five perished in this plane crash? They have relations who are going to watch them buried in a mass grave. They are not even able to see their dead bodies, let alone pay their last respect. Think about it. Horrible things have happened, are happening as we speak and will continue to happen in the future. That's part of life, and we must learn and adjust to live with them," she continued to pour out words of comfort that practically fell on deaf ears.

"Becky, can you please, in the name of God, narrate how you got this story and the details surrounding Jane's death? You said she died on her way to Italy. That doesn't make any sense. What is she going to Italy for? She never liked Italy for once in her life."

"You diligently asked me to get to the root of her disappearance, and that I have done. I am sorry. I honestly understand your state of mind, so I am not surprised you asked this question. Have you forgotten that your wife was kidnapped? So, all the actions we are discussing here were not her decisions. She was up against these marauders who are notorious for kidnapping and luring girls with fake promises to take them to Italy and other European countries for a better life.”

“Do you by any means gather any information on how she died?”

“I don’t think I know much, Jeff. All I can tell you is that she was one of the girls allegedly thrown into the sea when the ship carrying them ran into difficulty due to severe weather. You know the Mediterranean is one of the most dangerous migrant routes in the world. I was told that a quarter of the people on board the ship were thrown into the sea to lighten and stabilise the ship to make it more possible to counter the storm that was determined to sink it.”

“Do you by any chance know where this incident took place?”

“Not at all,” she said.

“All I want from you is to dig deeper to find out where this incident happened.”

“I don’t know how that is going to be possible, Jeff. This ship in question was operated by an illegal firm and criminal gang.”

“Whatever organisation it is, and whatever gang, the ship must be operated by somebody who was able to read and understand the routes and weather forecasts. Whoever that was in charge must have read and understood that they were approaching a life-threatening storm for them to do what they did."

"I am not promising anything, but I will continue to try. But I wonder why you want to know where that happened?"

"So, I can arrange to see if her remains can be recovered."

"Recovered? She screamed. This event happened over a month ago. Have you forgotten? I don't want to sound callous, but I am afraid there will be nothing to recover."

"I understand that. I know the flesh must have been eaten up by the sea creatures. But I believe that her bones will be lying somewhere in the seabed…" As he said it, he had a flashback, and he remembered Jane saying after losing her virginity to Douglas that she wished to be at the seabed with the goonches and piranhas feeding on her flesh. It was like a déjà vu that had become a reality. They were still speaking when Becky's mobile phone started ringing.

"It is her," Becky said quietly.

"Who?"

"The lady that has been supplying me with all the information."

"Please, can you seize this opportunity to ask her where the incident happened?"

She nodded and walked off to the kitchen to answer the call. She returned about twenty minutes later. "It wasn't easy, but I managed to get an idea of where the incident might have taken place. She said it was around the Tunisia—Libya border from the Mediterranean Sea in the north to the tripping with Algeria in the south."

"Impressive. That is useful information," he eagerly replied, even though he still needed a good sea map reader to confirm the area.

"The bad news, Jeff, is that this area is one of the deepest areas of the sea. She said that no ocean diver would be willing to dive that deep for fear of dying of hyperbaric sea pressure. Secondly, she said that the area was infested with all kinds of dangerous fishes, such as goonches and piranhas, and she was sure Jane's remains must have been devoured by these creatures by now."

Jeff cringed again as Becky mentioned goonches and piranhas, and he thought that Jane might have foreseen not only her death but how she was going to die and what would happen to her corpse.

The news hit him so hard. He sank deeper into his seat, and with his hands over his face, he cried unrestrainedly.

As he cried, he inadvertently allowed words that appeared as dirges to flow effortlessly from his mouth, "*My Jane. Only if I had been able to gather your bones to bury. I knew I shouldn't have let you embark on this journey — this sorrowful journey, this treacherous journey. I wish I knew. How did I let the sun go down on me? Why did I allow the stars to disappear from the sky? Now, I am shut out of the universe. The door of love and life has been shut and* slammed *in my face. My world has come crashing down. My heart is broken beyond repair. Now, love means nothing to me because I can't just love again. Not when I have loved you. Nothing is ever going to be the same again. You once told me that I was larger than life, but I knew that you were larger than the sea. How, then, did you allow it to swallow you up? Let the power of our love gag and choke the sea until it has no choice but to spew you up from the depths of its being. Every day, I think about you — about your tender kisses, your tender touches, our sweet pillow talks and sometimes, our silly pillow fights, our endless and meaningless walk by the seashore. Some nights, I cry myself to sleep. Every day is a challenge 'cause I have no idea how to get through it without you. How can I live without you? Can a body exist without the soul? Can a car drive without an engine? Can an eagle fly with its wings clipped? Now, I am like a toothless and clawless lion. You are everything to me, and now you are gone. I am nothing. My world and heart are broken, never to be mended. Good Lord, if my last wish could be granted, let me hold my Jane one more time in my arms.*

The more days passed, the more the reality that Jane was gone hit him. He decided to mourn her for a good seven days. He shaved his hair and ate nothing except fruits and water. He did that to see if the thought of her could dwindle but to no avail. Nothing could abate the feeling.

"As later gathered from a reliable coastal source, the ship Jane was travelling got into trouble near the Algerian-Libyan border as they approached a typhoon storm. The crew was now left with no choice but to reduce the load of the ship to prevent it from sinking or being swept aside. They decided to jettison some of the goods and some of the ladies into the sea. They never considered throwing Jane into the sea as they saw her as the goose that would be laying the golden eggs when they got to their destination. They were going to maximise their profit using her beauty — she would be offered to the highest bidders.

But as bad as the situation was, it came to Jane as a blessing. She never wanted to make the journey to Italy in the first place because she knew full well what the journey was all about — slavery at best, prostitution at worst — though the traffickers would always tell their victims that the journey was for greener pastures.

Jane had read, listened to, and watched documentaries about the trade of prostitution abroad — a trade she would prefer to die than take up. She couldn't imagine being pimped and used as a prostitute.

As the commotion in the ship reached an uncontrollable, frightening peak, she took advantage and grabbed one of the few life vests left. She quickly put it on and jumped into the Mediterranean Sea, damning all the consequences. She preferred drowning to practising prostitution. It was about 12:30 am in the morning. There were screams and wailings from the girls thrown into the sea, just as fishermen would cast their baits to catch a fish. Dignity and sanctity of life were jettisoned in equal measure.

It was when Jane hit the water that the enormity and reality of her action dawned on her. She realised the size of the task and the danger she had got herself into. The realisation was late.

The Rubicon had been crossed, and there was no going back.

The sea roared and rippled as she started her journey that had no beginning and no end. She was intermittently tossed by the waves of the sea. She was in the middle of the sea. Apart from the sky, in a 360-degree view, there wasn't any object in sight except a body of water and the ship, which continued to drift away from her vision. She could only hear the distressing wailing and calls for help from the girls thrown overboard as they battled to stay afloat.

Before now, Jane at least knew they were heading to Italy, but now, in the middle of the sea, she was alone as the cries of the girls jettisoned were no longer audible. They must have succumbed to the relentless power of the sea since they were thrown into the sea with no life jackets. The only thing that was still in view was the ship, which now had started to fade away from sight.

Jane didn't know where she was. Neither did she know what to do. She was at the mercy of the sea, and she was overpowered with emotions and fear. The fairy tales she was told while growing up began to play before her — the mermaid and ghost stories. But that thought was cut short when she was struck in her left leg by something she couldn't identify. She panicked. She hoped whatever it was hadn't cut the leg open. She remembered clearly that sharks and other sea creatures could smell blood miles away. She remembered clearly that two things you must avoid if you were in her kind of situation were to make noise and sustain a cut that would lead to blood getting into the water. She couldn't find out if she was bleeding because it was pitch-black now. But her pastor's words came alive in her mind when he said: *stars can only shine where there is darkness*. She saw herself as a star and had hoped she would brighten her world somehow, somewhat.

She had, in the last two hours, swum and trod the water intermittently. She felt she was at the end of her tether as the sea roared and barked amidst the raging storm, which by now was felt around her. She saw her world drifting away. But when she quickly recounted her life journey, it rekindled the sheer fire in her belly. She imbued herself with the courage to fight using all the swimming skills she learned while growing up, having been brought up by adoptive parents from Ijaw in the riverine area of River State. They swam like fishes. They were able to submerge underwater for almost ten minutes fishing, just like the Bajau nomads.

Just as things couldn't get any worse, it started to rain. That caused the sea to become more tempestuous. Jane's swimming skills had been stretched to the limit, but she had determined not to give in.

She was born and left in the bush by her biological mother. She survived in the bush for days before a hunter discovered her in a very poor state and rushed her to a nearby hospital, where she was treated for bronchitis and sunburn. It was after her recovery that she was transferred to a motherless babies home, where she was finally adopted by her adoptive parents, who later died in a ghastly motor accident just as she was graduating from university. Life had never been kind to her.

The rain was unrelenting. It came in quick bursts, interspersed with roars and thundering rumble of the sea. And Jane was caught in the crossfire. She was getting colder by the minute, and the fear of hypothermia engulfed her, but the constant surge of adrenaline kept her temperature reasonably stable. But she looked extremely fatigued and hungry, having been swimming and occasionally floating in the water for about four hours. She wasn't going to give up. She was determined to fight until there was nothing left to fight with. *If I am going to go down, I will go down with my head held high,* she encouraged herself.

But amid her trial, something happened. The rain was followed by a series of thunders and lightning. She felt frightened by the dazzling effects of the lightning when she remembered incidents where people had been struck dead by lightning just by walking on the road. Now that she was in the water, she felt even more terrified, knowing full well that the conduction of electricity was easier and more likely in the water. But as time passed, she suddenly realised that the lightning was harmless. Rather than she previously thought, she realised the lightning was there to assist, lead and illuminate the atmosphere generously for her, making it possible for her to see things around her again. Not that she cherished seeing the vast, raging water she had been surrounded by and battling with, but at least she was able to see the movement of the sea. And like manna from heaven, she saw two cellophane bags floating toward her as if they were guided. Each had some foodstuff like bread, biscuits, peanuts and bananas. They could be some of the belongings of the passengers thrown overboard. Jane felt bad at the thought, but she had to eat to keep going. She ate hungrily, having dissipated all energy in her tank. It was like a voice spoke to her to follow the flow of the sea instead of fighting or swimming against it. She felt peace in her troubled mind for the first time since getting into the water as she floated effortlessly.

One hour later, she saw something other than the water and the blue sky. The day was slowly breaking, and about two miles from where she was, she saw an island in the middle of the sea. She swam towards it and got there an hour later. On getting to the top of it as the day was breaking, she looked around and could not but appreciate the revolting, magnificent, deep blue sea. She couldn't believe she had been swimming in this majestic water for over five hours.

About three miles away from the island was a thick forest. The island came in hand as her legs were getting hamstrung with much accumulation of lactic acid following long hours of swimming.

After resting for an hour or two on the Pilau island and having waited in vain for an opportunity to get any help, she knew she had no choice but to head back to the sea and swim towards the forest.

Tying the faux leather bag containing two bananas and a handful of peanuts to her waist, she said a short prayer and then jumped into the sea one more time. What awaited her if she was able to swim ashore was something she hadn't contemplated, and she was not ready to bother herself with that. To her, she would cross the bridge when she got there.

Like a mother's hand guiding her toddler trying to take her first steps of life, so was she safely guided ashore by forces of nature.

There was no sign of human life when she finally came ashore. All she could see was herself standing on what looked like Kaihalulu beach, sandwiched by the sea and thick forests that appeared as dangerous as the sea. She would be bothered about the danger of the forest later. For now, she wanted to savour the victory of making it to the shore. She sat down and ate the last bananas and the peanuts, which were the last food left. She didn't know when, where and how she was going to come by her next meal, or, more likely, whether she was going to be the next meal of some strange creatures lying in wait in this monstrous forest.

CHAPTER 14

Drenched to her bone and looking lost, Jane stood there and weighed her options. She looked back at the sea as it rose and raged into majestic surfs before unfurling into a torrential splash as it reached the shore. She wondered how she managed to survive in it for hours. The trees comparatively sang, whistled, and danced amazingly to the gusty wind that accompanied the relentless rain and had ended up driving the cold deeply into her already saturated body. But her resolve to survive and the revolting adrenaline running through her system had protected her from going into hypothermia. She was encouraged by the lesson she learned from her pastor years ago, where he said: *it is through suffering that we reach spiritual maturity.* Nevertheless, she wondered how much more suffering she still had to endure before she could reach this maturity. Hardship and ill luck had coiled around her like a reticulated python would on its prey. And the more she tried to break away from the squeeze, the tighter the coil became.

She had tested and survived the tempestuousness of the sea, but she was about to find out what the thick forest had to offer. The popular saying: *There is no lowering your anchor until you have reached your destination* flashed through her mind, but she wondered if there would ever be a destination on a journey that seemed boundless and endless like the one she was about to embark on.

She inspired herself with the part of the scripture that says: *Like the gold in the furnace, the Lord put his chosen to the test.* She believed she was being tested, and she also believed, though unconvincingly, that she would live to tell her story. With that, she took her first step into the tall, dense, cork-oak forest. It was like a shot in the dark, but she had hoped it would be the silver bullet that would illuminate the horizon ahead of her and bring her agony to an end.

A few steps into the forest, she was startled by an object that fell in her path. If she were two meters behind, it would have landed on her head. *That's not the best way to start the journey,* she said, looking at the object that fell from the tree. Then another fell, and another, each few feet from where she was standing. And that frightened her. She moved away from the spot as quickly as her legs could carry her before stopping to look back. Momentarily, she was spooked and felt she was being haunted already. She then realised that they were coconuts, and she thought they could come in handy at some point, realising she had no food left and was not sure when the next meal was coming.

She went back and gathered the coconuts, three of them, and put them in her faux bag. While picking the coconuts, she heard creaking noises from under the leaves. She didn't know what the noises were until a crab appeared from under them, and then another, and another, until the ground was teeming with crabs. Jane was at a loss as to what to do with them. She loved crabs. It was one of the delicacies her deceased adoptive parents introduced her to. She was quick to gather as many as possible and put them inside her bag before continuing her journey. But she stopped to think what she was going to do with the coconuts. She had no instrument to remove the husk. About the crabs, she also realised that she had no resources or condiments to prepare and cook them. She knew she wasn't going to eat them alive or raw and prayed that her situation would not deteriorate to a point to think in that direction.

She was like one stumbling around in the dark, on a slippery slope. At times, she felt she was going round and round in circles as she weaved between and ducked under the trees and their branches. She felt she had walked past particular spots so many times and had gone under some trees as many times as well. *I am lost, she finally said to herself.* As if she knew where she was before.

She was still soaking wet. The mud and leaves squished under her feet as she walked aimlessly and endlessly, but not tirelessly.

In the stillness of the day, she had had that intense feeling and fear that she was going to be attacked by something. Nowhere felt safe. She felt she was being watched by boa constrictors from the top of the trees, flanked by the cackle of hyenas on the left and the pack of wolves on the right. She believed there was a pride of lions lying in wait in front of her, and she was going to walk into them before long. But her faith in Divine power and providence hadn't deserted her, though it had taken a hit by recent events.

By the time she had walked for three hours, with no refuge in sight, she was tired, desolate, afraid, and hungry and had no strength left to continue her journey. Her pace now wasn't any faster than the pace of the crabs crawling inside her bag. She sat down in the driest corner of the forest, soaked and shivering a bit from the cold. The thought that the night might fall upon her in the forest haunted her for a moment, and she dreaded it. She had spent the night in the sea and survived, but she was much more pessimistic that she would survive the night in her condition, in a forest that had all the trappings of harbouring everything ominous. Most dangerous animals were nocturnal, and ghosts thrived more at night, in the dark. She prayed that she would not witness that.

For now, what mattered most was getting something down her gut to re-energise. She opened her bag to bring out one of the coconuts. She was going to improvise with anything, even with her teeth, to get to the flesh of the coconut. Opening the bag, she was amazed that the husks of two of the coconuts had not only been peeled but the shell had also cracked open by the crabs. That was the time she discovered that the crabs were coconut crabs, a documentary which she had watched on the wildlife channel on the telly some time ago, which also explained why there were many of them under the coconut trees. Before now, she was blaming herself for not watching Bear Grylls's programme on television— *Man vs Wild.* Jane thought she would have learnt how to remove the coconut husks and all the tricks to survive in the jungle. But not anymore. She didn't need them. God had provided her with a natural Bear Grylls — the crabs, and that kept her hope high, and she believed she was being looked after by Divine power.

The crabs' actions were like manna from heaven, especially when Jane discovered that the crabs did not try to eat the flesh of the coconut despite how much they loved coconuts. But what now convinced her that she wasn't alone in this journey was the fact that the crabs went back to work at once to remove the husk of the last coconut. It seemed they were getting it ready for her next meal.

Just moments ago, she was thinking of the possibility of preparing, cooking, and eating the crabs. But that was now in the past. She saw the crabs as friends, helpers, and providers. She believed deep in her heart that they were sacrosanct and Divinely sent to be a source of her meal ticket. Consequently, she removed them permanently from her menu. She believed at that point that some unseen hands were with her on that treacherous journey, especially when she remembered the part of the scripture that says: *you are blessed when you are at the end of the rope, where there is less of you and more of God and His rule.* She knew quite well there was nothing left in her. She believed it was only God's intervention that could lead her to safety. But in all her belief and trust in the Lord, she still pondered why she was subjected to a life filled with misfortunes, miseries, and hardships.

She gathered some strength after eating the coconuts and was able to continue her journey. Just two kilometres from where she was, she sighted a smoke. And like the three wise men in the scripture, she followed it until she came to the source, where she met a lady who seemed to be in her early forties, cooking under a small, thatched house. Jane was gripped with fear. She concluded that she must be a ghost or at least someone from a lost tribe. But there was more panic in the lady's face than there was in Jane's when she set her eyes on Jane.

"Don't harm me," she spoke to Jane in Arabic — a language Jane could make nothing out of. The only thing she could understand was that she was asking for mercy by kneeling and flinging her hands in submission. She must have mistaken Jane for a mermaid, judging by her beauty and skin colour.

Jane gestured to her in the best conceivable way that she was only a human being, and that she came in peace.

Convinced that Jane was harmless, she pointed to a wooden chair and gestured for her to sit down. She then went inside the thatched house and got her something to change into, seeing how drenched and feverish she was. Jane thanked her for the help.

"My name is Hiba," she told Jane amiably.

"I am Jane," Jane told her with a smile.

The fire was soothing, and in a matter of minutes, the purple colour of her skin caused by

the cold gave way to her normal, beautiful
chocolate colour.

CHAPTER 15

Everything seemed perfect except communication, which Jane and her host struggled to navigate through. They managed to introduce themselves, during which she wanted to know why and how Jane found herself in the forbidden forest, just as Jane wanted to know why she was in the forest all by herself. Nature provided them with attributes they did not know they had. They started using sign language just like professional signers to explain things they couldn't explain in English or Arabic. Jane was able to tell her mission, and she was able to narrate her own ordeal. She was accused of sleeping with another woman and was ostracised by her community into the evil forest. She told Jane that the forest was like a cemetery where people who contravened the law of the land were buried, and she counted herself lucky to be alive.

Jane asked her whether she had seen ghosts since she described the forest as a cemetery. She said she hadn't, except on a few occasions she had seen flickering, multi-coloured lights at night. "If the lights represent ghosts, then I can say I have seen quite a few. If they were ghosts, then they must have known that I am innocent of the crime I was accused of because they have never bothered me in anyway," she concluded.

"What of animals? One would expect a dense forest like this to be inhabited by exotic and dangerous creatures. I learned while watching *National Geographic Wild* that animals like wild boars, hyenas and jackals are common in this part of the world."

"Not really. They are rare in this part of the country. I have only seen a herd of gazelles and hares a few times. Only once have I seen some warthogs numbering seven to ten, and it was only on two occasions that I saw a horned viper. I told Hassan about it, and he brought some snake-repellent trees and shrubs like lemon grass, garlic, marigolds, allium, and basil. They are not only repelling snakes, but they are also providing me with some vital food ingredients," she said, pointing at some of the lemongrass, garlic, and basil plants she had used to surround her little thatched house.

She said the only times she saw people were when they came to bury people or when Hassan came to secretly bring some food items for her.

"Who is Hassan?" Jane asked inquisitively.

"He is a good friend of mine. He is one of the few people who believe that I didn't do what they accused me of. He usually visits once a month."

"I hope I won't cause any problem if he sees me here?"

"No, he won't when I have told him your story. The only people we should be wary of are the villagers when they come to bury somebody. They don't usually come this way, though, but that doesn't guarantee they can't. If they by any chance see us together, they may kill us because that will confirm to them that I am unrepentant of the crime I was accused of."

"Oh my God," Jane exclaimed. "I don't want to bring my bad luck to you."

"Neither do I," she responded. "We are only victims of circumstance," she said softly.

By the time Jane had spent two weeks with her in that densely wooded area of the forest, they were like old friends. Their unfortunate circumstances had been key to their strong bond, even though they knew that their lives were hanging on the knife edge if they were to be seen together by the villagers. For now, they were immensely enjoying their companionship as they said goodbye to loneliness.

But Jane had on a few occasions been frightened by the weird activities in the forest, especially at night, that reminded her of the paranormal programme she watched a few years ago about the Cleveland National Forest in California. She couldn't believe she was not only in a similar wooded area but actually living in it.

"If my calculation is right, he is likely to visit sometime today," Hiba said cheerfully as they were having their breakfast that freezing morning.

"You mean Hassan?"

"Yes," she said, nodding simultaneously. "I hope he comes," she continued. "Our food bank is dangerously running low. I would have still got much left, but I have an extra mouth to feed now," she said, referring to Jane. And she smiled elaborately with a hint of embarrassment as she said it. "But I am not complaining because your company is worth more than food," she said to water down the impact of her comment about Jane living with her.

On a condescending note, Jane felt like a child, with Hiba referring to her as an extra mouth to feed. Worse still, she felt guilty as she saw herself as a parasite sponging off Hiba's meagre resources.

Hiba read the expression on Jane's face, and it made her feel bad because she was presenting Jane as a miserable scrounger. But she had not lied at the end of the day. It was just the way her words might have come across and might have been misconstrued by Jane.

More than the food and Hiba's comments, Jane's mind was even more preoccupied with what Hassan would make of her when he saw her.

She wondered if Hiba was going to be able to convince him of her genuineness and that she meant no harm. If Hassan misconstrued the situation, Jane had thought, then she would be in a mess. But even more worrying, she had believed, was the dilemma it would push her and Hiba into. Hassan, like an umbilical cord to a foetus, was the channel through which Hiba got her food. And she wouldn't like to be the midwife that would cut it. The thought made her feel so low. She silently prayed in her heart that she would not bring such ill luck to her host.

Left with no *tabouna* bread, Hiba brought out smoked mackerel they had prepared two days ago from their fishing expedition. Whenever the coast was clear, they would nip down to the sea to do some fishing with homemade fishing rods made from bamboo and local threads strong enough to hook in any fish weighing not more than two kilograms. Their baits had always been worms. They now used fishing as a hobby to kill off boredom and to strengthen their relationship. It had equally helped Jane to take her mind off Jeff whom she believed she had left in a quandary for several weeks after her supposed travel to England. She believed that Jeff was most unlikely to know about her kidnap, but she knew that he would be wondering why she hadn't called all these weeks if she was safe.

Hiba yanked the smoked mackerel into equal halves, removed the bones and then passed one to Jane. They had it with a cup of *Nana* tea made from a hint of sweetener and a pinch of saffron. Whenever they could, they would layer the tea with pine nuts.

Two hours later, Jane sighted some movement from afar. Her heart began to hammer vigorously against her ribs as the figure inched ever closer. "Who is that, Hiba?" she asked, pointing feverishly at the male figure approaching them.

"That's Hassan," she whispered gently amid exhilarating smiles.

Knowing it was Hassan helped to calm Jane's nerves. But she wasn't quite sure what Hassan's reaction would be on seeing her with Hiba.

As he came closer, Jane noticed that he had become wary and had begun to walk more cautiously with his eyes firmly fixed on her.

"Don't worry, Hassan, she is a friend," she said happily and confidently, noticing the apprehension in his face.

Hassan waved cautiously at Jane without saying a word. Then he put down the two big woolly bags he was carrying, which Jane believed contained the foodstuffs.

He was still not sure about Jane's presence. He wondered why Hiba should have a female visitor with her when she was aware she was accused and ostracised based on being with a lady. But he was even more bemused by how Jane came to be with Hiba in the forest.

Jane spinelessly waved back at him, still unsure what Hassan thought of her.

Then he turned and greeted Hiba before sitting down. They spoke Arabic all the way.

Jane couldn't understand anything they were saying. The little Arabic she had learned from her friend, Hiba, didn't come in handy because the pace of their communication and accent made it difficult for her to keep up with them. But that did not prevent her from understanding that she was the centre of their discussion.

Hassan, despite all his efforts, couldn't keep his suspicious eyes off Jane. There was profound doubt in his mind whether what Hiba was telling him was all true.

Jane didn't know what it was, but Jane noticed much relaxation on Hassan's face after Hiba said something to him.

He turned to Jane and asked, "Are you truly Nigerian?" He had some Nigerian friends in the past in his previous employment at Sousse.

His English wasn't the best, but it was a million times better than Hiba's.

"I am," Jane replied gingerly, still not sure whether he had fully accepted all Hiba had told him about her.

To Jane's relief, he told her that Hiba had narrated her ordeal. He felt genuinely sorry for her. Jane nodded her appreciation for his concern and understanding.

It wasn't easy for a man to make an impression on Jane, but Hassan did in a measure. He was a charming young man. He looked to be in his mid-thirties. He was tall, about 5 foot eleven. His immaculate white linen short-sleeved top and trousers complimented his tanned golden complexion. His set of teeth looked so symmetrical and transparently white that one would believe they had been enhanced by a renowned consultant dentist. But most of all was his shimmering blonde curly hair that harmoniously joined to his well-trimmed chin strap beard. His blue eyes came into view when he removed his aviator sunglasses. They were sparklingly beautiful, and Jane saw a semblance between them and the sea. He looked irresistibly handsome.

"You are coming with me," he said. "You are not safe here. If they found both of you together, the end will be brutal," he continued. And that frightened Jane.

Jane looked at Hiba as if she were seeking her approval, and she returned a look of permission.

"You must go with him. It is for your safety, mine, and all of us," she told Jane with eyes saturated with tears.

Jane, unaware of where her future rested, went and hugged her tightly and told her how grateful she was for everything she had done for her and how much she would miss her company.

"Please, Jane, you need to hurry up. Just gather your stuff as quickly as possible so that we can get going. Nobody is safe if we are found here. They will see me as a traitor."

Her panic quadrupled when Hassan said that. She hadn't anything to gather. She had only the blouse and pair of jeans she had worn since she arrived at the forest. Hiba had borrowed her hijab and blouse to cover herself whenever she wanted to wash her jeans and blouse or have a shower. She felt disgusted with herself for being a nuisance by exposing innocent people to undue danger.

"Hiba, I will be back soon. Take care of yourself," he said.

"Be careful yourself, Hassan. Goodbye, Jane. Hope you encounter good fortune. May God guide, protect, and bless you," she wished Jane.

Jane wiped off the tears that were now streaming down her cheeks. "God of justice will remember you, Hiba," she responded with a weak, trembling voice. She knew how uncomfortable she was even in the company of Hiba. She felt deeply sorry for her that she was going to be on her own all over again.

It took Hassan and Jane close to thirty minutes to get to the road. She trailed behind all the time, unsure of what awaited her on this unexpected journey with a total male stranger. She had escaped the danger of the sea and the forest, and now she was heading into uncharted waters with a complete, full-fledged young man she had just met. She didn't know his background because she never bothered to. She never thought that a situation like that would occur. The fear inside her bubbled and grew with every single step she took. She was not going to be consumed by it, she had told herself. She was now of the school of thought that says that you should make lemonade if life throws a lemon at you.

They walked another 12 minutes before they got to where he parked his car. It was a white, convertible sports Jaguar, which matched his white attire. He asked Jane to hop in without even looking at her. Jane sat at the back.

"Why will you not sit in the front with me?" he asked her suspiciously.

"I am comfortable here. Thank you," Jane replied respectfully.

The road was untarred, and thick dust was lifted off the road so they could barely see as he stepped on the throttle. They drove on the untarred road for fifteen minutes before joining a tarred, dual carriageway with road signboards reading Sidi Bou said and Dar Mimoun Bey. He signalled right to come onto the outer lane and then put his foot right down on the throttle. Jane felt they were flying instead of driving. She panicked and thought it was only a matter of time before they crashed. *What does it matter if we crashed anyway? That might be a timely intervention to end all this travesty of life,* she thought in her mind.

Twenty minutes later, he slowed down and then signalled right to come unto a tarred single carriageway. Five minutes later, he pulled up at a shop. Barely bringing the car to a stop, he jumped out of it like a movie star in an action movie.

If he was trying to cut a dash to impress Jane, he had failed completely. All his swagger of over speeding and manoeuvres had only rekindled the fear in Jane's mind that she might not be in a safe hand as her premonition had already warned her.

He disappeared and reappeared five minutes later with two ice creams. Again, without pleasantries, he handed one to her before sliding into the car flamboyantly.

"I thought you would need something like this, having been stuck with Hiba in that forest for weeks," he told her.

"Thank you," she said with much pessimism, believing the ice cream wasn't safe for her to eat.

He started the engine and was about to drive off when she mustered the courage to ask, "Is there no speed limit in your country?"

He laughed and said, "There is, but the speed limit is in the mind of every driver." Starting the car, he reversed with a screeching noise that mimicked the one you would hear in (James Bond films). Then he indicated again to join the major road. With the ice cream in his right hand, he decided to steer with the left hand, still driving at the same breakneck speed.

Forty minutes later, he signalled left unto a side road that led to a little hilltop and pulled up on getting to the top. "Here we are," he said as he switched off the engine. "This is Sidi Bou Said," he said as he stepped out of the car.

"It is beautiful," she said, stepping out of the car.

The city was picturesque with most of the houses painted blue and white. Standing on top of the hill, he pointed to her the famous Sidi Bou Said beach.

"That's equally picturesque," she responded, looking amazed at the impressive turquoise-blue sea glittering against the midday sun with hundreds of people basking and running around on the white-sand beach, most of them being holidaymakers.

She thought he had brought her to a tourist part of the country with hotels and funfair rides scattered here and there.

"Come with me," he told her in a voice that appeared like a command. "You must be hungry," he continued.

She was hungry, but the idea of going into a hotel with a man she had just met wasn't the brightest idea. But like a dog in a lead, she followed him submissively.

She felt a huge relief when he led her to his car instead of the hotel. He started the car, reversed, and drove away. Three minutes later, he stopped in front of a magnificent five-bedroom bungalow.

As he opened the door, two adorable little girls rushed to the door as if they had been waiting for him and excitedly greeted him, "Papa, Papa." The younger one was about three years old, while the other looked five. But the sighting of Jane instinctively made them cower behind their dad and cling to him tenaciously. Still holding their dad firmly, they looked at Jane keenly and suspiciously. Their dad had never brought home a stranger, a young lady, the least.

In Arabic, the five-year-old daughter asked Hassan who Jane was.

"She is a friend," he replied cheerfully.

Jane felt immense relief when she realised Hassan was a family man and couldn't have been up to no good as she had previously thought.

But as she was about to sit down on the sofa offered to her by Hassan, a young lady who looked to be in her thirties entered the lounge and expressed so much shock on seeing Jane. Her countenance dropped.

Jane shifted uneasily in her squat position — half standing and half sitting and greeted her cheerfully, but got no response or acknowledgement. Instinctively, she knew it was Hassan's wife.

She knew that, at that moment, it was no longer sensible to sit down. She wasn't welcomed.

The lady stared at her ferociously with her beautiful blue eyes now turned scarlet in anger. She then turned to Hassan and started talking to him rapidly in Arabic.

Jane knew she was having a go at Hassan by the flippant waving of the hands, shrill voice, and the monstrous, angry face.

Hassan couldn't withstand her barrage of insulting words. He raised his voice in response. What started as bickering was quickly turning into a full brawl.

Jane was caught in the middle. She didn't know what to do. She didn't know how to explain herself better to Hassan's wife.

"I can't understand Arabic, but I know enough to know that this altercation is caused by my presence, and I won't allow that to happen," Jane cut in. "I better leave two of you in peace. About the time I stopped bringing my misfortune upon innocent people. I can't stand here and watch beautiful couples like yourselves tear each other apart on my account. I am leaving, Hassan," she continued. Genuflecting and putting her hands together in an apology posture, she said, "I am really sorry, Madam, for causing trouble in your home."

Jane was disturbed by the fear that had engulfed the young children. Before now, the children looked uncomfortable, but now they looked both terrified and petrified. Jane wondered for a moment if that was the first time the children had seen their parents tearing each other apart in that manner. But she was even more troubled that she had sown the seed of doubt and suspicion in Hassan's wife's mind. She hated herself just thinking about it. To her, marriage is a sacred institution instituted by God, and she did not want to put asunder what God had put together.

Hassan blocked the doorway as Jane tried to leave. "Where do you think you are going?" he asked, voice high and concerning.

Jane, filled to the brim with emotion, wasn't able to speak, and neither did she want to shed tears. Again, she made a more determined attempt to leave, but he was having none of it.

"Where do you think you are going? Where do you know, huh?" he asked again.

"I have never had a destination. I am certain I am not supposed to be in your house. I have never had any directions from birth. I came into this world with nobody to call mother or father. My adoptive parents perished in a ghastly motor accident just as I was graduating from the university. My innocence and virginity were slyly and disrespectfully taken away from me by a man I called my boss, and who had all along acted as a father to me. My supposed journey to England by flight suddenly turned into a journey to Italy on a boat, and then I ended up in the forest with Hiba. I wouldn't be surprised if my presence was responsible for the problem the boat encountered, leading to loss of lives. And now, here I am in a peaceful home, trying to wreck it. Hassan, if you were a lady, you would be doing exactly what your wife is doing. How would you feel if your wife brought a handsome man home and told you she wanted him to live with your family?" Hassan's face instantly turned crimson in anger just hearing Jane make such an assumption. "Look at that anger and jealousy in your face, even when you know it is just mere supposition. So, do me a favour and let me leave to continue my unending journey. Why should you bother about my safety? Not even my biological mother bothered. She wanted me dead, but didn't know how to carry it out. If she had done the right thing by throwing me into the river close to where she abandoned me, the hunter wouldn't have found me alive in the forest days after she left me. If she had thrown me into the river, I would have been long gone and forgotten. I had been in the forest before, at the most vulnerable age of my life. My life with Hiba in the jungle wasn't the first time, and I am not sure if it is going to be the last," Jane said, sounding very pessimistic and emotional. "As far as I know, good luck has always been in short supply in my life, but I have never lacked sorrows and ill luck — I have them in commercial quantity, but I am sick and tired of bringing them to innocent, peaceful homes and people like you and your wife," Jane said, cupping her quivering mouth with her unsteady hands.

Hassan's wife struggled in vain to hold back her overstretched emotion after understanding Jane's background. She felt the pain of a fellow woman. "No woman should be subjected to this kind of ordeal. No woman should suffer like this," Hassan's wife lamented in her poor English, with some tears now escaping her eyes.

They eventually pleaded and convinced Jane to stay with them. "We are not your mother. We are not the sex traffickers. We are not Mr Douglas. We are people with hearts and souls. We will look after you. We will protect you," both promised her.

With a good atmosphere returning to the house, Hassan asked his wife, Hana, to prepare a nice meal for Jane, who was now seen as a special guest.

Hana was enthusiastic to carry out Hassan's order. She dashed out of the lounge to the kitchen with great exuberance.

When she left, Hassan whispered to Jane, "She is a fantastic cook. I don't tell her that all the time, though. It makes her head swell out of proportion."

Jane smiled. In Jane's mind, for a change, good food is something she had been blessed with. For the umpteenth time, the thought of Jeff and his unmatched cooking skills crawled back to mind. She felt pain at the loss of contact with her beloved Jeff. She thought of Jeff's position once more — what he might be thinking of her for not bothering to contact him since she travelled. She hadn't learned about the crash of the plane she was meant to travel with. The thought of Jeff was overpowering. She thought of asking Hassan to allow her to make a call to him using his phone, but she thought better of it. It was still early days to ask for such a favour. She would make the call tomorrow if her wish were to be granted. For now, she should savour her acceptance into Hassan's family.

Thinking about it all, Jane suddenly realised that it would have been impossible to make the call since she was unable to clearly remember the sequence of the last four digits of Jeff's phone number. The ordeal she had been through must have interfered with her memory somehow. She thought in her head that she might be able to think more clearly the next day after getting a good sleep for the first time in weeks.

Just over an hour later, Hana appeared in the lounge to inform Jane that the food was ready. "Come with me to the dining area," she told her in Arabic, which was quickly interpreted in English by Hassan. She could speak English, but hers wasn't as good as Hassan's, even though Hassan's wasn't the best, but it was certainly better than that of Hiba and his wife.

It was couscous spiced with harissa and layered with camel meat and some vegetables.

The dining area, just like the rest of the house, was immaculate, with a lot of space to spare.

Besides the American fridge at the top right corner of the dining room, the dining area had only a ceramic dining table with six dining chairs, which looked royal, exquisite, comfortable, and new. Jane knew at that moment they were a decent, organised, and neat family. The food, as expected, and like every other thing she had encountered so far, apart from the brawl that greeted her on arrival, was appealing and flavoursome.

Hana took her to the guest room at about 9 pm in the night. "This is now your room. Tomorrow, we will take you to town so that you can buy some clothes and shoes. For now, you need to go to bed and get some decent sleep. I can see you are very tired," Hana told her happily.

"I can't thank you and Hassan enough for your magnanimity and kindness. I owe you and Hassan all my gratitude."

CHAPTER 16

Hassan and Hana had waited for Jane to come to the dining room for breakfast the following morning, but there was no sign of her.

At ten o'clock, Hassan asked Hana to go and check on her.

"Good morning, Jane," Hana greeted after knocking on her door.

Hana's voice sounded quite distant to Jane.

"Are you okay, Jane?"

Jane, feeling out of sorts, said, "Erm, I think so."

"Are you coming for your breakfast then? It is past 10 o'clock in the morning, you know."

Jane felt horrible creating such a negative impression of herself as a late riser. But she couldn't help it despite all efforts to the contrary. She cuddled her face after managing to get herself in a sitting position in the bed, and knew right away she wasn't right. Her temperature was high enough that you could boil an egg on her forehead.

"You look awful and flushed. Are you sure you are okay?" Hana asked, looking genuinely concerned.

"I am not too sure, Hana. Just feel so tired and nauseous," she said, as she continued to conceal anything that would portray her in a bad light. She had thought in her head that it was always difficult to get a second chance to make a first impression. She tried to force a smile to show all was well.

Hana wasn't going to be deceived. She came closer and put the back of her hand on her forehead and screamed, "You are boiling." She didn't wait to get her response. She went and got Hassan instead.

Opening the windows to let in some fresh air, Hassan went to the medication cabinet in the kitchen and got a couple of paracetamol tablets and a glass of water. "Here, you must take this to bring down your temperature."

Hana left and came back with a tray holding a cup of tea and two slices of slightly buttered bread.

Jane felt embarrassed being served in bed. She wished she could shake off whatever it was that was wrong with her, but that was only wishful thinking. She wanted to throw up when she smelled the cup of tea and bread. "I can't eat anything. I am sorry, Hana."

"You must try. You can't have medication on an empty stomach," Hana encouraged her.

She courageously managed two bites of the bread and about three gulps of tea, and then the medication. She felt some relief an hour later. "It appears the medication and airing of the room had done the job," Jane said joyfully. She seized that moment of remission to take her shower and brush her teeth.

Hana told her that they were supposed to be doing some shopping that day, but added that it was now impossible for her to make the trip with them as she wasn't feeling great.

Jane once again expressed her immense gratitude to Hassan for keeping his word to look after her.

By the time they returned in the evening from the shopping, her fever had returned. This time, a lot worse. She was slightly coughing and holding on to her sides as she coughed. Hassan rushed and grabbed another two tablets of paracetamol, having seen that those he had given her earlier on worked.

This time, her fever was hardly touched by the paracetamol. The fever continued unabated. The temperature was over 39 degrees Celsius. She was still coughing. Delirium was slowly setting in, with her speech becoming slightly incoherent and disjointed.

Hassan and Hana looked at each other, and their faces at once contoured into an unpleasant spectre. They were running out of options.

As her condition took a turn for the worse, Hassan wondered what the next line of action would be. If they took Jane to the hospital, they would need some explanations to make as who she was to them during the initial medical clerking. Documents about her could be needed in addition. Inability to provide them could put them in a difficult position. They weren't prepared to take such a risk.

But as her condition continued to deteriorate over the next couple of days with no positive response to all the self-medication, Hassan had no other choice but to take her to a private hospital where there would be a better chance of hospitalisation without much requirement for medical history and demand for personal documents.

The fear of anything fatal happening to her haunted them. How could they explain her death to the authorities? There would be no birth registry of hers, nor would there be any documents to show her nationality. They could easily be accused of bringing illegal immigrants into the country. Hassan had equally envisaged what Jeff and Nigerian authorities would think of them when the news got to them— they might believe, and rightly so, that they had a hand in her kidnapping.

Hassan began to sweat and panic as the possibility of his thoughts materialising became increasingly possible.

Hana cast what looked as an accusatory look at Hassan as if to say he had landed the family in trouble by bringing Jane home.

Thankfully, there was no time for investigation of who she was when they finally arrived at the hospital because Jane, at that point, was literally fighting for every breath she took.

Her presentations and details of symptoms gathered from Hassan were enough to tell the doctors that she might be battling pneumonia. Having placed her on infusion and commenced intravenous antibiotics and some antipyretics, they hurriedly wheeled her on a hospital stretcher to the X-ray department, where they did a chest X-ray that confirmed the provisional diagnosis of pneumonia.

It was a race against time as Jane's lungs had been majorly compromised. That explained her pleuritic and chest pain, especially when coughing or during any physical exertion. She was restless with severe delirium and high temperature.

Jane ended up spending a week in the hospital. The doctors were so pleased by how quickly she recovered, considering how badly her lungs were compromised by the pneumonia.

There was massive relief in Hassan's and Hana's faces as the doctor drafted the discharge letter for Jane. They felt let off the hook by Jane's full recovery.

Hassan, Hana, and Jane all agreed that she caught the pneumonia while living with Hiba in the forest.

"You are one lucky girl," Hana said. "I don't think you would have made it left in that forest."

"I thank God for His infinite mercy. I also remain grateful to you and Hassan through whom I escaped death in the forest," she said humbly.

They drove straight to Hassan's parents' house to get their children, Mariam and Amina. They had been with their grandparents ever since Jane was admitted to the hospital. Their granddad, like their grandmother, had mobility issues. Hassan's dad had left-sided weakness after suffering a stroke a few years ago. Their grandmother, on the other hand, was struggling with osteoporosis and arthritis. They were in and out of the hospital because of one health issue or another. But they were still able to look after the kids with Hassan doing their shopping and other demanding chores.

Amina and Mariam were incredibly happy to go home with their parents, not that they weren't looked after by their grandparents, but for the fact they missed the usual funfair of playing around in their vast garden with so much fixed equipment like trampoline, swings, and slides. It was like a family reunion. There were hugs and kisses from their parents and Jane.

"We are getting takeaway tonight. We are all tired, and it's getting too late for anyone to go to the kitchen to cook," Hassan said.

"Yeah!" The children screamed excitedly. They had missed their takeaways since Jane's admission to the hospital. Their grandparents were old-fashioned and would cook all their meals no matter what.

With the passage of time, the children got used to Jane, having noticed that she was there to stay. Jane was like an auntie they never had because they had yet to meet their mum's only sister. Hassan was the only child of his parents. Their mum's only sibling lived in faraway France, and there was little or no correspondence between them.

The pneumonia Jane suffered didn't help. It had compounded her memory loss. She had tried in vain to recollect Jeff's phone number to give him a call. It made her feel so sad. Many thoughts were streaming through her head about what Jeff might be thinking about her. She had thought that he might be thinking she had got into trouble on arrival in England. But on second thought, she remembered that Jeff had full details of the university she was to attend in England. She knew that Jeff must have given the school a call, having not heard from her for months now. She panicked, knowing that the school must have told him she never arrived nor registered. The determination to contact Jeff multiplied with that thought. She felt for Jeff.

Hassan and Hana felt sorry for her for being unable to remember Jeff's phone number.

She could neither remember Tessy's number. *If I had been able to remember Tessy's she would have given me Jeff's phone number*, Jane had thought. She was still angry with Tessy for trying to snatch Jeff away from her. But that wouldn't have mattered now if Tessy could be the means of reaching Jeff.

Hassan and Hana told her not to worry. "As you recover physically and mentally, I believe you will regain your recent and past memories. Your health is paramount for now," Hana told her sympathetically.

Jane nodded in agreement. "I can't wait to recover fully, so that I can set the ball in motion to contact my husband," she said optimistically.

Hassan and Hana didn't renege on their promise to take care of Jane. They lived up to their words.

The kids were now completely used to Jane and vice versa. They would entertain Jane by performing their traditional dances, the *Nuba* and *Stambelli*, usually a belly dance that resembled Shakira dancing to her famous track, "Hips Don't Lie."

Jane, not being the best dancer in the world, would rather tell them tales by moonlight as she learned from her primary school teachers and deceased adoptive parents — her own little way of entertaining the girls.

Hassan had watched them secretly with some joy and admiration.

To Jane, it was like a home away from home, but the urge to get in touch with her husband, Jeff, continued to grow endlessly.

Hassan and Hana made sure she lacked for nothing. They had got her full wardrobe with assorted clothes, shoes, handbags, and underwear. Hassan even bought her a brand-new phone and a wristwatch. "This is now your home, Jane. You need a mobile phone in case you lose your way," Hassan said humorously.

Just two days after Jane's discharge from the hospital, she heard a thud in the wall and a stomp on the floor from the adjacent room around 2 am in the morning. She listened, but the sound died down instantaneously as if it knew someone was eavesdropping.

But as Jane was about to fall back to sleep, there was another unusual sound and muffled noise from the same adjoining room, supposed to be Hassan's and Hana's. Jane picked her phone up and looked at the time to confirm the time she had seen earlier. She listened harder. The noise was coming from their room. But she wasn't sure what the noise was all about. She was determined to find out. She tiptoed closer to the wall and put her ears right next to it. It was clear there was at least some misunderstanding going on between them. Then Jane heard what seemed like someone crying. That was short-lived as well, as it died down as soon as it started. And everything went quiet thereafter.

She again tiptoed back to her bed. She lay there trying to figure out what she had heard. *Were they fighting? Or was Hassan beating his wife? Or were they having an ordinary argument like any other couple?* Jane wondered.

The mere thought of Hassan beating his wife sent shudders down her spine. She was still pondering it when she fell asleep.

She woke up with fear. She couldn't wait to meet them in the lounge where they usually said their morning prayers.

They had just finished praying when she came in. Hana was full of bounce and excitement as she greeted her.

"The breakfast will soon be ready. I am making white porridge. You can add bread and milk if you want," Hana told her cheerfully.

"Another beautiful day. The sun is out already. Holiday makers will be having fun on the beach today," Hassan told her as he sat comfortably on the sofa, looking innocent and harmless as a dove.

Jane couldn't understand what she was seeing and hearing. She wasn't sure now whether she had heard what she thought she had heard earlier on in the morning, or whether she only dreamed about it.

Three days later, she was woken up again by a similar unusual sound and noise. This time it was louder. Stealthily, she crawled to the wall.

She didn't need to listen harder this time. The voice, the cry, the stomps, and the thuds were all louder than those few days ago.

"Shut your bloody mouth or I will shut it for you. If you wake the children or Jane up with your crocodile tears, I will skin you alive," Hassan screamed at her.

Jane put her hand over her mouth to prevent herself from screaming. *Is Hassan really a wife-beater? She inquired inwardly.*

Jane didn't know what he was doing to her. All she could hear was a muffled cry like someone being choked. Jane was shaking with fear and rage at the same time. She contemplated phoning the police. But she thought of all the consequences that would follow. Unless there was evidence of injuries, it was most likely that Hassan would deceive the police. Jane was confident, based on her earlier experience, that Hana would tell the police that she was fine. If that happened, it wouldn't be difficult for Hassan to figure out that she was the one tittle-tattling to the police, and she didn't need anyone to tell her what the repercussions would be. So, she sadly killed off the idea of getting the police involved. But she prayed fervently that Hana didn't come to major harm.

Jane couldn't get back to sleep this time. But what followed thirty minutes later shocked her to her bone marrow. There was yet another noise from the room. Like always, she listened intently. She could not believe her ears. The scream and moan of ecstasy from Hana was deafening as their bed rocked endlessly until a shuddering, moaning male voice came tumbling down to drown hers out. And the noise stopped.

"What? What was that? Has Hassan just had sex with Hana minutes after abusing her physically and emotionally? "

Jane thereafter heard Hassan run the tap for a shower. "You really deserved a shower and all to wash away your sin," Jane muttered in anger.

She believed that Hassan did the same to Hanna days ago, but couldn't confirm it because she fell asleep.

Jane hoped that this was not every night's thing. *If it were, then one would be right to ascribe Hassan as being hyper-sexual because most hyper-sexual individuals were known to be abusers,* she remembered.

Was he genuinely feeling sorry for me over what Douglas did to me when he is doing the same thing to his wife? Jane inquired within her.

Jane couldn't wait to see them in the morning. Jane believed that she wasn't going to be deceived again.

Again, Hassan and his wife were sitting leisurely on the sofa when she entered. The evidence was bare and undeniable. There was a little plaster on Hana's lower lip, a scratch mark on her exposed neck.

Jane looked at Hassan but was able to hold her tongue as she itched to make some accusatory remarks.

Jane wasn't sure where the wound and scratch marks came from — whether from wild sex or a beating. Jane decided to be calm and exclaimed in a low tone, "What happened to your lip?"

As if Hana knew Jane would ask that question, she was ready with an answer and said, "I bumped into the wardrobe and burst my lip last night."

"It is a nice job, she doesn't drink alcohol. I wonder what her fate would've been. She is so clumsy that she at times trips on her own feet," Hassan said slyly.

Unless both were into sadomasochism, Jane knew straightaway that poor Hana was likely to be in a controlled, coercive relationship and knew how dangerous it was for her to intervene.

If Jane hadn't observed these recent events, it would have been difficult to think otherwise because Hassan and Hana, in the eyes of every observer, lived happily. Outwardly, they treated each other with a great deal of respect.

Jane, now fully recovered, dolefully thanked them for everything they had done for her before announcing that she was going to visit the Nigerian embassy with a view to finding her way back to Nigeria. She was missing Jeff like crazy.

Hassan and Hana were sad to hear that, especially Hassan. "Well, we can't stop you, but I would appreciate it if you could hang on for a few months when I start my leave so we can take you round the city before your departure," Hassan told her.

Jane was missing Jeff terribly, but at the same time, she wouldn't ignore their plea to stay longer. They had treated her as royalty for all she could remember. So, she accepted their plea.

CHAPTER 17

Jane was very relieved when Hassan announced that Friday morning that they would be going out the next day to show her the city and all it had to offer. It was a special family outing, and everyone was agog with excitement. It had been a long time since they went on a family outing. They had almost forgotten all about it, but Jane's planned departure had re-enacted the feeling, and it was unanimously welcomed, even though they knew it would kickstart her departure to Nigeria.

They didn't need to go to another city for the funfair. Their city had it all. From rollercoaster rides to bumper cars, water slides, amongst others. It was a fun-filled adventure. After the rides, they moved to the beach where they had horse, donkey, and camel rides.

It was the last event of the day, the quad bike ride. Jane declined when Hassan asked her. She still remembered the rough driver he was and would not like to experience that again, worse still, on a bike. To her, Hassan burned up the road when he drove, and one could not help but have your heart in your mouth if you were his passenger.

"Since you are not keen on a quad bike ride, could you please keep an eye on the children?"

he pleaded with her. "I am taking Hana on a quad bike ride. We will be back shortly."

Mounting the bike, with Hana at the rear seat, he set off, and in a matter of seconds, they had disappeared into the narrow countryside road where traffic was light.

Jane hummed silently, "Why is he speeding all the time on anything mobile? Does he think he is made of steel? I think he is in the wrong job. He should be one of the drivers *in Formula 1.*"

Ten minutes later, while she was still standing with the girls awaiting the return of Hassan and his wife, there were gunshots which initially sounded to Jane as big fireworks, and that would have been in tune with the many activities going on in and around the beach. But what followed shortly after showed her that what she initially thought might be wrong, because the gunshots were quickly followed by a stampede where people at the beach were running and screaming.

Jane was still not completely sure what was going on, and did not know whether to run, stand, or hide. The children now were in flight mode as if they had read the situation better than her.

In a situation where one should be thinking and acting fast, she did neither as she froze in fear and had to be jolted from her stupor to full consciousness by a man in a ski mask.

"Who are you, and what are you doing standing there?" he asked Jane, posing with a gun that looked like Ak 47. He was scarily tall. She couldn't make anything of his face as the black ski mask he was wearing only revealed his fierce scarlet eyes. Nevertheless, she could tell he was a young man by his voice, which showed strong projection and resonance of his vocal cords.

She did not even know how and when he got that close to them. If he had wanted to take them down, he had all the chance.

"I am a housemaid looking after these girls," she said, clutching the girls. "My madam and master had just gone on a quad bike ride, and we are waiting for them," she continued, shaking feverishly, realising who the man could be.

"Are you that simple-minded that you do not know what to do in a situation like this? I hope you know this is neither Xmas nor Eid-al-Fitr celebration, where you would expect turkey or ram for yourself and sweets and chocolates for the children?" the man asked her sarcastically.

"What should I do, sir?" she asked, unable to gather her wits.

"You are very lucky you have got these little girls with you; I would have shown you how to treat somebody with no grey matter in the brain," he derided her, hitting her hard with the butt of his gun. "Next time, it will be the other end of the gun delivering the wake-up call to your muddled brain that will send you to the great beyond to meet your ancestors," he continued, now very angry and sounding impersonal.

She suddenly understood what was going on in the city, and that she had been told to leave the area, and she did at a run, screaming as she ran. The scales had finally fallen off her eyes, and her brain had fully reset.

Just as she thought the dust was settling down and a new vista of hope was opening before her, things for the umpteenth time took a turn for the worse. She ran as fast as her legs could take her, but would stop to wait for the girls to catch up, urging and beckoning them to hurry up. She knew the gunman would have killed her if she had hesitated further, but at the same time, she knew he wouldn't have been able to send her to meet her great ancestors because she hadn't any to meet.

But as the non-stop ratatat and the razzmatazz of the guns drew ever closer, she knew she had to carry Amina if they were going to move any faster and get to safety. Giving little Amina the piggyback, she encouraged Mariam to run as fast as she could, but she would occasionally hold Mariam's hand to force her to move at her own pace when she thought she wasn't moving fast enough.

She forgot how many times they fell while running. It was like a gory nightmare where one was being pursued by a man-eating monster, or someone witnessing sleep paralysis surrounded by poltergeists, the so-called noisy ghosts.

Finally, they managed to get to their house. It was then that she realised that she didn't have the keys to the gate and the house. Hassan had them. Her tummy churned, and her intestines curled and tightened in fear. The children looked at her in desperation. They wanted to get inside, away from the terror and tension in the street. She explained to them that she didn't have the keys.

"I am going to phone Papa to come quickly so that we can go in," she told the girls, who are now glaringly panic-stricken.

She put her hand in the pockets of her linen trousers to get the phone, but couldn't feel anything. She anxiously searched herself with her fidgety hands, but there was no luck. When she confirmed that she didn't have the phone on her, she quickly turned her attention to the girls. She twirled them round and round, as she searched them, believing she inadvertently gave it to one of them. It was only a desperate belief. She knew she never gave them the phone; why would she?

But she was now believing in non-existent miracle.

"Oh my God," she screamed, realising that she had lost the phone. She believed that the phone must have fallen out of her pocket when they were running and falling.

She turned pale. It was a double whammy. She didn't have the keys. Now she had lost her phone and had no means of reaching Hassan or Hana.

Mariam, at that point, asked her about their parents.

"They will shortly be with us," she answered reassuringly, trying her best to conceal the fear that had eroded her confidence.

But no amount of pseudo-confidence would protect them from standing in the street at that hour. Everywhere was deserted. They were the only people about at that hour. There was equally no sound except the rings and booms of gun shots that rained like hail stones on a zinc roof, interspersed by the sirens of the anti-terror squad unit of the police, who by now had stepped in to counter the terror attack.

Graciously, the fence of their house wasn't too high. Jane knew that they had no alternative but to climb over it. She didn't want any of them to be hit by a stray bullet.

With so much adrenaline running through her, her strength had quadrupled as she scooped the girls over the fence like a box of crisps before climbing over herself. She took them to the garden in the backyard, and they sat in the swinging chair in the garden to get their breath back.

That was a momentary relief, though, because minutes later, Amina asked her for food.

"I am hungry too," Mariam added.

They were going to finish the day in the restaurant after the quad bike ride, but not anymore.

The children's demand put her on the edge. The drama had completely wiped away her hunger, but she knew she had to do something for the kids, but what? She had no access to the house, she had no food with her, she had no money on her, and even if she had, how could she venture onto the street, and even if she could, there would be no shops open. She knew she was up against it as Amina began to twist and turn as she cried, repeating that she was hungry. Minutes later, Mariam joined Amina and cried even louder.

All attempts to calm them down fell through. The more she reassured them that their parents would soon be home so that they could go in and eat, the more and louder they cried.

She knew the only way to quell the situation was to say something about the attack. "If you continue to cry like this, that man with the gun will come here and kill all of us." She hated herself for choosing this option, but at least it worked for that moment, as they quickly wiped their eyes. They didn't want to die. Instinctively, they knew they were better off hungry than dead.

The sirens and gunshots were getting a lot louder, which only translated that they were drawing closer. She knew it was unsafe sitting where they were. She knew it was safer to lie on the floor when bullets were flying about.

The only structure in the garden that could offer them safety was the trampoline. Thankfully, there were some washed duvet covers spread out in the lining in the garden. She gathered them and spread two under the trampoline and covered themselves with the remaining one. The trampoline had momentarily provided the requisite sanctuary.

The children, still sobbing inaudibly, finally fell asleep.

Jane lay there watching them as they slept. She was consumed by anger, fear, and dissatisfaction with her inability to provide food for them.

But as time passed, her attention was drawn to what might have happened to Hassan and Hana. It had now been over two hours since the attack started. She knew that they should be home by now if everything was okay with them. Her tummy churned again, and her heart took a lurch thinking of anything untoward happening to them.

The more hours passed, the more the reality dawned on her, and she feared the worst.

Four and a half hours gone now, and there was still no sign of Hassan and Hana. Her fear grew exponentially. She looked at the girls lying on the ground as the prospect of becoming their guardian grew stronger and stronger. She was now looking at the worst-case scenario, where she believed that Hassan and his wife might have been killed. If she had her phone, she would have checked if Hassan or Hana had phoned her for an update, or she would have phoned them, but she hadn't.

Once more, the thought of becoming a adoptive parent or guardian haunted her like a ghost seeking revenge on her killer. She wasn't going to abandon these precious children to their fate.

"But how can I be a guardian to them when I have no work, no credentials, no money, nothing?" she asked herself so loudly that she woke Amina up. And this time, there was no stopping her. The hunger had turned her into a little monster. She got up and started remonstrating, stamping her feet repeatedly on the ground as she did. And that was enough to wake her big sister, who unceremoniously joined the hunger demonstration.

She was at a loss for what to say or do. She had absolutely nothing to offer them, not even water. She couldn't lie to them about the gunshots, nor the man with the gun, because everywhere was quiet and deserted, meaning that the attack was over.

She was torn to ribbons emotionally. She felt inconsequential, seeing herself unable to provide for the girls who were now under her care and could potentially be under her care for an unforeseeable future if her fear about their parents was confirmed. Then she stopped and scoffed at herself for having dared to think of having them then under her care when she was nothing and had nothing. She could only see herself as a bull shark that had had all its teeth extracted. Useless. Powerless. And the pain of her pathetic situation seared through her like scissors on a piece of paper, and the bile of anger rose to her throat, as the glum future stared her in the face.

As if all these weren't enough, she suddenly remembered Hassan's parents. His father had left-sided weakness after suffering a stroke a few years ago. Hassan's mother, on the other hand, was battling chronic osteoporosis and osteoarthritis. She was constantly in pain and had difficulty with her mobility. The last time they were there, she could only mobilise with a Zimmer frame, wincing with every step she took. It was Hassan and his wife who usually did their shopping and took them to the doctors for reviews of their medical conditions. She realised that the onus was going to rest on her to look after them as well if Hassan and his wife were dead. But when she remembered that it was Hassan who handled the provision of food and medications, she knew she would be of little or no help to them because she had no means of turning one dinar into two. Overshadowed and consumed by hopelessness, she could only look up to heaven and pray for Divine intervention.

While she felt overburdened by the thought of Hassan's parents, she was relieved about Hana's. Hana had mentioned them once when she said they lived in Marrakech in Morocco, where they owned a fish shop. She knew that there was a possibility the relationship between Hana and her parents could be strained. Her only sister lived in Monaco, France, and there was little or no correspondence between them. She thought it could be one of the reasons Hassan was treating Hana the way he did, knowing she had nowhere to go and nobody to come to her rescue. She wasn't going to be concerned about that. At least, Hana's relatives weren't going to be one of her problems.

She sat between the girls and squeezed them under her bosom, stroking and reassuring them that things would be okay. *But how? How can they be okay without food and drink, and without their parents?* she lamented, and she cried a little.

It was getting really late now. Darkness was now lurking around the corner. She couldn't imagine sleeping outside with the girls. On top of that, the monsoon-like wind and the overcast sky showed that rain wasn't far off.

Good, gracious God, how am I going to spend the night outside with the children, in the rain and on empty stomachs?

She was still ruminating over all sorts with no solution in sight when the security light in the garden came on.

"Papa," Amina screamed, sighting a male figure moving around in the dining room.

Jane's relief was immense. She hurried to the front door with the girls and knocked. And Hassan came and opened the door.

She was platonically tempted to give him a kiss and a hug when they entered the house, but she found no reciprocity in Hassan's face. She believed it was likely because of the emotional trauma he must have endured during these long hours, especially being unable to contact them. And that was his first question, as she had thought.

"Why did you not pick up my calls, Jane?"

"Because I lost my phone in the chaos," she answered subtly.

Hassan went and sat down on the sofa opposite. He lowered his head and covered his face with two hands and sobbed gently.

It was then that Jane realised she hadn't seen Hana. "Where is Hana?" she asked suddenly and curiously.

Hassan cried further.

"No, no, no. Don't tell me that. I don't want to hear it. Just tell me Hana is fine. Tell me she is ok," she demanded frantically.

"She is alive, but in a bad state. Both tibia and fibula of her right leg were crushed," he told her.

She cried. The children, seeing their dad and Jane crying, joined even though they weren't sure why they were crying. Hassan cuddled them and explained to them in a simple language what had happened to their mother without necessarily frightening them by going into details of the possibility of their mother losing one of her legs.

Jane, after pulling herself together from the shocking news, said to Hassan that she was still happy Hana survived the attack somehow.

"Her injuries were not from the attack," he quickly corrected her. "Our quad bike collided with a farm tractor at a sharp bend while coming back," he continued. "We were at the scene of the accident for over an hour because we got information from a friend that the city was under attack. I tried my best to arrest the bleeding using my little first aid experience with the help of the tractor driver. I just hope she makes it," he said with slim optimism. "It took so much time in the hospital to stabilise her. I just finished all the hospital admission protocols before coming back now, and I am going back to spend the night with her. I am not being pessimistic, but I want to be there with her in case anything should happen to her," he said, voice unsteady and face flaccid.

"Please stop talking like this, Hassan. You are scaring me, and please don't let these little girls get the clear picture of what you are painting. Hana will pull through by God's grace," she said optimistically.

What started as a wonderful adventure had now ended as a major disaster.

Hana's injury was so bad that the orthopaedic surgeons thought that she would need an amputation if the planned surgery was unsuccessful.

Jane once more thought that she had brought her ill fortune to a happy family. She believed the accident wouldn't have happened if Hassan hadn't decided to take her out to give her a treat as a special guest prior to her departure to Nigeria.

CHAPTER 18

Every thought about travelling back to Nigeria vanished with Hana's accident. Jane needed to be there for the family, more so, the children.

It was her time to show how much she cared for the welfare of the family. And she didn't disappoint. She was effectively used to the lifestyles of the locals. She knew where the nearby markets and shops were. She could speak little Arabic and French, enough to get by to explain basic things such as prices of food stuff, toiletries and getting a taxi or a bus. She was the one doing the shopping, cooking, getting the kids ready, taking them to school, bringing them back, and taking food to Hana in the hospital while Hassan got on with his work.

The children weren't only seeing her as an auntie now; they saw her as their mother.

Hassan couldn't thank her enough for the pivotal role she was playing to keep the family together in the absence of his wife. "You are a godsend to this family. What could I have done without you? My work, the children, Hana, and my parents. I really appreciate, Jane."

"One good turn deserves another, Hassan. I am doing what I am supposed to do."

The third week after Hana's admission to the orthopaedic hospital, on a Saturday, Hassan went to a neighbouring city with the kids and bought all the ingredients needed to prepare egusi soup. He bought garri as well.

By the time Jane came back from the hospital, Hassan had prepared egusi soup and made some garri, waiting for her return.

Jane stood at the door and exclaimed, "What a coincidence! Whatever it is smells like one of our local delicacies in Nigeria."

"Like what?"

"It smells like egusi soup," she replied, smiling.

"Yes, it is."

"What do you mean, it is?" she asked, laughing. She believed he was only joking.

"I mean it. I am not kidding. I prepared egusi soup and garri for you."

"Can I see then?" she asked curiously. "I thought you were joking. Where did you buy the ingredients and how did you manage to cook it?" she asked him, having confirmed he cooked egusi soup.

"I travelled with the children to a neighbouring city where there are few Nigerian shops. About the preparation, I learned it by watching YouTube."

Jane couldn't thank him enough for the food. "Not in a million years would I have expected to eat garri and egusi soup in your country."

"Glad you love it. My little way to show appreciation for the vital role you are playing in the family in the absence of Hana."

A few weeks later, as they sat in the lounge, Hassan opened up to Jane. He was full of praise for the invaluable help she was rendering to his young family in the absence of his wife. "The children would have been lost without you. You are kind, religious, soft-hearted, and dedicated." It took him some time before he made the next comment, "And most of all, you are delicately beautiful." That was the first time he commented on her beauty, and there was a deep sense of love in his eyes when he said it. He moved closer to her, close enough to take her hand in his, patting and rubbing it gently.

Jane looked surprised and uncomfortable. Firmly but politely, she withdrew her hand as he held onto it longer than necessary, looking her in the eyes all the time. Having got her hand back, she shifted away from him before thanking him for his kind words.

At that time of the year, usually between June and July, the most popular magazine in the country would always hunt for the best couple to appear on the front page of their magazine. It was an event that attracted the cream of society and foreign magazines from other parts of the world.

Hassan had tried his hand at modelling before with little success. This show of the best couple was one he couldn't pass up. He knew they would have a good chance of winning only if he could convince Jane to pair with him as a couple.

While Jane was having her dinner after putting Amina and Mariam to bed that Sunday evening, Hassan came and sat opposite her without saying anything.

"I don't like to be watched when I am eating," she told him politely.

"Can I go and come back then?" he asked.

"There will be no need for that. I am almost done. Is there anything you want to tell me?" she asked. He nodded but was unsure how to introduce the topic. She cleared the table, washed the plates, dried her hands, and came back. "Yes, I am all ears," she said, after returning from the kitchen.

He coughed, cleared his throat repeatedly, afraid of how to begin without annoying her.

"I am listening," she said with a light smile.

"I don't know how to start."

"Okay, let's leave it till tomorrow, then. Maybe you will be able to overcome your nerves then," she said comically, noticing the nervousness in his face and voice.

As she wanted to stand up to go, he stretched his hand and caught hers. That was the second time he was holding her, and she didn't feel comfortable on each occasion. Like the first time, she at once withdrew her hand and sat back down.

"Jane, there is this top show coming up in two months, organised by Carthage magazine, where they are seeking the best couple to appear on their front page…"

"And you want us to contest, right?" she interrupted him. She had never boasted about her beauty even though she knew it was there. So, it didn't take her time to figure out what he was about to say.

He looked surprised and then nodded.

Jane laughed uproariously. Pointing her right index finger at her head like a typical Nigerian, she said to him, "You are mad." She didn't know when she said it. It escaped her mouth before she could think it through. She watered it down at once and told him she never meant to be insulting or insensitive.

"I am sorry to have asked, but I genuinely believe we will win it. We have everything needed to come out on top," he said with a confident smile.

"Except the fact we are not a couple, or are we? I am not talking about potential here. I am only disappointed that you could be this callous and insensitive to have come up with such a bizarre idea. For crying out loud, your wife is lying critically ill in the hospital with every chance she could lose one of her legs, and here you are talking about us being a couple and going on a fashion and modelling show. How inconsiderate, Hassan?" she yelled at him, now rip-snorting mad.

"I know I shouldn't. It might look like we are financially comfortable, but we are not. I borrowed a huge sum of money from the bank recently for a business I thought was promising, using this house as collateral. Unfortunately, my money went down the drain. I was scammed. Now I have barely six months to pay back the loan, or this house will be taken away from me, I mean from us. My wife didn't know about what I had just told you. This is my opportunity to break free from this financial mess, and it's only you that can help me out of this hopeless situation," he pleaded desperately.

Jane exhaled harshly. She was tongue-tied. She thought it would be sheer madness and the most discreditable lack of gratitude to Hana if she consented to Hassan's bizarre request. On the other hand, all of them, including Hana, would be made homeless if Hassan were unable to pay back the loan. But the thought of the children being homeless was unthinkable. They were like her own children now. The bond between her and the kids was deep and sincere. The thought that they would be made homeless if Hassan were unable to repay his loan put her under pressure to consent to his proposal. But she wasn't sure how they were going to win this competition if they entered it. Again, she had thought that the organisers were most likely to ask for evidence to show that they were a genuine couple. "We are not a couple, are we? The organisers will surely ask for evidence that we are married, won't they?" she asked him unexpectedly.

"Let me worry about that. I am sure I will be able to find a way to raise a marriage certificate."

"You are going to forge one, aren't you?" And he nodded.

"It is a one-off thing, Jane, just to contest and win the $3.5 million. Nothing more, nothing less. Winning this will surely put all of us in good stead."

"You sound so optimistic that we will win."

"Of course, I have no misgivings about it. I am not trying to sing my own praise, but I am confident to say that I am not bad-looking. I have won a few modelling competitions in the past, you know. And for you, everything speaks for itself. A few of my friends who have been privileged to see you in person were unable to describe your beauty. You might not notice, but heads usually turn, and people stare whenever you are out with us. So, I am confident we will win if we enter the contest."

"Shouldn't your wife know about this as a mark of respect? She not only deserves to know but also to give her approval."

"No, Jane. If she knew about what I have just told you, all hell would let loose. She isn't as docile as you might have thought. Have you forgotten how indignant she was seeing you for the first time? Again, she is quite indisposed both physically and mentally now. Telling her this can only compound her health, which is bad enough as it is. I will explain everything to her when the time is right. I promise."

Jane reluctantly agreed and they entered the competition, and true to type, they won it and their faces, including the one they kissed, were on Carthage magazine and some of the foreign magazines that graced the occasion.

Months later, Becky had come in that evening with OK magazine. She didn't have time to read it as she was hungry. She dropped it on the coffee table in the lounge and hurried to the kitchen to prepare yam and egg stew. She was still cooking when Jeff came in. The first thing he noticed was the OK magazine. OK magazine was one of Jane's favourite magazines. He picked it up and held it close to his heart, as Jane's memories rushed in and filled his yearning mind. "Do you care for a cup of tea?" Becky asked, coming out of the kitchen.

"Not really. Thanks anyway."

"Hey! You are not supposed to read that magazine before me. I just bought it," Becky jokingly told him, snatching it from him.

"I am not reading it, Becky, as you can see. It just reminds me of Jane. It is one of her favourite magazines," he said, face icy-cold and crestfallen.

"Aww! And what a coincidence!"

"What coincidence?" Jeff asked.

"The lady on the front page is also called Jane with her husband, Hassan. Aren't they gorgeous, this Tunisian couple?" Becky said, throwing the magazine back at him.

Jeff never looked at the people on the front page of the magazine, all the time he was holding it. With Becky's remarks, he had to take a good look at the picture and screamed hysterically, "Oh my God! Oh my God."

"What?" Becky exclaimed, almost pouring down on herself the cup of tea she was holding.

"It is Jane, my wife," he said, unable to contain a mixture of excitement and anger. Excited because Jane didn't die as he was made to believe. Angry because she was with another man all the way in Tunisia.

Becky laughed so loudly. "Okay, I am sorry for laughing, but I couldn't help it. How can it be your Jane? Jane can't be in Tunisia, married to a Tunisian guy. This could be a mere semblance. Don't forget that Tunisian ladies are known for their beauty."

"Even if I were in a coma, I would still recognise my wife." He looked at the picture one more time and was shocked she was married to a Tunisian man whose surname was Slimane. Jeff was so annoyed that he made an anagram of Hassan's surname of Slimane, to *sillyman*. "He must be a silly man indeed to get his hand on my wife. I am going to Tunisia to get her back. This is not my Jane. Something awful must have happened to her to do this. She can't just forget me like that and get married to a foreigner." He knew that she would not have consented to Hassan's demand if she knew the magazine would go that far, knowing full well that Jeff would have a heart attack if he saw her anywhere close to another man.

Becky had now confirmed it was Jane on the front page of the magazine with the headline, "Young Tunisian couple scooped $3.5 million after winning the best couple of the year competition."

"How are you going to do this? I mean it's going to be a Herculean task to pull off. You can't go to a foreign country to dissolve an existing marriage. It is extremely dangerous, Jeff."

"Who cares if it is dangerous or not. It is my wife we are talking about here. Nothing, and I repeat, nothing is going to be in the way. If I die fighting for her, so be it. But I am going to risk everything to get her back."

"Jeff, you have to be reasonable. Yes, I know how much you love her, but have you stopped to ask how much she loves you? If she loved you as much as you love her, why would she marry that man, Hassan? Look at this inside picture. They are even kissing. And she looks happy."

The picture exacerbated Jeff's anger. "He must have done something to her," he insisted, but with a flicker of disappointment and jealousy.

Since winning the competition and the millions in his bank, Hassan's confidence had soared through the roof as he threw his weight around, including trying to be more intimate with Jane. Jane had persistently and smartly warded off all his flirtatious allusions.

But it wasn't too long before Hassan made his intent fully known to her. He had come home looking radiant and happy, like he had looked lately. He wore a black designer T-shirt with a pair of sky-blue denim jeans shorts, which had ragged edges. He wore a woven black leather necklace, which matched his Boss leather bracelet. The immaculate Valentino trainers gave him extra spring in his step. His parfum filled the room delightfully.

Jane found him exquisitely handsome and hunky. And that was the second time she had appreciated him that way.

He came to her while the children were playing in the garden. For the third time, he took her hand in his and looked at her admiringly. Jane had to tell him to let go of her hand because she couldn't withdraw it on this occasion, because the hold wasn't only intentional but also tenacious.

"Are you trying to make it out with me or what?" she asked him, reading the expression in his face.

"A lot more than that, Jane," he replied. Kneeling on one knee before her, he dipped his hand into his back pocket and brought out a little, navy-blue box holding an eighteen-carat gold ring and asked her to marry him.

His charm wasn't going to woo her. Like one made of wood, she was able to repel his charming magnet as she remained steadfast as the sun. Her oath of allegiance and faithfulness to Jeff wasn't going to be broken again by any man.

"You have a lot of nerve, Hassan. What do you think you are doing?" she asked him with a cold, furious face. "Please, you need to get up before the kids come in and see you in this weird position. Don't let them know that you want to replace their mum with another woman. Show them some respect. I would rather you didn't use Hana's indisposition as a smokescreen to seek another woman. That would be vile," she advised him, with a hint of dispiritedness in her voice.

Looking at Jane morosely, he pleaded, "Please, say yes."

Jane was boiling with anger. If she had the power, she would have given him a wake-up slap to reset his brain.

"Say yes to what? You are married, Hassan. Despite my situation, you mustn't forget that I am equally married."

"Please, Jane," he continued his plea, ignoring everything she had said.

"What has come over you? Haven't you got a conscience anymore? This is weird, inappropriate, and untimely. Your wife is still in the hospital fighting for her dear life, and all you could think of is getting married to another woman. I am deeply shocked at your behaviour."

"I will give you time to think about it if you think my request is ill-timed," he said, and left.

Jane shook her head and tutted in disbelief at Hassan's hard-boiled, depraved behaviour.

"Can I have a word, Hassan?" Jane asked him in the evening of the following day.

He followed her to the dining room, unsure whether it was good news about his proposal or whether she was going to tell him off. He believed the latter, judging by her look.

"What is the matter, darling?" he asked endearingly.

"Would you please stop talking to me like that?" she pleaded with him.

"Like what?"

"Like that. There is no need for all these darlings and endearments."

"I won't next time," he promised disgruntledly.

"Thank you." Jane sat down and pointed to the chair opposite. "You may be seated," she told him flatly.

There was overpowering silence in the dining room as she locked her unwelcoming gaze on him. Save for the humming sound from the American fridge in the corner of the dining room, and the Tik-Tok sound from the wall clock, it would have been possible to hear the drop of a feather.

She broke the silence and said, "I have this concern."

"What do you mean? What concern?"

"When last did you visit your wife in the hospital?"

He never expected the question and as such wasn't sure what to answer.

"Not that she complained to me," Jane continued. "I found out myself when Hana told me that you brought her some oranges three days ago when you last visited. She tried to cover up for you when I confronted her about her comments. It must have slipped out of her mouth. So, tell me, Hassan, when last did you visit Hana?"

"It is work. I have been very busy lately," he tried to excuse himself.

"Busy? But you have the bloody time to shop around to buy an engagement ring for another woman, huh? Why didn't you use that time to visit your wife?"

"You've got to understand…,"

"Understand what, Hassan?"

"Okay, I am sorry. I will see her later today if that would make you happy."

"I can't believe you needed someone to prompt and remind you to visit your wife. That's quite unfair and unreasonable."

"It is just that I am very distracted lately. I can hardly concentrate these days."

"What is distracting you from your lovely wife?"

He kept quiet for some time before pointing at her and saying, "You, Jane. You are my aphrodisiac, my distraction. I will regain my composure and reasoning if you say yes to my proposal."

Jane didn't know when she told him rudely to shut his mouth. "The earlier you get me off your mind, the better for you. I can't marry you. It is impossible."

"Why?"

"Because you are bloody married for God's sake, and to a good woman," Jane remembered how Hana had condoned his violence and abuse, probably since the beginning of their marriage. She also remembered how nice Hana had treated her since she arrived at their house. To Jane, it could only be a virtuous and docile woman like Hana who could accommodate his volatile and abusive behaviour.

"I am a Muslim, and I am allowed to marry up to four wives if I choose to. And you know I will look no further if you marry me," he convincingly assured Jane.

"But I am not a Muslim, or have you also forgotten that?"

"Then I will convert to Christianity."

"Good. But you know, as a Christian, you are not allowed to marry more than one wife."

"I will marry only you if that is what you want," he said, sounding senseless and lost.

"Then what happens to Hana, your wife?" Jane asked, trying to instil some sense into his absurd brain in case he had forgotten all about her.

"I will return her to her parents in Marrakech, and that is even if she makes it alive from the hospital. If you want me to become a pastor or a priest to make this happen, I will," he shamelessly promised.

"You are out of your mind. You have lost it. You need help, Hassan. Why would you abandon your religion because of a woman?" she asked him, looking furious and breathless.

"What of Amina and Mariam? You have confessed your undying love for them. Jane, if you can't do it for me, at least, you can do it for their sake. They see you as their real mother, as if they knew they would never have their mum back and even if they did, they are aware she is not going to be any good to them," he said with no emotion.

Jane, for a moment, on the strength of evil words coming out from Hassan's mouth, thought that it was possible that he might have intentionally caused Hana's accident to get rid of her so that he could get to her. After all, nobody saw the accident first-hand. He forged the marriage certificate. It might be possible that he colluded with the farm tractor driver to cause the accident; otherwise, why hadn't he suffered any injury at all from the accident?

Jane then exclaimed, "Their mother won't be any good to them? Really?"

"Why are you talking like this? You have your eyes and ears. That leg is extensively gangrenous, and the doctors have exhausted all options. They told me, and I am sure you are equally aware, that Hana is going to have that leg amputated to prevent further complications. Of course, you have your nose. You can smell her as soon as you enter her room. On top of everything going on with her, she has developed a grade four decubitus ulcer in the sacral area of her buttocks, and that is where the awful smell is coming from."

"I can't believe this," Jane said, tutting and shaking her head simultaneously. "How deep is your callousness, Hassan? I can see that you have ruled out Hana's survival. I don't think I am wrong to say you are preparing her funeral or have performed one already while she is still alive. This is inhumane to say the least."

He heaved his shoulders and pouted his mouth disgustingly.

"I am not going to be part of this God-forsaken arrangement ..."

"You are, Jane," Hassan rudely interrupted her. "You started all this, and you will see the end of it," he said, voice harsh, discourteous, and threatening.

Jane was taken aback by his sudden accusatory position and change of tone. She was speechless and could only stare.

He told Jane that she had ruined and caused problems directly and indirectly to individuals and families she had met, but vowed that his own family would not fall under her satanic influence, no matter how hard she tried.

"Whatever ill luck you have been bestowed by nature, I don't want to be one of your victims. I will hold you responsible for all the havoc you have wreaked in my family. If you don't clean up this mess you made, I will help the security services to hide you where you will never have any chance to harm anyone again. You have messed up my family. You have turned my world upside down, and don't think I will fold my arms and watch you run riot with your witchcraft powers in my home without reprisals. Believe you me, I will make you pay by hell or high water," he continued to threaten and lay curses on her.

Jane managed a plastic grin. She knew his plan was to break her both mentally and physically. She vowed in her mind to defend herself. But her defence and resolve were fraught with defects and doubts.

Hassan might not be too far from the truth after all, Jane had thought. *I have touched people's lives negatively for all I can remember. Like an infectious disease, I have infected everyone I met in one way or the other.* In her mind, she thought, *I am not on speaking terms with my best friend, Tessy, because of what happened between her and Jeff. Who was at the heart of it? — Jane. Jeff was inches away from losing his life in the hands of Douglas. Jeff murdered two people in the process and was sentenced to death as a result. On whose account did all these happen to Jeff? — Jane. Mr Douglas was sentenced to death after he was unveiled as a serial ritualist and human organ harvester. Should I count this against myself? Not really, that was the only good thing my presence has ever caused anyone. But I wouldn't say the same for Hiba, the lady I lived with in the forest. I knew I would have caused her death if we had been seen together in the woods. Even though Hassan and Hana are happy in their marriage, or so it seems, I have managed to wreck whatever was to be salvaged in their marriage with my ill luck. It was to entertain me that Hassan organised a day out that led to Hana's accident.*

But are all these enough for Hassan to brand me satan? Perhaps. After all, the bible says that satan has come to steal, kill and destroy. I have stolen People's happiness and peace. I have destroyed homes, including Hassan's. I am not sure I have killed, maybe by proxy, because it was on my account that Jeff killed two people so that he could save me. So, Hassan might be right.

Jane, at that point, was filled to the gills with emotion, but she promised herself even more vehemently that she wasn't going to cry on anyone's shoulder anymore, Hassan, the least. She remembered vividly how crying on Douglas's shoulder stole everything that mattered to her, especially her virginity. She felt so annoyed with herself for rejecting Jeff's advances the day she visited him at the hotel. In h*indsight, I would have happily given him my virginity on the day* Jane thought, regrettably, again.

Jane replaced her emotions with bravery, indifference, and coldness. She believed that Hassan would never be a soft land for her troubled emotions to fall on. She went to her room, locked the door, and cried as she let out her built-up emotions while thinking about what the future held for her here in Tunisia.

CHAPTER 19

Jeff arrived in Tunisia prepared. He knew it wasn't going to be an easy task to pull off. He knew finding Jane would be akin to finding a lake in the desert. He was equally aware of the danger lying in wait, even if he was able to find her. It was clear as daylight that Hassan wouldn't give in easily, especially now Jane had made him a celebrity, and husband to an incredibly beautiful lady. So, he knew that he was going to exert every ounce of effort to get her back. But nothing was going to deter him. He was ready to bite the bullet.

He took a cab from the airport to the head office of Carthage Magazine, which conducted the competition. He met two ladies in the reception area on arrival. He greeted them warmly and then shook their hands, which they offered him gingerly and nervously. Then, he told them why he was in their office. "I am here to find my sister who won the best couple award with her husband, Mr Hassan."

"How can we help you?" they asked him, wondering what they had to do with his visit. *That your sister and her husband won the competition doesn't mean they are employed here; they wandered in their hearts.*

As if Jeff knew what they were thinking, he told them that he was at their office because he lost his diary and phone en route to the country and was unable to contact his sister, Jane, directly.

The ladies looked at him suspiciously, unsure whether to believe what he had told them or not.

Jeff sensed their doubt about his genuineness and presented some pictures of himself and Jane to them just to prove his legitimacy.

"I have come to congratulate them on this laudable achievement as her only brother. I am so proud of her, have always been, but more so now she is up there with the upper echelons with this heartwarming achievement." They laughed admiringly and were pleased and happy for him for having a sister who was now seen as a celebrity. "They deserve it. Her husband is handsome but not as beautiful as your sister," one of the ladies said approvingly with a smile.

"Here you go," the other lady said enthusiastically, handing him a piece of paper that had their address and phone number.

Jeff thanked them and left. He thought of giving Jane a call, but thought otherwise, as that could be a tip-off to Hassan. He decided to take them by surprise, giving Hassan little or no time to react or plan a counteroffensive.

Hassan, before this, had made up his mind to finish Jane off, knowing he was getting nowhere to win her love. *Since I can't have you, no one can, and that includes Jeff,* he vowed in his mind.

He thought of reporting Jane to the police, alleging she entered the country illegally, knowing full well she had no passport or any form of identity. But on second thought, he realised it would be a huge miscalculation as he had appeared publicly with her on many occasions, including in the magazine. Secondly, he knew that she was likely to convince the authorities with her storyline if he reported her. He therefore thought of a second choice, which was to lure Jane back to the woods in the name of seeing Hiba. Then he would murder them and drag them into the sea. That, according to him, would leave no trace. At the end of the day, nobody would bother about them because of their prevailing circumstances. Hassan didn't even mind cutting his nose to spite his face, knowing full well that his action was going to end Hiba's life as well. All he wanted was to get Jane out of the picture and out of his mind.

Visiting Hiba was an idea that was warmly welcomed by Jane when Hassan told her. She had always wanted to see Hiba again. She missed her.

On their arrival in the forest, he got an emergency call from his office. He quickly took

Jane to Hiba and told them he would be back as soon as he finished at his office. He was livid with his boss, who demanded that he come to the office for an urgent meeting. He had no choice. He had to find out why he was needed at the office, and then he would return to the forest to finish his planned job.

"That's absolutely fine, Hassan, Hiba, and I will need some time to catch up anyway," Jane replied, smiling ecstatically.

Just as Hassan was about to leave his house to return to the forest after collecting his gun at about 2 pm, Jeff knocked at his door. He opened the door and was surprised to see a young man standing at the door. Jeff introduced himself as James, Jane's brother, avoiding the mentioning of Jeff in case Jane had mentioned it to him, especially as a husband.

Hassan smiled vaguely and extended his hand for a handshake. Intuitively, he knew who Jeff was and why he had visited.

"Come in, my brother-in-law," he warmly welcomed him.

It was a twist in the tale as far as Hassan was concerned. He never expected Jeff, but being a smart man, he knew that Jeff must have seen their picture in one of the entertainment magazines and had come to get her.

They regarded each other secretly. Jeff confirmed that he was even more handsome in flesh than he was in the pictures he saw in the magazine. And for a moment, he felt jealous at the thought that Jane might have fallen for his charm — the reason they were not only in the magazines as a couple but were also kissing.

In the same vein, Hassan wasn't comfortable with Jeff's physique, especially seeing that in addition to his handsomeness, he was even taller than him. They saw each other as rivals — the unhealthy version.

"Oh my God! I have a special visitor," Hassan exclaimed. "By the way, my name is Hassan. Come in, James. Please sit down and feel comfortable. This is your house. So, feel at home. Your sister has gone to see a friend. She might be back tonight or tomorrow. You know your sister is so social. She has made tons of friends here already. How was your journey?"

"Fine. Thank God for a safe journey," Jeff said amiably.

"You must be hungry and thirsty after hours of flight. Let me first get you something to drink, then I will prepare something for you to eat while we wait for the return of your sister."

Hassan had already taken Amina and Mariam to their grandparents to give him space to perpetrate his devilish act. Their presence would have attracted questions from Jeff. So, he was happy he had taken care of them before his arrival. Hassan, up till now, was playing his game well, like draughts; he was moving his seeds professionally. He had pretended to have been fooled by Jeff's fake name. Jeff didn't realise Jane had told Hassan her life story, including being an adopted child with no brothers or sisters. So, he knew Jeff was lying to him, and he knew why.

He took time with the drinks. That evoked some doubts and suspicion in Jeff's mind.

"Sorry, I took time. I was answering a call. Handing a glass of juice to Jeff, he raised his and toasted, "To my brother-in-law and his successful journey." They clinked glasses and sat down.

He took a gulp of the drink and said, "Drink. You must be very thirsty. I will get you some more when you finish that. I will spoil you rotten today. I will show you that your sister is in safe hands."

"I appreciate, Mr Hassan," Jeff said thankfully. Jeff wasn't stupid. *Why would he prepare the drink in the kitchen? What stopped him from getting the juice to the lounge and pouring it out for both of us?* Jeff asked why in his mind. Jeff thought that there could be more to it than meets the eye. Jeff was still hesitant with his drink when a call came to his rescue. Hassan's phone was ringing. He took a quick glance and discovered it was Jane. There was no way he was going to answer the call without giving himself away. He decided to answer the call outside. As he excused himself to answer the call, he took a quick look at Jeff.

Jeff knew why. To satisfy his curiosity, he took a gulp of the juice and made a face as if he had swallowed it. Hassan left with full confidence that his trap had made a catch. As soon as he left the room, Jeff quickly spat the juice in his mouth back into the glass. Thankfully, the glasses were replicas of each other, so Jeff had no issues swapping them.

When Hassan came in minutes later, Jeff had already drunk about half of Hassan's juice. Hassan quickly grabbed the other glass and took a gulp, then another, and said, "I have told you to feel free. You are in your in-laws' house. Finish that so that I can get you some more." Jeff took another gulp in his presence, then another. It wasn't difficult for him to decipher that Hassan was up to no good. His evil intent was written all over him.

Fifteen minutes later, Jeff shook his head repeatedly as if he were preventing himself from falling asleep. He looked dazed, with his hands flailing limply. He made repeated attempts to speak but couldn't. The words he later managed to voice were slurred.

Hassan picked up his glass and finished the contents, and then got up and clapped his hands in victory. "That was very quick indeed. Next time, you embark on this kind of journey, you should make sure the coast is clear," he said, making mockery of Jeff's drowsy state. He had put 25 milligrams of Valium in the drink. It was from the remnant of the medication given to him when he suffered anxiety, when he lost his supposed investment money. He went and peeped through the window that led to the garden and smiled wickedly. "Well, I will wait until it is dark enough before I venture out. He came close and confirmed that the overdose had taken effect. He had planned to get a pillow to suffocate him to death while he was still under the effect of the drug. "I will dig a shallow grave that will be deep enough to bury you and your shallow ambitions." All this time, he was texting someone whom Jeff believed was Jane. As Hassan made his last statement while still texting, the effect of the overdose suddenly hit him, and he crashed onto the sofa like a moose shot in the head by a Texas hunter.

Jeff quickly grabbed Hassan's phone while the screen was still on and needed no password. Jeff realised that the ladies at the magazine's office only gave him their landline numbers and not their mobile phone numbers. So, he searched for the text and call apps and found them. He confirmed it was Jane he was texting and calling all these times they were together. Jeff hit the call button but got no reply.

Jane was now getting angry that Hassan hadn't come to get her as he had promised. Jeff had no time to waste. He texted Jane using the phone.

Hello darling. It is Jeff. I saw your face in Ok magazine and decided to visit to find you to find out what's going on. I am in Hassan's house as I text you, but there is an issue. Hassan knows who I am, even though I lied to him that I was your brother. He poisoned my drink, but I was clever enough to swap our glasses when you called him. So, he ended up drinking the lot he meant for me. He is zonked and sprawled on the sofa right now as I text you. I don't know what to do. I fear he might wake up to discover that I had played a fast one on him. What am I supposed to do? I still love you dearly, Jane. Don't leave me for him.

Jeff.

Jeff pulled out his phone and typed in Jane's number as quickly as possible and texted her. Jeff was now using the Tunisian mobile network, Orange Tunisie.

Jane was excited beyond belief, but at the same time very afraid about Jeff's safety. She called Jeff and told him to leave the house as quickly as possible. Then she paused and asked, "Are the kids there?"

"Which kids?" Jeff asked, not sure what she meant.

"His kids, I mean Hassan's kids?"

"Has he got kids?"

"Yes."

"From whom?"

"From his wife, of course."

"From his wife? Which wife? Are you the second wife then?"

"Jeff, this is not the time for questions, arguments, or suspicion. It is your safety that is paramount for now. You need to get away from that house in case he wakes up from the effects of whatever he had put in the drink. That man is evil, Jeff. I will give you the details when we meet."

Jeff pondered momentarily in his mind why Jane was calling Hassan evil when she got married to him, appeared in the World Magazine competition, and even kissed him in public. But again, he was rational to think that all of that could be under coercion. He wondered how possible it was for Jane to get married to another man, let alone as a second wife. He knew it must be a situation out of her control. After all, Jeff still wondered how Jane was in Tunisia, living with Hassan.

"Where should I go? I don't know anywhere or anyone," Jeff said in panic.

"Anywhere will do, Jeff, provided you are out of that house."

He quickly left as advised and checked into a nearby hotel. The problem now was how they were going to meet. Jane was stuck in the forest. She had no idea how to make it back to the city on her own. The only time she walked out of the forest was when she left it months ago with Hassan. Suddenly, something clicked in her brain. She remembered that while coming to the forest with Hassan that morning, there was a signboard on the untarred road about 100 meters away before they entered the forest that read: 'Begumi game reserve.' She also remembered the name of the taxi driver who usually took her shopping, Mr Omar. Jane didn't want to phone the taxi to pick her up. She did not want to jeopardise Hiba's safety or to raise any suspicion. It would be better for Jeff to come first on his own, then they would book another taxi to come back together. She then called Jeff and told him to go to the taxi depot and ask for Mr Omar. She told Jeff to tell him that he was her brother and had visited to explore the country for the project he was writing about. He told Jeff to tell him that he wanted to visit the Begumi forest to learn about wildlife in the country.

As luck would have it, Mr Omar was the first person Jeff met on getting to the taxi depot. "Excuse me, sir, I am looking for one Mr Omar."

"Speaking. Is everything ok?"

"Yes, sir. I am Jane's brother visiting from Nigeria. I have come to visit my sister and to see and explore this wonderful country."

"That's great. Anything I can help you with?"

"I wonder if you can take me to the Begumi game reserve?"

"Begumi game reserve?" he screamed. "That's far away, my friend. What are you looking for in that evil forest? No one visits that forest, you know. It is dangerous and creepy."

"I know. My sister had already told me. It is just that it will be beneficial for the project I am carrying out on wildlife and climate change."

He told Jeff it was going to cost him 300 Dinar.

"That will be no issue," Jeff replied. They arrived at the forest around 4:30 pm.

"How are you going to get back?" Mr Omar asked him after dropping him off.

"I will ring you up when I finish."

"You would not like to be here when it is dark, young man. This is ghost land. Whatever you are going to do there, please be careful, otherwise, you might not have the chance to ring me back."

"I will be careful," Jeff promised him.

He reversed and left.

Jeff felt lost. There was no sign of life. Everywhere was exceptionally quiet. The only sounds he could hear were the chirping and chirruping of some weird birds.

Jane was almost making it to the road by then. She paid attention as she walked into the forest with Hassan earlier that morning. As Jeff moved into the forest, he stood at the entrance and phoned Jane to say that he was standing close to the signboard on the road.

Somehow, Jane, using natural instinct, plus little knowledge from following Hassan earlier on, was able to make it out of the woods.

On sighting Jeff, she screamed hysterically, "Oh my Jeff, oh my Jeff." She was running towards Jeff as Jeff was running towards her. Meeting midway, she jumped majestically into his arms, and he caught her like a magnet. Holding each other tightly, they cried, laughed, and kissed each other so passionately and intensely until they were almost out of breath.

At the corner of their eyes, a figure emerged from the back of a tree. Jane and Jeff were about to scream, thinking that they had seen a ghost, when he started laughing and clapping cynically. Lo and behold, it was Hassan.

"Bravo, my honourable in law. Isn't it a taboo for a brother to be kissing his sister passionately like that?" he jealously pointed out to Jeff. "Or is your country so immoral that incest means nothing to her people?" he asked him mockingly. Hassan had parked his car kilometres away and had sneaked behind trees until he got to where they were.

"Well, your game is up. You came all the way from Nigeria to take her away, huh? How narrow-minded can you be?"

Jane and Jeff stood still like mannequins at Hassan's sudden appearance. They wondered how quick he had recovered from whatever he put in the drink. But they were even more surprised how he had made it to the Begumi forest already. Jeff, at one point, had thought whether it was he or his ghost that they were looking at. Jeff thought he might have died because of the concoction he had drunk mistakenly. They continued to hold themselves while ruminating over Hassan's mysterious appearance.

It looked like Hassan read Jeff's mind and said, "It is me. I am alive and well."

Jane remembered he had a mini pharmacy cupboard in the kitchen and could have some antidotes to overdosing and poisoning.

"Well, like I said, the game and thrill are over, unless you want more time for some more kisses and hugs, do you?" He winked at them as if he were waiting for them to answer him. "Well, if you have finished, you might as well step aside, because I am taking her back home. It is getting late, and I don't want some nasty night insects to bite or sting her."

CHAPTER 20

This is not the first time I have been accused of trying to take Jane away from the wrong person. Jeff remembered Douglas accusing him of coming all the way from Lagos to Port Harcourt to take Jane away from him. *I have fought this fight before, and I am willing to fight as many more to defend my wife.* With his heart now pounding vigorously in anger, he broke free from Jane. He had heard enough from this imposter. He wanted to show him who the boss truly was. But before Jeff could come anywhere close to him, he pulled an immaculate, silver colour pistol from his double-breasted jacket and waved him to a stop with it. His mouth appeared contoured, and there was a sudden flash of anger in his eyes. "Make any stupid move and I will blow your f*ing head off."

Jeff stopped, took a step back with his hands held over his head in a surrender posture. Jeff knew he wasn't showboating from the vicious look that smeared his face.

Jeff and Jane knew that they were in trouble.

With the wind in his sail, spring in his steps, and convinced he held the aces, Hassan matched them back to the forest, and finally in front of the sea. On getting to the edge of the cliff that separated them from the sea, he ordered them to face him.

"I never wanted to do this, guys, it hurts badly. Sorry, it has to end this way," he said, trying to cork his pistol. Just then, there were loud grunting and thudding sounds from four warthogs behind him. He panicked and unconsciously turned back to find what it was. And that was all Jeff needed to turn the tide of events in his favour, and in one fluid motion, he was upon Hassan and gave his wrist a hard kick that made the gun fly out of his hand. A mighty battle ensued between them thereafter. It was nasty and bloody. Taking their tops off, they fought each other like lions trying to protect their pride. They were already bleeding from their mouths two minutes into the fight. Hassan also bled a bit from his nose while Jeff bled from the cut he sustained in the corner of his right eye. Hassan was as skilled in martial arts as Jeff.

Jeff was wrong to have thought that it would require a token effort to put Hassan in his place. He matched Jeff kick for kick, strike for strike, and punch for punch. Both were at the peak of their powers. Jane was panicking and sweating. She believed one of them was going to kill the other before long.

Jeff, now held in what looked like a sleep hold, screamed at Jane, "Get the gun and kill this evil man."

Jane would have loved to carry out Jeff's order, but she couldn't. She had never handled a gun all her life. How could she now? She feared she was going to shoot the wrong person or both, or even herself. Jeff was still held in that inextricable position and was making a grunting noise as he struggled to breathe. Panicking that Jeff was about to die, Jane screamed, "Let go of him, you wicked man."

Hearing Jane's scream was like a nikethamide injection that stimulated Jeff's respiratory depression. A power and strength from nowhere surged through him, and he managed to break free from the death hold.

As the fight continued, Jane could see that Hassan was beginning to lose his tenacity and was glaringly less defensive. His reactions and reflexes were slower than they were ten minutes ago. He looked so dazed and unsteady, you could knock him over with a feather. Jeff, like a shark, had now smelt blood and was ready to lick it. He had outclassed and outlasted Hassan. Hassan was hanging on by a thread, and it was only a matter of time before he was out for the count.

Jane had known Jeff as one with horsepower, but she had thought that his stamina was restricted to love making, where he would go on and on. Today, Jeff had proven that his stamina was boundless.

Hassan was staggering and stumbling like a punch-drunk boxer now. Jeff, taking advantage of Hassan's fading strength, gave him a roundhouse and reverse side kicks before finally giving him a powerful kick in the back that sent him staggering and plunging into the sea.

"What have you done?" Jane screamed in horror. "Do you want him to drown or what?"

"I haven't done anything like that. He kicked me and I kicked him back, and he fell into the sea. If he decides to drown, that's up to him. It is his decision, not mine," Jeff said nonchalantly.

"If you think I am going to stand here and listen to you talk out of your ass, then you better think again," said Jane ferociously.

"Meaning what?" Jeff asked, looking exasperated.

"I am going to save him, of course."

"Save who? Are you out of your mind?" he asked again, looking more bewildered.

She felt it was a waste of time listening to him.

He held her when he saw she was determined to take a dive. "What do you think you are doing?" he asked her.

"If you don't leave me right now, I will stop loving you," she threatened.

"What?"

"You heard me right."

He made another attempt to stop her. "You have to come back to your senses," he said persuasively.

"If you stop me one more time, I will not only stop loving you, but I will also leave you," she warned him emphatically.

"Really? Leave me? For him?" he queried, looking lost.

"Don't be silly, Jeff," she responded angrily.

"So, you truly love him?" he asked, his suspicion and confusion deepening.

"I don't love him; I don't love him. Get that into your greasy head," she swore at him.

"You are swearing at me because of this murderer."

"I am not aware of that. Nobody has ever told me that he had killed somebody in the past," she responded.

Jeff felt annoyed and humiliated by her comments and behaviour and said, "I am leaving the pair of you to it. Why did I even bother to waste my resources and time to make this trip? I am off," he said, disappointedly.

"If you walk away, Jeff, don't come back," she warned him.

He was halted by that warning and said despondently, "What do you really want? You can't love two men at the same time, can you?"

She shouted repetitively and more loudly, "I don't love him, I don't love him. Can you stop saying that? There is a big difference between love and saving life," she explained.

"I get that. But not in this kind of scenario, and certainly not for him. Have you already forgotten that we're seconds away from being lynched by this blood-sucking leech? Not too sure, perhaps I am the only person in danger here. I think he would have shot me and taken you home. Thanks to the godsend warthogs that arrived just in time."

"I can't continue this argument. If this man drowns, his children might become orphans with their mum now terminally ill, and I don't wish them that," she said. And with that last statement, she took a dive into the sea.

Hassan was just a mere swimmer. His swimming skill was nowhere near as good as his skill in Marshall arts. At this point, he had started to struggle to stay afloat.

When they say that a drowning man clutches to a straw, Jeff saw how true the adage was because as soon as Jane hit the water and came to Hassan, he clutched to her eagerly before she could position herself. She was now battling to break free from his tenacious hold. Jeff wasn't sure whether Hassan's clutch was out of desperation or whether he wanted to drown with Jane. From the edge of the cliff where he was standing nervously, he screamed, "Let go of her, will you?" He was tempted to jump into the sea to save Jane, but he just realised he was as stiff as a board when it came to swimming. So, he knew there was no way he could help her.

With last-ditch effort, Jane was able to break free. She made sure that she was behind him all the way until she got him to the shallow part about 150 meters away from the deep end, where it all started.

"Now what? Now you have saved him, what are you going to do with him? Go home with him or…?" Jeff asked, now stuffed to the gills with indignation. Jeff held on to the gun, making sure he stayed in charge and in control of affairs.

"I am calling the police," Jane said. She didn't wait to see whether Jeff approved of that or not. Jane informed the police of what had just happened. She told them to come down with paramedics. Hassan was conscious but didn't look great overall. Consequent upon that, she told the officer to come down with some medical staff, as one of them didn't look too well after being rescued from the sea.

When the police officers arrived in their blue and white van with the paramedics in another, Hassan put up an incredible performance that would take months to understand and maybe centuries to forget. He sobbed, cried, and told the officers that their arrival was timely.

"These foreign couple who claimed to be on holiday here lured me to this God forsaken land. They said I should escort them to this place for sightseeing and an excursion. When I wasn't looking, they pushed me into the sea to drown. Thank God I am a strong swimmer and was able to swim to safety to make this call. They are evil, officers."

Jane's eyes nearly popped out of their sockets when Hassan said that.

Then he began to cry even more frantically, and said, "Now, he wanted to shoot me but stopped when I told him that I had phoned the police." An allegation that needed no proof, as Jeff was still holding the gun. "I thought they were real friends. I was wrong. They lured me to this ghost, forsaken area so that they would leave no trace."

One of the officers came and tapped him on the back and told him that he was now in safe hands. They swallowed everything Hassan told them hook, line, and sinker, so much so that they didn't even bother to find out who made the call or how they knew one another. *They must have at least noticed it was a female voice. Even though I am not from this country, that would not change my voice to a male voice,* Jane argued in her heart. *Are they that dense, or are they trying to be extraordinarily patriotic or racist? This country is not known for that. Tourism is one of the major sources of their national income. They are welcoming, as shown to Jane by Hiba and Hassan's family. So what game are these officers playing? she* wondered.

They handcuffed Jeff and Jane without bothering to ask them any questions.

When Jeff and Jane wanted to say something, one of the officers told them to shut up. But Jane and Jeff thought the officer was about to follow it up with the usual police parlance, "For everything you say will be used against you in the court of law." But no. They rather shoved them into the police van. And while they were in the van, the officers shoved them around and about like boxes. The paramedics drove off, having examined Hassan and realised he had made a full recovery.

Jane couldn't believe the officers took the matter seriously. But she was even more stupefied by the barefaced lies Hassan told them about everything that happened.

As they sat in the back of the van, Jeff gave Jane a disappointing look, making her understand how senseless her action was to have phoned the police.

At the police station, still in handcuffs, Jeff and Jane were ushered into a crowded lounge full of people supposed to be under investigation for various criminal offences. Plain-clothed officers believed to be detectives as well as uniformed police officers were parading up and down, each looking very busy.

Jane's shoulders had begun to hurt because of the awkward position they had been in for a long time due to the handcuffs. She dared not make her feelings known to the officers whom she now believed might not pay any heed to her plight. She had already lost faith in their security and justice system.

They led Jeff and Jane to the next room, which was less busy than the first lounge. They asked them to sit on a long wooden bench. Jeff was pondering in his heart what kind of justice they were going to be served. He was wondering why it was only he and Jane who were brought to the police station. *Have they discharged and acquitted Hassan without even letting them say anything about what happened at Begumi forest? Jeff asked himself*. He hadn't finished thinking about it when Hassan came into the room looking spotlessly clean. They had taken him to his house to change before coming. For an ordinary visitor, Hassan could pass for a detective. Jane and Jeff shook their heads. But Jane had already made up her mind never to wallow in self-pity. Her heart was now made of steel, but she wasn't stony-hearted.

Hassan sat next to them. Jeff and Jane had concluded it was going to be a sham trial from what they had seen so far, so they were ready for the likely miscarriage of justice.

The officer in charge of the case was still opening an official file for the case when another officer barged into the lounge from an inner room. He took two steps back after walking past them, cocked his head to one side and took a closer look at three of them, and exclaimed, "What is going on here? Why are they here? And why is she in handcuffs?" he asked, pointing at Jane.

"Do you know her?" the officer in charge of the case paused to ask.

"Of course, I know her and the gentleman sitting next to her," he replied, pointing at Hassan. "Who doesn't? They are the couple that won this year's Carthage magazine competition for the best couple of the year."

"They are not a couple," Jeff barged in without waiting to be asked.

"Who are you?" The officer asked, looking angry at the way Jeff cut in on their discussion.

"I am her husband."

"Husband?"

"Yes. I am her husband," Jeff repeated himself jealously. He wasn't happy that Jane and Hassan were seen as a couple by the police officer.

"I know this lady is Hassan's wife. But you are doing her no favours if you are claiming that she is also your wife. You know why? Because you are portraying her as practising polyandry, an offence punishable by law."

"He was never married to her. This man is an imposter and a fraudster. He coerced and blackmailed my wife into all of this."

Things were getting complex but interesting all at once. The other officer had inadvertently started trying the case without the permission of the officer in charge of the case, and without formal prosecution. The in-charge officer was so intrigued by what was unfolding that he forgot that protocols and procedures were being broken. Closing the file he was opening, he asked Hassan, "What have you got to say in all of these? Are they true?"

"Of course not, officer. This man called Jeff is a wife snatcher. He came all the way from Nigeria to take away my wife," he said, trying to shed his crocodile tears again.

"Well, the cause of the disagreement is here. So, we might as well hear what she thinks about it."

"Do you know these men?" the presiding officer asked Jane.

"Yes, I do."

"Who are they to you?"

"He is my husband," she said, pointing at Jeff.

"And Hassan?" The officer continued.

"I live with him."

The officers looked at themselves and sniggered. You could see the reason for their wry smiles. Jane's answer didn't make a lot of sense. The in-charge officer took off his pair of glasses and said, "I don't understand. Jeff is your husband, but you live with Hassan, who is also claiming to be your husband. You better be careful with your answers, young lady. If you don't, you may be landing yourself in a big mess. Like my colleague had warned you earlier, if you are convicted of polyandry, that could land you in all sorts of trouble."

"I am aware of that, sir. All I am telling you is the truth and nothing but the truth," she reaffirmed her position. "Like my husband said, I was never married to this man, Hassan. He is married with two kids. He knows the truth. But if he is unwilling to tell the truth, I have witnesses to buttress my claims."

The other officer then asked, "If Jeff is your husband, how come you are living with Hassan?"

"That's part of the witness investigation I am talking about," she said confidently. "It was by chance and due to unforeseen circumstances that I am in your country and living with Hassan. One of my witnesses is living in the Begumi forest. My second witness is Hassan's wife, who is lying critically ill in the hospital after a life-threatening accident months ago," Jane said.

"Do not listen to what she is saying. This man must have cast a spell on her. Officer, you recognised us from the magazine. If we weren't married, we wouldn't have been allowed to take part in the competition," Hassan countered.

"Then, tell the officers how you procured the marriage certificate," Jane challenged him. "Officers don't take my word for it. Go to the magazine office and pull the marriage certificate, and use your forensic procedures to find out who is telling the truth. If he could con the magazine staff, he can't con you. But if all of these aren't enough to convince you, this will." Jane fired up her phone, scrolled through it, and said, "Listen to this, officers." Jane smelled a rat when Hassan introduced the topic of them getting married with a fake marriage certificate to enable them to take part in the magazine competition had recorded some of their conversation.

The officers had heard and seen enough to know who was telling the truth. Thinking more clearly now in the absence of prejudice, the in-charge officer said to Hassan, "But you said that this couple wanted to kill you by pushing you into the sea and all that. So, somehow, you are admitting inadvertently that they are the genuine couple and not the other way round."

Hassan had nothing to say. The evidence was overwhelmingly against him.

The officers equally had heard something in Jane's statement that they wouldn't like to sweep under the carpet. "Who is the lady in the forest you mentioned?"

Jane took the opportunity to narrate everything to the officers, including her kidnapping from the airport on the day she was supposed to travel to England, the hostage's travel to Italy on a boat, and how she finally made it to the forest where she met Hiba. Jane told the officers Hiba's story. She told the officers that it was through Hiba that she met Hassan, who was heroic in looking after Hiba, knowing she was innocent of what she was accused of. This man, Hassan, had been a good man until lust of the flesh consumed him and turned him into the barbarism we are seeing today. She told them that Jeff, fortunately, saw her picture in one of the magazines and decided to come and get her.

Jeff, seeing that they were now safe, told Jane that the plane she was supposed to travel on had crashed, killing everyone on board except one survivor who later died three weeks later because he sustained fourth-degree burns from the crash. Jane screamed loudly in shock on hearing the devastating news. "May their souls rest in peace," she said. "Thank you, Jesus, for saving me," Jane said with her hands put together in a prayer posture.

The officers removed their handcuffs and promised Jane that they would investigate Hiba's case. The officers weren't happy that some communities were using a kangaroo judicial system to condemn people for things like that because the law neither prescribed capital punishment nor ostracism for people practising gay/lesbianism. They equally stepped in to help Jane obtain travel documents. They promised to contact the Nigerian embassy in Tunis with a view to providing Jane with travelling documents to facilitate her travel back to Nigeria.

Finally, the officer in charge wished them well. Hilariously, he said to Jane, "You know what to do to keep men away from you."

"I know, sir. I will lose my teeth, cut off my nose, and go bald."

Everyone laughed, including Hassan. The officers told Hassan that they weren't going to press charges against him, but recommended that he be cautious with things like that next time. "It is not her fault that she is disarmingly beautiful," the in-charge officer said, and that attracted another bout of laughter from everyone in the room. "We have searched, and we can confirm you legally obtained your gun. However, we are relieving you of it because of what happened between you and this couple," the officers told him. They closed the case thereafter.

Hassan was over the moon that it skipped the officers' memory to inquire about the fake marriage certificate he used for the magazine competition, which could have led to his prosecution by the magazine.

Jane never wanted to leave as a bad houseguest without thanking her hosts. If not for anyone else's, she certainly would have loved to thank and say goodbye to Hana and her kids. But the possibility of that happening had been truncated by recent, ugly events orchestrated by Hassan.

CHAPTER 21

Jeff maintained a low mood throughout their flight back to Nigeria. Jane noticed but didn't bat an eyelid about it. The reason couldn't be difficult to discern anyway. She attributed it to the terrible ordeal they witnessed in Tunisia, at the hands of Hassan. However, she got worried in a measure when Jeff's mood remained overly low even when they landed in Lagos. She had expected a change in his mood with both of them safely back together in Nigeria after agonising months of separation, and after surviving the harrowing events in Tunisia. Painfully, she noted that in addition to his low mood, he looked flat and uncomfortable. She couldn't hold back any longer. "What's the matter, Jeff? Is anything bothering you?"

"Why?"

"You look detached … lost … tired…," Jane added.

Jeff made a concerted effort to wriggle out of Jane's scrutiny, but to no avail. He was lost for words. Jane knew right then that something was amiss, but she wished it away. How could she think of anything untoward after their ordeal in Tunisia? Nevertheless, she wanted to know why. "Stop ignoring me, Jeff. I need an answer," she insisted, refusing to bury her head in the sand.

"Can we leave it for now?" he pleaded, not knowing how to start.

That wasn't what she wanted to hear. His answer had only worsened her inquisitiveness. The anxiety in his eyes was enough to tell her that the problem might be bigger than she had thought. But she still wanted to hear it right away; no need to postpone the evil day. She had seen and heard it all — what else was going to be news to her?

He had been cornered. There was no way of avoiding giving her the answer she desperately needed. "I am living with a lady. I am sorry about that," Jeff finally said, now looking like an antelope surrounded by a cackle of hyenas.

Jane sniggered because what Jeff said made no sense to her.

"Stop laughing. I mean it."

"What do you mean?" she asked, still smiling lightly. She was still not convinced that he was serious.

"I really am sorry, Jane. I really am," he said, voice brittle as glass.

She now knew that he wasn't joking, and said, "If you are living with a lady, why did you bother to come to Tunisia to get me?" she asked, voice hard and stern.

"I came to get you because you are my wife, stolen by a con artist. Honestly, Jane, it is not what you are thinking."

"That's okay, mind reader. I am glad you know what I am thinking, and that has equally confirmed to me that you know what you are doing."

"Don't be sarcastic," he pleaded with her.

Jane was so distraught that she didn't want to hear any more details of his confession, like who the lady was or how long the lady had lived with him. She rather wanted to pay him back with some made-up confessions to pierce his heart just as he was piercing hers: *Should I start by telling him that he did me wrong by coming to Tunisia? That would be a lie. Telling him that Hassan loved me dearly would not be far from the truth. After all, he wanted to convert to Christianity from Islam and even promised to return his wife to her parents. Jane still believed it was possible he had staged the accident that had kept Hana in the hospital for months, probably to get to her. It was a possibility that Hassan thought that Hana would die on the spot from the accident. So, I would be right to say that Hassan was madly in love with me. Or should I tell him that I have been making love to Hassan? That isn't true. But would Jeff doubt me if I told him that? — Probably not.* Jane lacked the willpower to go that route and decided to confront the issue as it was.

"Well, since you have started confessing, you might as well tell me the whole truth now so that you don't contradict yourself later," Jane suggested, voice laden with hurt.

"There are no further confessions to make," Jeff said cowardly.

"Well, can I ask how long you have been living with this lady?"

"Erm…erm. I can't really remember," he answered lamely.

"You can't remember how long you have been living with her, Jeffrey?" She called his name in full as she normally did when he got under her skin.

"I think it was within the first few weeks or months of your travel," Jeff said after thinking so hard.

"Weeks, months? You are staying in the same house for that length with a woman whom I presume cooks for you and vice versa, and you want me to believe it is nothing to worry about. Is she not enough for you? I was accused of practising polyandry in Tunisia. Now you want to practise polygamy in Nigeria."

"They accused you. I never. I believed you. Why can't you do the same for me? After all, you had lived with Hassan in the same house for months after his wife's accident. So, I have the right to accuse you of what you are accusing me of," he protested, trying to convince Jane of his innocence.

"They are two separate, irreconcilable situations. We still had Hassan's children in the house, unlike your situation, where there was no hindrance whatsoever."

"Don't make us argue over things like this, Jane. What did the presence of the kids have to do with you doing something with Hassan? They go to school. They sleep at night. You even told me on the day of my arrival in Tunisia that Hassan took them to their grandparents. Even during daytime, you can catch a fast one while the children are playing in the garden or having a nap."

She was still terribly angry, but at the same time, she saw where Jeff was coming from. "Take me home. I cannot argue anymore. My brain is messed up," she said in a high, squeaky voice.

Jeff had neither the time nor the opportunity to keep in touch with Becky while he was in Tunisia. The problems he met in Tunisia were more than enough. He hadn't the nerve to mention Becky to Jane either. He knew the implications. Jeff didn't want any other issue to superimpose on the one that was already snowballing out of proportion.

Becky was carrying a bowl of custard and fried plantain for her breakfast from the kitchen as Jeff and Jane were entering the house. She was still wearing her sexy nightie. The look on Jane's face turned scarlet. Her eyes switched back and forth, from Jeff to Becky and Becky to Jeff. "Who is she, Jeff?" she asked, as pure anger stole into her beautiful face.

"It is not what you are thinking, Jane … Erm …Erm. I think we have thrashed this enough. It is not what you are thinking," he said, repeating himself.

"What am I thinking, Mr Psychic? I asked a simple question that only needed a simple answer." Anger was building up quickly, as shown in her countenance and voice. Everything Jeff had told her about Becky had flown out of the window.

He knew he was up against it. He knew hell was about to let loose if he didn't handle the volatile situation carefully. He knew that Jane would fight to protect what she genuinely believed was hers. On the other hand, he feared Becky's reaction if Jane got her back against the wall.

"I am Becky, Jeff's friend. Nothing more," Becky introduced herself with a broad smile, sparing Jeff the agony of making the introduction.

Jane's anger had now gotten the better of her, and she felt some blood vessels had ruptured inside her and were now draining through her skin. Seeing Becky in a transparent nightie, highlighting her thong underwear, tipped her over the edge. She was filled to the gills with jealousy. She couldn't control her anger. She flung her suitcase onto one of the sofas and, like a black belt holder in karate, she kicked the tray Becky was carrying, sending the custard flying in different directions, with some ending up in Becky's face.

Jeff feared the worst. "What has come over you, Jane?" he asked in panic.

"Even if I were dead, you couldn't even mourn me for a year as tradition demanded before hooking up with this. Are you that insensitive?" she said, gritting her teeth in anger as she did.

Becky calmly wiped off the custard covering her right eye with a hand towel and sat down in the swivel chair in the lounge. It was Jane's favourite chair. She bought it personally for her comfort.

Jane became madder seeing her sit on it. "Look at this street girl sitting down on my chair when she should be leaving the house. Get your bum off that chair and jump into the street where you belong," Jane screamed at the top of her voice.

What should have been a memorable moment was quickly turning into a nightmare.

Surprisingly, Becky in all of this remained as cool as a cucumber. Jane turned her attention back to Jeff. "What is the matter with you? What is this thing you have for girls? Where are your manners? You have the boldness to keep a young woman in our house for me to meet. It took you no time to forget everything we shared to hook up with this one, jerking her fingers at Becky. You couldn't even wait long enough to determine my fate before jumping into her arms. What were you even doing with Meghan at the Cosmo hotel the other day? Fab did say in my hearing that you had always had your ways with girls. I should have given deeper thought to that assertion. I should have known that a guinea fowl will always retain its white spots even if it has been battered by monsoon rain. The erroneous impression I had about you deceived me." She then came close to him, took his hand, and whispered, "I thought they said that appearance could be deceitful. Naturally, any girl could easily fall for your charming look. I know that. But could action also be deceitful? I guess not. The singular act of bravery you showed at Mile 2 market, Lagos, some years back stole my heart. You might have forgotten, but I haven't. You defended a girl who they wanted to stone to death for having illicit sex with a trader in the market. According to the mob, she was caught in the act and should be stoned to death. You were the only person who had a contrary view. You stood up to them, thereby putting your own life on the line to defend this defenceless lady. You were brave to ask them to produce the man he was having illicit sex with, since according to them, she was caught red-handed. You said that women should have a voice and should not be treated as second-class citizens. You ignited the rage of the mob, making them turn their anger on you, and that's how you sustained this scar in your spotless face," she said, caressing the scar. "This scar in your face, which you should wear as a badge of honour and bravery, was instantaneously imprinted in my heart, and I have never forgotten who you are since then. You could imagine the concealed excitement I felt seeing you in Enugu that day. I wanted you straight away and never wanted anyone or anything to come between us. And when you could not take your eyes off me at the capping ceremony, I thought it was destiny playing out and coming into fulfilment. And now this." Her emotions were clearly getting the better of her, and she fought hard to conceal them.

Becky saw that the house was at a boiling point and decided to put in a good word for Jeff to douse the tension. "Listen, Jane, I don't mean any harm ...," she tried to explain.

"Shut your bloody mouth," Jane cut her short. "Why can't street girls like you leave him alone? Is he the only young, handsome man in town?" she asked Becky, almost walking up to her to swing her fist at her.

"I just want…"

"I say shut your mouth before I shut it for you," Jane shouted at her before Becky could finish what she wanted to say. "Look at her sitting in my chair. Your presence irritates me," Jane continued her verbal attack.

Becky bit gently on her lower lip and managed a snigger.

"You won't be smiling and showing your teeth when I hit you hard and uproot some of them," she continued her rants.

Becky smiled again.

Jeff knew Becky was showing some maturity as expected in that kind of sticky situation.

Out of an abundance of caution, Jeff had to intervene swiftly before Jane could say anything that would lead to something unpleasant.

"Jane", Jeff said, "It is through this lady sitting here that I knew you were kidnapped and later thrown into the sea when the boat ran into difficulty. Without the facts she presented to me, I wouldn't have known about your unsuccessful journey to Italy on the boat. The police, up to now, don't know about your journey to Italy. They are not even aware you were kidnapped, nor are they aware you are with me now."

"How did you come to know her, and how does she know all these details? And point of correction before I forget, I wasn't thrown into the sea. I jumped into the sea by myself," Jane interrupted Jeff, trying to make Jeff understand that Becky didn't know all that had happened to her.

Jeff wasn't impressed with the way Jane was addressing Becky. "She is a lady like yourself. She was in the street because of circumstances beyond her," Jeff politely reminded her.

"Go to hell, Jeff for comparing me with a slut. She is a prostitute. What kind of a decent woman dresses like that in a man's house if she hasn't an ulterior motive?"

"Stop being nasty, and would you like to stop calling her names. She is not what you think. We are supposed to be our brothers' keepers," Jeff told Jane, sounding religious.

Jane laughed scornfully before saying, "Brothers' keepers? Really? This is a random street girl. She could be anything. You told me how vast and knowledgeable she is in criminal matters. Didn't that tell you something?"

"That isn't what I meant. She was only interested in your case because she wanted to find out what happened to you."

"My dear, Jeff, you are playing with fire. There is a difference between walking into trouble unintentionally and walking into trouble with eyes fully opened and in full consciousness. My friend at the university always said that she hated people who said 'if only they had known' when they actually knew all along.". She never liked the word, hindsight. She preferred foresight. And that is what you are missing here, Jeff. You don't ask a hungry lion to look after an antelope. An Irish Priest in our parish then, may his soul rest in peace would during confession advice the penitent confessing his or her sin of fornication to avoid staying under the same roof with the opposite sex as much as possible because it was a perfect and fertile ground for Satan to infiltrate dirty thoughts into the host or the guest. And that is exactly the atmosphere you have created here, Jeff."

"But I am not a lion, let alone a hungry one. Jane, you are everything, and everything is you. I will never seek comfort or pleasure in the bosom of another woman. Your bosom is more than enough for me."

"Don't sound like you are above temptation, young man. I do not know exactly what you are trying to convince me of. You want me to clap for you for keeping a lady in our house who wears not only a transparent nightie but one that displays her thong."

"Remember, Jane, she did not know we were coming today. Nevertheless, I will warn her not to wear that again. In all fairness to her, this is the first time I have seen her with a thong. She usually wears fitted knickers that cover all her bum cheeks."

Jane's jaw dropped, and her mouth gaped in shock. She was speechless for a moment. Then she screamed, "So, you know what underwear she wears— possibly the colours and makes? I am not continuing this discussion. You have two things you must do: First, you must send this harlot away now. Second, you must go and test for all sexually transmitted diseases before you can come anywhere near me," she said, looking at him condescendingly.

Meanwhile, Becky had heard enough and had gone to the room to gather her stuff to leave, but Jeff insisted she was going nowhere. He took the luggage from Becky's hand and returned it to the room.

"Really? Well, if you want to keep her, you can go ahead, but I am not staying. I can't share a man I call my husband with a street girl. Impossible. As you can see, my bag is still unopened. So, I don't need to pack anything. I am leaving the pair of you. I am going to find Doris. She is the only good friend I have because you have destroyed my friendship with Tessy with the same attitude. I think you like women. I really do. Otherwise, why do you play into their hands all the time?"

"I don't get you. What women are you talking about? That Meghan was with me at the Cosmo hotel, and Becky was in our house, do not make me a womaniser, do they? Of course, you know the true story about me and Tessy."

"I hope you are not expecting me to answer that question, are you? Do you want me to catch you on top of them before I know you love them?"

Jane finally tried to leave, but Jeff stood in her way and said, "You are going nowhere, Jane."

"Wao! Wao! Really? So, you really want to keep two of us. Well, that makes you a polygamist. But I am sorry to tell you your plan has failed woefully because I am not going to be part of it."

Jeff looked away in disappointment. He never believed Jane could accuse him of something so scandalous.

"Keeping quiet has said it all. I am leaving, and now, don't you dare try to stop me again, otherwise I will be ringing the police," she cautioned him.

Ignoring all her ranting and unfounded accusations, Jeff said, "Where has your kind heart gone? Like I said before, we should be our brothers' keepers. This girl is on the street not by choice, but by circumstances beyond her control. She never liked and has never enjoyed it."

"But she is surely enjoying it now, parading herself almost naked in your presence."

"I am not going to continue to declare my innocence, but one thing is clear: we mustn't forget our past. You and I know our past, and the parts others played in it to make us who we are today."

Jeff reminded her of how a couple accommodated and even fed them in the North when his parents could not afford house rent and food. He reminded her how his uncle and wife made sure he wasn't a school dropout by training him up to university level when his dad passed away. "Think about that, think about your own background. From birth till now. But let's just focus on the recent ones. Hiba accepted you in the forest. Forget about what Hassan finally turned himself into, but he and Hana wholeheartedly welcomed you into their home."

They were reminders that reset Jane's brain, and she felt a bit ashamed about her callousness toward somebody who needed some help. She apologised to Jeff for her unenviable behaviour towards him. "But you wouldn't have acted differently if you had come home and found me with a guy in his boxers, would you?" she weakly protested, frowning as she said it.

Jeff laughed so loud at her supposition.

"It is not funny," she said, still frowning.

"You are just too jealous. Why would you think that I will break your heart? It would be a lot easier for me to stop the sun from rising and setting than do something that will break your heart, infidelity, the least. You rock my world, and I will not trade you for all the tea in China. You know that, Jane," he told her reassuringly.

Jane laughed heartily at his encomium. She apologised one more time and sealed it with a kiss.

Becky was full of emotion coming out of the room after Jeff had gone in to apologise to her on behalf of Jane and had told her that Jane had accepted her stay.

"I am sorry, Jane. I never meant to cause any misunderstanding between you and your husband," she said, her voice sounding so docile and comforting. "I have told you my name. I don't need to ask your name because Jeff had already told me. Can I say that you are pretty? When the news broke in our dormitory that the kidnapped girl was so beautiful, I never knew it was this outstanding. Not trying to exaggerate, but there are adjectives inadequate to qualify you and (beautiful) is one of them. No wonder your husband was willing to travel to the sun and back to find you."

A sudden grin registered on Jeff's face. Jane smiled elaborately at Becky's eulogy and thanked her for that.

"Really sorry to learn all the difficulties you passed through. But you must be grateful for not boarding the ill-fated plane. It seemed like a blessing in disguise," Becky said.

"We thank God for His mercy and protection. He guides and leads His children," Jane said in reverence.

"Excuse me," Becky said. She left and reappeared ten minutes later with a bowl of indomie noodles and a bottle of cold coke. "I am not good at cooking, but I can at least prepare indomie and plantain. We would have enjoyed the plantain and custard I made, but you decided to practise your kung fu with it and made me wear them." And she laughed. And everyone laughed. Jane humbly apologised again for her unfriendly attitude.

Becky had now changed into a more comfortable, fitting dress, knowing how upstaged and annoyed Jane was seeing her in the transparent nightie minutes ago. "You must be hungry, and I think this can serve as an appetiser while you wait for Jeff to prepare a proper meal for you later. He is one hell of a cook. He can turn a broth of cruciferous bitter vegetables and eyes of a vulture into a delicious meal, and you will still lick your fingers and want some more," she said, putting the plate and the bottle of Coke on the side stool beside Jane. Jane laughed at the way Becky said it.

"Women and their home politics," Jeff exclaimed. "Where is my own indomie, or do you think I am not hungry?" he asked Becky humorously, with a wave of pride registering in his delighted face at Becky's accolade.

Trivialising Jeff's demand, Becky said to Jane, "Don't mind your husband. Eat so you can get some strength to tell us all the details about your ordeal."

CHAPTER 22

The more they lived with Becky, the more they discovered so many other positive attributes she had. What they weren't sure of was whether they were genuine, or she was merely putting them on to secure a roof over her head and have food on the table. She was getting increasingly involved in domestic chores. She would barely allow Jane to cook or perform any house chores. "Jane, I am ready to wait on you hand and foot. You have been through a lot in life," she would tell her as if hers were any better.

Slowly, but steadily, things started moving from better to mysticism. Jeff gradually began to look into Becky's everyday lifestyle more carefully. He found she was neck deep in funk music. She didn't only play them; she sang them, and beautifully too, which explained why she was at the Cuban club the day they met. He could remember that Sunday morning, he secretly found her singing and dancing to *Night to Remember by Shalamar* as it played on one of the local radio stations. He paid real attention to her dance moves. He was startled. He started listening to her voice more intently when she talked and sang. His discoveries worried him. He also remembered that Saturday morning, as he was having his breakfast, he heard a voice haggling with an *Aboki* (Hausa man). The voice sounded familiar. The only surprising thing was that he wouldn't have associated or linked the voice to the Hausa language. In his inquisitiveness, he drew the curtain a bit and peeped. It was Becky trying to buy a female wristwatch from the Hausa man hawking ladies' watches and jewellery. He was transfixed. His shock wasn't only that she was speaking Hausa, but the accent she was speaking it in. She sounded like an Alhaja. She was more fluent than the Hausa man, who was trying to cope with her speed. Thirty minutes later, a Yoruba lady who hawked well-cooked, stewed beans came shouting as usual, *Ewa ago yin.* She wanted some. She had always interacted with this lady in pidgin English and occasionally in proper English. The hawker wanted to pull a fast one on her, but Becky was having none of it. The hawker got angry and started complaining to a fellow Yoruba lady in Yoruba about how stingy Becky was, believing that Becky was an Igbo girl who did not understand Yoruba. How wrong was she? Becky got very angry at the way the hawker was slagging her off and responded in Yoruba language as a Yoruba guru. The hawker was stunned by Becky's eloquence in Yoruba and had no choice but to apologise. To make up for her blunder, she added an extra portion of beans to Becky's order. Jeff looked even more staggered than the hawker. He had never heard her speak any language other than English and Pidgin English, and occasionally Igbo. But these were just the beginning of more mysteries to come. A week later, Becky was making a call in her room. Jeff had no idea what language she was communicating with the person at the other end of the line until she said, "Adios" and hung up. Jeff knew nothing about the Spanish language, but at least he knew "adios" meant bye in Spanish. Jeff was so surprised and impressed.

As days and weeks passed, Jeff noticed that Jane was becoming more tolerant and comfortable around Becky. Occasionally, they had prepared meals together and had dined together. Sometimes, Jeff had seen them casually dressed and taking a stroll towards the beach. She was very chatty and wanton, especially when she had had a few drinks. Her talkativeness, like a lullaby, had at times sent Jeff to sudden sleep.

The whole situation came to a head when Jeff, coming out of the toilet that Saturday morning, saw a small golden-brown bracelet carefully placed on top of his portfolio. He was thoroughly shaken by the sight. It was his dead sister's bracelet she wore as a toddler, according to his mother. She was so fond of it that their mother kept it for her until she was old enough to look after it. She was so fond of it that the family in one accord agreed that it would be an honour to bury her with it when she passed away. Jeff feverishly wondered how it was now lying unscathed on his portfolio as if it had never been worn. He was scared to touch it when he saw it. Then a sudden courage surged through him as he remembered it belonged to his sister. He believed that his sister would never harm him, even in death. He then took it, opened his portfolio, and hid it.

Things continued to unfold at a mind-boggling pace. A few days after the bracelet conundrum, while he was with Becky in the lounge, she went to her room and reappeared ten minutes later with one of her bags. "I have been looking for my cheque book since last night," she said. "I have no idea what I have done with it," she resignedly complained. She was still blaming herself while ransacking the bag furiously, when a picture fell out of the mini photo album she pulled out of the bag. It caught his attention because it was a replica of his sister's picture when she was about a year old. On her left wrist was a replica of his sister's bracelet. Jeff froze. Becky didn't notice Jeff's consternation because she was so engrossed with what she was searching for in her bag. Jeff ran into his room from the lounge. He wanted to check out the bracelet. It was still there in his portfolio. And it perfectly matched the one in the picture he had just seen.

Five days later, Jeff had gone into her room to retrieve the universal TV remote she borrowed to operate the TV in her room the previous night. Jeff thought he heard her leave the house. He was wrong because she had just had a bath and was standing in front of the mirror in her panties, applying some cream, her back to the door. What he saw shocked him deeply. Noticing the presence of someone in her room, she turned, and cupping her breasts, she screamed, "What is the meaning of that? Why would you not knock before entering my room? Don't I deserve some privacy?"

Stumbling back in shock, and raising both hands in an apologetic gesture, he said, "I am sorry, Becky. I was looking for the remote."

A week later, after Jane had gone out for shopping, Jeff approached Becky subtly and began a normal discussion as usual. When he got her full attention, he started asking her personal questions. He had been told by the elders that dead people could come in diverse ways to visit loved ones or start a new life in an entire unfamiliar environment far away from where they came from. He also remembered being told that as soon as the dead person realised that they had been detected, they would vanish. He wasn't sure about the authenticity of the story. He wanted to use this opportunity to confirm it. He believed Becky was his dead sister in disguise. He loved her to bits while she was alive, but now she was no more, he wouldn't like to share his life with her anymore, at least from Christian's perspective. So, he wanted to uncloak her to show he knew who she was, so that she would leave. He created a sparkling, enabling environment that would allow him to address Becky, whom he believed was now a ghost. He got two glasses and poured her scotch whisky, which was her favourite brand. Taking a sip of his drink, he asked, "Where are you originally from, Becky? We are getting on a lot these days, and it is about time we knew ourselves a little bit better."

"Ok, if you really want to know, I am from Imo state."

"Imo state?" he asked, surprised and unsure whether she was telling him the truth.

"Have we met before?" he asked just in an attempt to make her take a hint that he had recognised who she really was.

Instead of disappearing as he had expected, Becky burst out laughing and said, "What do you mean by that? I met you at the gig, the night you saved me from the hands of those riffraff."

"I meant before that."

"Nothing I can remember. Why are you asking?"

"Never mind," he responded dismissively.

Lately, every now and then, Jeff would bring out his sister's bracelet to bring back good memories of her. That was what he was doing this Wednesday afternoon when the front door opened suddenly, and Becky entered. But before he could stash the bracelet away, she had seen it and went off the rails and said, "Because I am living in your house doesn't mean you have the right to be rummaging through my stuff when I am not here. I will never touch your stuff without your permission. Why have you decided to go through my things without my permission?" she queried bitterly.

But before Jeff could say anything, she brazenly demanded, "Can I have my bracelet back, please?" She snatched it from his hand and stomped off to her room.

What Jeff initially thought must have been wrong. Becky must have dropped the bracelet on top of his portfolio mistakenly, the way her childhood photo fell out of her bag the other day. He was baffled that Becky had a replica of his sister's childhood photo, and now the same bracelet, and like his sister, she had looked after it and cherished it the way his sister did. Her voice, laugh, gait, choice of music, the dance moves, but most importantly, the mark she had on her back— the exact spot his sister had hers. He wondered if all these were mere coincidences. On the contrary, her multilingual attribute has nothing to do with his late sister. His sister, Naomi, could only speak English and their dialect. But he suddenly realised that when somebody was dead, they became ethereal and superhuman, and everything was possible. He was in a quandary about what to think and believe at this point. *If she is not my departed sister. Who is she, then?*

It was just event after event. It was the last Saturday of the month. The government had ordered a nationwide clean-up on the last Saturday of every month. They were observing it. As they cleared the little shrubs in the backyard, a rat escaped from a tiny hole near one of the trees and ran straight through the door and then into the storeroom because Jeff forgot to close the door that led to the storeroom. Becky and Jane were dancing, jumping, and screaming their heads off in fear.

"You are afraid of a common rat, Becky? Can you just imagine that?" Jeff said, making a jest of her musophobia. "I know Jane screams at her own shadow sometimes. Never knew you were even worse."

Becky made a face before jovially saying, "Shut up, Jeff and go in and kill that rat; otherwise, I am not entering that house again."

Jeff, in the process of killing the rat, discovered that the storeroom was full of junk. He said to them, "It is clean-up day anyway. We might as well clean out the storeroom. We are scared of common rats, but this could be a nice hiding place for spiders, cockroaches, scorpions or even a snake."

"Stop talking like that. I am scared of rodents and insects, never mind crawling and creepy animals," said Becky, terrifyingly.

"Then, we need to tidy out the storeroom."

They agreed to the plan wholeheartedly. Everything was covered with cobwebs and dust. "I think we need to bin everything. Nothing seems redeemable here." He was flinging them out while Jane and Becky were busy putting them in a black bin bag. He had unknowingly flung a picture frame, and Jane was about to put the picture frame in the bin when Becky intervened and said, "I know we need to bin everything, but you are not supposed to bin pictures. Pictures are treasures, the older they are, the more value they have and the more story they tell." She retrieved the picture from Jane and screamed, "Where did you get that from?"

"Get what?" Jeff asked.

"This picture."

"Can I see? Oh, it is my Mam and her friend years ago. I don't even know where they took the picture."

"It seems you love old things."

"Yes, I do," she answered.

"Same here," Jeff said. "I used to go to antiques and artefacts auctions before to buy antiquated stuff, like the world clock in our room."

Later that day, Jeff heard Becky talking to herself quietly in her room. She didn't know Jeff was close by. "He said the other day he thought he knew me. I saw him with my bracelet. He was shocked and transfixed seeing me naked the other day. There was no sense of lust in his face when I confronted him. Now, a picture of my mother and his mother."

So, my mother and her mother were known to each other at some point. How did my mother know her mother and vice versa? Jeff asked himself. I will need to investigate this further. I must get to the root of this. It could only be her mother or my mother who could resolve the conundrum, Jeff thought.

Jeff knew it was only his mother who could unravel the mystery because Becky detested with passion anything about her family background, and he knew it would be a waste of time to ask her about her mother.

Jeff told Jane all he had heard and observed lately.

"It appears your mother might be the solution to this puzzle," Jane said after listening to him. And he agreed.

He decided to travel to the village the next weekend. When he got home, he was told his mum was busy on the farm, as would be expected at that time of the year, the farming period. He sent one of the young boys in the village to fetch her from the farm after greasing his palm with some money.

Jeff's mum was so excited to see him. She was carrying a basket full of vegetables and fruits on her healthy, grey hair, with her whole body covered in mud. "You finally decided to come and see your mother," she said cheerfully, dropping the basket on the ground. "Come and give your mother a hug. I know I am covered in mud, but that will not stop you from giving me a hug." They laughed. Then she took a closer look at him and said, "You look troubled. Is everything ok, my son?"

Jeff didn't want to pretend. He had to hit the nail on the head without much ado. "Not really, Mama. It is by the grace of God that I am still alive today. I have been deluged by a series of unpleasant and frightening events for some time now. It is like one week, one trouble."

"Wait, my son. Let me wash my hands and sit down," she said, looking very worried as a concerned mum. "Get yourself a seat, son. We need to sit down."

Jeff took time and narrated all the ordeals he had been through— from the hassles in the office, to his imprisonment, and of course, mysterious Becky.

She broke down in tears. "I thought that you were so busy with work to see me all this time. The network was and still is so bad, the reason I couldn't reach you, and I thought it was the same reason you hadn't been in touch. Never knew my son was passing through hell. My enemies are after my son. They will not succeed in Jesus' name." She started quoting several chapters and verses of the bible as perfect as you would expect from renowned pastors and priests, and reassured him that no weapon fashioned against him would prosper. She placed her hand on his head and laid uncountable blessings and protection over him.

"Thank you, Mama, for your prayers and blessings, but you have not said anything about the mystery lady living with me and Jane."

"Who is she?" she asked. The smirk on her oblong, fleshy face was a contradiction to the concerns she had just shown.

"Mama, this is a serious matter. I don't know why you think I am joking."

"You know young, handsome man like you will be chased up and down by these city girls who are looking for men to marry or hook up with," she said with a mischievous grin.

"You need to see this picture and know whether, by any chance, you know this lady in the picture. That might help to unravel this mystery."

"Why didn't you bring the picture, or are you just looking for a way to lure me to the city even when you know that city life isn't my cup of tea?"

"Whatever you make of it, mother."

His mother, seeing how concerned he was, thought better of her ideas and asked him to narrate his story again.

"So, you weren't even listening in the first place?"

Her countenance changed after listening to him, and she asked, "What is this girl's name?"

“She said her name is Becky.”

“I mean her Igbo name?” his mother asked again.

“She wouldn’t say, or should I say I didn’t ask.”

“Becky! That doesn’t ring a bell at all. I am not trying to ridicule your complaints, my son, but this could be a random lady who is exploring all avenues to hook up with you. You know husbands are scarce to find these days, and every woman is making frantic efforts and using every gimmick and ploy to get a man she will call a husband,” his mum said, smiling.

“Are you coming with me, or do you prefer I continue to wallow in quandary and turmoil as I have done for some years now?”

“I will come with you, my son. God forbid, I will allow you to bear this pain alone.”

CHAPTER 23

"Good evening," Becky greeted Jeff's mum on their arrival from the village, recognising her from the picture they were looking at a few days ago.

"Which of the girls are you talking about, my son?" Jeff's mum whispered while the two of them were in the kitchen preparing gumbo dinner, consisting of freshly picked okra, wild mango seeds and assorted (Mangala) fish and beef. "You see, you have surrounded yourself with beautiful girls. What do you expect? They will be giving you plenty of pleasure and throbbing headaches at the same time," she said, cheeks puffed up as she tried to stifle a laugh that was brewing inside her. "I hope you are wise enough to make a good choice when it comes to the one you will tie the knot with when the time comes." Jeff's mum was meeting Jane for the first time after their court marriage. She refused to acknowledge that their court marriage made them husband and wife. As far as she was concerned, Jeff and Jane were just friends until they had performed and fulfilled all the traditional marriage rites as their custom demanded. For her, Jeff was still single.

Taking a good look at the ladies again, she said, "The one wearing a green top, referring to Jane, looks like a guardian angel. God created her on a Sunday when He had no other duty to perform. Simply put, she is a quintessential creature of God's creation. If she is half as good as she is beautiful, then you have hit the jackpot, my son. She is extraordinarily beautiful. Her face sparkles like a morning star. Her smile is as beautiful as the sun rise in June. Jeff, my son, you have eyes for beautiful women. I think it runs in the family. You are a lady-killer like your father. No wonder they are hovering over you."

"Mama!"

"What?"

"Can you be serious for once?" Jeff suppliantly cautioned her. "I have nothing to do with the one in red top, if that is what you are implying. I told you the circumstances surrounding our meeting. Why do you still believe that I am having any intimate relationship with her?"

"I am sorry, my son. It is common knowledge that most naughty men like variety when it comes to women. However, I want to believe you are not one of them. But if you are, I want to believe that the one in green top is the main chick and the one in red, the side chick."

"If you were an alcoholic, I would have thought you had been drinking all day and would have recommended gastric lavage to clean up the alcohol in your gut; or maybe take an easier option without a medical procedure and give you some freshly made spongy bread to soak up the alcohol from your tummy. I don't know why you are talking like this. Why have you decided to treat this dire matter with such Levity, Mama? At the end of the day, you know I am married, whether you agreed with it or not."

"I am only pulling your legs, son. I only want you to feel relaxed because I have noticed how nervous and stressed you are."

"Okay, Mama, it is the one in red top that I am on about. She said her name is Becky."

"First things first. Can I see the photo you mentioned to me?"

Eagerly, Jeff went to his room and brought the picture.

Having dried her hands with the kitchen towel, she took the picture from him and looked at it with squinted eyes as she was not wearing her eyeglasses. Feeling a bit woozy out of nervousness, she asked him to fetch her a chair. "I need to sit down, my son." She looked at the picture one more time after sitting down. Then she looked at him one more time and said, "Did I hear you say that the lady with me in this picture is her mother?"

"So, she said."

Jeff's Mum left him in the kitchen and scurried to the lounge where Becky and Jane were watching a movie and said to Becky, "Sorry to interrupt what you are watching, but can I know your name, my lovely, young girl?"

"My name is Becky," Becky answered flatly.

"You are not called Becky. Tell me your name, I mean your Igbo name?"

Jane stopped watching the television and got hooked on the unfolding events. Jeff had joined them from the kitchen after turning off the gas. They were all watching and listening with rapt attention.

"I have no Igbo name," Becky answered begrudgingly.

Jeff's mum knew at that point that she wasn't telling the truth or didn't want to. She couldn't help but start sobbing gently.

Jeff was taken aback by her mum's reaction. "Why are you crying, mother?"

"Because she will not tell me her name."

"How can I tell you a name I haven't got?" Becky answered harshly, raising a frustrated eyebrow at Jeff's Mum.

"You recognised me in the same picture with your mother, didn't you? I thought that would have meant something to you?" Jeff's mother modestly told her.

"I have seen photos of my mother with other women. You are not the first. What made yours different?" Becky asked indifferently. She viciously ground her teeth in anger and left the lounge, staring down at Jeff's mum as she left.

"She is my daughter. She is called Nkoli," Jeff's mum said softly.

"Your daughter? What do you mean by that?" Jeff asked, looking so confused. He didn't wait for the answer, he rather followed Becky to her room. "I am sorry about all this."

"So, you went to the village to bring your mother to torment me with this, even when you know how it hurts me?"

"Not really. It is just that I am a bit perturbed by recent revelations."

"What revelations?" she asked, face brimming with fury. "We can't go over these again. You know as much as I do that so many things are amiss, Becky."

"I don't want to add insult to injury, but are you really called Nkoli?"

With the snail speed of someone trying to escape an assassin in sleep paralysis, she slowly dropped the book she picked from the lounge and turned to face him and asked, "What did you just say?"

"I don't intend to hurt your feelings," he quickly apologised, seeing how troubled she looked on hearing that. "That's what my mother said."

That was her real name. She picked up Becky as a form of dissociation, trying not to have anything that would remind her of her immediate family.

"Did she agree she is called Nkoli?" Jeff's mother asked him when he joined them again in the lounge.

"She didn't say anything, mother. She expressed much surprise and started crying when I asked her."

"Well, my son, I think we have bitten more than we can chew. We have a big problem on our hands."

"What do you mean, mother?" he asked worryingly.

"It is a long story. But the short version of it for now is that we might be living with a ghost."

"Living with a ghost? How?" Jeff was engulfed in fear when his mother repeated herself. He knew there was something odd about Becky. Now it seemed his fear had been confirmed. He developed goosebumps all over his body, and his hair stood on end.

"If she is Nkoli, as I strongly believe she is, it means we are certainly living with a ghost. I can guarantee you won't find her if you go back to her room, knowing she has been uncovered because this Nkoli and her stepparents were killed in Kano years ago, when the extremists killed many Igbo Christians living in the city. I was reliably informed by one of the survivors of the massacre that they perished in the ugly carnage. I have privately mourned her death because I didn't want to bother anybody with the details. That's why I never batted an eyelid when you raised the issue. I had thought it was no issue, knowing full well it couldn't be. But now, I am scared and worried as you, my son."

"Stop talking like this, Mum. You are scaring me. Now, I am frightened to go to her room."

"You don't have to if you are that scared," his mother advised him cautiously.

Jeff slept with one eye closed most periods of the night, with weird images forming at the back of his mind. He had never seen a ghost all his life, but he had heard a lot about them. Now, he was in a position of sleeping under the same roof with one. Something he could never have imagined. He didn't know the exact time, but he finally fell asleep around 4 O'clock in the morning. He felt a bit jealous of Jane because she slept through the night, though she clung tenaciously to him the way she never did before, and he knew why.

Jeff's panic reached fever peak when there was no sign of Becky up to 10 O'clock in the morning. They had all had the most unexciting breakfast of beans cake (akara) with custard and were sitting uncomfortably close to each other in the lounge. None of them had the courage to mention her name, let alone go to check on her. They didn't even have the motivation or desire to switch on the television or tune in to any radio station. They were frightened to their spines, though his mother tried her best to conceal hers. The look on Jane's face told the whole story.

Jeff wasn't any more comfortable with the hair-raising atmosphere they had found themselves in. About time he did something to enshroud himself with some dignity. *You are the head of the household and this cowardly behaviour of yours is unbefitting and damning. About time you confronted the problem head-on,* he inwardly perked himself. His friend's dad had always said that it was the living that you should be afraid of, not the dead. Since Becky had not been seen or heard from since the last time he saw her yesterday, it was most likely that she had gone, as his mother had suggested.

"I am going to check on her," Jeff boldly announced to his Mum and Jane, though the look on his face showed the decision wasn't sitting comfortably with him.

"Oh my God," Jane screamed. "Please be careful, Jeff," she added, her face looking more ghostly than the one Jeff was about to check on.

"Are you sure of what you are about to do, son?" his mother asked, blood running cold. "We can invite priests, exorcists, or ghost whisperers to help with the investigation, you know. I don't want you to get into trouble. You are now my only child left. Like I told you yesterday, it is a long, complex story. I will get to the details bit by bit shortly, but the summary for now is that Nkoli is your blood sister. She was the twin sister of your sister, Naomi."

The news went through Jeff like a hot knife on a block of butter. He couldn't stand steady, nor could he focus. He had to sit back down.

"Don't flay me, son. I am not proud of my action, but you must hear my story first before you draw any conclusion."

Just weeks ago, they were all dining, chatting, and having banters with Becky. Today, the mere thought and mentioning of her name was like an anathema. This event unmistakably reminded Jeff how quickly situations could change.

Jeff defiantly decided to check on Becky against his mother's advice. "I am sorry for the disturbance, Becky," he humbly apologised after mustering the courage to knock on her door. But there was no answer. Everywhere was silent as a graveyard. He then said a little prayer, made a sign of the cross, and then opened the door with his unsteady hand. He felt giddy. He could barely look in. He was really imagining things that weren't there. The more the image of Becky being a ghost formed at the back of his mind, the more his goosebumps became evident. When he eventually stepped into her room, it felt agonisingly cold despite the early morning sunshine rushing into it via the ventilated hollow blocks. In a glazed, dewy vision, he noticed what freaked him out …. The bracelet. It was distinctly and meticulously placed in the middle of Becky's bed. He switched on the light and took a second look just to assure himself he wasn't under any illusion. He decided to take it, but lacked the courage. He couldn't fathom out what the repercussions would be if he meddled with her bracelet. The anger she displayed the other day when she saw him with it was still fresh in his memory, and that's why he wouldn't understand why she left it behind. Overwhelmed with fear, he left the room and went and got Jane and his mother after informing them there was no sign of Becky except the bracelet.

"The bracelet?" Jane screamed.

They cautiously entered the room and were able to look everywhere just to make assurance doubly sure.

As the saying goes, there is always safety in numbers. Surrounded by his mother and Jane, Jeff had the courage to pick up the bracelet. Like Naomi, Nkoli was equally his blood sister as had been confirmed by his mother. Like Naomi, she valued her bracelet.

Jane looked at him in awe. She couldn't believe that he would have the boldness to touch the bracelet. They stood rooted to the floor, gazing at one another. Jane was the first to gather her thoughts to say something.

"What are we still doing here? We need to get out of this room. I feel so uncomfortable," she said as she intermittently hugged herself and chafed her exposed hands constantly over each other from the shoulders to the wrists to restore some warmth into her frozen body. Like someone witnessing out-of-body experience, her goose pimples bulged out in her bare skin, realising they had been living and dining with a ghost for months.

They walked out of the room the way they walked in — in a single file, holding one another just like the newly hatched ducklings would follow the mother duck.

When they overcame the shock of their discovery, Jeff's mum told them the whole chilling story.

CHAPTER 24

With Becky and all she stood for out of the picture, and his mother gone back to the village, Jeff and Jane were able to turn a new leaf and start a new normal life like any other person down the street.

"Finally, we can live our lives like every other person," Jane said that Sunday morning as they listened to the preaching on God's TV channel. "When last did we sit together on a Sunday morning eating quietly and watching television like this?" she asked, feeling contented with the way things were going.

"I can't remember, Jane. Surely, it has been many a day," Jeff answered joyfully.

Things got better and better as months passed. With normalcy fully restored in their home, they instinctively resurrected their usual lifestyles that they had almost forgotten. They started going to the pictures, visiting pubs on weekends, walking on the beach, and much more. Their sex life was given a boost. With Becky and his mother now gone, they had the whole house to themselves. Their sex adventure now was unrestricted. Sex was no longer restricted to their room. They had it everywhere, in the kitchen, lounge, bathrooms and even in the corridors when neighbours had gone to sleep, exploring every sex position they could imagine as they did. They would, when they chose to, walk about in the house in their boxers and knickers with nothing on top.

"That's how to bring yourself close to nature," Jane hinted joyfully one of those days as they cuddled up to each other on the sofa watching *Coming to America*.

Better still, Jane wasn't into full-time employment. She was just a freelancer for some movie industries, either as a director or a make-up artist. Jeff also had all the time in the world. He had no steady job as yet. He only performed at big hotels every other week to earn some money. So, they had more than enough quality, family bonding time, which had eluded them for quite some time now.

Jeff was on one of his usual rehearsals with other artists at Ikeja for the upcoming live performance at the Elon hotel. He was hungry after five-hours rehearsal. The rehearsal arena was somewhere in Ikeja, a completely new area he wasn't conversant with. He was driving and asking passers-by where the nearest restaurant was. After driving for ten minutes in a relatively traffic-free Bisola road, he stopped when he saw a big, decorated signboard with the inscription "Den Garden Eatery."

A man in his mid-fifties approached the gate and opened the electric swing gate for him. He drove in cautiously and managed to find a couple of empty parking lots.

The first thing he noticed when he stepped out of his car was that his sky-blue Cherokee was by far the most obsolete, out of date, and most probably the cheapest in the whole parking lot. It was like a meerkat in the midst of a pride of lions. No wonder the gateman regarded him with contempt when he opened the gate for him.

The ultramodern building, from what he saw, looked like a three-storey building with each rectangular plate like floor slanting on top of each other rather than resting on it. It looked delicately slim, beautiful, and contemporary. But that was the beginning of the amazement. It was when he entered the building that he realised that he might have made a mistake in entering. The atmosphere that greeted him left him dumbstruck. The tinted glass wall interacted beautifully with the revolving lights, and like an illusion, they continued to flash assorted colours on the wall and ceramic floor. It wasn't only the flashing lights that he needed to contend with, but also the illusionary images of people constantly on the move and dangerously close to one another. He was scared to move. He was careful with every step he took to ensure he didn't step on anyone's toes. He felt inferior to everyone he saw. It was like a gathering of senators and ministers after a plenary session.

"How did I find myself here?" he asked himself hesitantly. He thought of heading for the door, but it was too late because a well-tanned English lady was already next to him and with a catchy smile asked him to follow her. He followed her sheepishly like a cow being led to the slaughterhouse.

"Here you are, table 24." Beside her were two Caribbean ladies exquisitely and smartly dressed in yellow short-sleeved shirts and purple/black scarves tied in a V-shape fashion around the neck. They wore smart black slim-fit trousers to match. One was with a glass tray that had six glasses of wine arranged in two rows. The other was with a square white colour tray with some deliciously looking fruit and vegetable appetisers with what looked like artichoke dip in the middle. Their Caribbean accent took his breath away.

"You can choose your champagne. The first row is thirty percent alcohol, and the second is non-alcoholic. The choice is yours," she said with a spine-tingling smile highlighted by her screaming yellow colour lipstick.

Champagne! Jeff almost thought aloud. He remembered Mark telling him some time ago that he attended Okacha's birthday party, where a bottle of Champagne was sold for two hundred and fifty thousand naira. He knew he was in trouble. He had only fifteen thousand naira cash on him and an Oceanic bank card that had only twenty-five thousand naira. He wasn't sure whether that would even be enough to pay for the champagne and the appetiser, never mind the main course and desserts. He was visibly alarmed.

As if one of the girls sensed his worries, she spoke in a strong patua accent, *"Feel like gumbe drum widout the goatskin."*

"What?" Jeff asked, thinking the lady had sworn at him.

"Don't worry. It is only a proverb."

Jeff asked her what that meant.

Her smile became more elaborate, and she said, "It means you feel out of place." And she was correct. "Anyway, the champagne and the appetisers are on us."

Jeff momentarily heaved a sigh of relief when she said that. But on second thought came the realisation he could even be in bigger trouble. They were not a charitable organisation. A restaurant that served her customers free champagne and appetisers would certainly make sure that somehow, they were going to get their money back in some other way. And the only way to do that would be to charge exorbitantly for the meals and desserts. He wanted to call Jane to come to his rescue, but realised she was out to repair her phone, which was disabled and unable to make or receive calls. The thought that he was in a position of using all the money he had on him and going to need more financial help to settle his bill diminished his appetite, and he felt miserable. Taking a glass of non-alcoholic champagne from the tray, he sat down and managed to say thank you.

"You are welcome," the other lady replied as she dropped the appetiser on his table.

Jeff was glaringly scared to touch the menu on the table. Then, things got completely out of hand, because standing and looking down at him was Becky, dressed impeccably in an immaculate white jacket and black skirt. He was speechless as waves of nausea and dizziness washed through his face.

"Why the stare? Aren't you happy to see me?" she asked, as she sat down on the chair opposite him.

Jeff looked petrified, and she noticed it and said, "You look alarmed. I will leave if I am making you uncomfortable. I have only joined you so that we can have lunch together and to keep you company, realising you are here by yourself. Where is Jane, by the way?"

"She is out to repair her phone and to do some shopping afterwards. No, I am comfortable," Jeff reassured her with a look that countered his speech. Ordinarily, he would have been annoyed with her the way she left, but not when he was aware of the circumstances surrounding her disappearance.

"I am hungry, Jeff. I haven't eaten anything since morning. Just coming from a friend's house."

That was the last thing he needed to hear. He wasn't sure how he was going to pay his bills. If she was going to have lunch with him as she was presenting, it meant she might be expecting him to pay for her meals as well. But he was even more concerned about the possibility of sitting next to a ghost.

"You really want me to leave, don't you?" She asked dejectedly, noticing that he still looked nervous.

Jeff put on a brave attitude and smiled vaguely. "No," he replied. "It is just I haven't got enough money for myself, never mind the two of us."

"Who asked you to pay? This is Senator Ifediora's birthday. Everything is free from now till 6pm. How did you get in because you sound and look like a gatecrasher? Senator Ifediora is going to kill the gateman when he realises that he let someone in without an official invitation," she hyperbolically said. "You could be a hired assassin, a robber, a kidnapper, or anything," she said jovially.

Jeff lifted his eyebrows inquiringly at her. He believed she had gone back to prostitution after leaving his house. He believed that the politicians had organised some call girls through their agents to grace the occasion, and she was one of them.

Could she have allowed those miscreants to molest her at the Cubans the other day if she were a ghost? And why did she approach me now? She was supposed to avoid me if she were a ghost. Jeff enquired worryingly.

Craving her indulgence first, after regaining some composure, he said, "I don't know whether this is the right moment or place to ask this question. But why did you decide to leave like you did, just as our relationship was blossoming into a cordial and enduring one?"

She screamed blue murder hearing that, and said, "Oh my God! Here we go again. You are back on your hobbyhorse! I came here to say hello, and not to talk about me. Can you do me a favour and let that topic die a natural death, please?" She didn't even want to mention the topic. That's how much she detested anything about her past, especially her family.

"Where are you now?" he asked, trying to change the topic. He didn't want to open an old wound.

"I am not telling you in case you find me and start to make that enquiry you like so much. I want some peace of mind."

"I promise I won't."

"Cross your heart, Jeff."

"I promise on my honour."

He did not know why he travelled to Ikeja with his portfolio. He only did so when he was making long journeys that required spending some days. He then realised it could be that he was somehow designed by fate to meet her that day. He had the bracelet she forgot when she left. He told her that he had something that could make her day even better.

"Like what?" she eagerly asked.

Opening his portfolio, he took out the bracelet and with a gratifying smile, he said, "Here you go. Your bracelet you forgot on the bed, the day you left. I kept it carefully, not because I thought I would ever see you again, but because of the mere fact that you treasured it by the way you reacted the day you found it with me."

She remained quiet and was at a loss for what to say. She began to observe Jeff obscurely. When she regained her wits, she said, "That's not my bracelet. My bracelet is in my bag. I saw it this morning."

Then, they locked an exploratory gaze on each other. Maybe she was thinking what he was thinking. After prolonged silence, she rested both hands on the table. Leaning forward toward him, she asked, "What is going on, and what exactly do you want from me?" She was as confused as Jeff. She couldn't understand how Jeff had a replica of her bracelet.

"If it wouldn't get on your nerves, can I ask the same question I asked months ago?"

"Hope you are not going to break your promise, are you?" she asked in a modest bearing.

"I wouldn't like to, but I wish to know a lot more about you,… Your family background."

Unenthusiastic to give an immediate answer, she put in, "I am going to get some food before we are left with the scraps and leftovers. I am here to have a good time and enjoy good meals. I will be more lucid and focused to discuss this burning issue with a full stomach."

Jeff was lost in a stream of joy, learning that she had made up her mind to speak about it.

She came back with two plates of pepper soup prepared with ram meat. She put them down on the table and went back. This time, she returned with two large cabernet cocktail glasses. "Do you think this cocktail is going to be anywhere near as nice as your woo woo?" she asked, handing one over to him. She had tasted Jeff's cocktail, woo woo months ago and couldn't believe he made it.

Jeff laughed audibly. "This is a five-star restaurant. How do you think that my cocktail will be better than theirs? Yes, I know I can cook, but that doesn't mean I can make better cocktails than the staff of a five-star hotel. They are trained professionals for goodness' sake."

"I would like to bet on that," she said, laughing heartily.

The glorious atmosphere he found himself in and his earlier experience and encounters with Becky unquestionably had injected him with some courage and had significantly calmed his fear of being in the company of a potential phantom.

"Yes, my name is Nkoli, if that is what you want to know or hear," she finally admitted after having a few gulps of the cocktail. "Does that make you feel better, Mr Chibuike?"

"Why address me like that?"

"Like what?" She petulantly asked.

Watching her countenance carefully, Jeff said, "I hope I am not awakening anything sinister in you."

"You are not. I called you by your surname because you are after my past, as if your life depended on it or you were going to publish an article about it."

Jeff gave out a sudden chortle. And she smiled back.

Her face tightened and looked deadpan. There was suspense in her look. She gave him a stare that startled him and unequivocally made him feel, one more time, he could be in the company of a ghost.

"Now listen, Jeff," she warned. "I am going to narrate my story. Nobody knows my background here in Lagos. Nobody. But recent circumstances and your persistence have now compelled me against my wish to narrate my story." She sat back, threw her head back as if she were stopping herself from being emotional. Then, she leaned forward again, her face close to his, regarding him with a look that seemed to ask for his loyalty and sincerity to keeping what she was about to tell him a secret.

Jeff felt nervously unsteady and returned a look of reassurance that he would keep the story to himself. In his mind, he was ready to offer anything to her, even a moon on a stick to make her discuss her past and family background.

"Why do I think you are a muck-raking journalist or a writer, Jeff?"

"None of the above. I am not after your past to take you down a peg or two. I am just a man driven by curiosity and a quest for knowledge."

"Exactly what I mean. These are some of the basic attributes of a journalist," she said calmly.

Shaking her head repeatedly, she said, "I can't believe you have put me in a position to talk about my past. I had before now sworn to myself that my past was dead, buried, and never to be resurrected. I think they call it dissociation in Psychiatry and psychology. I lied to them in the dormitory when they asked me about my past by telling them what they wanted to hear."

"What did you tell them?" he curiously asked.

"You are so inquiring and inquisitive, Jeff. What do you want to hear? What I told the girls or the information you have always craved for?"

"Pardon my silliness, Becky. I am ready to listen to your story."

"It is a long, complex story, but I will try to condense it as much as I can without leaving out major details.

"I was born in Kano to Mr and Mrs Amalu," She began grudgingly as her fingers raked through her newly permed hair.

Jeff leaned back against the chair and folded his hands across his macho chest, his ears attentive and as sharp as a tack.

"My father, Patrick, was an assiduous, caring, down-to-earth man," she continued. "A devout Christian and a philanthropist. He didn't become a philanthropist by virtue of his wealth, but by his unparalleled good nature and selflessness. He would prefer to go hungry than see anyone around him suffer." She stopped momentarily, tapped her foot a few times on the floor, then blinked repeatedly.

Jeff could see she was struggling to narrate her story, but he didn't know how to ask her to stop. He wanted to hear it all.

Then she continued, "The Igbo community in Dala district of Kano state, where we lived then, gave him an Igbo title (Ozo Igbo Ndu), meaning the man who strived to preserve the lives of his people. He was a trader and traded mostly in women's traditional wrappers such as *Abada*, *Ankara,* and *George*. He also dealt in female bags such as clutch bags, travelling bags, and locally made jewellery. He excelled exceedingly in the business, partly because of his dedication to the business and the love people had for him. He enjoyed exceptional patronage not only from the Igbo community but from other tribes of the country. His business was booming so much that my mother, Nwakaego, had to abandon her petty trading of cosmetics to join forces with him. I saw how difficult it was even with my mother joining the business, and I wished I were old enough to help. The business continued to grow rapidly. The struggle to cope with business activities and keep the family together had started to take its toll on my dad and mum. Though I was the only child, it was clear as day light that I was receiving less and less attention. His friends noticed and warned him of the dangers of leaving me in the care of other people while they got on with business. My father paid heed to the advice and decided to hire two apprentices. My mother was relieved of her post in the business and was put in charge of my welfare. There was unquantifiable joy, peace, and love in the family. I lacked for nothing. My father made sure that I was on par with the other children born to the upper echelons in the community. I wore the best of clothes and shoes. I had the most expensive toys. He would take me on tailor-made holidays where I would do horse and camel rides and go on mini roller coasters. I was sent to a private school. On top of all that, my dad arranged for private lessons in Spanish and French. I could speak Igbo language because my parents were Igbos. I was versatile in the Hausa language because I was born and bred in the Hausa state. My father wasn't satisfied. He wanted me to speak the three major Nigeria languages, so he paid for private lessons for me to learn Yoruba language as well. I didn't disappoint him. I learnt the three languages and in a matter of three years, I was as fluent in those languages as I was in writing them. My dad was immensely proud of that and had bragged among his friends and co-traders about this laudable achievement.

My mother, on the flip side of things, was more astute and future-thinking especially in money matters. She was keeping an eye on my dad's spending, ensuring that he didn't overindulge in his philanthropism and magnanimity.

My mother would always remind him whenever he went on a spending spree to help people in need that he had a family to look after as well. She had constantly reminded him that charity begins at home and that a man unable to take care of his immediate family was worse than an infidel.

Being the only girl and only child, my mum made sure that I was religiously and culturally brought up. She was dexterous in all spheres of human endeavours. Her cooking skills stood out amongst other Sterling qualities she had. She was the best cook until I met you. Not too sure, but I am confident it could be one of the things that endeared her to my dad. They were a perfect match. They were constantly compensating for the other's shortcomings. It was a perfect home. A home anybody would like to be part of.

Then came the dark Saturday. It was a weekend we were all looking forward to ... a weekend planned for my birthday. Being a Saturday, we all decided to go to the shop to help."

"Nobody saw it coming," she continued. "It took everyone by surprise. The extremists had decided to unleash an unprecedented mayhem on the Christian community in the area. They were quoted as saying that our crime was indoctrinating and spreading the Western world's lifestyle to the rest of the community.

Christians in the ensuing carnage were either hacked down like trees with machetes or shot down like bucks as seen on American wildlife channels. We were surrounded with no escape routes. They went from one shop to another in a synchronised, organised fashion, killing as they went. There was a spillage of blood and wailing as they perpetrated their carnage. We prayed and sang as they approached our shop. They smashed our shop. They dragged the two apprentices working for my dad, whom they believed were their own, to safety. And instead of shooting us like they had done to others, two of the men took me to a forest where I was held hostage for months. The other two stayed with my parents. I didn't know what they did to them. I heard gunshots after I left with the men, but I wasn't sure whether they were for my parents or other victims."

Jeff anxiously asked her what became of her parents. He did not want her to confirm that they were killed.

She returned an expressionless look, shook her head repeatedly and started crying.

"I can feel your pain. Now I know why you have always avoided the topic. What became of them? Did they survive the attack?" he asked solemnly, wishing that she would not confirm his fears.

"It would have been miles better if he didn't," Nkoli regretted.

"You wish he never did? Really? Why would you say that?"

"My good old father, I erroneously thought hung the moon and stars wasn't after all. He was a trained soldier before he relocated from the East to the North, where he later abdicated the post of a brigadier in the Nigerian army due to corruption and high-handedness in the service and went into business. On the day of the attack, the assailants attacked them with their machetes, inflicting deep gashes on them. They didn't bother to kill them, perhaps because they already had me as a ransom.

They survived the attack after some weeks in the hospital.

My dad and mum thought that I was killed by the men who took me away, as all efforts to find me proved abortive. I was in captivity for well over three months before I managed to escape with the help of one of the gang members." She paused at that moment to blow out air. Tilting her head backwards, she fanned herself with her hand as she fought back the tears.

Jeff knew why. Becky was struggling to tell the harrowing ordeal she went through at the hands of her captors. He was deeply touched by her acute distress and said reassuringly, "Pass. I don't want to hear the details."

Becky recovered and continued, "Things didn't exactly turn out the way I had thought when I got reunited with my parents, who then had relocated to another part of Kano called Sabongeri.

We didn't know precisely what happened. We didn't know whether it was post-traumatic stress disorder, new friends, unfamiliar environment, or something else, but it was clear that my dad became a different person — he became wild, conscienceless, inconsiderate, and vicious. It started gradually with raising his voice at my mother and me for trivial matters. Before the attack, he was cool-headed and would suffocate anything that would make him operate on a short fuse ... he was a jolly man to the core. The converse now was the case. He could not control his short-tempered behaviour. He was like a seeking missile, always looking for something that would enable him to unleash his new vicious character. He became insatiable. It didn't matter how much we tried; he would still find something to complain about.

Then, it went from bad to worse as weeks passed. There wasn't much difference between him and a perverted lunatic. He started accusing my mother of sleeping around with his business partners. A reason he would adopt to beat her, though batter would have been a better word … and then leaving her with bruises and black eyes. Each time I tried to intervene on behalf of my mother, he would drag me into it and make sure I had a fair share of his belligerent hostility."

She took a breather. Her hazel, dazzling eyes darkened and narrowed at the same time. She tilted her head backwards again. Her lips quivered uncontrollably as she struggled to get her words out. She didn't want to show her weakness despite being so close to tears. With the head still tilted, she put her hands over her face and remained silent for about ten seconds, trying to comport herself.

"Take your time, Nkoli. You know you can stop this story if it is too much for you to continue," he told her, seeing how difficult it was becoming for her to continue the story.

She gathered her mojo back. "I am fine," she said, shaking her head and blinking repeatedly to push back the tears. "It was a new area and a new era for us. A complete new hostile world we never envisaged we would ever be part of. We knew nobody, practically no one, except a few neighbours who would say good morning to you when they woke up on the right side of the bed. Conversely, he knew everyone, including the uniformed men, as well as all the nooks and crannies of the town. On very few occasions, we managed to lodge complaints at the police station, and we were told to go home and settle whatever the problem was amicably. 'It is a family matter. For two of you, you should learn how to give men their due respect. Your husband is the head of the family and must be given his due respect,' one of the police officers unconcernedly told us when we managed to escape to complain at the police station.

As if what we were enduring wasn't enough, he upped his antics and introduced what I never contemplated that would be our portion in a million years. He stopped having sex with my mother." She took a short break to fine-tune her voice, which was losing its resonance.

Taking advantage of the breather, Jeff asked, "And why didn't you and your mother leave at this point? Not sleeping with your mother obviously meant he was getting it somewhere else. This could easily have resulted in your mum being infected with sexually transmitted diseases, including the much-dreaded HIV."

"You didn't allow me to finish, Jeff. He wasn't getting it somewhere else. He was getting it from my mother."

"How? You said he stopped sleeping with your mother. Now, you said he was getting it from your mother."

"I haven't made any complex statement difficult to understand, have I? You know what I meant. Well, if you want me to spell it out, then I will. He started raping my mother. What baffled me was the fact that he was performing this savage act more regularly than when he used to make love to her."

Jeff was left with a gaping mouth, trying to assimilate what he had just heard.

"Then he stepped up the gear. At this point, there was much wind in his sail. He seemed unstoppable. He managed to get a gun, and like a depraved, wild felon on the loose, he started inviting me forcefully to witness the barbaric act he was performing on my mother. I would cry, sob, and beg on behalf of my mother, who appeared toothless, cowered, and immensely subdued in shame. I wanted to do something to help my poor mother, but the presence of the gun prevented me from making any wrong moves. I knew the way he was that he wouldn't think twice to pull the trigger.

I remembered mustering courage while I was with him in the house alone, and asked him why he was the way he was. I asked him where his good nature had gone. I asked him who had stolen his golden heart. I was crying as I did.

He looked devilishly and impishly at me and raised his voice vulgarly. Pointing his finger in rage at me, he said, "Never in your life will you have the effrontery to ask me that stupid question again. Have I made myself clear?" I nodded helplessly in fear.

As if what was happening wasn't bad enough, he decided to go maniacal and did the unthinkable. It was clear now that he had made us his project. Nothing made him happier than seeing us suffer and cry. This time, he was more interested in me than any other thing. He drafted me into his plans. When my mother was at the market or had gone for food shopping, he would use the opportunity to get at me. 'You are now a woman, and I need to teach you what you would expect later in life,' he shamelessly informed me as he forcefully took my virginity that fateful afternoon. I was heartbroken that it was a man I called my dad who took my virginity, which I managed to protect even in the hands of my abductors. And then, it became a recurring event. "If you say anything to your mother or anybody about what we are doing, you are dead. Have I made myself clear?" I nodded cowardly without even looking at him."

Jeff was physically shivering at Becky's storyline. Like a radial stream, tears flowed unrestrainedly from his misty eyes. At a point, Jeff wanted to tell her to stop. The story now wasn't only outrageous; it was exceedingly sickening. "Stop, Becky. I have heard enough," he finally begged her. "The only thing I want to hear is that he is dead. He doesn't deserve to be alive."

"Not now. You never stopped harping on the same string, trying to learn about my family history and background. We have crossed the Rubicon, Jeff." Then, she remembered that she still had the cocktail. She picked up the glass and had a few more gulps.

Jeff now regretted asking her to narrate her past. *If I knew how bad the situation was, I would have opted to narrate my own story to her and spared her the agony of reliving this horrible experience,* Jeff thought.

She continued her story, sobbing and wiping her eyes intermittently with the inner part of her elbow, having finished the paper towels available on the table.

"Again, for umpteenth time, he pumped up the volume and tightened up the screw and grip he had on us. This time, he started using us to entertain his guests. *"Zabi Wanda kake so,"* meaning choose the one you like, as he pointed at me and my mother. We were helpless ... with nowhere to run to and no one to come to our rescue, we became his sex slaves.

When one's soul is sold to Lucifer and his cohorts, then be ready to expect the unexpected. Because in the coming months, the man I called my father graduated from being a beast to becoming a ritualist. Things continued to evolve weirdly before our eyes. By now, it was clear to me he had managed to put Lucifer in the shade by what he was villainously able to accomplish. He systematically kicked my mum out of the room. At first, we did not attach any importance to that. He had done worse things. That was our assumption until that Saturday afternoon when we saw smoke coming out of his room. He had forgotten to turn off the iron after ironing his clothes. We had no choice but to break down the door to gain entry. We switched off the iron. My mum demanded we leave the room as quickly as possible. "We are going to endure his wrath if he catches us in his room," my mum said with appalled countenance.

"We are caught in the web already anyway," I aptly made her understand.

"How?" she asked.

"As you can see, Mum, the door is broken, and we can't fix it, can we?"

"You are right, my daughter. But our punishment will still be less than the house going up in flames," she retorted.

"Just as we were leaving the room, something caught my attention. At the corner of my eye, I saw behind the wardrobe something that looked like a coffin. I stopped to take a second look to confirm. I was right. It was a three-foot cream coloured coffin smeared sporadically with red substance I believed was blood, with birds' feathers stuck to it. I couldn't tell what animal blood it was. Curiosity got the better of me against my mum's advice as I ventured to open the coffin after I had said a short prayer. What I saw made me throw up. It harboured three human skulls. One of the skulls was so tiny that you could tell it was a baby's skull. Poor, innocent souls. It was harrowing to see.

My implicit confidence in God undoubtedly saved the day. I was sure we weren't supposed to see what we saw. We were saved by God's grace.

That was the last straw that broke the camel's back. I didn't want to tempt fate any longer. The signs were everywhere for us to see that we were in imminent danger. I knew it was time to dive into the Mariana Trench of the ocean if that was what it was going to take to escape from him. In the face of all of these, my mum remained resolute and immovable as a statue as all attempts to co-opt her into the escape plan fell through."

"We need to get away from here, Mum, before we are killed by this loathsome man who has sold his soul to the devil. One day, we are surely going to be sacrificed to his gods or whatever he is worshipping. It is only a matter of time, mother," I tried to instil fear into her.

"We have nowhere to run to, my daughter. We have nobody here in Kano. Even if we do, your evil father will still find us because he has several means and avenues to find us. And you know what that means if that were to be the case. We must continue to pray to see if the Holy Spirit will touch his estranged heart."

"Let's escape to the east then, to your family," I frantically suggested.

"I wish I had a family, and a place called home, my daughter."

"Meaning what, mother?"

"Exactly what I mean. Your father came from the Osu community."

"Osu community? What does that mean, and how does that concern our escape?" I inquisitively asked her.

"I never thought a situation that would compel me to explain this would ever rear its ugly head when I married your father. Well, my daughter, the Osu community is a community whose indigenes are seen as sacrificial lambs to the gods or shrines. They are more or less excommunicated from the rest of the people."

"I then realised why my mother had always avoided any discussion about her family politely."

My mum said, "With both of us being deeply religious and knowledgeable, we wouldn't allow such derogatory and bizarre beliefs to hold us back when we fell in love. Your father whisked me away from the clan to Kano state, where we did our marriage, since it would have been difficult to perform it in the east. My family disowned me and vowed not to do anything with me because I married him."

"When it was obvious that my mother wasn't on the same page with me and wasn't ready to move, I decided to take a unilateral decision and run for dear life with some money I borrowed from our few good neighbours.

That was how I came to Lagos, a land of opportunity, as some would call it. Things surprisingly didn't work out as I planned. I ended up using up the little money I had on paying hotel bills while I tried to find a job. Driven by anger, frustration, and hunger, I had no choice but to hit the street when I hadn't a dime left to pay my hotel bills.

That was the business I went into to save myself from starving to death. That was what I was doing the day you saved me at Mile Two Market. I was the prostitute you saved, Jeff."

Jeff's head was tossed up in the air. The information was now too much for him to take in.

"How did you know I was the person who saved you at Mile Two Market?" Jeff asked, shell-shocked. "They put a sack over your face as if you were a horse being led to the slaughterhouse. So, it was impossible for you to see me."

"I wouldn't have known if not for Jane."

"Jane? How do you mean?" Jeff asked.

"Remember the day Jane returned with you from Tunisia. You had a great altercation with her when she saw me in your house. It was during the rift that Jane mentioned how you saved a girl in the market as she was inches away from being stoned to death. I was the lady Jane was on about. That was how I got the scar on my face. I do not know if you noticed the shock in my face when Jane said it. I knew that without you, I wouldn't have been alive today."

A wave of uncontrollable emotion swept through Jeff, and he wept loudly and brokenheartedly, hearing that bit.

"Yes, you saved me that day, just as you were there at the Cubans to rescue me once again from those evil men. Without your intervention at the Cuban's club, we couldn't be sitting here discussing this sensitive issue. You have always been my guardian angel." And he agreed he was.

"What has become of your parents?" he asked, still feeling mawkish.

"My mother is late."

"And your evil dad?"

"Absolutely no idea. To be honest, I could not care less what has become of him."

Jeff wasn't shocked by her answer. He then stared at her for quite some time and said, "Such a series of sad events. But how would you react if I told you that your mother is alive and well?"

"We have had a lengthy, disturbing discussion. Do not make it worse by being unreasonable, Jeff. I just told you my mother was late. My friend sent me a video of her funeral. It has been an emotional rollercoaster day for me. So, don't add insult to injury."

"I am not kidding. You should know it would be sheer folly and the height of irresponsibility for one to start babbling about a serious matter like this at a time like this."

Her eyes lit up with a mixture of doubt and belief. "Then explain that to me."

Jeff stood up and walked up to her. With his heart now melted as wax before the fire, Jeff wrapped his hand round her and wept yet again before saying, "You are my sister, Nkoli, my biological sister. You are the twin sister of our sister, Naomi. That explains the two bracelets. That's why your step mum was in the picture with our mother. That was why God sent me to Mile Two Market and Cuban's club. God sent me to go and save my sister on each occasion. That's how we both sustained the scars on our faces. You must remember the day I walked into your room as you were getting dressed. You expressed dissatisfaction with the manner I barged into your room. It appeared as if I was moping, but I wasn't. I was stunned by the mark on your back, which was exactly the same spot as in Naomi's. For me, the bracelet conundrum was Naomi's subtle way to acknowledge your presence and reunification with your biological family"

Becky was speechless and could only look at Jeff in shock, but with a degree of relief. And they shed some tears again.

"I am going to narrate my own story. Like yours, mine is a long one," Jeff told her, after comporting himself. "Our mother took time and narrated the full story to me and Jane before you left the house. And like your own narrative, I will try to condense it as much as I can."

"By the way, before I forget, how did you leave the house unnoticed the day my mum confronted you about your name...? We all concluded that you disappeared because our mum hinted that she was reliably informed that you and your stepparents perished in the attack."

"She laughed cheekily and said, "Now I know why colour quickly drained from your face when you saw me here. Oh, you thought you had been accosted by a ghost. You are so chicken-hearted, Jeff."

"Who wouldn't, Nkoli? Tell me. After all, you almost jumped into the gutter seeing a rat the other day." Their laughter echoed across the room."

"I sneaked out through the back door when I noticed everyone was fast asleep," she said softly.

"Oh well. We thought you had disappeared. Anyway, back to my story. It gives me joy to tell you that our mum is called Felicia Chibuike. She was married to our dad, Mr Osita Chibuike, who worked in the railway corporation. A couple of years after their marriage, he was transferred to Kano. It was an impromptu and difficult transfer. Little or no arrangement was made for a smooth transition. The quarters for the staff were not only far from the city but were also overrun with hoodlums, bedbugs and rodents. Our mother told us how they would always sleep with one eye closed as they constantly anticipated somebody breaking into their house. Moreover, the roof of the house leaked profusely, so their bed was always soaked when it rained.

On that fateful payday, my father had taken my mother to town for a meal. Payday wasn't guaranteed by any stretch of the imagination. At times, our dad would go for months without any pay. It was on this outing that they met Mr Amalu and his wife, Nwakaego. They started talking. It was in their discussion that they learnt about our parents' predicament. And it broke their hearts that our parents were suffering that much. They were comfortable, and they willingly decided to accommodate our parents in their vast house.

"We have many rooms to spare. We are not going to let the pair of you continue to live in abject squalor like this," Mr Amalu joyfully informed our parents.

First year of our parents' stay in their house, our mum was diagnosed with renal failure. Dialysis was out of the question because of its exorbitance, and most of the time unavailable. Donors were scarce. Mum was dying as her condition worsened. Our dad wanted to donate one of his kidneys, but he wasn't a match. Secondly, the doctors were not keen on him donating even if his kidney was a match due to our father's failing health. Mr Amalu volunteered, seeing that Mum was slowly dying. Again, he wasn't a match. It was Nwakaego's that matched, and she willingly donated one of her kidneys, a donation that snatched Mum back from the cold hand of death that had already gripped her.

It was in the third year of our parents' stay that Mum got pregnant with me. Unfortunately, it was the same year that Nwakaego was diagnosed with endometrial cancer. It was aggressive. Thank God it was detected early enough. The only way round it was for her to undergo a hysterectomy with some other recommended cancer treatments. She recovered fully from it, but the only snag was that she was never going to conceive. Months later, our mum had me. She took in two years later. Nine months later, she had you and Naomi. It was a mixture of gloom and happiness for both families. Our parents were living on meagre, inconsistent salaries from the railways. It was becoming increasingly difficult for them to put food on the table. Railway workers could at times go for over four months without pay. Mr Amalu and his wife, in contrast, were pretty comfortable but were very unhappy because of childlessness. They started contemplating adoption. Our parents heard about it. Mr Amalu and his wife had treated us so nicely, helping our parents with feeding at times, and refusing to ask for rent. And that was when it happened. Our parents reached an extremely hard decision. They knew it would be impossible for them to take good care of three of us due to limited resources and Dad's failing health. They met Mr Amalu and his wife and informed them of their willingness to give them one of the twins as their own daughter. "It is a hard decision for us to make. We are willing to give out one of our daughters, partly because we cannot fend for them, but the main reason was the mere fact that your family gave my family life and life shall we give back to your wonderful family," my mother happily informed them.

"But above all this, we will be assured that our daughter will be in the best hands for the rest of her life," our dad chipped in."

Nkoli hiccupped a sarcastic laugh. "Really! Best hands for the rest of her life," she echoed back Jeff's words.

"You wouldn't blame our parents. That's what they genuinely thought," Jeff replied to her sardonic comments. "Our mum then bought those two bracelets and made those marks on you and Naomi on your backs the day you were officially handed over to them. You and Naomi were about two months old when this historic event happened. Our mum still helped to wean you even though you were theirs officially.

Two years later, Dad was diagnosed with terminal tuberculosis. Consequently, they were forced to move back to the East, where he passed away peacefully a year later."

"That's so sad," she lamented, anguish in her face. "But you omitted any details about my twin, Naomi. Where is she? Everyone mentions her passively."

"No, no, no. That is a whole new story for another day, Nkoli. Let's just savour our reunion for now."

They had spent hours on end telling their stories and rejoicing in their reunion that they forgot about how long they had stayed. They were so carried away that Jeff even forgot about Jane.

"Nkoli, I need to go home now," Jeff said, realising the day was almost gone, and that Jane must be wondering what had happened to him. "You are coming with me," Jeff told her.

"But how is that possible? Jane still believes I am a ghost."

"That's my plan. I know she won't talk to me. Neither will she allow me anywhere near her because I switched off my phone when you agreed to tell your story and forgot to switch it back on. Look how many phone calls and text messages she has made and sent. She will be fuming. The plan is to divert her anger to fear. I will get in first and close the door. Then I will be ready to absorb her outbursts. While she rips my head off, you will make your ghostly entry. That surely will not only shut her up but will make her seek refuge in me. You know Jane is scared of anything, never mind coming face to face with a ghost."

Nkoli laughed loudly, thinking about Jane's supposed reaction on seeing her. "I hope she is not going to have a heart attack," she said, still laughing heartily.

Jeff got in safely as planned, as the door wasn't locked. But Jane, as a heat-seeking missile, noticed that someone had entered the house and appeared from the kitchen looking crimson like the comb on the head of a cockerel. She grabbed Jeff and hooted viciously at him. "Where have you been all day, with your phone switched off? Oh, your battery died. Isn't it? Maybe a flat tyre? Or, even more likely, you have found another babe? It is either you are finding them, or they are finding you," she said condescendingly.

"Don't be so derogatory, Jane," Jeff said, trying to pull her towards him.

"Don't you even try to touch me with those hands …," she viciously warned him. She began to punch him repeatedly, screaming and swearing at the same time.

"I have just realised you have a trust issue," Jeff told her.

Then Nkoli came to his rescue, but not without scaring life out of Jeff because she made her ominous entrance from their bedroom instead of the front door as they agreed. She had entered through the back door, just the way she left. Her appearance was like a phantasmagoria as she looked like a real ghost against the faded fluorescent light in the lounge. Jeff was as frightened as Jane and was about to scream when he finally realised it was Nkoli. She was good at everything she did. She dressed like a ghost one usually sees in Nollywood movies. She walked effortlessly as if she were floating. Everything came to an abrupt stop with her entry.

With the same hands Jane had been throwing punches at him, she tenaciously grabbed and buried her face in his chest, unable to raise it up to look at Nkoli.

"Please, Becky, don't hurt us. Just go away and leave us alone, please," Jane frantically begged, shivering like a leaf blown by a hurricane wind. If there was still any speck of doubt in Jane's mind about Becky being a ghost, her majestic, spine-chilling entry put paid to it.

"Why are you beating him? You never asked him why he came back late. That's so unreasonable. I must teach you a lesson you will never forget," Nkoli said in a slurred, dragged, echoing, ghostly voice.

Jane grabbed Jeff further. If it were possible for her, she would have buried herself right inside him. Then Jeff spared her further torture by laughing aloud and said to her, "Jane, Nkoli, my sister is not dead. I have been with her all day. The circumstances of meeting her took all the time." He briefly narrated what happened between him and Nkoli.

Jane felt great relief hearing the details.

"But you went too far. Did you think that was a knee-slapper? You could have given me a heart attack with that your expensive drama," she slammed him.

Jeff laughed again.

"It is not funny," she said as she threw a few more kid-glove punches at him. She went and hugged Nkoli, and they held each other for a long time.

CHAPTER 25

This reunion brought with it an unprecedented, heart-warming relationship. Jane and Nkoli got even closer to each other than before. They were now like childhood friends. Save for Jane's dislike for funk music, they shared the same interests in other things. Most striking and strange to Jeff was their great love for fishing and swimming. He remembered coming home that Saturday evening and finding two fishing rods and a plastic bucket half filled with slow-moving tilapia and catfish. Neither Jane nor Nkoli was on hand to explain how these fish got there. An hour later, they walked in looking scruffy but excited. Obviously, they hadn't changed since coming home from their weird fishing expedition. They had gone to the nearby local market to buy condiments to prepare the famous fish pepper soup.

"Never knew I was living with professional anglers. How come I am just discovering, and for how long have both of you been in this exciting profession?"

Jane and Nkoli laughed joyously and answered, "Donkey years." "I learned how to fish when we were still in Warri, Delta state, before we moved to Lagos. Traditionally, swimming and fishing are learnt intuitively in that part of the world," Jane said proudly.

Nkoli, on the other hand, got hooked on fishing after seeing the famous Arugungu fishing festival when she was still a child.

Fortunately, one of the nearby Lakes was teeming with all sorts of fish, such as rainbow trout, common carp, catfish, and tilapia. Occasionally, Salmon, cods, and medium-sized tunas have migrated from the ocean into the lake. That made it a hotspot for anglers, with Jane and Nkoli now joining the ever-growing number of teams. They saw it not only as an opportunity to bring to life their hibernated fishing skill, but also as an opportunity to promote their bonding.

"When are you taking me to the village to see Mama? Or don't you think that I deserve to see her following all these revelations?" Nkoli asked him suddenly as they had their dinner.

"Of course, I have been trying to contact our mother to inform her of our coming, but all efforts to reach her have been unsuccessful. The mobile network in the village isn't anything to write home about and has never been, despite all the promises made by the network providers. I need to make mum aware of our visit to spare her the horror and psychological trauma that might result from driving in with you without prior knowledge, because up till now she still believes that you are dead."

He told Jane of the plan. She didn't only buy the idea, but she also agreed to make the journey with them.

Jeff knew the situation might be too much for their mum if they walked in with Nkoli without prior knowledge, especially now she was getting on in age. So, they decided to leave Nkoli in the car on arrival. That would give him and Jane time to explain things to his mum before bringing Nkoli into the scene.

Though Jeff's mum wasn't expecting them, by God, she was extraordinarily ecstatic seeing Jeff and Jane.

"That's more like it. True son of his father. The son who knows what pleases his mother. The one and only handsome son of his mother. The one who stands head and shoulders above the rest," she eulogised Jeff endlessly. "I have been expecting this visit," she continued.

Squeezing herself in between Jeff and Jane, she gave them a welcoming, warm hug, amid fulfilling smiles.

Despite Jeff's mum getting on in age, she hadn't forgotten how to look after herself. Her city lifestyle of yesteryears hadn't quite deserted her.

She looked gorgeous in her new plaited hair that was held together at the back with a bubble.

You could tell the difference between her costume and that of her younger sister, Nneka, who visited from a neighbouring village where she was married to. No disrespect to her, but she looked like an old grey mare despite being Jeff's mum's younger sister. She had virtually lived all her life in the village with a poor educational background and exposure, and you could easily tell from her simple *cut-and-sew Ankara blouse.* Pointing towards the sky was her obsolete Afro plaited hairstyle tied with mere silky black thread, which was conically packed together. Her make-up wasn't too far from the Igbo mural painting worn by some women during the post-colonial era, derived from (*uli*) tree. But what she lacked in looks and fashion, she made up for in her unblemished oratory. Her figures of speech and adages flowed effortlessly as if they were sown into her like seeds. She hardly finished a sentence without adding a proverb to give richness, resonance and meaning to it.

"I was thinking how long it is going to take you before you do the right thing. As you can see, you are not getting younger and again, you are not the only man who has an eye for a good thing. I was getting worried some smarter men will snatch her under your nose if you continue to dilly-dally," his mother said. She was still reluctant to acknowledge their court marriage. As far as she was concerned, Jeff and Jane were still single until the traditional marriage rites were performed. But apart from tradition, Jeff's mum also wanted to use the traditional marriage ceremony to present Jane officially to the community. According to his mum, Jane was so beautiful to be married secretly. She wanted her village people to know that her son was married to the most beautiful woman of their time.

Jane hid her face. She was obviously embarrassed by Jeff's mum's remarks.

"This visit couldn't have come at a better time. I really have been looking forward to it," she reiterated. She then turned to Jane, looked at her lovingly and started pouring all sorts of praise, most of which centred on her beauty and what a good wife she expected her to be.

Nneka, Jeff's mum's sister, who visited from the neighbouring village, couldn't contain her excitement either. She went with Jeff's mum's line of thought, believing that the main reason for Jeff's visit was to introduce Jane as his future wife, as custom and tradition demanded.

Referring to Jane, Nneka said, "*Nkea buya, akwa ugo. Oma agbananari anyi* (This girl is special, precious as an eagle's egg. We are not going to allow her slip through our fingers). But remember, Jeff, *Onye mee osiso, omenari odachi. Which translates: if you act swiftly, you will avoid regrets and disappointment."* In other words, she was encouraging Jeff to hasten the marriage rites.

Jeff didn't want to argue with his mother anymore about marriage. "We will perform the traditional marriage and church wedding when we are ready," he reassured her.

Nneka turned to Jeff's mum and said, "When Jeff marries her, your bragging right as the most beautiful lady in our town will cease to exist. Hasn't she made you and all our beautiful women look ordinary and plain looking?"

"I will not contest that," Jeff's mum joyfully replied. "After all," his mum continued, "No reasonable parent would like to surpass their children in any aspect of human endeavour, and that includes beauty and handsomeness. Their children will surely continue the legacy… they will be more beautiful and handsome than Jane and Jeff in Jesus' name."

"Aaaamen," Nneka, her sister, chorused loudly and excitedly.

Jeff fixed his gaze on his mum. At first, it didn't mean anything to her. But when he continued looking, his mum paused and asked, "Why are you looking at me as if I wore my top inside out, or someone who had discovered a hidden treasure?"

"I think I have, mum."

"I know you have, son. The treasure is sitting next to you. What treasure will be greater than her?" she said, pointing at Jane. Jeff laughed, Jane laughed, infectiously, they all laughed at his mum's remark.

"Mum, you need to sit down. We came prepared. Our bag is full of goodies. It might be true that the treasure is sitting next to me, but what if I told you that we had as much treasure, if not more, in the car? Well, mum, when I say that the treasure in the car is huge, I meant it by every single letter of it."

Her flippant face of nonchalance gradually metamorphosed into worry and inquisitiveness …. a sense of urgency declared in her countenance. She was now eager to hear what it was. "Then prove it to me," she demanded eagerly.

Without much ado, Jeff said to her, "Nkoli came with us. She is in the car. And for good and bad reasons, she is alive, not dead." Jeff wasted no time explaining everything to her as he noticed the disquiet and discomfort in his mum's face.

"Don't play such an expensive joke with your mother. I am sure you know it is not good for my age," she solemnly admonished him, trying to maintain what seemed a compromised composure.

"I know. I am not silly, mother. There are things you don't joke with. There are limitations to jokes. I can't be that callous to say things like these if they weren't true," he reassured her.

The pensive, thoughtful look that showed in her face confirmed to Jeff that she believed him. She untied one of her wrappers and used the edge of it as a handkerchief to wipe her tears, now convinced that Jeff meant what he said.

"Nkoli, my daughter, you have to forgive your mother," she said when she met her, still unsure what Nkoli's reaction would be seeing her as a mother who gave her away to another family. "We didn't do it intentionally," she continued, "Never. We were pushed to take that hard decision due to abject poverty and circumstances beyond us. If you don't forgive us, I will understand. Worthy Parents should never have taken the option of giving their child away under any circumstances. I really am sorry. I am ashamed of our action and decision. I am even more traumatised now that your brother has narrated the monster, good Patrick later turned out to be."

"If I were bearing grudges, mother, I wouldn't have bothered to make this trip to see you," Nkoli said reassuringly. "I can't deny the fact that I am broken-hearted and hurting, especially recounting the unfathomable ordeals I passed through in his hands," she continued with eyes saturated and flickering with unshed tears. "Everyone in my situation should be. But the bottom line is that we as Christians should practise what we preach… one of which is the spirit of forgiveness. I appreciate that it is hard. But like seed, we must let the past die so that the future can germinate and live."

With apology rendered and accepted, they all walked back to the house.

"You came prepared, my children and my future daughter-in-law. Your bag is full of goodies. Oh my God! Today of all days, I can't boast of anything, not even garden eggs or kola nuts. I just came back from the market and was about to cook dinner when my sister called. And we have been doing some catch-up talking about the glamorous traditional marriage of the king's second daughter last weekend. The traditional marriage is still talk of the town, but it will soon be forgotten when the pair of you come up with yours in no distant time," his mother said, pointing at Jeff and Jane.

"That's correct," Nneka agreed before adding she couldn't wait for a date to be announced for their traditional marriage. She was still speaking when four boys of the same age bracket entered the scene. They could be any age from five to seven. Three of them were shirtless with their shorts ripped here and there. Being the harmattan period, their skins were just like a chalkboard — so dry and dusty that you could write visibly on them. They were just returning from playing football, as the fourth boy explained when Nneka asked him where he had been since morning. He wore an old Barcelona jersey with "Messi" inscribed on the back. He went and sat on Nkoli's lap uninvited to the surprise and envy of the other boys. "Can I call you auntie?" he asked Nkoli politely.

"If you want to," Nkoli replied wholeheartedly.

He felt relieved. He didn't want to call her by her name as that could be construed as a lack of respect according to their culture and tradition.

"What did you buy for me, auntie?" he asked bravely and unexpectedly.

"Jesus!" Nkoli exclaimed. "I am sorry, boy, I haven't got anything for you. I didn't know I would meet you. I promise I will buy you some biscuits and a new football next time."

"Please, add football boots," he pleaded meekly. "Make it Adidas if you can," he continued. "I have never played with football boots. I want to know how it feels playing with one. I want to be the next Lionel Messi," he ambitiously claimed.

"Why not! Good ambition. I will get you a full football kit. That's a promise," Nkoli reassured him. "What's your name, by the way?" Nkoli asked him dotingly.

"Nwadili for short, but if you want the full name, it is Nwadilinneya, meaning I will live for my mother."

"Aww! What a lovely name," Nkoli responded. Jeff's mum kept stealing quick glances at the intrinsic relationship that was unfolding rapidly between Nkoli and Nwadili. Jeff was equally watching with some interest.

"Your mother must be fond of you, giving you this beautiful name."

"I think so," Nwadili replied resignedly. He left Nkoli and disappeared into the backyard. He resurfaced eight minutes later carrying an old, rusty plate. He carried it with old cloth that looked like a rag because it was hot. Stretching his hands toward Nkoli, he said, "It is my leftover *Abacha*. I left it for later, but you can have it. You must be hungry, coming from the city. It must be a long journey, mustn't it?"

"Yes, it was really a long journey," Nkoli replied, while cautiously accepting the plate with the cloth to avoid burning her fingers. Then she looked at everyone in surprise. She couldn't understand the strange affection. "That's very kind of you," Nkoli replied, looking nonplussed. "Where is your lovely mum anyway?" Nkoli asked.

"I don't know. They said my mum had gone to see God up, up in the sky. She is yet to come back. I am still eagerly waiting for her return. I don't know why she decided to go up, up in the sky to see God. My friends' mums only go to the city. And when they return, they return with bread, biscuits, and gala meat. But my mum, on the contrary, had decided to travel upward to see God."

Nkoli knew his mum had passed away. She felt deeply sorry for him and cuddled him close to her chest.

"Will you take me to her, Auntie?" Nwadili asked respectfully.

Spooked by the question and feeling like one a curveball had been thrown at, Nkoli said, "It is a very far, far place, Nwadili."

"That's what I get each time I ask anyone. I wonder why my mum decided to embark on a journey that she couldn't come back from. If I could fly an aeroplane, I would just take off on my own to bring her back here. Why would God not let her come to see me all these years?" he asked, almost remonstrating.

"Because God loves her so much," Nkoli said persuasively. "We will come back to your mum's story later. What about your dad?"

"My father? I don't know either. Everyone says I am too young to know about my father. That is weird, isn't it? I must be a weird child whose mother has abandoned him to see God and who is too young to know anything about his father. I want someone to tell me that all these are just smoke and mirrors."

Just then, a girl of about 12 years came along and told one of the boys that his father wanted him.

"You see what I mean, Auntie. Andrew's father wants him," pointing to the boy, the young girl had come to fetch. "Andrew is the same age as me, he knows his father; his father knows him. Why is my case different? Auntie, don't bother about my mysterious parents; otherwise, your food will go cold."

Deeply touched, Nkoli looked at him, then at the food. Jeff was imagining what was going on in her mind… the food…the state of the plate it was served and much more. She couldn't afford to say no to this meal that was respectfully, cheerfully, and wholeheartedly served to her. "You haven't given me a spoon or fork, Nwadili."

Nwadili laughed unrestrainedly and said, "Auntie, you don't need a spoon or fork to eat Abacha. If you do, our ancestors will be mad at you."

Nkoli nearly fell out of her chair laughing.

"It is tradition. And please don't even think of changing it," Nwadili warned Nkoli, tutting and shaking his head in disbelief that she had the guts to ask for cutlery to eat abacha.

They all roared with laughter at Nwadili's witticisms and remarks.

"Really! How am I going to eat it then?"

"With your hands, of course. I will get a bowl of soapy water so you can wash your hands."

"Nwadili, she is not the only visitor here, you know," Jeff cut in just to draw his attention a bit away from Nkoli. "Where is ours?" Jeff asked him kindly.

"None. This is the only abacha left, and it is too small to share between you."

"And you think Nkoli is the only one hungry here, ehh?"

"Men can endure hunger more than women," he cheekily replied.

"And what about Jane? She is not a man, is she?" Jeff asked him comically.

"Oh! Jane? Is that her name? I thought they said that very beautiful woman with exceptionally smooth skin is called (*tomato Jos*)."

They were all crying-laughing at Nwadili's funny comments.

"No, I wouldn't give her abacha because I don't think she knows what to do with it. She is more or less a stranger, unlike Auntie Nkoli, who is from here. I would have given her chicken pepper soup as a special guest if there were some," Nwadili said, referring to Jane.

Jeff's mother left the scene at that moment. She had seen and heard enough. Jeff knew why she left. He followed her to the room. "Naomi is here with us. She is surely in our midst; don't you think so?"

"I am aware of that, mum," Jeff replied with misty, unfocused eyes. They sobbed briefly and then wiped down their tears before rejoining others in the sitting room.

Jeff gave Nwadili some money. "Go get yourself and your friends some biscuits and chewy at Boni's shop." In Nwadili's absence, they narrated everything to Nkoli. "Nwadili is Naomi's son," Jeff began the sad story. "She died giving birth to him," he continued. Nkoli put both hands over her face and wept loudly and bitterly. Pulling herself together shortly after, she said, "Blood, they say, is thicker than water. No wonder the swift connection. He knew instinctively who I am. But why wasn't he allowed to know what happened to his mother? He is not the only child who lost his mother during childbirth."

"I know. It is the circumstances surrounding the pregnancy and birth of Nwadili. We think he is still too young to take in all the information. It might be too much for him. We will tell him everything when the time is right," Jeff's mum assured Nkoli.

CHAPTER 26

Nkoli was the first to wake up the next morning. Jeff, seeing Nkoli awake that early, thought her sleep might have been punctuated by the unfamiliar environment, a common factor that affects the majority of people. She curled up on the sofa in the sitting area, wrapping herself up with a fleece throw blanket to generate some warmth to counter the cold harmattan weather.

But Jeff's assumption was incorrect. Nkoli told him that she stayed awake all night thinking about Nwadili and what they were going to do about him, his education and general upbringing.

"I don't think it is right to leave Nwadili to grow up in the village," Nkoli told Jeff as they were about to go back to Lagos. "He needs a good education and proper upbringing. I just want to take him with us. If it is too sudden to do it right away, we may rearrange to come back at a future date, … What do you think?"

"I lean in favour of the latter, Nkoli. Allowing Nwadili to be brought up in the village is something I have always detested and dreaded. However, the topsy-turvy events in my life have hitherto prevented me from bringing him to the city. For now, it seems difficult when you give real thought to our condition. None of us has a steady job and time to take adequate care of this young man. It won't augur well to bring this boy to a big city like Lagos without first ensuring that his care, safety, and education will not be compromised. If we treat his upbringing with levity, he might end up with the wrong company, and that will be a disaster for him and all of us and more so, his mother, Naomi. We need a solid base to make this come true. We need to sort ourselves out first. Remember, it is difficult for a drowning man to save a drowning man. Naomi will be raging in her grave if we do not give this little boy the best head start in life. We owe her that duty, don't we?"

Nkoli regarded him with a solemn look of resignation and surrender… a look that affirmed she was on the same page with his line of thought.

Back in Lagos, Nkoli continued to pester Jeff about her twin sister, and on each occasion, Jeff had smartly avoided the discussion. He didn't want any discussion to remind him about Naomi he loved dearly.

"It's clear from my standpoint that you are not comfortable discussing our sister, Naomi," she said.

Jeff knew he couldn't avoid it forever. He decided it was better to talk about it and forget about it.

"Well, Nwadili asked questions when we were in the village, remember?"

"Well, Nwadili, being a precocious and intuitive child, asked so many questions and made so many remarks— some of which were soul-searching, some mind-boggling and some heart-warming. You need to say categorically which one, Jeff."

"Remember him saying (I must be a weird child whose mother has abandoned to see God and who is too young to know his father). He also asked if someone would tell him that things happening in his life were just smoke and mirrors. He is quite right to make such assumptions. I am also immersed in the same stream of thought about our own lives that seem no better than his. It has been one horrible event after another. Look at me. Look at you. Look at Mum. Look at Nwadili. The same series of sad events snuffed life out of our sister, Naomi. The cold hand of death snatched Dad away from us even before he turned fifty."

"I know all these bits. I wish they were all smoke and mirrors as well. Unfortunately, they are not, and they are not going to be. However, I still want to know the circumstances that led to the death of my twin sister, please."

"Naomi lost too much blood while giving birth to Nwadili, as you already know," Jeff began, "But there was much to that." He took a deep breath. Telling the story was one thing. How Nkoli would construe it was another.

"Was it the mistake of the medical team?" Nkoli interrupted with a worried, sad look.

"Not necessarily. It was meant to happen because the hospital to the best of my knowledge took care of things as they should. When they found out that Nwadili was a big baby, they opted for a Caesarean section. However, there was postpartum haemorrhage associated with the delivery of the placenta, which they could not stop because of Naomi's poor blood clotting factor."

"Poor soul!" Nkoli exclaimed with a heavy heart as she fought back the tears. "What about the husband in all of this? I remember Nwadili saying that he was told he was too young to know about his father. What was that all about?"

"Because he discovered Nwadili wasn't his."

"Nwadili wasn't his? How? How did he find out? Before or after Nwadili's birth?"

"After."

"So, he must have been suspicious of something before or during Naomi's pregnancy, correct? Naomi wasn't promiscuous, was she?" she cautiously asked, eyes spiky and penetrating.

"No, she wasn't." DNA revealed that the child wasn't his."

"So, what happened?" she asked, looking confused and angry all at once.

"Naomi, our sister was raped."

Nkoli laughed contemptuously and said, "Don't give me that bullshit, Jeff. Please don't. I am sick to death of hearing such dire narratives. They are now so repetitive and sound like a broken record."

"I know. I am equally tired of it. It is one of the reasons why I have been dragging my feet to tell you all about it."

"Raped? By whom? How? When? Where?"

Jeff could clearly see that she was filled to the gills with indignation. "You have to calm yourself down," he suppliantly pleaded with her.

"Forget about calming down and tell me how Naomi was raped," she demanded angrily.

"I am going to, but you must calm yourself down first. You are not the only one feeling this way. I am still hurting and will forever mourn Naomi's death," he said calmly.

"Naomi was one of the employees in one of
the new generation banks in Enugu called Elite
Bank. She was successful in the interview, where
the bank finally employed a hundred staff out of
about five hundred people who applied. It wasn't
much of a surprise because she graduated with
first-class honours in Banking and Finance at the
University of Nigeria, Nsukka. But as you know, in
our country, especially in financial institutions,
your intelligence isn't a guarantee of getting or
keeping a job, let alone progressing in a career,
especially in these new generation banks. And so,
it was proved on that fateful day. Owners and
chief executives of these new generation banks
would stop at nothing to attract and reel in
potential affluent customers, some of which would
be to encourage young female employees to do
whatever it took to persuade the potential rich
customers to bank with them, even if it came to
sleeping with them. Such was the notoriety these
new generation banks were known for. And such
was the predicament Naomi was up against that
day. Before then, she had used her peerless
ingenuity and creativity based on innovative
banking systems to convince well-off and highly
connected individuals in the society to Bank with
them while dissuading them from the sexual
reciprocity they usually demanded. These
shameless he-goats would use the debasing
parlance to justify their evil act (scratch my back

and I will scratch yours). I still remember one of the ladies, a newlywed in the banking sector, being told by a customer that she should forget using marriage as a deterrent from enjoying sex when the lady told him that she was married, and that sleeping with him would be tantamount to adultery. He derogatorily replied that they were adults and that adultery was for adults. Such was the level of their unchastity. That's how insensitive, inconsiderate, and ungodly they were." On that day, Naomi ran out of luck as she was lured by this monster into his love nest with the collusion and help of the conscienceless bank executives and the hotelier. It wasn't Naomi's first time meeting clients in a hotel. She had been clever and intelligent enough to stir herself out of trouble using her God-given intelligence and oratory. She had single-handedly turned many clients' ventures into world-class business empires by teaching them the new, simple techniques in contemporary businesses. But that day in question, her efforts proved abortive as this evil man had carnal knowledge of her against her will. It was a matter of life and death. Such was the desperation of this evil man to sleep with Naomi. "The choice is yours, Naomi," the customer told her with a disrespectful smile. "Do as you are told and walk away richer and with your life, or be ready to pay with your life if you dare turn down my request," he warned her. "I know girls more beautiful than you who would perform a cartwheel to sleep with me because they know that they will say goodbye to poverty thereafter. You are no better than the next girl down the street. So, stop parading yourself as one from another planet," he said to humiliate her.

"I am not the most beautiful girl. I know that. But I know my worth. I will never compromise my faithfulness and womanhood because of money. I am not hungry, and my husband is taking good care of me. I promised my husband that I would remain faithful to him all the days of our marriage," she told him, refusing to be intimidated.

"You are making things unduly difficult for yourself, young lady. I haven't got all the time in the world to stay here and argue endlessly," he warned her, gritting his teeth in the process. To show he wasn't joking, he pulled out a semi-automatic gun from his portfolio. Then he stopped and looked at Naomi, who now looked petrified. He reintroduced himself to Naomi and told her that he was running out of patience. He said to her that he was only trying to be gentle and persuasive, but if she continued to be unyielding and foolhardy, then he would have no choice but to pull the trigger. He told her that his gun had got a silencer attached to it, so nobody would hear it go off when he pulled the trigger. He told her that he would inform the police, who would arrange for her remains to be removed.

Naomi froze at his boldness to inform the police of the heinous crime he was about to commit.

"Yes, I am the biggest shareholder of this hotel nationwide. With the hotel management, the police and of course your bank in my pocket, you have no chance to resist me or fight back. Married women had thrown themselves at me just to get my attention. They beg me to sleep with them with their husbands aware because they know that their lives and that of their husbands will never be the same thereafter."

Naomi had always been thanatophobic, and that morbid fear of death got the better of her. She had no doubt in her mind that this raging man was going to kill her if she didn't comply. But before she went in to see this man, she had a premonition that something sinister might happen to her. Sensibly and intuitively, she decided to activate her voice recorder. True to type, he took Naomi's phone and powered it off to prevent any interruptions. Then he defiled her like a sex-starved stallion."

"I don't need a penny from you. You are evil," Naomi swore at him when he asked her to give him her bank account so he could transfer a substantial amount of money after defiling her.

"Alternatively, I can give you a blank cheque if you want," he said slyly, pouting his mouth and shrugging his shoulders.

"Go to hell with your cheques and money and leave me alone. You have done your worst. I know I am powerless, but God will judge you," Naomi cursed him as she sobbed and cried.

On her way out, she met one of her classmates at the university. She noticed that Naomi looked devastated and brokenhearted.

She took her to a corner and sat her down. "It seems you work here," Naomi asked her when they were both seated.

"Yes, I do."

"I guessed by the uniform you are wearing."

She then asked Naomi why she looked so sad.

Naomi narrated everything to her.

"He is not going to get away with this," Fidelia, her schoolmate, promised.

Naomi told her not to waste her energy. She told her the status of the culprit in the society and that it would be a wild goose chase to seek justice on her behalf. "When he told me his status and how he had the police in his pocket, I knew that the recording I made would be inconsequential."

"What did you record?" she asked Naomi anxiously. Not even her impenetrable eyes and inscrutable countenance could hide her anger. She could feel the pain of what happened to Naomi in her bones.

"Everything," Naomi responded.

"Can I listen?" she demanded. After listening to it, she nodded satisfyingly and said, "That will do. He might think he has the police in his pocket, but he hasn't got the army. He will pay for this. What happened to you is disgusting and heart-rending, but I think it happened at the right time — a time when there is a quiet revolution sweeping across the army and the police. I am equally excited that the human rights activist, Barrister Chigbo, as we speak, is blazing the trail in the fight against crime and corruption in our society. He carries this aura and charisma that everybody listens to him, including the president and members of the House of Assembly. This might interest him. I will draw his attention to this. I am sure as death that he will throw his weight behind this campaign. He likes to champion the cause of the underdogs and the oppressed. I am confident that he will ensure that this miscreant is nabbed, tried, and jailed accordingly."

"How do you mean? Are you sure of this?" Naomi asked.

"Yes, the new commander of the 82nd Division of the Nigerian army in Enugu is my uncle. He is like a dad to me. My uncle, like Barrister Chigbo, is a human rights activist, and he is making a lot of changes already in the army to regain its lost glory since assuming office. But the icing on the cake is that the new police commissioner posted from Benin City to Enugu is a no-nonsense man as well. He vehemently detests bribery and corruption. Both were present at the swearing-in of the new judges of the Supreme Court just weeks ago in Abuja. There, they unanimously agreed to join forces to tackle corruption in the state head-on. I am phoning him right away to explain what just happened to you. I think that will be a good ground to kick off their campaign against bribery, corruption, and crime in our society. By the time they finish with this monster, the rest of the public will realise that there is no sacred cow in the society anymore."

And that was exactly what happened to him. The evidence against him was overwhelming, including the swab sample Naomi gave the team investigating the crime that matched the rapist. He was arrested, charged, and sentenced for his despicable crime.

Naomi's husband grudgingly accepted Naomi back, knowing all the circumstances. He believed that the child could still be his. However, when Nwadili was born, there was still a hint of doubt and jealousy lingering in his mind. He wanted a DNA test to confirm the paternity of the child. Unfortunately, DNA revealed that the child wasn't his but that of the rapist who is now in prison. Naomi's husband was quoted as saying that Naomi should have been wiser. To him, Naomi should have known better and should have avoided meeting a stranger in the hotel, knowing the likely outcome. He said that common sense should have prevailed. Rational thinking should have warned her of the danger associated with such a visit. He therefore concluded that Naomi didn't do her own bit to avoid what happened to her. He categorically said that he was not prepared to raise another man's child. He made it clear that on no account should anyone from our family try to contact him in whatever role. He did say that Naomi's name was a sore and will always remain an anathema to him forever, and would not like to be reminded of anything associated with her, and that included Nwadili. There you go, little sister. That's how our poor Nwadili is unaware of who his father is up till today."

"Which prison is this savage serving his jail term?" Nkoli asked offhandedly, trying to hide her anger.

"Of what importance is that to you?" he asked her in a toned-down voice.

Exhibiting profound calmness to kill off any suspicion or evil intent she might be harbouring, she said, "Just to make sure he is in the correct place where he will be tortured enough for his crime."

Jeff reassured her he was serving his fourteen-year jail term in the correct prison.

"Just fourteen years. Why not life? He murdered someone. He is supposed to be jailed for life for his heinous crime. You are going to accompany me to the prison, Jeff."

"No matter the length of time he spends in prison, we will never have Naomi back in our midst again. That's why I earnestly enjoin you not to bother to visit him. It will only revive and open an old wound. Remember that the roaring noise of a lion is never welcomed in the backyard of a shepherd. It spells danger. Don't poke the sleeping bear, dear sister. I know you too well, Nkoli. You are going to cop an attitude. Yes, you are going to cause an uproar when you set your eyes on him. I can see and feel the anger in your eyes. Such a visit can only compound your ill feelings about what happened to our sister," Jeff told her persuasively.

"I am assuring you that I won't cause any trouble. I just want to see who Nwadili's dad is, and who is also responsible for our sister's death."

"That's not a clever idea. It will only leave an everlasting bitter memory, and that's not what you want. That's the reason I refused to attend the court sessions throughout the trial. I don't want anything to remind me of what happened to Naomi. Remember I told you we were close. I am still deeply devastated by her death. Again, on what ground are we visiting anyway? The prison officers will never in a month of Sundays allow us to see him, knowing that we are blood relatives of his victim."

"We are not that foolish, are we? We are coming as his friends from Kaduna, where he is from, according to you. You said he hails from Kaduna state and came to Enugu to open another branch of his transport industry."

"Yes, I know, but you only lived in Kano, Nkoli. Okay, how much do you know about Kaduna? You know you will be prepared to answer some specific questions to convince the prison officers that you are actually from Kaduna. They are not just going to take your word for it. You claim we are not silly; the prison officers aren't either."

"I know all the cities and towns in Kaduna: from Zaria to Kachia, Kagoro, Kafanchan,

Kagoma, you name it. It is the same as asking someone from Enugu state about Anambra state or vice versa."

Jeff knew he was fighting a losing battle to dissuade her from visiting the prison. If Nkoli knew all these places in Kaduna supported by her unmatched Hausa speaking ability, it wouldn't be hard to convince the prison officers that they were genuine. "But what if, for argument's sake, they want to know who I am? I know nothing about Kaduna apart from the capital, which is also Kaduna, and of course, the only two popular Hausa words (Zo and kudi), which mean come and money. Nothing more, nothing less."

She laughed. "Don't worry about that, Jeff. I will tell them that you are my husband from the East. There are many Igbo girls married to Hausa men."

"What of tribal marks? You have none in your face."

"You are now showing your in-depth naivety and lack of knowledge about Hausa religion and culture. Hausa Christians can go without tribal marks of any sort. In fact, tribal marks are gradually waning away for both Muslim and Christian Hausas. Again, Hausa Christians are more likely to marry outside their clan and communities, and that will explain why I married you."

It seemed she had an answer for everything. Jeff chuckled, and she laughed. Despite Nkoli's cool-headedness in addressing the issue, Jeff still had a chunk of belief that she was going to turn the prison upside down in annoyance. The anger in her face said it all. Something kept telling him that she would avenge all their family misfortunes on this vicious prisoner.

CHAPTER 27

It was straightforward. Easier than falling off a log. Like she had thought and believed, it was a doddle to convince the prison officers that they were friends of Mr Sanni Michael. Nkoli had mesmerised the prison officers with her unblemished Hausa language when one of the prison officers spoke to her in Hausa just to clear the little doubt lingering in his mind. Nkoli was not only good at speaking Hausa, but she also spoke it flawlessly with a typical Hausa accent. Any remaining doubt in the minds of the prison officers was wiped off by the smart hijab scarf she wore over her head, neck, and part of her chest.

Convinced beyond all reasonable doubt that they were genuine, the prison officer said, "Stay here, guys, I will get him for you."

"How did you even know his name? You said you never attended any of the trials," Nkoli asked on second thought.

"Yes, you are right. I got his name from the local papers."

"What are we going to say to this prisoner when he comes to meet us, especially having told the officers that we are his friends?" Jeff asked Nkoli, feeling unsettled. "Mr Sanni Michael doesn't know who we are and is going to give away an expression of unacknowledgement on seeing us, and that undoubtedly will set off the alarm that will land us in all sorts of problems. I doubt we are going to be allowed to leave the premises as they might believe we are harbouring evil intents for making the visit."

Nkoli looked a bit bewildered at Jeff's line of thought. Alarmed by Jeff's supposition, she swallowed some air, rubbed two hands briskly together before clutching the back of her head.

Jeff guessed she never gave a thought to that. "We are digging a hole for ourselves. This dangerous journey could land us in a big mess," he reiterated, voice soft and convincing.

"You are making sense, Jeff. To be honest with you, I never for once thought about it this way, I mean, the repercussions if he fails to acknowledge who we are. We need to leave," she said regrettably. She stamped her foot firmly against the floor in frustration and said, "I am not happy that I am not going to meet this savage of a man."

But their decision was too little, too late because walking gingerly and edging towards them was an old, ill-looking man flanked and supported by two inmates.

Jeff told the officer that they just remembered they had an appointment they needed to attend urgently, and they would have to come some other day to see their friend.

"What is the need of disturbing this very ill man to come and see you guys?" the middle-aged warden asked disappointedly.

"Is that the man we have come to visit?" Nkoli inquired confusedly.

"You just told me, Mr Sanni Michael is your friend. Don't you know again who you have come to visit?" the prison officer asked angrily, and now a bit suspicious of them.

Jeff and Nkoli looked at each other nervously. They believed that they had landed themselves in trouble.

Then the old man saved the day as he began to shed some tears seeing Nkoli. He didn't even have the strength to cry because he was that lethargic.

"The inmates gently lowered him like a box holding fragile ornaments onto one of the padded chairs opposite them and left with the prison officer.

Nkoli froze and felt ghastly recognising him. Her lips appeared instantaneously dry and colourless as if someone who has been given an HIV diagnosis.

Jeff panicked at the pictures she was seeing.

"Is there something I am missing here?" Jeff quizzed worryingly. "What is going on, Nkoli?"

Nkoli regained some composure and said, "I know him, Jeff… I f…king know who he is."

"You know him? How?"

She kept quiet. The quietness and wry smile on her face were more vocal than the roar of a wounded lion.

"First of all, he is an imposter. His name is not Sanni Michael, he is Dan Dauda." She suddenly rose from her chair as one propelled by an unhindered force and grabbed the old man by the throat.

"Oh my God! What do you think you are doing, Nkoli? You want to commit murder in the prison yard. What has come over you? Have you completely lost your mind? You promised to be sensible and to keep your emotions in check. Will you let go of him before someone sees what is going on here?" Jeff lashed out at her.

"Let me kill him and go to prison, Jeff. Let me be the sacrificial lamb. I am better off dead than allow this man to regain his freedom and get out there to commit more atrocities."

"I would rather you didn't, Nkoli. That will complicate issues." Jeff could barely look at Nkoli's face…. It depicted disgust and hatred. "If you want to go to prison, that is your choice. I am not ready. You have forgotten that I am on this mission with you. If you are arrested, so will I, and that's something I am not ready for."

Then the old man spoke out. "You will gain nothing from killing me, even though I deserve death. And just a point of correction, Nkoli, I am not an imposter. Sanni Michael is my real name. I will come to the details in a moment if you give me audience."

That rekindled Nkoli's anger. She felt a big slight and landed a big right-hand punch to his face that burst his lips.

Jeff had to intervene at this juncture. He knew the impending repercussions of what was happening between Nkoli and the old man. Jeff knew it was either that he did something urgently or risked Nkoli and him joining the old man behind bars. Using his manly strength, Jeff loosened Nkoli's grip on the man's throat. "What do you think you are doing, Nkoli?" he asked, a flash of anger and disbelief in his face.

"You would do a lot worse if you were in my position, Jeff. He doesn't deserve to be alive on the strength of the atrocities he had committed."

Jeff wasn't in doubt that this man represented evil in her sight, but at the same time, he believed that his sister was going about it the wrong way.

"Whatever your reason, this kind of violence will never be admissible for trying to kill someone you have come to visit. How do you know that the officers will not even believe that the main reason for our visit is to kill him?"

"It is easy for you to sit there and rant because you have never had any dealings with him. That's why," she reprimanded Jeff.

Jeff didn't look nonplussed; he was stunned by what he was seeing. They had come to visit the man who was responsible for Naomi's death, and now, from Nkoli's reactions and revolting anger, she knew who he was — a dangerous man. Whatever it was, Jeff knew Nkoli was going about it the wrong way when he spoke again. "Nkoli, I am sorry I am not going to take your side if you decide to be maniacal and senseless like this. As you can see, this old man is more sensible than you. Can't you see how calm and composed he is despite your huffy attitude? Can I know who this man is? I need to know what this man represents in your life to cause this much grief and hatred."

"Do you really want to know? ... he is a ritualist, a gambler, a rapist, a kidnapper, and a gigolo. Lest I forget, he is into human and sex trafficking as well ... he is evil personified."

If this man weren't sitting before Jeff, he would have thought he was Douglas. There wasn't much difference between him and Douglas based on what Nkoli described about him. Jeff had now started putting two and two together, and the answer was only pointing in one obvious direction. *Could this be Patrick?* Jeff imagined in his heart. "He is Patrick, isn't he?" he finally asked.

"He is not. He is worse than Patrick. He was Patrick's mentor."

Jeff's mouth gaped as he contemplated a person worse than Patrick.

"I recently discovered while chatting with a childhood friend on social media that it was this man who actually nurtured Patrick into the evil man he turned out to be," Nkoli continued. "Can you see now why I want him dead, because he represents nothing but danger, not only to us but to everyone? This ugly monster was the same man Patrick was using more regularly to rape me and Nwakaego in Kano. He was his regular customer."

Jeff could barely contain his anger hearing that bit. His blood boiled, realising the magnitude of his offence. His action somehow led to the death of Naomi and directly led to Nkoli leaving Kano and finding herself in all kinds of trouble, including turning into a prostitute. Jeff shot him an evil look and said in his heart, *You are getting what you deserve.*

The old man in all of this looked away in shame as he kept unbelievable calmness while pressing down his burst lips, which were still bleeding. Bringing his right thumb from his mouth to confirm the bleeding had stopped, he then said, "Nkoli, no human being that passed through your ordeal could have acted differently. But there is no need to burst your blood vessels like you burst my lips. Nemesis, as you can see, has eventually caught up with me. Don't make yourself a murderer on my account. I am already getting what I deserve. You have your eyes, haven't you? You can clearly see that I am a walking corpse…. cancer has eaten me up. The doctors said that I had a few months to live. So, you see, you came at the right time."

His face looked sober but with some guilt and regret. His hands shook at every movement … his mouth quivered each time he allowed a word to escape from it, showing off his sunken eyes and bony cheeks.

Nkoli, obviously not satisfied with his terminal illness, turned to Jeff and asked, "Is there any other place people go besides hell when they die?"

"Heaven, of course," Jeff quickly replied.

"Will you just cut it out and be more reasonable. Of course, everyone knows about heaven."

"Oh yes, I remember, Catholics believe that some go to purgatory when they die."

"Purgatory? Where is it?"

"In Catholicism, it is a place of purification for sinners before they are allowed to go to heaven."

Nkoli laughed uproariously in derision and said, "That is surely a jest, Jeff." "This one," jerking her fingers at the man. "Purgatory will have no place for him. Nothing can purge him of his iniquities. I think Lucifer is going to contend with him when he gets to hell."

"One thing I can say in all of this is that God is not man. It is not up to us to decide where one goes after death. It's God's decision. God will have mercy on whom he will have mercy. I truly regret all my horrible deeds. I am not proud of my wrongdoings. I wish I could take them back. I have confessed all my sins to God. I am now born again," he said serenely.

"You are born again because you know your time is up. I have heard it before. When people like you have riddled themselves with all kinds of sin, they then turn to God for forgiveness. Don't you think you are cashing in on God's mercy?" she asked him glumly.

"Don't let the past and unforgiving spirit keep you from accepting Christ," the old man said, sounding religious.

"Shut your mouth or I will punch it again. What do you know? What do you think you are doing, you common criminal? Don't make me believe you are trying to preach," she shouted at him, sarcasm in her voice.

He shrugged his shoulders resignedly. "Like I said, you came at the right time because Patrick passed on a lot of information to pass to you before he passed on. He died a repentant man. May the good Lord accept his poor soul," he devoutly prayed with two hands joined together and head bowed in veneration.

"We need to leave here, Jeff, we really need to go, otherwise I am definitely going to commit murder," she said, hearing him mention Patrick and seeing him preaching for salvation.

"You must not let your emotions get the better of you," Jeff admonished her.

"So, you want me to sit here and listen to someone that raped me and my twin sister? You want me to sit here and listen to him blabbing like a sot? Is that what you want, big bro? Are you for real?" she asked, voice sharp as a razor.

"Do you want to hear about your father, Patrick?" the old man asked her calmly.

"Go to hell with your story," she replied with venom in her voice.

"I would have thought that you would be in a better mood to listen about Patrick, your father, now you know he is dead," he serenely enjoined her.

"For the love of God Almighty, can you shut your trap and stop referring to him as my father. Just call him Patrick," she warned him ferociously.

"I know he is not your biological father. He told me."

"He told you?"

"Yes, he did before he became born again."

Nkoli gave out a smile that bore so much pain. Jeff could see she was trying her best to hold her anger, which was snowballing out of control. She held her two hands together and placed them over her face. Shaking her head disconcertingly, she said, "The world should celebrate the exit of an evil genius," referring to the passing of Patrick. "Unfortunately, the world still harbours the most notorious criminal," she said, pointing her finger at the old man. "You need to die. You are clearly not worthy to be alive, and you know it," Nkoli asserted convincingly.

With the same calmness and a faint smile, the old man replied, "Of course, I know. You don't need to reiterate it, neither do I need to re-admit that I deserve death. What I am more concerned is what happens to people like you that deserve to live," he explained, pointing at Jeff and Nkoli in a voice that could be misconstrued as slight. But he wasn't trying to be sarcastic in any way. He knew the hardships his evil deeds had caused so many souls, Nkoli and her stepmother the most.

"I can't even believe I am still sitting here having this conversation with you."

"I am not holding you against your wish, nor am I forcing you to listen to me. But it would be nice if you could swallow your hatred and anger just for a moment to listen to what I have to tell you. The choice is yours," he finally said, puffing his wasted chest out and extending his bony hands in opposite directions. He sounded genuinely born again, but you could still see an element of arrogance and bravery in his voice and body language.

Nkoli turned to Jeff, looking more baffled than riled up by the old man's remarks. Her body language told Jeff she was asking him to make the decision, so he did.

"We are ready to listen to your story. Make it brief, though; we haven't got all the time in the world," Jeff said flatly.

"Neither have I," he responded. Putting one hand on his chest, as if he were trying to support his point, he coughed continuously as one suffering from whooping cough or tuberculosis and said, "I can't hold a lengthy conversation because my heart and lungs are immensely compromised. Again, the prison officers may be on their way to take me back to my cell for my medication. So, I will hit the nail on the head without rigmaroles. Don't worry, I won't miss important points," he reassured them with a weak smile.

"Patrick, before his death, had a terrible nightmare," Mr Sanni began his story that invoked more anger than sympathy on the strength of what Nkoli could remember him for. "In the dream," he continued, "He lay in the wilderness inhabited by all kinds of animals, from the dangerous ones to those that almost appeared tamed and docile. He was completely incapacitated and helpless. The very wild, vicious ones like the hyenas and leopards would go for a hunt and would bring home the kill, where Patrick was laid and began to devour them. Though the animals observed the pecking order when they fed, they would still ensure the weak ones got turns to feed. The strong ones were like the army guards ensuring the enemies didn't trespass or encroach. They were very protective of the youngsters, the aged, and the weaklings. When there was rumbling and chaos, the alpha male or the matriarch stepped in to quell the fuss before it escalated. Waking up from the sleep but still in a twilight state, a voice broke through the silence in his room and said, "Beasts of the wild provide, protect, and cater for the young, old and weakling in their midst. Did you do the same when you were in that position? Weren't you surprised that the animals would wander afar to look for their meals despite you lying right there before them? They could have easily feasted on you if they wanted, but they didn't. In your situation, you exposed and attacked the people you were supposed to protect."

"Then, he became fully awake before he could answer the question, with sweat pouring down his back as if he had been submerged in a pool of water. But the crux of the matter was the fact that he was actually unable to move any part of his body on full awakening, making him think he was still having the nightmare. The more he tried to free himself from what seemed like sleep paralysis, the more he found himself trapped in that catatonic stupor-like condition. Then a thought came to him to analyse the dream and the question he was asked at the end, and he knew what to say at that point. "I am sorry, Lord," Patrick prayed repentantly, with tears in his eyes. That was all he needed to set himself free from his lame body."

"So?" Nkoli queried.

"So, God forgave him," the old man answered.

"Just like that?" Jeff asked indignantly.

"Yes. Just like that. You see, my son, God is not a man and will never be. In our eyes, Patrick's sins seemed unforgivable and irredeemable, but not with God. Patrick humbled himself and acknowledged his sins before God. That's all God wants from you and me," he said humbly, pointing at himself, Jeff, and Nkoli.

"No. Just point at yourself," Nkoli interjected discourteously. She didn't want to be seen to be in the same boat with someone like him.

"God's mercy is unquantifiable and incomprehensible. He doesn't reason like us. He doesn't concern himself with the length of time you spent in a sinful state. He is only concerned with the moment you confess them and turn away from them," Sanni continued.

"And?" Nkoli prodded. You could see she was far from being convinced that somebody like Patrick could be forgiven for all the atrocities he committed by just making a simple sentence consisting of just four words.

"Two days after the first dream," he continued. "Patrick dreamt again where he was commanded by the same mysterious voice to get rid of all occult materials in his possession. He was also commanded to make restitution of all monies and earthly materials he had obtained during his occult practice. He obeyed the command and literally started his life from scratch … a pauper. A year later, he ran into one of the apprentices who served him when he was still a good man. To abridge the story, this apprentice had become a business mogul owning chains of businesses nationally and internationally. He remembered the good old days when Patrick was still a good man, a God-fearing and benevolent man. He took pity on his pitiful, indigent situation. Without a second thought, he decided to engage him as a business partner, knowing how industrious he used to be. The favour of God was clearly with Patrick. Everything he touched turned to gold and diamonds. In no time, he became exceptionally progressive in the business, even beyond the wildest imagination of his business partner, Alhaji Bello.

Patrick spent every energy he had to convert me. It took time, but when I saw how easy things were going for him, I couldn't help but concede to his pressure. And true to type, my life changed for the better both spiritually and financially.

Unfortunately, Patrick was struck by a weird illness that ate him up in a matter of months. When it was clear he wasn't going to survive the ailment, he decided to make a Will, which I was so much involved in, not because of what I would gain from it, but the role I was going to play in it. So, there you go."

"I am not too sure you are abridging the story, but can you hit the nail on the head as you promised?" Jeff pleaded with him, now realising that time was no longer their friend.

He raised his voice to draw the attention of one of the prisoners who was passing by. "Can you get me one of the prison officers if you can, young man?" he asked the prisoner.

"With all pleasure, sir," the prisoner responded, and ran off to fetch a warden.

"You are well respected here in the prison," Jeff cajoled him.

"Most of them know who I was in the outside world, and they know their palms will be greased handsomely if they run little errands like this," he said with a look of a shrewd business tycoon.

He told the prison officer in what sounded like a command to go to his room and fetch him the box under his bed. He went and returned three minutes later with it.

"Here we go. This is the juicy box," he said hilariously, taking delivery of it from the officer. Gently and carefully, he opened the box and pulled the documents that held full details of Patrick's Will and handed them over to Nkoli.

"As you can see, the Will was drafted in two parts. The first part was for Nkoli, if she could be found after he passed on. The second part was that it should go to charity, most especially people who had suffered any form of abuse, especially physical and sexual abuse."

"You can imagine how glad I was when I set my eyes on you. Don't try to dissect the meaning of the Will here. You will need to take it home and have a good read of it. All I can say for now is that you will need an expert in economics, business, and finance to oversee the management of the business empire he had bequeathed to you. It is worth billions of naira. You will also need an estate manager to handle the vast lands and properties. Also, you will need a financial expert and accountant to manage his monies in Nigerian and foreign banks."

Just as Nkoli was contemplating what to do with the influx of wealth and information being put into her care, the old man opened the box and brought out what melted Nkoli's heart. It was her first doll — a teddy bear she was presented with on her second birthday. Despite the doll looking scruffy, dingy, and fluff-less, it was still able to evoke huge and pleasant memories of her growing up and the attachment she had to the teddy bear. Then he brought out assorted pictures of Nkoli, Patrick and Nwakaego when she was only a toddler and their happy pictures on holidays.

Jeff could see that each presentation was like a balm that clearly soothed the pain in Nkoli's bruised soul. Anger was slowly and steadily being replaced by solemnity.

Then, he showed Nkoli the first letter she wrote to Patrick, where she adored and called him the best dad in the whole wide world. Then, he presented Patrick's response letter where he called Nkoli special and the apple of his eyes and how he would remain her pillar and protector all the days of her life. Then he finally presented the letter Patrick wrote on his deathbed:

"To a wonderful daughter. A shining, bright star. You never got what you deserved. I failed you morally and spiritually. I went against all my promises. I was overcome and consumed by my evil passion. I succumbed to the spur of the moment. At a time, I should have led by example, I let myself be open to the evil men and women who took full advantage and destroyed in a matter of months what took us years to build. My heart bleeds in anguish. My heart feels hollow and deeply hurt by my actions. It is all right if I am not forgiven. But please, don't let my evil ways deter you from giving your life to Christ. My promise is that I will always pray and watch over you from up there."

Patrick.

Jeff was lost for words. Nkoli was clinging feverishly to her heart, which seemed melted by the events unfolding before her.

Then the old man continued and said, "That's Patrick's story. My own story isn't as straightforward as his. I don't need any introduction. My conversion lasted while Patrick lived. As they say, nature abhors a vacuum, because as soon as Patrick passed away, I got back to the notorious *sundown confraternity* and got reinfected with their deadly, ugly ways of living once again. Nevertheless, I kept my new name, Sanni Michael, which I took the first time I got converted and was later born again. I didn't go Scot-free the second time I joined the confraternity. Of course, that's why I am where I am today. Nonetheless, I am indescribably happy and indebted to God's infinite mercy, who decided to give me a second chance even though I am paying for it with my life now. If you would accept my offer, my Will is drafted in one part. Half of my wealth is yours, while the remaining is for charity and to help people who have suffered any form of abuse and neglect. I, however, made a clause in the Will where I recommended that the lawyer willed everything to charity if you were not found. That is my humble way to ensure that people, especially the vulnerable, don't fall victim to people like me. I will give you our lawyers' contact details. They will finalise everything while I am still here. Don't worry about the source of my wealth. It is genuine and untainted. All illegal wealth I acquired had been restituted already to the orphanage by my lawyers."

Then, he finally opened the bag and brought out a bag that made Nkoli cry. It was her first school bag that she used in the nursery. "Put all the documents there. Patrick highlighted the significance and how you were and still are very fond of the bag."

Nkoli was overpowered by so many old memories the events had invoked. "I forgive you,

Sanni. I forgive Patrick wherever he is. I forgive everyone I have been bearing any form of grudge. This is the most sober moment I have ever witnessed all my life," Nkoli exclaimed. The thought of St Paul came alive in her mind that moment. She remembered all the atrocities he committed while he was Saul, and how he ended up the strongest apostle of Christ after his conversion and repentance.

They were momentarily drowned in a spontaneous moment of tranquillity. Sanni supported his bowed head with his hands. Lifting it up thereafter, he took a humble look, first at Nkoli and then at Jeff.

Jeff guessed he knew what was going on in his troubled mind. He wanted to ask about Naomi after he understood that Jeff and Nkoli were her siblings.

He lacked the courage. Apologetically, he said, "I don't know how to say it, I don't even know whether I have the right to ask," regrets and unworthiness conspicuous in his expression. Then he summoned courage and asked, "How is she?"

Another round of silence swept through them. Both Nkoli and Jeff lacked the willpower to answer.

"I should have allowed things to stay the way they were, shouldn't I?" he asked regrettably.

"Not really. You deserve to know the outcome of your handiwork," Jeff sarcastically replied with a lump of anger once again in his throat.

His eyes flickered through Jeff and Nkoli in exasperation as if he knew the impending answer to his question.

"Yes, Naomi died giving birth to your baby," Jeff informed him disconsolately.

He couldn't say a word. Like one in a drug haze state, he bent down and blinked away a few teardrops on hearing about Naomi's death and said, "What else can I say? My evil is now complete. I am deeply sorry for everything." The guilt that accompanied the news swept through him like a typhoon on a plain field, making it impossible for him to make any enquiries about Naomi's baby ... like the gender, whereabouts, and so on.

CHAPTER 28

It was a monumental inheritance to put it mildly. There was a lot of paperwork, emails, phone calls, formal and informal meetings, legal and estate consultations to formalise the handover of businesses and transfer of shares, money, and estates. It took about eight weeks to put the transfers and the handovers into proper perspective. It would have taken a lot longer if not for Sanni's involvement using his lawyers, accountants, and estate management consultants in the transfers and takeovers.

Nkoli distanced herself from active participation in the business scheme of things, even though everything was willed to her. She had seen this as an opportunity to further her education, which was truncated by a series of unfortunate events in Kano. She willingly entrusted the management into the care of Jeff and Jane and would only get involved on weekends or when school was not in session. Jeff and Jane, nevertheless, had always made sure that Nkoli was informed about any major decisions about the business empire, and would abide by Nkoli's decisions or at least humbly challenge them if they genuinely thought or believed that such decisions and contributions would be detrimental to the business.

Jeff and Jane were committed and had continued to run the business flawlessly, though with the constant help from magnates introduced to them by Sanni.

The business heavily involved lot of meetings, consultations, and travels. As Jane was returning from one of the business trips that beautiful Saturday morning after supervising the delivery of some consignment of Mercedes' spare parts from Germany in one of their warehouses at Ladipo auto market, she felt symptoms she had never felt before, but had heard about them in the past. She wanted to ignore the sudden shooting pain and spasms she felt in her tummy and lower back. But when they came in quicker, stronger successions minutes later, she knew she had to pay more attention to the symptoms. She was about twenty-five minutes away from home by then. She decided to speed up, but the traffic was heavy, preventing her from accelerating as she would have wanted. She needed to get home as quickly as possible to check herself out. But what followed shortly after made her change her mind. She felt wet in her Jeans. She had never had any issues with her bladder. She had always had full bladder control. She wouldn't understand why she was wet down below. What came to her mind was difficult for her to take in. A combination of waves of contractions and wetness could only mean one thing. But she was so scared to think about it, let alone believe it, because up till that time, she had never felt any significant symptom related to pregnancy. She had always had an irregular menstrual cycle. According to her doctor, she had a condition called polycystic ovary syndrome (PCOS). Her menstrual cycles were so irregular that at times she would go up to four months or more without any. But what was even more mind-boggling was the fact that she saw her period two months ago.

Though Jane didn't know anything about cryptic pregnancy, she at least knew at that point she should be changing her destination from home to the nearest hospital. Thankfully, St Matilda's hospital was closer to where she was than home.

The contractions were getting stronger, more regular, and more distressing as she drove to the hospital. She was screaming in pain and fidgeting and had struggled to concentrate on her driving. Her driving was now erratic as she squeezed through cars and buses. It was by a hair's breadth that she missed having a head-on collision with an oncoming lorry as she drove into the opposite lane trying to overtake a bus. The lorry driver blared his horn so loud and cursed her as he swerved away from driving into her.

Jane thought it was a waste of time to clear off the road to make an emergency phone call because there was no breakdown lane to do so. The roads were completely jammed with traffic. Even if there was an emergency lane, Jane knew that it would take three times the time to get the help she wanted. She had no choice but to keep driving. Her back was now against the wall. She mustered the courage to keep going, gritting her teeth in pain, and ignoring the impending danger.

She made it to the hospital twenty minutes later — twenty minutes that seemed like forever. Opening the door and forgetting, or didn't bother to close it, she ran when she could, crawled when overwhelmed by spasms, and cried when the pain was unbearable. She didn't care whether the car would be stolen, nor did she care that she was wringing wet from the amniotic fluid that had just broken. All she was after was to know what was wrong with her. Amid her pain and discomfort, Jane took solace in the fact that she was going to be a mother if what she was suspecting was right. But breaking the news to Jeff would be the icing on the cake. Jeff had been broodier than a woman. Jane, on many occasions, had seen him buy gifts and chocolates for the children. She had seen him at times playing football with their neighbours' little kids. Jane usually felt guilty for not being able to give him a child of his own. Jane knew Jeff would have even loved it better to be playing football with his own child.

Jeff had always wanted a baby, and now I am about to give him one, Jane thought, a thought that helped to reduce the pain and discomfort she had been subjected to.

A staff nurse of the hospital, coming back from her break, saw what was going on and knew at once what Jane's problem might be. She had been in the business long enough and had seen similar scenarios in the past. Other staff joined her when she shouted for help, and they assisted Jane straight to the labour room. With no time to spare, Jane was helped into the birthing couch where they conducted preliminary investigations and palpations.

Jane's labour time was unprecedentedly short and smooth, especially with her being a primigravida. If not for the high-pitched, rhythmic cry of her baby, she wouldn't have known she had had him. Being her first pregnancy, they had expected the labour to have lasted longer than that. But within one and a half hours of admission, Jane had already reached 10cm dilation, and with the encouragement of the two nurses and an obstetrician, Jane had her baby with the least discomfort and no complications. It was a bouncing baby boy and weighed 2.8kg. The nurses were over the moon about the successful delivery. Since it was an emergency delivery, they didn't have the time to make phone calls. They went ahead based on the much information Jane was able to provide as her labour pain allowed her.

After cleaning the baby up, they wrapped him in a blue swaddle blanket before handing him over to his mother. He was strikingly handsome, the hair almost blonde with sparkling blue eyes, and tiny hands he wiggled over his face as if he were trying to shield his eyes from the bright light, which was still alien to him.

The nurses and the obstetrician believed Jane was married to a white man.

"Congratulations," they said with smiling faces after the delivery. "He must be excited to hear the good news," the nurse said gladly, referring to her husband as she handed the baby over to her.

"I bet he will," the obstetrician said gladly, face beaming with a longing smile.

Jane's smile disappeared as soon as she set her eyes on her baby. She looked at the baby, and then at the staff. She didn't know whether to cry or scream. She was tempted to accuse the staff of swapping her baby, but resisted it. She was wide awake and fully conscious as she had him. She saw and witnessed everything first-hand, from start to finish. It would be sheer stupidity to think that her baby was swapped. Again, St

Matilda's hospital had an untainted reputation. The hospital's good reputation followed it like a shadow. Jane knew and believed it was her son, but how?

The medical staff saw Jane's discomposure. They noticed that her reaction was at odds with what was supposed to be a heartwarming moment. They had expected beautiful smiles from her beautiful face. Rather, they saw sadness and fear.

"Can we have your husband's number to break the good news to him, please?" one of the nurses demanded.

Jane couldn't answer her. She began to sob instead. A few hours ago, she was overly excited and couldn't wait to break the good news to Jeff. Now, she preferred to be led to the gallows to mention what had just happened to him.

Jeff wasn't in town. He had travelled to Abuja to attend the annual board meetings, destined to last the whole week.

The staff at that point began to put two and two together. One of them asked, "Are you married?"

Jane wiped her tears and runny nose and nodded.

The nurses and the obstetrician didn't need any more evidence as to why Jane's mood wasn't in a good place. They knew straight away that the little boy wasn't her husband's.

"But why?" The obstetrician asked her. "You are too beautiful to be doing stuff like this. Why? I am convinced that no reasonable man would look at another woman when he has a wife as beautiful and elegant as you are. I should have expected the same from you. You look so honourable and decent to be living this kind of life. Being pregnant means that you are not even practising safe sex. You could have easily contracted and passed on some sexually transmitted diseases to your husband," the obstetrician continued.

That turned Jane's sob into full-blown wailing. She couldn't believe that she was being accused of infidelity. "You won't understand, I didn't cheat on my husband. I didn't," Jane vigorously defended herself.

"So, the child is your husband's, then?" The obstetrician intervened.

"He is not," Jane said in a quiet, guilty voice.

"*Abeg! Forget it!*" one of the nurses exclaimed sarcastically in Pidgin English. "There is nothing difficult to understand here, Madam. The child is not your husband's, and you have not cheated on him. Can't you see how irreconcilable that sounds? Before today, I had heard our people say that there is no virgin in a labour room. Today, you have negated that proverb. The only choice you are leaving us with is that you conceived without sin. That could be sacrilegious and blasphemous if that is what you are claiming, because that state of purity belongs to only one Lady in the scripture — the Virgin Mary. So be careful about what you say," the other nurse continued the verbal assault. And they smirked mischievously. They were clearly making a mockery of Jane now.

Jane cried even more. Her cry jolted the little boy, and he began to cry even louder. As he cried, natural instinct took over. He wanted to suckle as he moved his mouth from one end to another. Instinctively, he started to tear at Jane's clothes with his tiny hands as he craved her attention.

"Please, can you stop this ... tears and feed your baby," one of the nurses told her. She wanted to say crocodile tears, but was able to stop herself before she said it.

"Don't let him go hungry, please. He is not responsible for your...," the other nurse chipped in. She wanted to say waywardness.

Jane suddenly gathered her mojo back. She knew she hadn't cheated on Jeff. She knew how the pregnancy was conceived. She remembered that Friday evening clearly. Hassan had come home and willingly volunteered to cook. "You have been so busy today, Jane — getting the girls ready — taking them to school — bringing them back — going to the market — cooking for everyone — taking some food to Hana in the hospital where she was looking after Hassan's dad when he was admitted for surgery to remove the gall stones in his gallbladder. Have some rest. I will cook and serve you tonight," Hassan told her.

Jane remembered feeling exceptionally tired and sleepy after the meals, so she barely managed to walk herself to her room thereafter. She thought it was because she was too tired from being too active all day, but it wasn't, because she remembered waking up drowsy at about 2am in the morning to find Hassan about to leave her room with only a bath towel tied around his waist, with folded tissue paper in his hand. "What are you doing in my room, Hassan?" Jane asked, looking bemused and confounded in her sleepy state. She noticed that her nightie was rolled up so that one could almost see her knickers. She quickly rolled it down with her eyes still firmly fixed on the dumbstruck Hassan, who now looked like a person who had swallowed a live scorpion. "What are you doing, or what have you done? I should have asked." She snarled at Hassan, who was nothing to her now but a sly dog. Jane wondered how he got into her room, only to remember she might have forgotten to lock her room due to her excessive tiredness, or he had always had the spare key to her room handy, waiting for an opportunity like that to present itself.

"Nothing, I am only looking for the remote control, sorry, I meant shower gel," Hassan finally managed to answer, aghast like one who has seen a ghost.

"Nothing? Remote control? Shower gel? With tissue paper in your hand? Oh my God! What have you done, Hassan? And when did you start keeping remote control and shower gel in my room? You look lost and guilty. You know you are up to no good, mooching about in my room at this odd hour, almost naked," Jane said, voice laden with anger. The time also coincided with the usual time he beat her wife up and then banged her minutes later and then ran the tap for a shower. Everything was pointing in that direction and following the same sequence, and pattern, except he didn't beat her up first as he would with Hana.

Jane believed he had done something to her and was about to leave to have a shower, as he would always do after having sex with Hana.

She would have gone to check herself out in the toilet, but she believed that Hassan must have wiped her clean with the tissue paper in his hand, and she was seriously tempted to ask him to give her the tissue paper as the evidence of what he had done could still be there. Again, she lacked the courage for the obvious consequence that might follow if she did.

He hasn't beaten me, but I think he had done the other one, Jane had thought. Jane concluded it was that night that Hassan perpetrated the evil deed. Jane had no doubt about it, especially after their encounter with him in Tunisia, with him spiking Jeff's drink. She believed Hassan had spiked her food that night to have his way.

"We can't leave things the way they are, madam, I am afraid," the obstetrician voiced out her concern, interrupting Jane's train of thought. "We need the details of your next of kin just in case. We don't want to be blamed for not following procedures," the obstetrician insisted.

"Who is your next of kin, please?" One of the nurses asked, still looking disappointed with Jane's infidelity, which they were now gradually escalating to prostitution.

"It is my husband," Jane answered shyly.

"Can we have his name and phone number, please?"

"You can't call him, please. If you tell him what has just happened, he will die of heartbreak. For starters, he didn't know I was pregnant, and neither did I. I am sure he can't handle it."

"So, what do you want us to do?" the obstetrician asked her, now looking more confused than her.

"I don't know," she answered.

"Neither do we," the staff said in unison. "We need someone who is related to you who can stand in just in case the need arises."

"Okay, okay, I am going to phone someone that might help," Jane warily assured them. She thought of Tessy, but remembered what Tessy did to her relationship with Jeff. Something told her that Tessy might seize the opportunity to slag her off and walk her way back to Jeff if she told her. The only credible options were Vera and Doris, her childhood friends, but they were living far away now in the East, though she was unreliably informed that Vera had moved back to Lagos. Of what help could they be in this kind of twisted situation? She wasn't sure. She called Vera, nevertheless, but it went straight into voicemail. Jane left a message for her to call her as soon as possible, citing an emergency. Jane told the staff that Vera would call her back, even though she knew the possibility of that happening was slim.

The little boy seemed awake but calm after being breastfed — a task Jane unwillingly performed. Without the insistence of the staff members, Jane was unlikely to have breastfed him. Not that she hated the child, but for the mere fact that he was Hassan's and reminded her of him.

While they were waiting for the call back from Vera, one of the nurses asked Jane again why she cheated on her husband. "Isn't he good enough in bed, or what?"

"He is," Jane answered, but felt disgusted with herself for answering the rude question.

"Then why?" She continued to pester her.

"I did not cheat on my husband. Why are you asking me again?" Jane replied with a raised voice.

"Ehh!" They screamed sarcastically. "You didn't cheat on your husband, and you are with a white baby, and you don't want your husband to know about it. Really? We don't want to sound derogatory, but your explanation sounds ridiculous."

Jane was very annoyed with the staff now. She had had it to her teeth and did not want to cover the secret anymore. So, she told them her whole life story, but still maintained that Jeff must be kept out of the whole thing. Jane told them that Jeff had suffered so much because of her and wouldn't like to add this present saga to the list.

The staff were touched by Jane's story and were sad that a man could be that callous to perpetrate such evil on a vulnerable lady seeking refuge in his home. They understood Jane's plight after listening to her heartbreaking story and decided to go with her line of thought, which was to keep the baby in a motherless baby home. They would lie to the hospital management and the motherless baby's home that Jane disappeared and abandoned the child after birth in the hospital, and that they discovered that she gave them wrong details about herself, except Hassan's details, whom she wanted them to contact to come and take his baby.

"Well, we can't take the baby to a motherless baby's home without a name. Do you have one in mind to go into his birth certificate?"

"What can I say? I have to give him his father's name." Jane named him Hassan Slimane Jr after his father. Jane gave the staff Hassan's details and pleaded with them to ensure that they contact him to come for the baby. She said that she wouldn't like the child to be in a motherless baby's home when he had a full-fledged father. Jane wrote a letter that they would give Hassan when he arrived to take his baby:

What can I say? There we have it. You have achieved your goal, and in so doing, ruined my life. You have brought to my domain what I have always dreaded. My heart is pierced and wounded by your selfishness and lack of self-control. Now, your wish has been fulfilled. I have got you a baby boy. Isn't that what you have always wanted? It is only God who will judge people like you. I wish you knew and understood the saying: that true peace of mind is achieved by resisting passion and not yielding to it. The only request I am making is that you bring him up the right way. Teach him to be content with what he has. Teach him to respect women and treat them right. Teach him the virtue not to be ensnared and consumed by the concupiscence of the flesh. Teach him to uphold the truth in all circumstances. Let our little Hassan know that uprightness is a virtue. Don't let him be a wife-beater. Let him know that children learn what they live and live what they learn. If you have the courage, tell him why I am not in his life, but most of all, tell him always that his mummy loves him dearly.

Jane.

Jane was in luck because Jeff had travelled to Abuja for a one-week board meeting. Jane had told Jeff and Nkoli that she bumped into Vera and was spending the week with her. It took Jane only two days to fully recover from childbirth and she was discharged.

What followed made Jane even more worthless. She couldn't look Jeff in the eyes when he returned a week later from Abuja. She was guilt-stricken.

It didn't take Jeff time to notice that Jane wasn't her normal self. He had observed her ruminating and looking vacantly into space at times. "What is the matter, Jane?" he asked offhandedly.

Jane hesitated. How could she tell him what her problem was? She took an option that went through her like a hot knife through butter and told him a fat, ugly lie. "Honey, I haven't been myself since returning from Vera's aunt's house. I think it was food poisoning or something. I have been throwing up ever since. No appetite. No strength. No motivation. I haven't been to the office since then."

"Oh dear. Why didn't you phone me, Jane? You know, I could have excused myself and come back to assist."

"You mustn't be involved in everything about me. It is only food poisoning at the end of the day," Jane concluded her lies, which attracted huge sympathy from Jeff, who blamed himself for not being there for her when she needed him by her side.

Jane felt abysmally guilty for her tale of lies to the man she loved so dearly.

But more lies were yet to come in the coming weeks when Jeff made some sexual advances towards her, having not made love to her for over two weeks. He thought Jane would be craving it as he did. She was, but the skeleton in her cupboard had been an obstacle. She heartily apologised as she compiled another set of lies that Jeff had no choice but to take in. She told him that she still felt awful and that she had done some lab investigation that revealed that she was suffering from malaria. She went ahead to tell him that they also found titres of typhoid fever in her blood.

Jeff screamed when she mentioned typhoid fever. "We need to go to the hospital right now. You can't continue to tempt fate. You nearly died from pneumonia in Tunisia. Now you have been ill for over two weeks. We need to go to the hospital so that the doctors will take a closer look at you to know what is going on."

"They only said insignificant typhoid antigen, not full-blown typhoid. Relax. I will be fine. Just need a few more weeks of complete rest to recover," she said to buy herself out of sex or any close intimacy with Jeff. She knew that Jeff always fiddles with her breasts while making love to her. She was still lactating a bit and wouldn't like Jeff to know about that, as that could lead to questions that would have no convincing answers. Again, the perineal tears following childbirth needed to heal completely.

Her series of lies didn't make her proud. She was ashamed of them. She felt horrible and accused herself of betrayal and insincerity. But she had taken solace in the fact that it was better to lie than tell the truth about what happened. Meanwhile, Jane was secretly taking lactation-prohibiting medication to stop her lactation.

CHAPTER 29

By the second month, Jane's lactation had completely stopped, and perineal tears had completely healed. Life seemed normal again in the house except for Jane, who was still harbouring the guilt of withholding vital information from Jeff, her best friend, soulmate, and husband.

Jane was constantly in contact with the nurses who delivered her baby. They told her that her baby had been moved to Ivory Motherless Baby's home. They provided her with the address so that she could visit if that was an option she would like to explore. It was a choice she didn't hesitate to take. At least that would offer her the opportunity to monitor her son's growth and development pending the time his father comes to get him. She was visiting the home at least twice a month. At times weekly, depending on her schedule. She had been in her son's situation in a Motherless Baby's home, and knew all it entailed. She knew it wasn't the best place in the world. Consequently, she made sure that her son was well looked after, even though she remained anonymous.

Didn't they say that blood is thicker than water? So, it was proven. Though Jane tried to hide her identity, the staff had started smelling a rat at the unusual, instinctive bond developing between little Hassan and Jane. Among hundreds of visitors who visited the home, the staff had noticed that little Hassan would cling to Jane like a leech on the skin of its host. Most of the time, he would cry when Jane left, and staff had on a few occasions seen Jane crying as well, though she tried her best to conceal it. The staff who knew the story of little Hassan began to narrow her down as the lady who abandoned him in the hospital, and they already knew why.

Hassan's handsomeness continued to blossom as he got older. His nose wasn't only as straight as a much-cherished Greek nose, but it was also long and pointed down proportionately. It was so perfect.

On one of her visits, Jane had heard the staff say that little Hassan was too handsome to be abandoned. They had also said that his dad must be strikingly handsome. Jane felt bad listening to them. "I don't think we should be amazed if, as we are suspecting she is his mother. Can you imagine a baby from her and a handsome man?"

"I can imagine. The offspring will look like little Hassan," the other staff replied. And they giggled delightfully.

The home was continually under pressure from potential adopters to take little Hassan home, but the home had made it emphatically clear that he wasn't for adoption.

Jane was panicking that the influential people in the society might take him away with their notorious influence and wealth. Jane didn't want him to be with nonbiological parents when he had full-fledged biological parents who should be caring for him.

Little Hassan was the attraction and centre of attention. Hardly would any visitor or adopter visit without asking after him. On top of his handsomeness, he was delightfully cheeky, smart, and bubbly. Proper handful, but in a good way. He was like the leader of the group, as every child wanted to play with him.

He was steadily attracting attention not only within the home but outside. Big baby food companies had fought to sign him to appear in their baby food and sanitary products. Even children's fashion companies weren't left out in the pursuit to have him in their adverts and products. Before long, little Hassan was on billboards, television and even magazines. From cursing little Hassan's dad for not coming to take his child, the home was now praying that he never came. Little Hassan had not only blessed the home with unquantifiable gifts and money, but they were also becoming incredibly famous all over the country with his pictures in children's magazines, billboards, and on television. They lacked for nothing. Their account was constantly being loaded by Jane, who remained anonymous. Though the home didn't know who the benefactor was, they at least knew it must be because of little Hassan.

A year later, there was a yam festival held annually in Jeff's village, a traditional ceremony of thanksgiving to God for bounteous harvest, and Jeff had decided to travel that year as he hadn't for years now. He wanted Jane and Nkoli to witness it for the first time. It was a big occasion which usually attracted not only the indigenes living abroad but also friends and well-wishers from neighbouring villages and towns. It was like a mini carnival with different musical and dance groups as well as masquerades of all kinds of shapes, colours, and heights. Foods and drinks were usually in superabundance, and people usually ate and drank from the same pots and basins, though those who wanted to be served individually for personal reasons were allowed to do so. The event was so colourful and entertaining that Jane had no adjective to qualify it. She and Nkoli had been to various events in the past, but they had never seen anything as invigorating and mind-blowing as that before. They were lost for words, and Jeff was very happy to have invited them, now seeing how intrigued they were witnessing this occasion. The little, twin white girls danced their way to the hearts of onlookers. They stole the show as people clapped and cheered each dance step. Nobody believed that white girls could dance to the traditional music so beautifully as they did. They looked whimsical and beautiful in their turquoise colour tie and die skirts, and white short-sleeved ashoke embroidered blouses with sky blue scarves that could not hold their blonde, long hair in place as it tumbled majestically down their shoulders.

"How could they be this good in our traditional dance?" Jeff asked his mum, nudging her to gain her attention.

"Because their parents must have taught them the dance steps," Jeff's mum replied, pointing at a black couple.

"Their parents?" Jeff responded, looking astonished. "How could a black couple give birth to white girls? I know you are just pulling my legs, mum."

"I am not. I mean it."

"If you mean it, it means that the husband is really daft to accept them as his. Hasn't he got eyes? Or is something wrong with his brain? Or is he under his wife's spell or what?" Jeff asked, looking disappointedly angry, and feeling ashamed on behalf of the girls' dad.

"Why are you so bitter that his wife gave birth to white babies?" his mum said, noticing how vexed Jeff had become.

"So, she told him those kids were his, and he believed her. She is a cheat and a manipulator, mother."

Jeff's mum saw how indignant Jeff and Nkoli had become because of the white babies and had to tell them the story of the expatriates in their communities centuries ago, how Americans and Europeans infiltrated their communities all in the name of religion and the slave trade. She told them how the expatriates capitalised on the naivety of their young girls. How they frolicked and slept with our girls at their whims and caprices, and got them pregnant in the process. She said that there was an explosion of white babies in their communities then and maintained that few of their people still carry these genes, a reason this couple gave birth to twin white babies.

Jeff never knew about this. However, he insisted that if he were the husband of this lady, he would still demand DNA to keep his mind at rest, especially when he discovered that those kids were born in America, and also knowing how common infidelity was in today's marriages.

For Jane, that story opened a new chapter, and vistas of hope emerged before her. Jeff's mum was so detailed in her story about the exploits of the expatriates in their homeland then, and Jane for a moment thought whether that could have a hand in little Hassan's white complexion. She also remembered the nurses telling her how angry Hassan was when they told him that she had a baby for him. According to the nurses, it was on second thought that Hassan finally apologised to them and promised that he would come down to take his baby. Jane thought he must have realised it was a baby boy, which his wife couldn't give him. Jane remembered vividly how he had wished he had a baby boy to continue his lineage and inherit his wealth. *Could little Hassan be Jeff's?* Jane optimistically wanted to believe. She vowed to get to the root of it.

It was two weeks away from little Hassan's birthday. Jane discreetly went and did a huge shopping for his birthday, including ordering a home kit paternity test. She would not like things to stay the same without making an effort to confirm little Hassan's paternity, and she had believed her efforts would not be in vain.

Those fourteen days were like a quarter of a century. It dragged forever. No wonder they say: a watched kettle never boils.

She couldn't sleep the night preceding little Hassan's birthday.

There was this intense eagerness in her mood when she finally got out of bed. It was her running around that eventually woke others up. She happily prepared and served everyone breakfast. As usual, she had lied to Jeff that she had an appointment with one of her clients at Ilupeju, which was close to Ivory's motherless baby's home. And as usual, Jeff had no reason to doubt her.

She was filled with an equal measure of happiness and grief. She had imagined the enormity of her joy if the paternity test confirmed Jeff as the biological father. She had also imagined her disappointment should the test reveal that Jeff wasn't little Hassan's dad, which could only mean that Hassan was indeed the dad as she had always thought and believed.

Two days before the day of her visit, she shaved Jeff as she had done every now and then in what she termed pampering and grooming time and had kept the razor and the hair out of sight, in her handbag. She had bought a toothbrush with which she would secretly brush little Hassan's teeth during their private, quiet time. She knew that the molar teeth were some of the best spots to collect a DNA sample. She also came with a little scissors to snip a tiny hair from him if she had the chance. Then she would take the samples to the lab for analysis. Jane had already bribed one of the lab scientists to carry out the test without needing Jeff's signature and involvement. Jane had added bribery and counterfeiting to her new way of life. She wasn't in doubt that her new way of life was taking a turn for the worse, but nothing was going to be in the way of confirming little Hassan's paternity.

She was quite surprised to find everywhere so quiet on getting to the Motherless baby's home. The staff put up an appearance that showed things were okay. Jane knew things weren't. If the staff could pretend, children couldn't. They were exceptionally quiet. The usual singing, running, and jumping around in the children's playground by the children barely existed. She could count on her fingers the number of children who were playing. Even those that managed to play in a most uninspired manner. Normally, at that time of the day, the playground would be teeming with excited children, screaming and running around frantically. The playmaker had gone. Little Hassan made the staff, children, and even visitors tick with his cheeky, bubbly behaviour.

Some of the children who knew Jane very well got excited when they saw her. They knew how close little Hassan was to her. They thought Jane had brought him back, but to no avail.

Jane's inquiring eyes were scanning the environment like forensic police officers looking for a clue in a murder case.

One of the staff whispered to her colleagues, "She is looking for him. I told you she is the mother. Can you see how distraught she is because she hasn't seen him?"

"You didn't tell us. We all know. It is just this incident has confirmed our suspicion," the rest of the staff quietly replied, and they felt so sorry for her.

One of the staff said to her, "He is gone."

"Gone to where?" Jane asked, looking lost. She wasn't even mindful of the fact that the staff didn't mention who was gone. Like a cleverly set trap, it had caught her. She had inadvertently given herself away.

"His father came three days ago and signed all the documents and took him."

The news cut through her like a sharp razor. She managed to hold her emotions. She didn't want to confirm to the staff that she was little Hassan's mother. But that was too little, too late. The staff had already drawn the inference.

"It is just that I have bought him some presents today, being his birthday," Jane said. Her last statement was a further confirmation to them who she was to little Hassan. They knew that she was the mother; otherwise, how would she know his exact date of birth?

Jane went and brought all the gifts and handed them to the staff, and left as quickly as possible, as her emotions had started to fail her.

"Oh my God! Why is everything in my life upside down? Why didn't Hassan wait until I had done this test? And why would it take Jeff's mother this long to mention the expatriates?" she asked ruefully and dejectedly. And she hated Jeff's mum for a moment, even though she knew full well that it wasn't her fault that the revelation of the foreigners in her town centuries ago was delayed.

As she drove home, she was thinking of the next step to take. She didn't want to blame anyone for Hassan taking little Hassan. She approved and consented to it verbally and in writing. But she wasn't going to let Hassan have her baby, who stood some chance of being Jeff's.

Jane had lied to Jeff about the birth of little Hassan; now she was ready to tell a bigger, and even more horrifying lie as she prepared to embark on a journey to Tunisia to find her son. She was going to keep it topmost secret. She dared not mention going to Tunisia to Jeff. She knew it would be total madness to do so, even if it were a journey to collect a ton of diamonds. She still remembered the ordeal they had been through at the hands of Hassan in Tunisia.

It took about a year before Jane had the opportunity to start her journey to Tunisia. She wasn't going to tell Jeff she was travelling to Tunisia. Such travel would never make any sense to him.

Jane had told Jeff that she was travelling to the USA the same week Jeff was to travel to Stuttgart, Germany, for consultations and ordering of some Mercedes buses and spare parts. She told him it was to help at their New York branch since the administrator was still on maternity leave.

She made sure it was a day after Jeff had travelled to Germany so that he would not have an idea that she wasn't actually travelling to America. But she also lied when she told Jeff that she would also seize the opportunity to visit her old schoolfriend she discovered on Facebook, who now lives in New York. Jane concluded that she would make sure that she and Jeff would be communicating via Messenger, where it was less likely for him to pay attention to phone numbers. She concluded she would be calling Jeff probably three times a day so that he would not have any need to make any call to her. Jane, fully aware how much Jeff loved her, knew that Jeff would not bat an eyelid even if she told him plainly not to contact her. Alternatively, she might choose the time difference between Germany and the US as an excuse to limit their calls.

Jeff had always trusted Jane with his life and had never had any reason to doubt her. Nonetheless, her guilt like a load was weighing her down like one carrying a ton of bricks on her shoulder for constantly lying to him. To her, she was abusing the trust Jeff placed in her, and she was dying emotionally and psychologically as a result.

Suddenly, the picture of Hassan and all he stood for flashed before her. She remembered that he was a loose cannon, and like a bomb would detonate at the slightest trigger. She remembered he was a wife-beater, he spiked people's drinks, he forged documents, he had a gun, and he nearly killed them at the Begumi forest. If Jeff wasn't able to swap the drinks, he would have killed him. At that moment, she was gripped with fear. She saw the danger associated with this trip. To her, it was like trying to take a kill from a pride of lions single-handedly. But more worrisome to her was the fact that nobody would know what happened to her if anything went wrong with this journey because she was still determined not to mention it to anyone, Jeff, the least.

Jane didn't lack consequential thinking about the journey she was about to embark on, but her positive thinking had oiled her resolve not to relinquish her quest to find her son. She was never in doubt that there would be consequences — they were as sure as death, but she remained optimistic she would not lose her life trying this venture that looked like a professional stunt about to be performed by an amateur. *If reward outweighs the risk, they say, then you might as well take it. If I could prove that Jeff was the father of little Hassan and bring him home, that would be the placating hallmark moment that would wipe away all the guilt and all the lies I had told him,* she encouraged herself. To her, the game was worth the candle, even though it appeared as a magical thinking on a rational mind.

Jane travelled the night after Jeff's. Her flight took off that night around 21:45 hours from Murtala Mohammed Airport. They had one stop in Istanbul, Turkey, before boarding another flight that brought them into Tunisia the next day. *Why do you need to travel to another African country through a European country, forcing you to obtain a transit visa to make the travel?* Jane wondered, realising that they would have a stopover at Istanbul before boarding another flight to Tunisia.

Jane couldn't believe she was in Tunisia. But when she saw the inscription in the arrival hall

(Welcome to Carthage airport), she knew she was. A sudden sense of panic cut through her system, causing her to breathe rapidly. The thought that this could be the end of the road for her was enormous. But there was no going back. She was already in Tunisia, and she had come to find her son, and possibly take him back to Nigeria if everything worked out as she had planned and believed. But first of all, she had to contend with Hassan. She left Tunisia on a sad, sour note. Hassan might still be hurting egoistically. His ego was deeply bruised by her, Jeff, and the Tunisian police officers. Jane thought this could be Hassan's chance to get the much-sought revenge. But life events had so hardened her that she could bite the bullet and sit comfortably on top of raging ocean waves. *If I die on this mission, I shall have died looking and fighting to get my son, a son I believe could be my* husband's. *Jeff has always fought for me. Now, it's my turn to risk my life for something that would make him happy for the rest of his life,* she thought.

She took a taxi from the airport to Hassan's house. Nothing seemed to have changed. Nothing was new to her. She had lived for months in the country before and had learned a lot about their culture and way of life during that period. She knew important landmarks, and she could also speak a little Arabic and French.

Jane purposely carried a huge luggage not for convenience but to convince Hassan that she had not only come to stay for good, but also to be his wife as he had always wanted. Her heart was almost in her mouth as a male figure approached the semi-opaque glass door when she knocked on the door. She braced up to meet Hassan, and she believed little Hassan and Hassan's daughters would be right behind him. But that was not to be. It was entirely a new face that looked younger, shorter, and obviously beefier than the owner of the house, Hassan. He looked puzzled, seeing Jane with a huge suitcase standing at the front of the door. "Can I help you?" he asked politely but with a suspicious look.

"Yes, please. I am looking for Hassan, the owner of the house," she said, scanning through him nervously.

"I don't know who he is. Never met him."

Jane looked around herself suspiciously to confirm she was at the right place, and she was. "Who are you then?" she asked him hesitantly.

"I am his tenant. I got told the owner had travelled to the USA with his family, and I had rented the house through his agent."

Jane stood motionless for a moment before gathering her thoughts again and asked, "Who is his agent that rented the house to you? Can I have the agent's phone number, please?" Jane wasn't ready to give up her quest to get her baby back or at least confirm his paternity. To her, it didn't matter if Hassan had moved to Antarctica. She would still find him insofar as he was with her son, that could be Jeff's.

"Who are you, and where are you coming from? Did he know you are visiting?" the gentleman asked her, wondering why Jane had come to see someone with such big luggage without first confirming that she would meet the host.

Too many questions for her to deal with. She avoided all his questions and gave a short answer. "I used to live with him some time ago."

"As what?"

She paused and took another look at him. She didn't feel comfortable or happy being interrogated by this fella, who qualified at best as a stranger to her.

"As a friend," Jane answered unwillingly, her eyes twitching in anger.

"How did you not know then he had travelled?" he asked with a hint of suspicion.

Unwilling to continue the discussion that was leading nowhere, Jane went back to her earlier question, "How can I meet the agent or the caretaker of this house, please?"

"The caretaker lives two streets down the road."

"Can you point me in the direction, please?" "

"Let me call my daughter to take you there."

Jane thanked him for his help.

The young girl took turns with Jane to pull the big luggage. "Here we are, this is the caretaker's house," the young girl said, and she knocked on the door. Jane squeezed a dinar note into her hand and thanked her for her help.

Jane screamed while Hiba hugged her tight as they saw each other. "Jane! What are you doing in Tunisia?" Hiba asked cautiously, but with a wide smile.

"I have come to see Hassan, but was told he had travelled with his family to America."

Hiba raised two hands to heaven in thanksgiving and said, "Thank God for His mercy and intervention."

"Why?" Jane asked, surprised by her gesticulation.

"Because Hassan is not here to see you. He swore with his life that if he found you anywhere that he would kill you for all the trouble you caused him and his family. It wasn't long before he forgave me. He threatened at one point to kill me because he met you through me. He is spitting fire and brimstone. But before I continue, I must thank you for setting me free from the forest. Hassan said it was through your revelation that the police came to know about me and finally came to my rescue."

"You deserve more than that, Hiba," Jane responded. She hesitated before asking about Hana. She thought it must be because of his wife that he was so crossed, and who wouldn't? Jane blamed herself for Hana's ordeal. She gazed momentarily at Hiba and asked, "How is Hana?"

Hiba paused, and then shook her head pitifully, and said, "She passed away from her injuries. Hassan believed and even told some of his friends that you were responsible for her death."

Jane was touched by the news, and she shed some tears.

Regaining her composure from the sad news, she asked about Hassan's kids.

"The girls are fine, but he brought home the most handsome little boy I have ever seen just over a year ago and claimed it was his son, but wouldn't tell anyone how he got him, not even me, his closest friend and caretaker."

"Where is the little boy?" Jane asked.

"He relocated with the rest of the family."

"He is my son," she announced to Hiba in a whisper.

"Who is your son?" Hiba asked in shock, unable to believe her ears.

"The little boy. Listen, Hiba, you can see my luggage. I realised I made a huge mistake, and I sincerely regret all the trouble I caused Hassan. He is a good man. He rescued me from the forest and welcomed me into his house with open arms. I have come to apologise to him and see if he will let me live with him as a wife, especially now, I have learned that his wife had passed away, and more so, we have a son together. I really need to be there for him to pay him back for everything he did for me."

Hiba was still shocked and disappointed with Jane's story, especially having a son for Hassan. She could not believe that Jane and Hassan cheated on their respective spouse.

"What of your husband?" she asked Jane suddenly, wondering why she wanted to become Hassan's wife.

"He divorced me when he discovered I had a son for Hassan," Jane lied indifferently.

"So, what are your plans?"

"My plan is to find Hassan, apologise to him and pray that he accepts me back into his life. So, your part, Hiba, is to give me his address and phone number and some other details so that I can find him."

Hiba gave it a wary, lengthy thought before answering. "I will, but be careful, he is still very angry with you for what he claimed you did to him and his family."

Jane spent the night at Hiba's, and they talked into early morning hours discussing this, that, and the other, including how the police came to her rescue in the forest, the details of Hana's death and burial, and Hassan's relocation to America, until they finally fell asleep.

CHAPTER 30

Two days later, Jane set off on her journey to Las Vegas, Nevada.

She gave real thought to this journey that appeared as dangerous as walking into a bask of hungry crocodiles. She saw Hassan as a keg of gunpowder and knew it would be sheer folly to approach him with a naked flame. She knew that to convince Hassan that she was genuine, and that she had come to stay, and to be his wife wasn't going to be a doddle. She knew she had to break protocols and cut corners to have the slimmest chance of achieving her mission. As a result, she agreed to give Hassan a kiss, which he had asked for so many times when they were in Tunisia and was denied on each occasion except the platonic one, she was compelled to give him at the magazine competition to meet the competition requirement. Now she was going to give him one without him asking for it. She was going to cry on his shoulder against her resolve not to cry on any man's shoulder after her ordeal with Douglas. She would then apologise for all the trouble she caused him. She was going to use for the very first time her natural endowment to seduce a man to get what she wanted, but she wasn't going to sleep with him. Jane had always been a looker to anyone who looked at her. But it was a quality that she had been reminded of more by friends than herself, where she was told how heads always turned whenever she was out and about. Today, she kept those qualities in mind and was determined to use them to actualise her dream.

Now at his door, she prayed that Hassan's mood would be in a good place when she met him. Nevertheless, she braced herself against any possible aggressive reaction from him when she eventually knocked on the door of his detached house in Fremont Street around 6.30pm in the evening. Her heart raced and thudded forcefully against her ribs as a male figure approached the semi-opaque glass door, almost a replica of his door in Tunisia. She was ready for anything. Events had made her develop an appetite for life, even though some of them were becoming increasingly difficult to stomach.

Surprisingly, the opposite was the case. Hassan felt he was seeing double on seeing Jane. In fact, he thought he was daydreaming. Like an ambushed soldier, he was rendered powerless by Jane's sudden and unannounced visit.

Jane knew that Hassan was a creature of quenchless vanity and innately lustful. With that at the back of her mind, she wore a stylish, attention-grabbing dress. It was a sleeveless, backless bodycon emerald green dress that revealed more than just a catch of sight of her breasts. Her natural Afro hair was a replica of Diana Ross' 70s hairstyle. Her sterling silver and emerald green drop earrings and silver stiletto shoes matched her dress. The rimless ombré sunglasses were the icing on the cake. But more engaging were her luscious lips. With a splash of colourless wet lipstick over them, they looked so full as if they were about to burst to let out the fluid. Her natural, full lips had made those spending a fortune on Botox and lip filling jealous. She exuded elegance and beauty, and she had hoped that Hassan would be drawn to her as a moth was drawn to a flame.

True to type, Hassan was swept off his feet and totally blown away by Jane's beauty and stylish dressing that he totally forgot everything that happened in Tunisia. He fed his eyes insatiably on her exposed, spotless skin, and fantasised his lips on hers. All the bitterness and grudges he had against her evaporated like steam. He had always wanted her. All he was presenting to Hiba and his friends was what Jane presumed to be reaction formation. With his wife dead, he felt lonely and wanted a lady to fill the vacuum created by her death, and who was more qualified than Jane? It was an opportunity he had always wanted. Now that the opportunity had presented itself on a platter, he couldn't help but grab it with two hands.

"Many thanks for letting me in," Jane said, as he merrily ushered her into the hallway that led to the exquisite, vast lounge.

"Just sit down, Jane and stop all this apology," he responded, feeling elated, almost crazy.

"No, no, Hassan. I am not proud of my deeds. Don't make me feel good when I shouldn't," she interrupted his speech.

"C'mon, Jane. You have got to stop…"

"Listen, Hassan," she cut in again. "I have come to apologise and ask for your forgiveness to accept me back into your family — into your life — and as your wife."

The explosion of euphoria that rushed through him like a flash flood nearly made it impossible for him to process the information correctly. He came closer, took her hand, and looked boyishly into her eyes. He wanted to confirm what he was hearing. In a positive response to his innuendo, Jane leaned into him and allowed her head to rest on his bare chest before she spoke again. She felt his warmth, and the smell of his aftershave filled her senses delightfully. In a quick, secret reciprocity, she seductively and intuitively let her hair rub against his bare skin, causing him to breathe faster and deeper.

"Hiba had told me everything. I am deeply sorry about Hana. I feel guilty. But I am here to recompense for my wrongs," she pleaded warmly. Leaning on him and putting her left hand to his bare chest, she gently lifted his chin with the right hand and then planted a shallow kiss on his lips, and she felt his hard-on on her lap at once, and she moved away quickly before he became uncontrollably excited.

Hassan couldn't believe that Jane had not only come to live with him but had also agreed to be his wife.

But she warned him to take things easy and not to rush her into anything intimate.

Feeling like a jackpot winner, he nodded his consent and reassuringly promised her that he would abide by her wishes and orders.

Hassan was still like someone in a sweet dream and would soon wake up from it, only to realise it was a dream. But it wasn't. It was real. Jane was with him in flesh. However, he wasn't too naive to sweep everything under the carpet. He wanted to know what had become of Jeff. "Where is your husband, Jeff?" he asked, trying to make sure Jeff was completely out of the picture. He didn't want a repeat of the drama that took place in Tunisia. He was still feeling ashamed about it. It was an experience that had left a bad memory in his mind, a sour taste in his mouth, and humiliation in his eyes.

Jane came prepared. She knew that Hassan, at a point was going to enquire after Jeff. "You mean my ex-husband?" she corrected him smartly. "Where do you expect? And what do you expect? He found out that I had a child for you and left me. But before he left, he was battering me and practising his karate skills on me every now and then. I thought he broke one of my ribs in one of the attacks when he kicked me so hard, sending me crashing against the wall. If we were near the sea, I am sure I would have fallen into it."

Hassan momentarily looked away in shame and wished he hadn't heard that piece of truth.

She paused for a moment and then pulled out her phone from her handbag and showed him some of the counterfeit images of her bruised face and black eyes he sustained from Jeff when he attacked her. "On one of those days, he nearly killed me like he wanted to kill you that day when he kicked you into the sea to drown," she told him, trying to stop herself from crying.

It was a harsh reality Hassan didn't want to hear about or be reminded of. She had smartly told him that Jeff was stronger than him.

"But the love I have for you made me dive into the sea to save you. I love you, Hassan," she continued with her fake, undying love.

Hassan wasn't too proud to be reminded how Jeff beat him up and kicked him into the sea, and had wished that Jane would stop making those references. Despite the harsh reality of her reminders, he was nevertheless certain that he would have drowned without Jane's assistance. And that's what counted.

If presenting herself as an imposter or con artist was what it would take to get her son back, Jane didn't mind.

Hassan screamed, "That animal did all these to you. Wait until I get him next time. I will make sure I put some bullets into his fucking brain before he comes anywhere near us."

He wasn't in denial that Jeff was a beefcake when it came to physical combat, but he still refused to eat the humble pie. He drew Jane to his bosom and reassured her with comforting words that she was now safe in his care.

Little Hassan and Hassan's daughters took to Jane straightaway just as much as Hassan. They all recognised her.

Jane was a bit taken aback by Hassan's behaviour in the presence of little Hassan. He had treated him a bit differently from the girls. Little Hassan was much more pampered by Hassan even in his natural high-handedness and strictest behaviour, where he had shouted at him and even beaten him, but not as frequent as he beat the girls. She noticed that close father-son bonding, especially one to be the heir to his fortune. It was clear that he was building his wealth around little Hassan at the expense of the girls — the typical African man's behaviour. Jane believed that she would thwart his plans if she were able to take little Hassan away from him so that he would refocus on his girls. But she wondered about the possibility of him building an empire and saving money in an expensive city like Las Vegas. If he were dreaming of building an empire and bequeathing wealth to little Hassan, he would have to relocate first to a modest city to realise this dream. She believed in the adage: *A society grows great when old men plant trees in whose shade they shall never sit.* Even though Jane knew full well that she was never going to be a permanent member of Hassan's family, she was still determined to encourage him to relocate to a city where he would spend less and save some money for his children.

Such a strong bond between Hassan and little Hassan was further evidence to Jane that Hassan must have done something to her that fateful early morning in Tunisia. His behaviour towards little

Hassan showed unequivocally that he believed that little Hassan was his son. And that fuelled Jane's hatred towards him, and she had given him the filthiest look anytime she could avoid his eyes and would call him a monster under her breath.

But the more it was glaring to Jane that Hassan could be little Hassan's father, the more she was still determined to go ahead with her quest to find and confirm little Hassan's paternity. And she had hoped that her laugh would come last if Jeff were eventually proven to be her boy's dad.

"You have eyes for beautiful things," Jane said to him as they sat in the garden that Saturday morning, having a cup of tea, with little Hassan kicking his ball around.

"You can say that again," Hassan quickly replied, looking seductively at her.

"Don't look at me like that, I wasn't talking about myself. I said beautiful things, not beautiful women," she cheekily scolded him to disabuse his mind of his erroneous impression. "I meant your house. I was impressed with your house in Tunisia, but this has made it look ordinary and almost ancient. Look at the size of the garden. You can play five-a-side football here, you know. It is huge and well-kept. The icing on the cake was the well-crafted waterfall that empties into a see-through stream. The interior décor is not far off from that of the SLS hotel in Dubai, especially the dream cloud premier bed," Jane said euphorically.

Hassan grinned with pride and delight when Jane said something about the bed. "But you have refused to sleep in it. And if we are going to be playing five aside football in the garden, then we must start putting this bed to use without further delay," he replied, laughing mischievously, knowing that it was one of the best beds in the world for good sleep and sex.

Jane's voluptuous lips at once curved into an alluring smile at Hassan's innuendo. "Keep the filthy thought to yourself," she said, refusing him eye contact he desperately wanted.

She then asked, "I wonder how much you pay for rent here?"

"A lot."

"I am not surprised. Why wouldn't you when you decided to rent a house in Las Vegas, of all places — and with a fibreglass swimming pool? I hope you haven't used up all our money from the competition for rent?" she pretentiously asked him.

"It is not only the rent that has depleted my money, but also my habit…"

"First of all, you must stop saying my money. It is our money," she reminded him. And he nodded. She then went back to his statement and asked, "What habit are you on about?"

"Gambling. Gambling," he re-echoed the word.

"Did I hear you say gambling?" she screamed. He nodded again, avoiding her furious face.

"Now that you are part of me, I need to come clean and tell you the whole truth. I lied to you when I said I used the money I borrowed from the bank to invest in a business and got swindled. The truth was that I spent the money in casinos and pool houses."

"Oh my God!" she exclaimed flaccidly. "Why did you decide to rent a house in Las Vegas, the headquarters of casinos and gambling, when you know you have gambling issues? That's akin to intentionally getting into a river infested with float of crocs. What happened to places like Texas, Missouri, Tennessee, and New Orleans…? I am not having this. We will have to move, Hassan. How much of our money do you still have left?" she asked him, looking angry and disappointed.

Hassan hesitated before saying, "None. That's why I am working for three agencies to be able to pay my rent, bills, and put food on the table for the children."

Jane frowned at him for being so wasteful. To have skin in the game, she brought out her phone and did some transactions from the bank details Hiba gave her. She then looked at him and said, "I have transferred two hundred thousand dollars to your account. But you must promise me that you will use part of it to find new accommodation that we can afford. Don't forget you have a family to look after. Their success in life hugely depends on us, the parents. That can't be achieved by gambling all our resources away. I am here now, and things must change. Please understand that," she told him authoritatively.

Hassan nodded suppliantly and smiled timidly like a pupil in the presence of his headteacher. He stood up, went to her, hugged her, and thanked her repeatedly for the life-changing money she transferred to him.

If there was any lingering doubt or suspicion about Jane's visit, this kind gesture completely removed it. The icing on the cake was the thought that he was potentially going to be married not only to the most beautiful woman he had ever seen, but also to an extraordinarily rich woman. *She must be a millionaire to part with two hundred thousand dollars just like that. Jeff must be rich. Jane must have gotten a lot of settlement money from the divorce,"* Hassan thought.

Jane read the expression in his face and was satisfied that the money she transferred to him was a worthy bargaining chip.

She never let her guard down throughout her stay in Las Vegas. The night she thought and felt Hassan drugged and raped her in Tunisia played continuously on her mind. She would never understand why he was in her room that odd hour with only a towel tied around his waist with folded tissue paper in his hand, looking at her bemusedly — the usual odd hour he usually beat her wife up and then made love to her as if they were into sadomasochism. Against that backdrop, she decided to stay and sleep downstairs even though she would have preferred upstairs, which, looking through the windows, would give her the panoramic view of the neighbourhood. And she also missed the comfort of sleeping in the Dream Cloud Premier bed.

She wore a tight pair of jeans during the day, and a tight pair of shorts at night with her nightie and dressing gown on top. She had equally but smartly made sure that she cooked and served her food and drinks. She didn't want to take any chances. She could only trust Hassan as far as she could throw him. She had come to solve the mystery surrounding little Hassan's conception and not to put herself in a similar position where Hassan would have a chance to repeat what she believed he did in Tunisia. She believed that eating any food prepared and served by Hassan was never a clever thing to do because she still believed that he spiked her food in Tunisia. Nevertheless, she missed the couscous meals prepared by him so much that she had been tempted on a few occasions to eat some of little Hassan's.

As it were, Jane believed she had things under control. But things weren't going to be as straightforward as she had thought or wished. A couple of minutes after Hassan excused himself to go in to get ready for work after finishing his cup of tea, Jane had a call on her mobile phone. She wondered who was calling her that early. She coiled up in fear, looking at the screen. It was Jeff. She didn't know whether to drop the phone, switch it off, or run away from the premises. It was a scenario worse than walking on a tight rope over a deep river, as she thought Hassan would meet her while still talking to Jeff. But when Jane took a closer look at the screen and discovered Jeff was making the call from the USA, she felt her brain immobilised, her heart compressed, and for a moment, she felt she had been buried alive. She thought she had convinced Jeff that they would only communicate via Messenger. She had been calling and messaging him regularly, thinking that by doing so, he wouldn't bother to contact her, but she was wrong. Jeff's Facebook had been hacked, and he had stopped using Facebook and Messenger for any form of communication. She had also told him that she was going to New York to do some administrative work as the administrator was still on maternity leave, and she would also use the opportunity to see a friend who had just moved to New York. But now, she was in Las Vegas, 2445 miles away from New York. There was nothing she could do but continue her new lifestyle of telling porky pies. Otherwise, how could she tell Jeff where she was? She had imagined Jeff walking up and finding her in her nightie and dressing gown, having a cup of tea in the garden with a man, let alone Hassan, with little Hassan running around as their child. She knew what the repercussions would be. But her thought quickly shifted from Jeff to Hassan, whom she suddenly realised could be even more dangerous if he discovered that she had lied to him. She had told him that she had ended everything with Jeff. She needed nobody to explain to her the consequences. That put her on the edge, and she was submerged in anxious steam with her head spinning like the vanes on a windmill. She knew heads would roll if Hassan or Jeff discovered what she was up to.

She was still looking for a way out of the mess when the phone stopped ringing. And just before she could take a breather, it started ringing again.

She had no choice but to pick it up. "Is that you, Jeff?" she asked, trying her best not to give herself away as someone unsettled.

"Where are you? I have checked our usual hotel in New York, and they said you didn't check in," Jeff asked concernedly.

"Oh, I forgot to tell you that I decided to cancel my trip to New York when my friend told me she now lives in Las Vegas. Again, I found out that the admin had come back from her maternity leave, so there was no need for me to stay in New York," Jane again lied through her teeth.

But Jeff didn't buy it. He didn't feel too comfortable with what he had just heard and screamed, "Las Vegas?"

"Yes. Sorry, I forgot to tell you. But what are you doing in New York, by the way? You are supposed to be in Germany," she cleverly asked him, trying to shift the attention from herself.

"The American coordinator phoned to say he was a bit under the weather and couldn't travel to Stuttgart, Germany. So, I was able to convince the panel to change the venue to New York to enable him to attend. But the main reason was for me to meet up with you in New York, knowing that you are here already. I wanted it to be a surprise. Such a shame," he lamented.

To Jane, surprise was an understatement for Jeff to meet her in Las Vegas. Anything would be better, except death.

"Anyway, give me the address so that I can come and pick you up when we are done here," he requested, concernedly.

The panic button was switched back on with that last request from Jeff. But she had determined to lie as long as it would take until she got her son back from Hassan or at least found out who his real father was. She now saw herself as a pathological liar and prayed earnestly she would be able to wean herself off it and regain her sincerity and trustworthiness when this was over.

"Don't bother coming here. It is such a long journey. Besides, I still have a lot to catch up with my friend, Vicky, and her friends. When am I going to have this kind of opportunity again? Let me make the most of this rare opportunity, sweetheart. Just get yourself home, and I will fly back later," she said convincingly and calmly to avoid anything that would stir up any suspicion in Jeff. And Jeff agreed with her. His love and trust in Jane were undiluted and everlasting. So, he didn't bat an eyelid or try to think outside the box.

Jane was still clinging to her heart when Hassan surfaced, looking cute in his work tunic with a splash of smile on his face. "I am off, Jane. Will be seeing you at 9pm tonight. Love you," he said, trying to kiss her on the lips, but Jane moved her lips quickly away from him and gave him her cheek instead.

CHAPTER 31

With the coast clear and the atmosphere conducive, Jane got the ball rolling. She had found a reputable laboratory and had had the privilege to speak to one of the geneticists in the laboratory before sending the samples as directed, after making the required payment online and meeting all requirements.

She was informed that the result would take two to five days to be ready. It was a five-day wait that looked like five years. Jane couldn't have a decent sleep after sending the test away for investigation. She was constantly checking her emails, where she was told the result would be sent.

She started sweating profusely like one in a marathon with profound palpitations when she received an email from the lab in the afternoon of the third day. She was so nervous and unsteady that she could scarcely breathe. The tremor in her hands was so severe that the phone felt like a ton of bricks in her hand. Her palms were sweating and twitching. Consequently, her bladder filled up and she needed the toilet.

She screamed and danced as if one who had been on a drinking session when she finally managed to read her email to see the result was positive, and exclaimed, "Thank you, Jesus. You are worthy of my praise. Who is like you, my God and my Redeemer?"

Though the paternity test confirmed Jeff as little Hassan's dad, subconsciously, she still believed that Hassan did something to her that fateful early morning, but she wasn't going to worry about it, at least for the moment. What counted was that little Hassan was Jeff's. And that she didn't cheat on him. If Hassan got his way, it was through rape which he achieved by spiking her food. And she thanked God that Jeff's seed had already been planted and had fruitfully germinated into little Hassan before Hassan's seed. Jane was equally glad that the STD test results she had done, including the HIV all came back clear.

While Hassan was at work and the children were at school, Jane used the opportunity to ransack the house to find little Hassan's birth certificate. The next day she travelled to the Nigeria embassy and obtained a Nigeria passport for his boy. When one of the staff at the embassy asked her why they had different surnames, she told her that she wasn't married to his dad. The staff believed her because they saw her name and signature on his birth certificate.

As soon as Hassan left for work the following morning, Jane wrote a long letter to him explaining everything. The summary of which was that she had taken little Hassan to his biological dad in Nigeria. She kept for him all the duplicates of the results that confirmed Jeff's paternity. She told him that he could conduct his own paternity test if he had any doubts about the ones she had done. Finally, she wished him well and encouraged him to continue to look after his girls. She advised him to move somewhere he would be able to afford to secure a bright future for his girls.

"Why is our brother not dressed up for school?" Amina asked Jane as she took them to school that frosty morning.

"Oh! Your little brother has a hospital appointment," she told her flatly. She also informed the school that little Hassan had a hospital appointment on that day.

When they came back, she asked little Hassan to gather his favourite toys. She had secretly packed some of his clothes and shoes the previous night. With everything set, she said to little Hassan, "Hurry up, let's go, my son."

"Where are we going, mum?" he inquisitively asked, looking at the big luggage in the lounge.

"Home," she answered.

"Home? With this big luggage? I thought you said we are going to the doctors," he quickly reminded her, having heard her say that to Amina earlier on.

"Home, son," she replied cautiously.

"But we are home, mum, aren't we?"

"I know, but we are going to a better home to see your father," she said, looking nervous about his questions and his wavering attitude.

"My father? How many fathers have I got?"

"One," she answered nervously. Now she was tempted to drag him off the chair to get going, but she thought better of it. She knew the way things were going that little Hassan might create a scene, and the whole aim would be defeated.

"We are going to see your real, good dad, who will treat you right, who will not shout at you, who will not beat you. We are going to your real father, who will buy you all your favourite toys, including video games." She noticed some days ago that Hassan had a go at him when he asked him to buy him some video games. Hassan told him that he wouldn't like him to be distracted in life. He wanted him to grow up into a responsible adult — a man with dignity and focus — one he would be proud of, and who would be eligible to take over the mantle of leadership when his time was up.

The Nanny had also confided in Jane how hostile Hassan had been with the girls, and occasionally with little Hassan, whom he treated less harshly.

Then little Hassan said to Jane, "You keep saying your real father. What do you really mean by that?" But before Jane could say a thing, he interrupted her and continued, "I am only asking because I know that the opposite of real is fake. How can the father you are taking me to be my real father when I am named after my father here in Las Vegas? He is the one who came to Nigeria to get me, and I overheard the staff say that I was lucky to have found my real dad. So, I don't know why you are taking me from my real dad to another real dad."

Little Hassan's level of intelligence got Jane on edge. She was dealing with an adult in a child's body. His questions were flying in at a breakneck speed, each overly sensitive and requiring skill and care to answer.

"If my real father is in Nigeria, as you put it, does it mean my name is going to change to his own name when I get there? And why did the staff say that I was lucky to be reunited with my real dad if I had a real dad somewhere else?"

Jane was now sweating not because of the hot weather but because it was becoming increasingly uncomfortable and difficult to deal with little Hassan. Then she got some courage to answer his question. "I thought Hassan was your real father then."

"Muuum! You thought …?" Then he laughed and smirked. Then he stopped, looked at Jane and apologised. "I am sorry, mum."

It was difficult for Jane to think in that direction, that little Hassan was insinuating she was wayward.

Jane was still standing in awe in little Hassan's presence when he asked, "How do you know now that the dad in Nigeria is my real dad?"

Jane was dumbstruck and fidgety.

"Or have you done the test?" he suddenly asked when she hesitated to answer him.

"How did he know all these? Isn't he too young to be speaking and thinking like this?" Jane wondered. It wasn't only the questions he was asking that bothered her, but also the composure he showed as he asked them.

He continued and said, "I am surprised to have two fathers, fake and real, but I am glad I have only one real mum who is kind, caring and loving. I still remember like it happened yesterday when you would visit me at home with different sweets, ice cream and toys, including this one here in the bag, and we would cry when you were about to leave. I love you, mum." Gently and comically, he added, "And you are also very beautiful, and I am proud to be your son. I hope the other father you are taking me to is as handsome as the one here, and I hope I will still see my pictures in the billboards when I was little, when I get to Nigeria."

Jane didn't argue with that. How could she? Hassan was still five, about to turn six, and he was already referring to his billboard pictures as if he were little. He talked and reasoned like an eighteen-year-old boy as far as she was concerned.

She was deeply touched when he said that he loved her. She cuddled him warmly, and, in a whisper, she replied, "I love you too, my son. I am immensely proud to be your mum. You are everything, and everything is you."

From his squeezed-up position, he looked up to her and said, "Don't worry, Mum, we will be okay."

But they weren't going to just yet, because as Jane was coming out from the toilet, the front door opened, and Hassan entered looking like one in a hurry.

With her luggage already out in the lounge, their two passports and the letter she wrote to him on top of the coffee table in the lounge, she knew the game was up. Two Nigerian passports, big luggage, and a goodbye letter were more than enough evidence to confirm her intentions. For the umpteenth time, her heart squeezed, and she died a little. But God was on her side because Hassan needed the toilet badly.

"I am bursting for a wee," he said, as he rushed straight to the toilet.

In one scoop, she gathered their passports and the letter and squeezed them hurriedly into her handbag. But that was only one hurdle cleared amongst so many remaining— the luggage, little Hassan, the taxi outside waiting for them and many more. The first thing he noticed after coming out of the toilet was little Hassan. She panicked not because she didn't expect him to ask why he wasn't in school, but because of the answer little Hassan was going to give.

There wasn't time for her to tell him to say they were going to the doctors if Hassan happened to ask, because Hassan was in and out of the toilet in a flash. And even if there was time, she didn't think she would have had the nerves to start teaching him how to lie. Hers was bad enough. But if that was what it would take to prevent Hassan from being suspicious of her moves and intentions, so be it.

"Why is he not in school?" Hassan finally popped the question as she had expected.

"He has an appointment at the doctor's for his immunisation," she hurriedly answered before little Hassan could say anything contradictory.

"And the luggage?"

"I have been ransacking the house for his immunisation record book. That's why I brought the luggage to check in case I mistakenly put it there last week when I was tidying up the house."

He nodded. But she couldn't confirm whether his nod was that he believed her or that he was suspicious of what she had told him.

"Why are you home this early?" she asked him to shift the spotlight from herself and little Hassan.

"Bloody bastards, they cancelled my shift." But before Jane's panic snowballed out of proportion, Hassan, the complete opposite end of the spectrum in terms of emotional disposition and composure, added, "But the other agency found me another shift."

She didn't know whether the new shift was day shift or night shift. If it was night, then it meant that her plan had been foiled. But even if it was day shift, she wanted to know what time of the day the shift was starting because she knew that their flight was scheduled in the next three and a half hours. She knew time wasn't on their side. She was tempted to ask him the time of the shift, but she was cautious not to show herself as one trying to get rid of him. A normal couple would see that as an opportunity to stay together and have some fun. But more worrying to her was the fact that little Hassan could say something incriminating or revealing about their travel. She was tense, and her bladder filled up again even though she had just used the toilet. But she was scared to leave little Hassan with Hassan in case he said something he wasn't supposed to say. She saw a major disaster on the horizon if Hassan discovered what she was up to. She was as sure as death that he would avenge all his pains, including the death of his wife, whom he believed she was responsible for.

She was bursting for a *wee* now but was scared to visit the toilet. She had two options— either wet herself in the lounge or leave little Hassan in the company of Hassan.

But little Hassan came to her rescue by asking if he could play games on her tablet upstairs.

"Of course, you can, my son," she happily responded while excusing herself to use the toilet.

Hassan had only come back to get the name badge for the new shift and was on his way out as she was coming out of the toilet. Jane was about to heave a sigh of relief when Hassan told her he was leaving for work, but the taxi driver was at the door to tell her that she would miss her flight if she continued to delay and that their company would not be held responsible. But she was there just in time and spoke to the taxi driver first. "Just another five minutes," she told the taxi driver.

"I don't want to be…"

"We won't be a minute," she interrupted him cleverly before he spilt the beans and wrecked her whole plan and possibly ended her life.

When Hassan finally drove off, Jane held her heart gingerly and wondered how she hadn't suffered a heart attack up till now. And she wasn't trying to sound high-flown when she said it — she really meant it.

Little Hassan rushed down when he noticed that Hassan had gone. "Come on, mum, hurry up before he comes back again," he said, surprising his mum one more time, who now knew that little Hassan moving upstairs was a calculated attempt to avoid Hassan's prying eyes and possible interrogations.

She thought Nwadili was precocious as a child, but she now believed that little Hassan might be one up on him. *Precocity must be running in Jeff's family, or has mine got anything to contribute to this unmatched astuteness and intelligence of little Hassan? Maybe. But how can I be sure when I have no biological family pedigree? Even though I have no idea about my biological background but I am at the minimum sure that this little genius is my son, and he means the whole world to me,* she said proudly in her heart.

CHAPTER 32

Jane was so happy to make it to the airport with her son in one piece. "Thank goodness," she exclaimed, satisfyingly after checking in with her son, and sitting comfortably in a long-padded bench overlooking the hangar with different aeroplanes from different airlines on display.

It wasn't long before she noticed that her son was attracted to a little girl opposite with her parents. They were watching each other eagerly and admiringly. Jane had also noticed them exchanging smiles. She pretended as if she didn't know what was going on, but she wasn't sure if the girl's parents were also pretending until the girl's mum looked at her, winked and smiled wildly, and that was a confirmation that she was not only aware but was intrigued just like herself.

The little girl pointed her toy gun at little Hassan, squinted her left eye as if she were a hunter aiming at an antelope, before pulling the trigger and then screamed, "kpshhew," to mimic the gunshot sound.

And little Hassan responded by opening wide the mouth of his dinosaur and closing it sharply, screaming, "Oh, sharp!" proving the sharp bite of the dinosaur. That was enough to show they liked each other as they broke free from their parents.

They ran around, screaming hysterically as they did. "Look at my dinosaur. It has nasty teeth, and it can give you a nasty bite with them," little Hassan said, bringing the dinosaur close to her face, before yanking the mouth open and closing it quickly to show how it tore its prey apart.

The girl, in response, squeezed the trigger of her toy gun, and it made a continuous rattling noise which the girl described as a pump action that would exterminate little Hassan' dinosaur. "That's how I will pump some bullets into its head." And they both giggled merrily at their pretend acts. They even did a hide and seek game where the girl would hide behind her little sister's push chair, while little Hassan would cover his head with his mother's jacket, believing it would make him invisible even when his legs were glaringly showing.

Jane was thrilled. She was happy that little Hassan was doing something that reflected his age. "That's more like it," she said. She was so happy to see him doing something of his age instead of sitting next to her, asking questions PhD students should be asking their lecturers, and answering and offering solutions to questions and problems that should be left for conflict resolution specialists.

Just as Jane thought they were over the hill and far away, she suddenly realised how dangerously close they were to the iceberg and needed a special manoeuvre to steer their ship away from plunging into it. The danger was at hugging distance — they were close to it as the bark to the tree. It started as a drizzle just moments before they started boarding. It was when Jane and little Hassan were cozily seated in the plane that she noticed that the drizzle was gradually growing into proper rain. Minutes later, they noticed it had graduated into sleet. Then it stopped for a few minutes, during which the flight attendants started performing the pre-departure rituals about flight safety and all that.

Jane's attention was distracted when looking out of the window, and she noticed that it was snowing slightly with snowflakes flying about in the sky. Jane had never seen snow. She had only seen it in the news and movies. She was so excited and quickly drew little Hassan's attention to it. He was exceedingly excited to see it, too. For the little time he had lived in Las Vegas, he had yet to see snow. He had read and watched movies about the snowman and had always wanted to build a snowman himself, just like the boys and girls in the movies. He had heard about snowball fights and had wished he had had the chance to take part in them.

"That's amazing," little Hassan said delightfully, looking out of the window.

"Why didn't it fall all these days? Why now that we are inside the plane?" Jane protested.

"That's cruel," little Hassan agreed, face puckered in disappointment.

But their excitement was soon to be cut short when the snow continued to gather momentum, it was coming thick and fast, and before you could say Jack Robinson, it began to lie. The beautiful green grass surrounding the tarmac was now literally covered in even more beautiful white colour. And so were the roofs of the buildings in the airport.

"That's beauty to behold," Jane said, looking out of the window. And little Hassan nodded and itched to get out to play in it.

It wasn't too long before the attention of all the passengers was drawn to what was going on out there. The snow had by now graduated into full-blizzard with over 90 miles per hour wind. Though the meteorologist predicted snow, nobody knew it would be of that magnitude.

It was little Hassan who first spoke out. "Mum," he said, "Do you think that the plane will still be able to take off in this condition?"

It was only then that Jane realised the danger that stared them in the face. The snow was now nearly 30 cm in thickness. The passengers could barely see through their windows as they were covered with snow, which continued to lash down unabated.

Jane panicked at the prospect that the journey was hanging on a knife's edge. She knew they were in trouble if the blizzard was going to interfere with their journey. If the flight were going to be cancelled, which, if truth be told, was looking increasingly more likely, then she would have to go back home with little Hassan with all the attendant consequences. Looking at her watch, she realised it was about two hours before Amina and Marianne finished at school, and she was the one who should be picking them up at school. But that wasn't in her plan anymore. She knew that they would be airborne before then. She knew that the school would be phoning her when she didn't turn up to get the girls, and when they couldn't, then they would have no other choice but to contact Hassan. But all this was going to change unless something changed quickly in their favour here at the airport. But she was out of luck because nothing was changing. The only thing that changed was the blizzard gathering momentum and the wind getting stronger.

Now the flight attendants were nowhere to be seen. Everywhere was quiet. The only sound the passengers could hear was the humming and roaring of the plane engines, which Jane knew was not for takeoff, but to keep the passengers and crew members warm. And that was confirmed when a voice came through the public address system to announce that the takeoff had been delayed until further information was received from the control room.

That piece of information went through Jane as a dagger to the heart.

The silence was once again broken ten minutes later when Jane's phone rang. It was Hassan.

"Have you seen the blizzard?" he asked her excitedly.

Her heart jumped into her mouth when she realised her mistake. She had brought out her phone when a delay in the takeoff was announced, and passengers were allowed to use their phones and tablets until advised otherwise.

"Why did I bring out the phone? And why did I answer this call knowing it was Hassan?" she asked herself, frustratingly. "Yes, we have seen, Hassan. It is amazing," she finally said, unsure whether it was the correct answer to his question.

"Are you guys still at the doctor's?"

That was another question she never thought she would ever need to answer. For her, she was done and dusted with Las Vegas, but the snow had thwarted that belief. She did not know what answer to give to this question. Though she wasn't sure where Hassan was making the call, she knew that she must not mention the doctors in case he offered to come and pick them up. And if he did, he would not only discover that they weren't at the doctor's, but that they never attended any appointment, and that would be a red flag that would open an assortment of problems.

"No, we left the hospital 30 minutes ago," she finally answered, now struggling to keep her hand and voice steady.

"Where are you now then?" he quickly asked, giving her no breathing space to gather her thoughts.

Like a cornered boxer, she knew she was on the ropes, and all she was trying to avoid was a technical punch from Hassan that would knock her out. "Oh, we are in the mall now, doing some shopping while we wait for the snow to stop," she said.

The woman sharing the same row of seats with her and little Hassan had to look at her, aghast with disbelief at her lies.

"Why is she telling all these white lies? Why would she tell whoever it is on the line that they left the doctors thirty minutes ago when she had been with this little boy in the airport for nearly two hours? And now, she had told the person that she was doing some shopping when she was sitting next to me in the plane," the lady murmured under her breath. Even though she wasn't sure who was on the other end of the line, she was inclined to believe it was somebody close to Jane and Jane was not telling the person the truth. And she wondered if little Hassan sitting at the window aisle had anything to do with her lies.

It was a double whammy when Jane eventually noticed that the lady sitting next to them had taken some interest in her discussion with Hassan. She had noticed some unwelcome, suspicious look on her face.

The lady's suspicion was confirmed moments later when Jane quickly switched off the phone when the sound that usually preceded the public address system came on in the plane.

Obviously, Jane did not want Hassan to hear the announcement that would follow the sound because it would give her away.

Just as the announcement finished, Jane's phone started ringing again.

"Sorry, Hassan, I think it was the bad weather that discontinued the call," she lied again.

The lady next to her said, "Oh my God." She never meant Jane to hear it, but it came out unconsciously against her wish.

Jane looked at her in shock. Now, it was clear as daylight to her that this lady had some interest in what she was discussing with Hassan. It was not only Hassan she was contending with, but also this lady sitting next to her. And her fear was confirmed when the lady sought the attention of one of the flight attendants. She whispered something in her ear when she came to her.

Jane knew the game was up. She believed that the lady had registered her concern and suspicion about her and the possible child abduction. But Jane had learned to roll with the punches. Nothing was new to her.

Minutes later, the flight attendant came back with a blanket and gave it to Jane, and then asked, "Is he alright?"

Jane knew it was an unwanted service to create an enabling and friendly environment before they would pounce with her arrest. Consequently, she became very defensive. "Does he look ill to you? Yes, he is fine as you can see," she told her aggressively.

"Woo! Woo! woo! There is no need for it, beautiful lady. I just noticed he felt cold and has brought the blanket to keep him warm. That's all."

"Okay. Thanks," Jane said, showing no genuine gratitude and offering no apology for her rude behaviour. She was now fighting a war that didn't exist.

Three minutes later, the lady next to her lifted her hand to beckon the same flight attendant. Again, she whispered something to her. Jane didn't know what, but the flight attendant's reply didn't help to calm Jane's nerves by any stretch of the imagination because the flight attendant said, "Don't worry. We are searching. We will let you know if we find any."

Jane knew at this point that her name and that of little Hassan must have been logged into their system to reveal some information about them. She knew ultimately that they would contact Hassan to ask him if he was aware of this travel.

When the flight attendant left, Jane muttered distinctively, "I wish some busybody would just mind her business."

And the lady in a faint voice replied, "*Ole, eke.*"

Jane could not speak Yoruba, but at least, she knew she had called her a thief and a liar in the Yoruba language, which was still better than calling her a kidnapper or child abductor. But even if she called her child abductor, she knew she would be making a false accusation because she was sure she was only taking her son to his biological father.

Jane was tempted to land a devastating punch on the lady sitting next to her. She would not understand why this busybody of a woman would go without a mark that would permanently remind her of the day she got involved in what did not concern her. She wanted to leave as a souvenir an indelible mark on her face for poking-nosing into other people's affairs.

She wished she were fluent in Arabic. *This mischief-maker wouldn't have been able to get involved in a discussion that was inconsequential and to no effect to her if I had discussed with Hassan in Arabic,* Jane thought in her mind.

Jane knew at least that she would be safe if she was handed over to the security service upon her arrest for child abduction, unlike the death sentence she was certain to face in the hands of Hassan if he discovered that she tried to run away with his son.

Then she thought of Jeff and all he would make of all this when he discovered that she had been lying to him all this time. She knew full well it would be over between them if she were arrested and her case aired on international television and published in international newspapers and magazines as a suspected child abductor. There would be no reason or explanation she would give Jeff to convince him otherwise. The fact that he was not informed beforehand would weaken her defence and make her look like somebody who had an ulterior motive right from the get-go.

The lady hadn't said anything sinister or incriminating to the staff to implicate Jane, as she later discovered. The lady had only been asking for a couple of sanitary pads because her monthly period had just come on.

It was a huge relief when a voice announced to the passengers that the plane would be taking off before long. The snow had now stopped falling for the past twenty minutes, and tens of snow plough vehicles had been deployed to clear the tarmac of snow.

Forty minutes later, their plane was airborne, bound for Nigeria, and all Jane could see beneath her was the snowy, white colour of Las Vegas' landscape and its skyscrapers that now looked like huts fast disappearing before her eyes.

CHAPTER 33

They safely landed in Nigeria early hours of the next day. She had told Jeff about her arrival, and he had shelved every plan he had for the day to welcome her home.

"Should I come to get you at the airport, or…?" Jeff asked her, joy and eagerness in his voice.

"Have you forgotten I left my car at the airport?" she reminded him.

"I entirely forgot." They hadn't seen each other for almost three weeks now. Jeff's heart yearned for her, and he couldn't wait to get his hands on her, to feel her warmth, and kiss her passionately. On the converse, Jane's heart was torn to ribbons by all the lies she had told Jeff lately, but more worrisome was how she was going to present and introduce little Hassan safely to him.

Her tummy took a lurch as she tried the door handle. The door was locked. So, she knocked, and Jeff merrily approached the door believing it was Jane, and it was, but with a twist. His joy and enthusiasm at seeing his wife back from America were cut short when he saw her holding a child.

Boldly, she gave him a warm, genial kiss, pretending nothing was amiss. Jeff, still in shock, didn't even know how to kiss her back. "Can we enter please?" she asked, as he stood like a statue at the front of the door, mouth agape, and eyes wide open. He had lost his power of speech. Stiffly and slowly like an operated robot, he moved away from the entrance to let them in, but his eyes were glued to the little boy she held. He thought he had seen him somewhere before, but couldn't remember exactly where.

Little Hassan looked at Jeff suspiciously before sitting down. He wasn't convinced of anything good about Jeff as his mum had described him. "I am hungry, Mum," little Hassan demanded cowardly.

She got him some ice cream from the fridge. "Quench your hunger with that while I prepare food for everyone," she told him, rubbing his hair gently, before pinching his cheek fondly.

Jeff was still in shock after managing to close the door. He was rooted to the spot, unable to take a single step. In fact, no part of the body moved except his eyes, which darted from Jane to the little boy sitting on the sofa.

It was when Jane wanted to go to the kitchen that Jeff finally recovered from what appeared as a trance and asked in a faint voice, "What is going on, Jane?"

"Finally. I thought you were going to stand there all day and watch us like a movie," she said coldly.

In Nigeria, there is an adage that says: when a child is given a gift far too much for his age, the child will ask the giver who he should give the gift to. Such was Jeff's state of mind. What he was seeing was far beyond his comprehension.

"Who is he?" he asked gingerly.

"He is our son," she answered unassuredly, in a low tone.

That answer finally made him snap out fully from his twilight state, and the floodgates of hell were unleashed. "Who is our son? What do you think you are doing? Have you lost your mind?"

She was given no time or chance to respond to his questions that were coming in quick succession. "That we have no child and thinking of adoption is not enough reason for you to embark on it single-handedly. How disrespectful is that? You got this one because he is famous, and you think his fame will make me overlook your nonchalance and disrespect, huh?" He had now remembered and recognised him as the billboard baby, as they referred to him then. "You better take him back where you got him from. I have profound respect for you, and I expect the same from you. Don't treat me like a fool because I am not," he said, voice rising with every word.

"Dad!" little Hassan said in an attempt to make him tune his voice down.

"Don't call me dad because I don't know where she got you from," he scolded him.

"Shut up, Jeff, shut up," Jane screamed back at Jeff, now losing her head.

"Mum!" Little Hassan called out.

Jane's face fell. She knew what little Hassan must be thinking now, especially being precocious. She told him she was taking him to a better home and a better dad. "I am sorry, Hassan, for all this embarrassment," Jane apologised to him.

"Hassan? Did you call him Hassan?" Jeff asked hastily and feebly. It was the last name he wanted to hear.

"Mum said we would change it to your name. Call me Jeff, Jeff Jr," little Hassan said.

Jane vaguely remembered discussing such with little Hassan, but it was vital he said it, nevertheless.

"Can you tell me who your father is?" Jeff asked him, hoping it wasn't the Hassan he knew.

"You mean my fake father?"

Jeff nearly laughed the way he said it despite his anger. But his anger was rekindled when he said, "He is Hassan Slimane."

"Hassan Slimane!" Jeff exclaimed. The thought that Jane had made a baby with Hassan took all his willpower away, and he slumped into the sofa with his hands over his face. He had been preoccupied by that thought; he had fought for ages to repress into his unconscious mind with little success — the thought of Jane sleeping with Douglas and in the process losing her virginity to him. It was a thought that had made him jealous, angry, and betrayed each time it crept into his mind. And now, she had come home with a baby called Hassan to compound the already complicated situation. He could only see Jane as one stoking a fire in a house filled with dry straw. Jane, at that point, looked dirty and worthless to him. And all he wanted now was not to push her out of the door but to grab her by the hair and fling her out of the window. His impression of her was rapidly changing with every passing second. He had begun to see her as a casual lay against what Fab described her as when they met at the Cosmo hotel in Port Harcourt. The thought that Jane tried to save Hassan while he was drowning was reawakened, making him believe Jane might have actually made a baby with Hassan.

"Fab once told me you were not a casual lay. He said you were one of a kind. But now, I cast serious doubt on all of that. That is surely false praise. No wonder my friend once told me that a woman is like a ripe tomato, but you need to spin it right round before eating it, just in case a part of it is rotten. Now, I understand what he meant."

Jane sniggered painfully at the picture Jeff was painting of her. Her heart sank. She could not believe he was describing her as a loose woman and as a nobody. He had not beaten her, but he had certainly weaponised his mouth, and like a soldier in the medieval age, he was throwing his rondel dagger at her heart where it hurt most. He hadn't called her a whore either, but it was easy for anyone to infer that, and that included her little son who had earlier on in Las Vegas made a cloudy reference to that. *If little Hassan wasn't sure of what he suspected her of in Las Vegas, Jeff's statement now seemed to have confirmed that to him,* Jane had thought. Though her heart and pride were profoundly broken and bruised, Jane, nevertheless, felt it was inappropriate to keep little Hassan there listening to Jeff calling her demeaning names. She decided to take little Hassan to the next room.

At that point, Jeff briskly walked up to her, grabbed her wrist, and screamed, "Don't you dare try to walk away from me with that thing. I am still talking to you."

"Are you also going to beat me and this thing? You call this lovely boy a thing?" she asked, as tears began to gather in her eyes. Her heart sank even deeper. She likened herself to a fish that stayed under water but would never drown. She promised herself not to go to the bad, no matter what life threw at her, even from the man she loved more than herself.

"Call me anything but leave this innocent, vulnerable boy out of it," Jane pleaded with him.

Little Hassan obviously looked terrified and concerned. Little Hassan, at that point, felt that he had been lured away from his relative comfort in Las Vegas to a house on fire. Before now, little Hassan thought his parents were class, now they were nothing but crass.

 Jane knew how little Hassan was feeling and couldn't stop apologising to him. "Don't mind your dad, son, he will soon come back to his senses and away from this transient madness."

Her last statement had some positive impact on Jeff, who now saw his action as putting the cart before the horse. He realised he should have searched his mind before drawing conclusions or making careless statements and references. He realised little Hassan was one of the babies at

Ivory Babies' home — and that he was a household name. He then wondered how little Hassan was Hassan's and at the same time at the motherless baby's home in Nigeria. "But why is Jane calling him their son when he was named after Hassan?" he wondered.

Jane was still sobbing as she held little Hassan between her legs with his head resting on her chest.

Little Hassan couldn't take his eyes off her face, which was now soaked in tears. "Don't cry, Mum," little Hassan continued to encourage her as he wiped away many tears from her face with his little fingers.

Jeff was now caught in two minds. He didn't know what to do — whether to stop further investigation about little Hassan and accept everything Jane had said, or to continue his inquest. He leaned towards the latter reluctantly. Apologising to Jane, he then asked, "You are supposed to be arriving from Las Vegas? How did you manage to get here, and then to Ivory Baby's home to get him? And how on earth is this child named Hassan Slimane if Hasan had nothing to do with him, or has he?" He felt nervous when he asked the question and prayed that Jane would refute his assertion and tell him Hassan had nothing to do with little Hassan.

"No, Dad. We are coming from Las Vegas. I left Ivory's motherless baby's home years ago. That was when my fake father came and took me to Tunisia," little Hassan said, giving Jane no time to answer Jeff. "Isn't it, Mum?" he asked, looking at Jane to agree with him.

"It is, son," she sheepishly responded, still avoiding any eye contact with Jeff, who had left her desolate and dejected by his accusations.

Jeff's anger was once again revived by little Hassan's comments. Jeff was now getting a clearer picture of what was going on. "Oh, you have been with Hassan for nearly three weeks in Las Vegas. It seems you have always been in touch with him all this time; otherwise, how did you know he now lives in Las Vegas? Or did you go to Tunisia to find him? Please don't tell me you did," Jeff pleaded, believing that Jane would tell him she didn't, but the look in her face confirmed his fear.

He paused and fixed his ferret-like eyes on her. "So, you went to Tunisia on your own? So, you have been lying all this time that you were with your imaginary friends in Las Vegas?" Jeff's disappointment was bare. "How could you, Jane?" he asked, heartbroken.

"It is true, Mum had been with us in Las Vegas. But it is also true she never did anything silly with my fake dad. Mum slept in the lounge downstairs throughout her stay in Las Vegas. I trust my mum, but at the same time, I can understand why you are so angry. It is natural for any man in your situation to be jealous. You must let go," little Hassan humbly advised Jeff.

Jeff and Jane, in unison, let their heads stoop in shame, seeing little Hassan acting as a mediator to broker peace between them.

Jeff didn't know whether to laugh or tell little Hassan to stop meddling in adults' discussions, especially noticing he was making references far too advanced for his age.

Jeff wanted to see things from a different perspective, but the fact that this child was named Hassan, and Jane giving her virginity to Douglas, defeated that idea, and he flipped that moment.

"I am not having this. I am not. I cannot be fooled twice. I am going upstairs. I can't stand your presence. I can't," he said angrily, with a hint of jealousy conspicuously written all over his face. And he stormed off.

Jane had heard enough. She quickly grabbed a sheet of paper from the bookshelf and wrote; *I am gone with my boy — don't bother with us — Jane.* And she dropped the letter on the coffee table.

Jeff didn't realise that she had gone with her boy when he heard the door shut. It was on second thought that he decided to come downstairs to confirm whether someone had entered or left the house. He saw only Nwadili, who now lived with them, coming out from the toilet.

"Where is Jane?" Jeff asked him when he could not see her or little Hassan. The luggage was gone as well.

"I don't know, uncle; I saw her moments ago driving off with a little boy. She looked terribly angry while the little boy looked frightened. She didn't say anything to me."

"Oh my God! What have I done?" Jeff asked, looking spaced out. He looked like one thrown off the cliff as soon as he saw Jane's letter. "I am dead," he screamed.

The first thing she did was to block Jeff's number. She didn't want to hear his voice. She was devastated and heartbroken as she drove, and little Hassan had continued to console her that things would be okay.

Jeff feared the worse when he couldn't get Jane on the phone. He believed it was unsafe for her to be behind the wheel in her present state of mind, and in the dark as the day was still breaking. He quickly phoned the police to say that his wife had driven out of the house in a down-in-the-dumps state of mind, and he feared something would happen to her. He quickly described his wife, the little boy and finally gave them the description of the car and the plate number.

About ten minutes later, there was a report to the police that a navy-blue Audi A6 car had driven under a parked lorry close to Lekki Lagoon. Jane, in her blurred vision, anger, and confusion, had lost concentration and had plunged under the trailer. She saw the parked trailer late and was too dangerously close to it when her little boy screamed, "Watch out, Mum!" He thought his mum had an unobstructed vision of the trailer as he did. His warning was too late.

The police rushed to the scene, where they confirmed it was the car Jeff described. The problem now was to know how long the accident occurred, and the possibility of pulling the car from under the trailer and most importantly, the condition of the occupants.

Jeff fainted when the police broke the news to him.

Thank God, Nkoli had just returned from her friend's birthday party that early morning. In panic, she quickly phoned the paramedics, who arrived in good time. They helped to resuscitate him.

When he was fully stabilised, he was driven to the scene of the accident alongside Nkoli, but Jane and her boy had already been moved to a nearby hospital, where X-rays showed no evidence of physical injury on Jane, but she remained unconscious and could only beam a weak smile from time to time. The nurses and the doctor on call rushed to her bedside when her BP monitor started beeping due to a sudden drop in her blood pressure. All interventions to bring up the BP proved abortive. Jane was drifting away. Her BP and pulse continued to plummet.

The hospital had to phone Jeff using the number the police gave them. Jeff answered the call. He was informed of Jane's deteriorating condition.

They arrived fifteen minutes later. By then, Jane's breathing was getting shallow and a bit laboured. The body was slowly going purple, evidence of poor circulation of oxygen in the tissues. That explained why the body was getting cold, especially the lower extremities.

The doctor cornered Jeff and Nkoli, and after putting comforting hands on their shoulders, told them that they had done their best and they should brace up for the worst. He attributed Jane's condition to possible psychological shock.

Jeff screamed, "Do you mean my wife is dying?"

"I am sorry. You have to take heart. Anyway, I won't keep you any longer. I have to let you go and see her before she goes. Go now and touch and talk to her because senses of touch and hearing are the last senses to go when one…" the doctor quietly informed him, consoling him all the time.

Jeff couldn't believe the doctor had written Jane off, and that Jane was dying. He was heartbroken and blamed himself for everything.

Jeff and Nkoli raced to Jane's bed, led by one of the nurses.

Jeff was speechless when he saw Jane's deplorable condition, and he was left with a welter of remorse that would possibly haunt him for the rest of his life. Though Jeff wasn't a medical doctor, he had basic knowledge about types of shock and their features. What he saw did not match the doctor's diagnosis. He ordered the nurse to get the doctor at once. The doctor rushed, believing that Jane had passed on.

"What is going on here? I think your diagnosis is wrong. Why would you call this psychological shock?" he asked, as a flash of anger stole into his face.

"You must show some respect, young man. It is our policy that no staff of this hospital should be subjected to any form of abuse. You should be blaming yourself for everything, not us. You told the police of your verbal abuse against her in case you have forgotten," the doctor told Jeff angrily.

"Great. So, it is the police that is making the diagnosis here, not you? So, you relied on the police information to make your diagnosis. Police work is to prevent crimes and prosecute criminals. Police investigate crimes, doctors make diagnoses and treat illnesses," Jeff reminded him ferociously.

"I appreciate your frustration, but if you continue this way, I will have no option but to phone the police to throw you off the premises," the doctor threatened him.

"Really? We will see who throws who. For now, I want my wife to be examined thoroughly, please, because what I am seeing is hypovolemic shock, which means that she might be bleeding internally. That's why the blood pressure is low with accelerated pulse, rapid breathing, cold hands and feet, and pallor of the skin. In fact, I feel so silly arguing with you instead of phoning consultant surgeons to rush to this hospital to try to save my wife."

Jeff contacted their family doctor and explained what was going on. Jeff understood that the medical team here had no clue what they were doing. Their family doctor was traumatised by the news. Using his good name and connections, he made emergency calls to highly qualified surgeons and colleagues, and they rushed to the hospital to take over proceedings from the hospital personnel who had now humbly stepped aside after they were informed who Jeff and Jane were.

Before now, people said that Jane and her son cheated death after seeing the picture of the mangled Audi car from which they were pulled out without major injuries. But they were wrong. It was just because the doctor misdiagnosed her. In fact, death at that point was at the doorstep knocking on the door, and Jane was about to open the door for it.

While they anxiously waited for the arrival of professional surgeons, Jeff grabbed Jane with both hands. Leaning over her, he said, "My fortress. My sunshine. My life. Where are you going? I am here. You can't leave. How can you leave me? Of course, you know I am lost without you. I am sorry for everything I have put you through. Forgive me, Jane." And he cried frantically. Jeff's words were impactful.

Jane slowly opened her dimmed eyes and smiled weakly before closing them again. At least the doctor was knowledgeable about human senses and responses because it was obvious Jane, in her dying state, recognised and responded to Jeff's voice and touch. At that point, there was a rattled noise from the BP machine attached to her left arm as it started to recalibrate. Slowly, but steadily, the BP started to come up.

It had taken Jeff's touch and voice for her vital organs to come alive, but the cold hand of death, like the sword of Damocles, was still hanging over her, ready to strike.

The MRI scan showed Jane had ruptured her spleen. It took the surgeons just over four hours to rectify, arrest the internal haemorrhage, and mop up the fluids in the interstitial space in the abdominal region. The spleen was then repaired, after which they finally stitched her back up.

Her son miraculously sustained only a fracture of the left wrist, as was confirmed by the scans ordered by the team of surgeons. It was a minor surgery.

The first thing Jane asked after recovering from the surgery was about her son, and she was told he was undergoing surgery for the broken wrist. She cried when the staff told her. She hoped they were telling her the truth.

Jane screamed on seeing Jeff after full recovery, "Get him out of here now." She even screamed louder when Jeff wanted to hold her and apologise.

"All I want is my little boy, not him. All we have done is cause each other pain and misery. I am sick of it. I have, to the best of my ability, kept my nose clean and to the grindstone to make this relationship fruitful, but to no effect. About time we parted ways. Go and leave me alone," she told him fiercely and despondently.

His presence on this occasion was very irritating to her, a sharp contrast to how she felt at the Cosmo hotel.

He was led out of the ward by the staff on Jane's insistence.

"It is our policy to respect the wishes of our patients. Yes, we know you are her husband, but now, she doesn't want you anywhere near her."

He was devastated as he was being led out of the ward, regretting all his actions. He couldn't believe she had ordered him out of the hospital's ward, and he was gripped with fear that she wasn't going to order him out of her life for good.

Nkoli had to step in when she gathered all the information and understood that the matrix and genesis of Jane's and Jeff's problems stemmed from a lack of trust. She promised to broker peace between them, such that it would bring a lasting and trustworthy relationship.

Jane's heart was finally touched after Nkoli narrated how Jeff suffered a syncope after hearing they were involved in an accident and needed the paramedics' intervention to recuperate. Jane's heart melted when Jeff walked in after a protracted plea from Nkoli on his behalf.

Jeff looked languid and traumatised as he walked unsteadily to Jane's bedside.

Jane took a quick look at him, and a strong stab of emotion stole into her face, and she was frightened by how much he had changed in a few hours. He was a mere shadow of himself, and that broke her heart. The piteous picture he presented was enough to show her how much he loved her, and she opened her weak arms wide to welcome him. He buried his head in her chest and cried.

"Jeff," Nkoli screamed. "Be careful how you lean on her. She had just had a major operation."

"I am fine, Nkoli," Jane reassured her.

She managed to lift Jeff's face to confirm her suspicion. She believed he was crying, and she saw some tears, and she quickly put his head back in her chest. She didn't want others to see the tears of a grown man, especially that of her husband, who was as strong as an ox, an additional attribute that had endeared her to him. She always felt safe in Jeff's arms, knowing that he could fight off any danger, even if the assailant had a gun. Holding and rubbing his back gently, she whispered in his ears, "I am sorry." And Jeff said the same to her. "I should be the one apologising," he told her.

She lifted his face off her chest again, and they exchanged a lengthy, guilty look at each other, and in an unbelievable synchronicity, their thumbs crossed each other to reach their faces to wipe off the tears. This time, she didn't mind if people were watching.

"Now, listen, you naughty, jealous lovers. About time you weaned yourselves off this unhealthy jealousy. Time to begin to heal and build the trust," Nkoli admonished them, amidst laughter from everyone, including the staff present.

"I don't think anybody can argue that we are children of circumstance, considering our background. Consider mine, Jane's, Nkoli's, Nwadili's, our dad's, and of course Naomi's. It has never been easy for any of us. We must come together as one United family and be supportive and protective of one another," Jeff said after apologising again to Jane.

With anger and jealousy now gone, Jeff began to think more lucidly and reasonably. For starters, he remembered that he had never seen Jane's pregnancy. So, he concluded that everything happened in Tunisia, which could only mean that Hassan was the dad. But on second thought, he wondered how the child came to live in Ivory's motherless baby's home, where Hassan took him back to Tunisia. *If he was born in Tunisia, how did he find himself in Ivory's motherless baby's home?* he asked himself. He thought at that point that it was only sensible to ask Jane who was in the best position to clarify all these mysteries, because finding exactly what happened was like walking through a maze — proper mumbo jumbo. In all his disappointment and confusion, he still tried to resolve the issue without escalating it any further because he loved Jane so dearly. Again, he wouldn't dare say anything that would upset her again, especially now that she was still recovering from major surgery. In fact, he knew it was wrong to bring up the issue at that time, but he was extremely inquisitive to wait until she had made a full recovery.

"I am sorry to ask this silly question," Jeff apologised once more to her as he tapped and rubbed her cheeks repeatedly.

"You are apologising after calling me all the names under the sun, the love of your life, your soulmate. You promised and confessed that you will always grin and bear my shortcomings. But you dishonoured your words. You said I make you tick. Do I still, Jeff?"

"Of course. You did, still do and will forever do, Jane. Pardon my insensibility and silliness. It will never happen again," he pleaded ruefully.

Jane, after being comforted and reassured by Jeff, then narrated everything to him, from the cryptic pregnancy to having the baby and telling him lies about bumping into Vera. She told him that she thought that Hassan raped her citing the incident that early morning in Tunisia. She told him she lacked the courage to tell him that she was raped by Hassan and getting pregnant as a result. She said that Jeff had done a lot and suffered a lot on her behalf, and she felt guilty about putting him through such a tough time again. She reminded him of the day his mum mentioned the story about the exploits of the expatriates in their towns and villages — impregnating young girls. And she thought that might explain little Hassan's white colour. "And that is how we got to where we are now. I embarked on this journey amid a series of lies I told you. I am sorry about them. I knew it was extremely dangerous, but I took the risk to bring you this bundle of joy," she said with pride and joy. "It wasn't easy, but I did it. All the DNA results confirmed you are the true dad." And she asked him to open her luggage, where all the DNA results were. "I went with your hair, and the swab I took from your mouth while you were asleep. I am sorry for doing that. That's an invasion of your privacy. But here we are with the result of all the danger I passed through," she concluded with a proud smile.

Jeff sat there looking at her like an alien. He was obviously disappointed by the lies, but happy with her bravery and the end product. "I can't believe all this. You had the courage to find Hassan on your own. Unbelievable!" Jeff said, still in shock.

After lunch, Nkoli, full of excitement and pride, took Jeff Jr for a walk in the hospital premises, introducing him proudly to anyone that greeted them, and would almost bump into others that didn't, just to gain their attention so she could introduce him to them.

While Nkoli and Jeff Jr were out, Jeff seized the opportunity. He stopped for a moment and let his eyes fall on Jane's.

"What? Why the look again?" she asked.

"Just being silly and inquisitive again. I am not trying to kick up dust. All these are now in the past. It is just that I want to know how you managed to convince Hassan to accept you in

Las Vegas. He was badly hurt by what happened between him and us in Tunisia. He must be suspicious and angry to see you. What did you say and do to douse his anger and remove any form of suspicion? Did you charm him with your beauty? Or did he see your arrival as gold in the hills?" he asked her, laughing as he said it.

She lowered her head and simpered shyly. She had already apologised for all the lies she told him. She was not ready to start another now, especially now that they had restored peace. She decided to tell him the whole truth. "I told him that I had come to apologise for everything and that I was ready to be his wife."

"And?" he asked, pushing further for more confessions.

She bowed her head and said, "Why do you want all these details? Like you rightly said, all these are now in the past, aren't they?"

"I know they are, but I still want to know everything, and if you truly love me, you will tell me everything, I mean, everything." His inner thought was telling him she did more than she was telling him.

"I don't want to upset you, Jeff, but at the same time, I don't want to lie anymore."

His heart skidded a bit, and he could only manage a pseudo smile. He wanted to know everything that happened between her and Hassan in Las Vegas, but he was obviously not prepared to hear that she slept with him.

She paused for a few seconds, took a breather, before telling him she kissed Hassan once, which was the day she arrived in Las Vegas. And she told him that it was the quickest and most platonic kiss one could give anyone. "I kissed him to draw him in and kill any form of suspicion in his mind," Jane expressed.

"You meant the second time you kissed him," he said, reminding her that she kissed him when they went for the magazine competition.

She covered her face, embarrassed. She had forgotten all about that. "To be honest, that kiss was even more platonic than the one I gave him in Las Vegas." Jeff agreed with her.

"Jealous. But thank you for telling me the truth, my sunshine."

"I am deeply sorry for kissing another man. It hurts me so badly. Let us take solace in the reason I did it. Personally, I believe our boy is worth all the risk and trouble," she said solemnly.

"Indeed. Didn't know all this time that the much-acclaimed billboard baby is my boy. Come here, my little piece of happiness and pride," he told Jeff Jr as he walked in with Nkoli. "I am glad and proud to be your dad. I hereby rename you officially Jeff Jr as you suggested, my little sunshine. You must forgive your dad for his rants and tantrums."

"I forgive you, Dad," Jeff Jr responded with an exhilarating smile.

"Isn't he handsome, Jane?"

"Like his dad," she said as she propped herself up in bed and hugged both and continued to make her unreserved apologies for everything.

"We are also sorry for everything you have been through," Jeff and Jeff Jr apologised to her.

"My late adoptive dad once said that the person who loved less in a relationship was usually the one in control of the relationship. He went on to say that there was always jealousy and suspicion where a couple loved each other equally. I totally agree with that. Our situation has confirmed all his theories. Look at us accusing each other and feeling uncomfortable anytime one of us is in the company of the opposite sex." She cited Nkoli and Hassan. And they laughed over it.

Jeff agreed with her and quickly suggested that it was time they did something to kill that jealous attribute both had. Jeff said that such jealousy could have cost them the relative comfort and wealth they were enjoying if he had sent Nkoli away as Jane insisted. He added that he would not have had the glaring prospect of identifying who Nkoli really was, his blood sister, if he had agreed to send her away as Jane demanded.

Jane also added that Jeff Jr wouldn't have been with them if she had allowed the fear of how Jeff would feel get the better of her if she travelled to Tunisia to find Hassan.

They promised each other to work on their trust issue.

Jane was discharged a week later. It took her another four weeks to recover fully.

Jane and Jeff couldn't wait to get their hands on each other. It was about two months or thereabouts the last time they made love. There was this mesmerising glow in Jeff's eyes as his thick brows pulled together in anticipation. Jane knew why. It was Jeff's signature tune to suggest he wanted to get it on. She bit down gently on her lower lip teasingly — a signal that she was in the mood for love. Their love magnet could only pull them in one direction — to their magnificent Dormeo king-size bed upstairs. They left Jeff Jr in the lounge with some ice cream and the tablet to play his favourite games.

They needed each other desperately. They nearly tore each other's clothes, breathing heavily and whispering sweet nothings to each other's ears as they did. There was little or no time for romance. Usually, Jeff had a slow hand during foreplay, where he would explore Jane's body carefully like a sculptor carving a sculpture on some wood. But not on this occasion. Their hormones were already raging like an uncontrollable Californian wildfire and needed nothing else to get them to work.

The act over, Jane said, "That was electric. I enjoyed it. I can barely stand. My knees are still buckling under the effect and excitement of what we just did. It reminded me of the one we did on the night of my botched travel to England."

"No way," Jeff argued convincingly. "Not that I didn't enjoy what we just did, but it was nowhere near the one we did on the night preceding your travel. In fact, I lost count ..."

She blushed at the way he said it. She couldn't dispute his assertion, now remembering it was the night she had her first squirt, where she squirted like a fountain and nearly blinded Jeff with it.

They laughed hilariously, thinking all about it.

"I am sure it was the night Little Jeff was conceived," Jane said. And Jeff nodded his consent.

Nkoli could not hold her excitement knowing that Jeff had a child of his own. She was even happier that Nwadili had got a cousin and a playmate.

Nwadili and Jeff Jr were a formidable force. They got on like a house on fire.

Jeff, heaving a sigh of relief, declared, quoting Second Corinthians, "We had been pressed on every side but not crushed, perplexed but not in despair, persecuted but not abandoned, struck down but not destroyed. In this treacherous journey, our love boat had been hit from different angles by different missiles. Holes made, water sucked in, but happily enough not enough to sink the boat. Even though fish lives all its life in water, we still need water to clean it before we consider it fit to cook and eat. This shows that as much as we strive towards perfection, we will never attain it. It takes only a little life event to expose our imperfections, vulnerability, and lack of faith. Thank God the storm is finally over. Our enemies are no more."

They were reliably informed that Douglas was eventually executed on the order of the state governor a few weeks ago after the governor refused to succumb to all the pressure from Douglas's men to at least reduce his death sentence to life imprisonment. On the order of the government, the police, in conjunction with other security agents, succeeded in eliminating Douglas' entire criminal network to the relief of the citizens of the state and the whole nation in general.

"This is the dawn of a new day — an important, promising watershed in our marriage life. We have swum ashore now and hopefully will remain safe. To God be all the glory," Jeff said, and Jane chorused a big Amen.

THE END